SUGAR

LYDIA MICHAELS

Copyright © 2020 by Lydia Michaels

All rights reserved.

No part of this book may be reproduced in any form or by any electronic or mechanical means, including information storage and retrieval systems, without written permission from the author, except for the use of brief quotations in a book review.

SUGAR

Contemporary Romance

www.LydiaMichaelsBooks.com

BOOKS BY LYDIA MICHAELS

Falling In

Breaking Out

Coming Home

Sacrifice of the Pawn

Queen of the Knight

Breaking Perfect

Simple Man

La Vie en Rose

Calamity Rayne

Blind

Untied

Forfeit

Lost Together

Atonement

First Comes Love

If I Fall

Something Borrowed

The McCullough Mountain Series

Hurt

For every woman who would rather be a shark than a mermaid.
Never be afraid to show your teeth and bite back.
Fins out!

1

AVERY

I could feel his stare weighing on me, heavy and warm like a blanket I didn't ask for but appreciated all the same. He watched from across the hall, watched me like a man who saw something he fantasized about possessing. A beautiful car, a valuable company, a woman, either way, I was only an object to him. That was fine. Impersonal, the way I preferred my relationship with neighbors.

My hand trembled as I slid my gold key into the slot of the deadbolt, securely locking my door. The ornate moldings throughout the building imposed a sense of security as well as a sense of lavish luxury, so my sudden unsteadiness wasn't due to fear, but rather the result of my hot neighbor's nearness in our shared, narrow hall.

This man should *not* stir the feelings he roused inside of me.

Don't look...

Sliding the ornate key into the narrow pocket of my Dior clutch, I tried to hide my body's response to his attention. He pretended to sort a handful of mail outside of his apartment door, his tailored, bespoke clothing the usual high-end office attire, but he didn't strike me as a self-important snob. Just a result of good circumstances.

Regardless of his background, he got up and went to work every weekday and sometimes on weekends. The golden stubble covering his jaw was proof of yet another long day's work.

Snapping my clutch shut, I pretended not to notice him, and fought the urge to dissect him with my eyes.

No one read their mail in the hall. They grabbed it from the lobby and dumped it on their counter when they walked through the door. Yet he eye fucked each envelope with the same intensity one reviewed a life or death contract. I doubted he read a single word.

Bingo. With a flick of his thick lashes, blond enough to give his blue eyes a dramatic gilded fringe, his gaze left the mail and landed on me. I looked away because there wasn't time to play the demure flirt, and the last thing I needed was another man in my life.

We lived in a civil war era mansion renovated into apartments, located on Delancey Street in the Rittenhouse section of Old City Philadelphia—a place college students shouldn't be able to afford. But I wasn't an ordinary college student. Exploits, the sort most women couldn't imagine—wouldn't want to imagine—dominated my social life.

This was the second time he and I crossed paths since I moved in, and it surely wouldn't be the last. I should say hello, introduce myself, do the upper class, neighborly thing, but there wasn't time. A luxury sports car waited for me out front, and I couldn't keep my client waiting.

A shiver raced down my spine as my neighbor's attention lingered, and my eyes slowly blinked. The heat of his stare teased at the base of my back, exposed by my ebony, couture midi dress.

I could feel him watching me as though he could see through my clothing. He left me feeling ... exposed, as if he might detect the faux jewels and second hand couture and discover the real me. Why did he have to look at me like that?

I knew my ass looked phenomenal, and it should for the amount of time I spent sweating it off at the gym every dawn. But my curves and this dress weren't for him. *I* wasn't for him. And by the look of his high-end, tailored suit and unquestionable attractiveness paired with his young age, I knew, without a doubt, he wasn't for me.

He hailed from prestigious lineage, perfectly suited for some pretty, little, pedigreed female, born and raised around old money, pampered and gently disciplined to always pick up the correct silver spoon at a formal table, and never go slumming in the places I'd been. Yup, I definitely wasn't his type.

Keeping my lashes low, I approached the elevator doors. My lips formed the thinnest smile as I tossed him a brief sideways glance, and my heart lamented the death of possibilities that could never be. His mouth opened by the slightest degree, and I felt the corner of my smile pull tight with genuine satisfaction.

Yeah, he's gawking. If only he knew...

Girls like me didn't know the meaning of vanity growing up, but the city had taught me well. I couldn't deny it felt nice to have an attractive man's full focus. Rarely short of attention, his awareness somehow struck me as different. Less manufactured and more valuable perhaps.

His looks ranked him as a dangerous female connoisseur, so undeniably handsome there'd be little challenge for him to find a date. Affluence and good looks with a hint of arrogance hid in those deep blue eyes. And the sheer size of his hands, the breadth of his shoulders, and the smolder of his gaze... His inarguable appeal sucked the air right out of our private, little hallway.

My manicured finger nudged the elevator button to a golden glow as the antique dial ticked up to our floor. My will trembled, as I demanded I not look back. I worked damn hard to get here, and I couldn't afford any distractions. Literally.

Six seconds left.

His throat cleared just as the brass dial hit our floor and the doors parted with a delicate ping. The slender five-inch heels of my Prada pumps crossed the threshold, my mind waiting for the precise moment I'd make eye contact, knowing full well it would be sharp and jolting, like a roller coaster letting go at the top of a steep hill.

Eyes down, I stepped over the threshold and turned, still not giving him the satisfaction of my full attention. I'd mastered the art of coy and unknowing long ago, but normally there wasn't much risk involved. Something told me he was different from my usual mark. Perhaps it was the fear that he somehow knew *I* was different.

I might look delicate, but I could make a grown man cry. Therefore eye contact was a gamble I shouldn't take with him.

But I wanted to see his response to my gaze. I wanted to try to read him the way he was trying to read me.

How would he respond if I met his stare head on, without a hint of shyness? Would he suck in a sharp breath, hold it? Look away?

My insides clenched with acute anticipation. I needed to experience that intoxicating split second in time when he knew I noticed him—when *I* chose to do so.

I wasn't a bitch, and I wasn't self-centered, but I lived alone in a scary world with a dirty history, and my façade remained the only veneer separating me from a muddied past. My appearance served as an opaque distraction hiding the girl I used to be from the world I desperately wanted to belong to.

I'd mastered the role I needed to portray, my chance to bury my past once and for all. I refused to go back to where I came from, back to being that girl. Avery Johansson had become my present and my future, she remained the only woman he and every other man would ever see.

Tipping my head at just the right angle to show off the contours of my high cheekbones and smoky eyes, I slowly raised my gaze, pretending to notice him for the first time. My fingers already called the doors to close, but I couldn't resist.

Our eyes met and my knees softened. Our gazes locked. Intense, provocative desire thrummed through the charged air as this silent game of *how good we could fuck* played out in a snapshot of time that would never come true.

He drew in that breath just as I'd hoped he would—a reward for him, a reward for me. A shame we'd never actually be more than neighbors.

The elevator doors glided shut. "Wait—"

The door closed, and I let out a relieved sigh, a twisted smirk pulling at the corner of my mouth. I loved playing cat and mouse, but only when I held the role of the cat.

I wouldn't necessarily classify him as mousey or timid. Despite his indisputable good looks and palpable, pretty boy propriety, something savage lingered under the surface, something untamed. It was dangerous to taunt a tiger. Maybe that's why my panties were wet because I knew I was doing something I shouldn't.

A satisfied heat coiled in my stomach as I stashed away all thoughts of my sexy neighbor and focused on the evening ahead. But the thought of him didn't go away easily. I carefully folded each memory into the tightest origami and tucked it somewhere out of reach. I'd never resist the temptation to keep considering all the various positions we could find ourselves in, dwelling on his every sexy detail down to the delicate divot of his upper lip.

My neighbor certainly qualified as handsome. Masculine yet beautiful. Devastating blue eyes. A true distraction that lingered long after I willed myself to stop imagining him—naked—at my feet—on his knees.

The elevator jostled and slowed as I drew in a bracing breath and tightened my posture just before the doors opened to the lobby. Shoulders back, tits out. Showtime.

Pasting on a pleasant smile, I sashayed out of the foyer and offered the concierge a polite nod as he held the door. All personal details about myself were masterfully disguised as I took that first step into the evening, autumn air.

The sleek Aston Martin Rapide idled silently by the curb as I carefully navigated the brick and cobblestone sidewalk in my pumps. My date, a man with passable looks, a receding hairline, and a designer suit I knew he didn't choose himself, appeared beside the driver's door and grinned.

His gaze measured me from head to toe, undeniable approval reflecting in his eyes. Not devastating eyes like the pair that studied me upstairs, but older eyes, worn by time and the stress that came with a hard-earned fortune and little time to play.

"Avery," he greeted affectionately, gently clasping my elbow and leaning in as if intending to kiss my cheek but not daring to actually put his lips on me. "You're stunning, as usual."

The musk of his cologne lingered by my skin, a scent I'd be wearing all night once I sat in his car. It wasn't an unpleasant fragrance. To be honest, I liked it more than most. But a man's natural scent, clean from the shower without a trace of femininity, remained my favorite scent of all. I wished someone would let men know I wasn't the only woman who felt that way.

"It's nice to see you again, David. I've missed you." I hadn't, but the lie slipped easily as I flawlessly fell into my role.

He opened my door, his chivalry noted and appreciated—an occupational perk I often enjoyed. Once behind the wheel, he glanced at me and smiled. I returned the gesture, meeting his every anticipated expectation.

"Dinner first?"

I'd already eaten, but he didn't need to know that. "Sure. Where would you like to go? You always find the best-hidden gems in the city."

He didn't. He went to all the usual rich and famous haunts, but making him feel superior and unique remained the goal. Reminding him he wasn't my only sugar daddy would be an extreme *faux pas*. I knew better, and that's why I excelled at my job.

"I have the perfect place in mind."

The car shifted, its quality and design evident in the way the leather seat hugged my body at the slightest turn. Another luxury I relished, one I never imagined years ago when I left my home in Blackwater.

Shelving the brief recollection of my old, dilapidated mobile home—*manufactured home* to be more PC—I focused on the present. That shelf where I kept the memories I never talked about, grew more cluttered with unwanted forget-me-nots of my past every day. Unreturned phone calls from Momma, friend requests from old acquaintances left in social media purgatory, and too many dusty recollections to count kept a gnawing sense of guilt alive in my gut. But I kept squeezing my dirty past anywhere it would fit, *'cause I ain't never going back to that hellhole...*

This was where I belonged and planned to stay.

2

NOAH

It took a minute—a solid, cock-swelling sixty seconds—after the elevator doors closed for the breath clogged in my lungs to release. Missed my chance again. What the hell was wrong with me?

Shoving into my condo, I tossed the junk mail onto the marble-topped secretary. My conscience ran on autopilot as my feet carried me to the window facing the street. Hugging the molding, I brushed the curtain aside and narrowed my eyes at the sight of a sleek Aston Martin pulling away. Even the cars she traveled in were sexy as fuck.

Once the vehicle pulled away, my fingers loosened the knot of my tie, and I pretended to push all thoughts of my new hot neighbor aside as I rummaged through the cabinets for dinner. But as I set the barley and wild rice to boil my mind returned to visions of her sweet ass swaying in that tight little dress as she sashayed into the elevator.

She saw me. She had to have seen me. We seemed to be playing some sort of game, and I couldn't tell who held the lead.

The image of her looking up and holding my stare for that split second glance sent a jolt of hot blood pumping to my cock. Oh, yeah. She saw me. Then she got in the car with another guy.

Okay, so she might be dating someone. A complication, but not a game ender. I needed to find out if she was new to town or merely new to the building. This guy might not be the man from the night before. That model Aston Martin retailed for around the two hundred thousand mark and the Mercedes that took her out last night retailed for over eighty grand. Either she only dated luxury car salesmen, or she only dated men who were loaded.

My mind reorganized and categorized every detail about her as if this could somehow make the facts accumulate. I needed more. She had me so distracted, I'd settle for a negative detail, something to drop her from goddess level and put her within my human reach.

She couldn't be more than twenty-two. But not a lot of single women in their early twenties could afford to live here alone. This one just appeared. Boxes arrived. Furniture followed. Then she showed up carrying a designer purse and a leather messenger bag, leaving me and Winston, the doorman, gawking after her. It wasn't the last time she left me gaping like a semi-aroused idiot either. Tonight she'd done it again.

Salad made, I headed to the den and grabbed my iPad. Kicking off my shoes and anchoring my feet on the coffee table, I cued up a search. I'd snagged her name off the mailboxes a few days ago. Avery Johansson. Christ, even her name screamed sexy.

The search pulled up the usual Twitter and Facebook accounts, but none of the profiles fit. I expanded my search to the other social media outlets, but they also proved to be dead ends.

"Who are you, Avery Johansson?"

Tossing my iPad aside, I shifted the weight of my slightly swollen cock in my pants. Whoever she was, I intended to have her. Sure, I had plenty of other options. My contacts held ample names of available, hot women. But this particular woman scored beyond a ten. She easily captured the total package.

Toned legs that went up to her throat, an ass I could make a meal out of, big, sexy, *don't you want to fill my mouth* eyes, and lips that could keep a dick warm for winters at a time. She was perfect.

Not used to women requiring this much strategy, I got a small thrill from the idea of a hunt. First, I needed more than a hallway pass by to get to know her. I wanted a chance to touch her, look into her eyes without the threat of a door closing between us. I needed to lure her into my domain. Picturing her in my space caused my insides to hum with hopeful satisfaction. If I could get her there, I might keep her until morning.

By the time I finished eating and had the dishes washed, I'd come up with a plan. I'd host a party. Nothing fancy and I could pass it off as a work thing, providing the perfect opening for personal details.

Avery appeared to enjoy successful men. I'd accomplished a comfortable level of success for my age, enough not to feel threatened by *her* success or the success of the men she passed the time with. Going by her clothing and living situation, she'd accomplished quite a bit at an early age.

Unsure what would get her naked faster, I decided to balance the party between upscale chic and trendy and prepster casual. I needed a wingman, someone with a little insight into women.

My thumb dragged over the screen of my phone, opening my favorites. There, beneath my parents and sister sat the number of my go-to gal. She answered halfway through the first ring.

"If this is about the papers you forgot on your desk, I already had them overnighted," Lucy answered.

Shit. I totally forgot about that. "That's why I pay you the big bucks."

She laughed, a cross between charming appreciation and the subtle hint she was overdue for a raise. I'd give it to her. As an invaluable personal assistant, Lucy always moved five steps ahead and anticipated my every move.

"I have a project I need you to get started on—something fun."

"My pen is poised. Whatcha' got?"

"I want to have a staff party here at the condo. Something nice, but not too formal. Give them something to talk about on Monday."

As I tossed out ideas, she bounced them back with better ones, and within ten minutes, the details were worked out. Of course, I didn't tell Lucy my motives. One, I didn't want her to think less of me, and two, I didn't want to work under a microscope once I lured my hot neighbor through the door.

Once Lucy understood the objective, and we got the ball rolling, I returned to fantasizing about Avery. I imagined her toned body and blonde hair. She'd be wrapped in my sheets come Sunday morning. I didn't care if that made for an awkward workweek afterward. I needed to have her, and I wasn't going to stop obsessing until I did.

3

AVERY

I stared through the tinted window of Christopher's Porsche, admiring the brick homes towering down Society Hill. *I live here.* The thought never got old.

The exquisitely maintained townhomes along Delancey Street were so picturesque, day or night, with their high gloss painted shutters and waving American flags. Sometimes I felt as if I'd been transplanted from a government crisis into a Norman Rockwell centerfold.

"Can I walk you up?"

My gaze drifted from the handsome road dotted by antique streetlamps to rest on my date's hopeful smile. He behaved like a gentleman, but I suspected others often missed his softer sides. Disinterested in what hid under that designer suit, and fully aware of the wedding ring on his finger, I played the sweet innocent who always abided the rules.

A polite smile softened my eyes. I couldn't wait to wash off the ten pounds of mascara weighing down my lashes.

"Thank you, but I don't want to trouble you. Parking's a nightmare, and it's only a short walk to my door."

"I don't mind. I'm sure I can find a spot nearby."

Keeping my expression friendly, I noted the non-verbal invitation he fished for, careful not to fall for the bait. He would park, walk me to my door, try for a kiss, and use his best moves to secure an invitation inside. If I were privy to his imagination, there would be some pretty intense petting that would undoubtedly lead to sex. But that wasn't our arrangement, and I remained unshakably grounded in my own mind, which only entertained fantasies motivated by my own personal benefit.

"Christopher," I said gently, brushing my fingertips over the back of his hand. "You know that's not how this works."

"Maybe we should renegotiate our arrangement."

Maybe we should, but I wasn't a fool, and I never agreed to anything after cocktails or midnight. "We could, but I think that's a conversation best had in the light of day."

By then he'd reconsider because *everything* came with a price and I'd yet to appraise the true cost of my dignity. Chances were, no matter how rich the client, none of them could afford the whole package. My heart wasn't for sale.

Appearing to accept I wasn't going to budge, he eased back in the driver's seat, out of my personal space. "I'll call you."

"I hope you do. Tonight was wonderful. Thank you." Only because I rejected him did I press a kiss to his jaw, a consolation he wasn't used to receiving from me. "Goodnight."

"Goodnight. I'll wait until you're inside."

So thoughtful.

I exited the car and pulled my wrap over my shoulders. The air held a chill for mid-autumn, and I longed to strip out of this dress, and these five-inch heels then snuggle into my fuzzy slippers and sweats.

As the doorman greeted me, I glanced back to give Christopher a wave, sighing as he pulled away. Some nights were more exhausting than others, but the perks of my job always far outweighed the drawbacks.

On the elevator to the third floor, my finger slipped into my wristlet to glide along a crisp envelope. Whoever said cash was cold comfort didn't understand the warmth of a renovated eighteenth-century gas fireplace or eight hundred thread count sheets.

I wasn't a snob. Snobs didn't appreciate the finer things. I appreciated every luxury I came by, each one a jagged reminder of where I'd been.

This envelope, like several others that came before, would go home to Blackwater—another consolation to make up for my recent avoidance. My mother would be satisfied with the money and forgive me for not calling as much as I probably should.

Stepping onto the ivory tile of the third floor, I gasped as my foot slipped and my ankle twisted painfully. A quick pinch shot through my heel and my little purse flung from my hand. I went down with the grace of an antelope attacked on the nature channel.

The cold tile floor smacked against my knees and palms as I caught my weight and my arms and legs sprawled inelegantly. Of course, the door across from mine opened.

"Jesus, are you all right?"

Large, masculine, bare feet stepped into my line of vision, and I quickly swiveled to sit. I slipped my heels off, struggling to stand without exposing any concealed body parts.

"My shoe broke." I stood, applying too much pressure to my ankle and hissed with pain as I lost my balance.

"Careful." A large hand gripped my elbow and steadied me, jolting my body with an almost electric shock as my eyes lifted and stared into his.

Everything I was, everything I thought, everything I believed I knew, disappeared, as his gaze swallowed me whole. I felt myself drowning in an ocean of arctic blue, those full lashes the most majestic shade of gold, prettier than the belly of a blushing cloud. I wasn't breathing, but I didn't have to. Drowning had never felt so good.

I jerked my stare away and breathlessly took account of all my belongings. My purse lay crumpled on the floor behind him.

"Th—thank you."

Embarrassment curdled in my stomach as I joltingly pulled my arm out of his steadying grip. The flawless picture I'd painted a few nights ago had been smeared with the image of a graceless klutz. I needed to get into my apartment and out of this hallway.

"Did you hurt yourself?"

"Only my pride."

My palms stung, and my knees would likely wear a nasty bruise by morning, but it could have been much worse. I gave my ankle a slow wiggle before putting weight back on the leg. I stepped gingerly, testing my tender ankle.

"No wonder you fell." He lifted my hand holding the unbroken shoe, and another bolt of electricity sizzled up my arm. "Look at these things. They're stilts!"

I pulled my shoe back and scowled at him. That was a mistake.

His crystal blue eyes pinched at the corners. Such creases weren't caused by age, but by charisma, charm, and a good sense of humor. There literally seemed to be some sort of magnetic pull coming from those eyes, so I forced my gaze lower. His lips were full, surrounded by the perfect amount of dark blond stubble. He had a foot of height on me. Of course, I wasn't wearing shoes, but neither was he.

My head tipped away, and I couldn't hide the flush warming my cheeks, not with my pale hair twisted into a tight bun. "I'm fine. Thanks."

My gaze returned to my wristlet and held, silently begging him to go back inside so I could gather my belongings and nurse my wounds in private. Mainly, I wanted to ice down my wounded ego.

His head turned, his stare following mine. And then I looked at his hair. The tousled, flaxen waves struck me as Nordic, and maybe he was. It made sense, given his height. He bent to collect my purse, his body folding low and springing back up with the grace of a jungle cat.

He personified a golden lion, appearing soft and beautiful but lethal all the same, a predator in his own domain. I swallowed, only to find my throat bone dry. I, apparently, had been cast as the clumsy, cornered antelope. Running would only entice the hunt, and I wasn't a fan of feeling like prey.

"You dropped this."

My focus lingered on the ridiculously long fingers clutching my tiny purse, and a frisson of excitement spiked in my blood, changing my inner temperature from uncomfortably warm to scorching hot. I cringed at the docile way my body responded in his presence. *I* was the alpha.

I didn't want to take the purse for fear I might touch him again, but apparently, he didn't register my personal boundaries.

Clasping my free hand, he lifted it, pressing the wristlet into my palm and curling my fingers around the material. The slightly rough but warm pad of his thumb pressed into my skin. The contact disappeared before I could truly decide if I liked or hated it.

"I'm Noah." The deep timbre of his voice sent a shiver up my spine.

Clumsily, I took a step back. "Thank you, Noah. I'm sorry if I woke you."

"You didn't. I've been meaning to introduce myself since you moved in, but you always seem to be on your way out."

I nodded because my vocal cords had dried up like an old mollusk. I could almost taste the sand clogging my throat.

Blinking up at him, I got lost in his expectant stare.

Damn it! Stop looking at him!

It happened so suddenly, like Alice falling through the looking glass, my bearings seemed there one moment, gone the next. I couldn't stop falling into his all-consuming stare.

When we were kids, my brothers and I would play Tag at the old quarries. When the person who was *It* chased me, my heart would race a million miles a second as I hauled ass back to base. My heart raced like that now. I yearned for sanctuary. I needed to get to base.

A sharp mental smack landed in the back of my head as the last of my common sense showed up to save the day.

He's not for you! Stop looking at him like that before you ruin everything! Do you want to move? You don't shit where you eat!

Without another word, I turned and hobbled to my door, my bare feet slapping along the cool tile, and my face pinching with every limping step. With a trembling hand, I removed my key and completely missed the lock, stabbing just past the deadbolt and taking a gouge out of the finish. I tried again, my heart pounding in my ears and fingertips.

I wasn't a fool. This wasn't some mere burst of sexual attraction throwing me off. It couldn't be. My sole desire remained to appear as if I belonged, to prove I had the right to be there, the eloquence to not stick out like a sore thumb, and the privileged upbringing to never need to explain myself. Busting my ass like a first-rate bimbo wasn't exactly sending that message.

"We still haven't been fully introduced."

Head down, I licked my lips as the door gave way. Without saliva, my mouth stayed ash dry. Swallowing uncomfortably, I forced myself to face him head on.

"I'm Avery. Avery Johansson." Despite my riled hormones, I kept my stare neutral—not too strong and not too passive.

"It's nice to meet you, Avery Johansson. I hope to see you around."

With a tight nod, I backed into my apartment and shoved the door shut. My hand gripped the knob as my fingers slackened around my shoes, sending them clattering to the hardwood floor. I panted quietly.

Shutting my eyes, I rested my clammy palm on my chest where my heart beat like a tribal drum. My head fell back, and I sighed.

Some people were too damn perfect—especially *him*. I couldn't embarrass myself like that again. And I certainly couldn't afford to get near him again. He affected me differently than any other man I'd met since moving to Philadelphia. I didn't like it.

Sagging against the wood, I groaned. Why did he seem so different?

"God, he's pretty." A total distraction and I was an idiot for teasing him, never once thinking he'd remain my neighbor and the joke might be on me.

I blew out a breath. "I might have to move even if I don't fuck him."

4

AVERY

As the manicurist applied a second coat to my nails, my phone flashed, notifying me of an email. Careful not to smudge the fresh polish, I swiped the pad of my finger across the screen and navigated to my inbox. Micah. Short and sweet in true Micah style.

Tonight. 6:00. Black tie formal. Can you make it? ~M.

I quickly responded, letting him know I'd be ready and waiting. The message sent and my phone pinged seconds later with his reply.

Good girl. Money's in your account for attire and jewelry. I'm picturing you in something red. See you in a few hours. ~M.

Moving to the dryer, I glanced at the time. Five hours. I could make that work. "Is it possible to fit me in for a wax?"

The manicurist checked the appointment book, and within ten minutes, I was gritting my teeth through a Brazilian. I hated being waxed, but I loved the ability to afford such indulgent spa treatments. And held myself to a certain high standard, that of a woman of means and strict beauty rituals. These were the differences between the girl I was and the woman I aimed to be. I opted to have my eyebrows threaded since I had a date in a few hours. There wasn't time for puffiness.

Buffed and polished, I scheduled a return appointment for hair and makeup at four. Two hours to find a dress, shoes, and all the accessories necessary for a black tie affair.

A notification came directly to my phone that funds had been electronically deposited. *Nice.* If anything, Micah, my most generous client and most important Daddy, took great care of me. Twelve hundred dollars of *make myself pretty* money. More than enough.

First stop, a consignment boutique in Society Hill that carried only name brand labels. I needed to look like twelve hundred bucks while spending as little as possible. I had other plans for the balance.

They knew me at the boutique and knew I usually shopped on a time crunch. As I walked in, the clerk, Twyla, dropped what she'd been doing to help me.

"He wants something red tonight." They never asked who *he* was and why should they? It was none of their business.

"Oh, we have this adorable new romper—"

"It's a black tie function."

Twyla deflated and twisted her lips, her gaze scanning the neatly organized racks. She suddenly perked up. "We just got a new shipment in. I think I saw something red in satin back there. Hopefully, it's in your size. Let me check."

I moved to the shoe display while Twyla searched for a dress. A great pair of nude Nappa heels for only forty dollars caught my eye. They likely retailed for a couple hundred. They were a size too small, but for a deal like that... I took them off the shelf and moved to the jewelry display, not seeing anything fitting with tonight's theme.

"Avery, you're in luck!" Twyla reappeared, carrying a devil red gown draped over her arm and nearly trailing on the polished floor. "*And* it's a size two. But it might need a hem." She lifted the gown and hooked it on an ornate sconce.

"Oh..." Drawn into the sultry ripples, I ran my fingers along the gently pleated chiffon. It wasn't satin but somehow better. "Can I try it on?"

"Of course."

Once in the dressing room, I shimmied out of my clothes and Twyla helped me with the zipper. The dress fit like a second skin and draped perfectly along my curves.

"What do I do about this?" I gestured to the plunging neckline that plummeted to my lowest rib.

Twyla arched a brow. "Nothing. You look incredible. That dress was made for you."

Now, for the painful part... "How much?"

"Retail, it originally went for nine. I can go as low as one-fifty for you. One seventy-five if you want it pressed. Two if you need a hem."

"The nude Nappa pumps out there. I left them by the jewelry—"

"Perfect!" Twyla snapped her fingers and disappeared, returning to the dressing room a second later with the heels in hand.

Mindful of my still tender ankle, I slipped the shoes onto my feet. Finding my balance, I stepped onto the pedestal facing the half octagon of mirrors.

"How do I look?"

"My God. What I wouldn't give to have your body just for a day."

I smiled at the sweet compliment, but no amount of flattery removed the longing for a Philly cheesesteak and a chance to sleep in rather than hit the gym every day at dawn. This *body* took a ton of work.

"Thanks. I'll take it."

"And lucky you, with those shoes, you won't need any alterations."

I left the gown with Twyla so it could get steamed and delivered to my apartment in an hour. I took a cab to Jeweler's Row.

I only shopped for wear and toss jewelry. If the paste held the stones for one night, I got my money's worth and walked away with money in the bank.

Settling on a stunning black choker and sophisticated studs, I'd found the perfect compliments to the red gown. Everything I knew came from watching others, fashion sense like, sometimes less was more.

As I left the store and hailed a cab, I reevaluated my spending. One-seventy-five on a dress, forty on shoes, eighty-five on jewelry. And hair and makeup shouldn't be more than one-thirty—including tip.

I prided myself on being a generous tipper since I, too, benefited from the practice. My total cost came in under five hundred but looked over a thousand, a successful shopping spree if I ever saw one.

I made excellent time and saved over seven hundred dollars to put toward tuition—plus the money I'd make tonight.

Leave it to Micah, the man who introduced me to the sugar baby profession, to also remind of the perks. The price of financial independence only cost me a little time each week.

I never expected to be a sugar baby or, more impressively, a college graduate. When I earned a scholarship and packed up my childhood bedroom back in Blackwater, I had doubts that I'd succeed. I feared I'd eventually return to that shithole called home.

My brothers left years before, long after my mother drank herself into a depression that deteriorated into abuse. But I couldn't abandon her completely. Maybe I was fucked up, but she needed help and I was the only person willing to help her.

But I was never going back. I lived with the mentality of an animal willing to gnaw off its own leg to escape a bad situation. Blackwater was a graveyard of broken dreams and disillusioned folks with more faith in scratch-off tickets than labor laws.

I'd been a kid when I realized getting out meant depending on myself and clawing my way to the top even when exhaustion and hunger held me down. I'd do whatever it took to break away from that past, even if it meant leaving others behind.

My life didn't have time for moral reflection or guilt. I was too busy surviving. Everything in this world came with a price, and the one thing people were always claiming they couldn't buy was *youth.*

I was young enough, pretty enough, and I had enough brains to know sometimes you had to rob Peter to pay Paul. Being a sugar baby meant borrowing against my youth to afford a better future.

Less than one year of college left, and I'd be a certified teacher, qualified to earn a respectable income and live a normal life anywhere I pleased. Once I landed a real job, I'd never have to return to Blackwater again, and I'd never have to fake attraction again.

"What do you think?" The stylist turned my chair away from the make-up artist, and I faced a reflection too pretty to be me.

"Wow." It never ceased to amaze me how easily they could transform a backwoods trailer park nobody with once mousey brown hair and freckles into a classy, sexy siren. "I don't even recognize myself."

My hair, no longer light brown since having numerous blonde highlights threaded throughout, spun like expensive silk into a wavy bun with impressive height atop my head. And my makeup was drop-dead perfect. Smoked out eyes with gold shimmer accents around the corners, heavy lash extensions, deeply contoured cheekbones, and the perfect nude shade of gloss to give my mouth the sort of pout men went crazy for. Micah would be *very* pleased.

Of all the men I kept arrangements with, there would always be something special about Micah. Dark skinned, quiet, sophisticated, with eyes full of secrets. He'd been my first Daddy and would probably be my last. Of all the Daddies I kept, he remained the only one with whom I shared a special bond. He'd be the hardest to leave.

He never smiled, but he also never failed to express praise. As my leading client, he taught me how to be one of the best sugar babies in the city. I let him get away with more than my other clients ever would.

The doorman called up at precisely five fifty-nine. "Miss Johansson, you have a guest in the lobby."

"Thank you. Please send him up." Micah would always be welcomed past the front desk. It was his name on the lease, after all.

Collecting my wrap and slipping on my heels, I met him at my door. "Always on time."

"Avery." He took my fingers in his hand and pulled me into a slow twirl. "You never fail to impress me. Gorgeous."

"Thank you." I allowed him to adjust my wrap and press a kiss to my cheek.

I couldn't help permitting the kiss. Micah could easily make me beam with pride. Mature and debonair, he defined a class act.

"Shall we?"

Not once did he try for more than my company. He wasn't in a relationship. And, aside from being married to his job, he led a fairly uncomplicated life. I believed our simplistic arrangement survived three years because of its uncomplicated nature.

I trusted him, something I didn't do easily. He encouraged and guided me in the gentlest manner possible. And, in a way, I believed he depended on me, too. Men like Micah didn't rely on many people, something we had in common.

He took my keys as we exited the apartment, and I waited as he fastened the locks. My gaze snagged on the moving dial above the elevator, and my heart stuttered.

Someone was coming.

There were only two of us on this floor, so chances of it being Noah were pretty high. His imminent approach filled me with an uncomfortable emotion, one I struggled to identify and had a hard time hiding from my date.

Micah passed me my keys, and I tucked them into my clutch just as the doors to the elevator parted. My breath escaped in a relieved sigh as a man I didn't recognize entered the hall. The scent of Chinese food wafted from the brown bag he carried, and I knew we only had a few seconds before my neighbor opened his door.

Set on avoiding Noah, very aware of the things he made me feel, the way he looked at me like he wanted to taste me, the way something dark awakened inside of me when I felt his stare on my body—and all the ways we were incompatible, I kept my gaze down. I didn't need complications and Noah couldn't be anything else.

I had my own game I wanted to play—be the untouchable goddess across the hall. When the game changed, I didn't want to play anymore.

Noah was the sort of man who looked comfortable in designer clothes, drove a beautiful garage-kept car, and seemed used to getting his way. The opposite of my type. So why was I obsessed with him?

He was the sort of man I accepted as a client, not the sort I invited into my bed. But, oh, to tie him to my bed...

Never. Going. To. Happen.

Noah was dangerous. If I kept reminding myself of that, the warning might sink in.

Micah rested a familiar hand on the base of my spine as we entered the elevator and turned.

The deliveryman knocked, and Noah's door opened. My breath drew deep and held as my neighbor stepped into the hall.

Noah's potent blue gaze clashed with mine, and the world went utterly still.

"Is everything okay?" Micah's stare needled at my side, but my gaze remained locked with Noah's, trapped in that sticky stillness.

No babies were born, no tears were shed, no birds flapped their wings, and no wind blew. Eerily motionless, time stuttered for that shared second between us, and the moment belonged to only us, no one else could touch it.

And then the spell broke, snapping like a stretch of elastic pulled too far. All of the energy in between lagged and drooped as his gaze drifted over my gown and lifted to Micah.

Noah's lips firmed, and I could taste his displeasure. Not my problem, I reminded myself. I had a job to do, and doing my neighbor wasn't part of it. And I didn't do guilt.

Micah leaned forward to press the button.

We shared an address, nothing more. I had no business behaving like some starry-eyed tween and knew better. If he knew who I really was, he'd know better, too.

The doors closed, and I forced myself to forget about Noah and focus on my date.

"Are you friendly with your neighbor?"

My gaze lifted to Micah's face. "Why do you ask?"

"You didn't say hello. Do you not get along?"

"We only met once. I hardly see him." *Because I'm excellent at avoidance.*

"No need to get defensive, Avery. I was only asking a question. If there's a problem with your neighbor, we could see about having you moved to a different floor."

I swallowed a laugh. The high demand building didn't have vacancies unless someone passed away or got evicted. No one voluntarily left such luxury. Even the apartments on the surrounding blocks had waiting lists. Yet, I somehow knew Micah could have me moved within one business day.

"I love my apartment, Micah. I'm sure my neighbor and I won't have any issues."

"Good."

He escorted me through the lobby, and my gaze snagged on the copy of *Cosmo* resting by the row of brass mailboxes. My guilty pleasure. I intended to devour the magazine in bed tonight after Micah dropped me off.

5

AVERY

After another pleasant evening out, Micah escorted me to the elevator, and my gaze lingered on the row of mailboxes, not a single piece of mail littering the mantle. Someone better have stuck my magazine in my box, or there was going to be a problem.

After a polite goodbye and a soft kiss on my brow, I said goodnight and stripped out of my gown. Plucking the pins from my hair, I searched for my slippers. There was really nothing quite as lovely as pajamas and slippers.

Heading back down to the lobby, not caring about my appearance at one a.m., I unlocked my mailbox and—

Empty.

Frowning, I scanned the antique tables decorating the pristine sitting room of our lobby. Nothing.

Beyond the lobby sat the main vestibule. The doorman sat behind an ornate desk with his back to the security monitors, his focus on his phone and an amused grin pulling at his caramel lips.

"Winston, did someone throw away the mail that was on the mantle?"

He looked more alertly in my direction, straightening his posture and adjusting the visor of his black Pershing hat. "No, ma'am. That would be a federal offense. Are you missing something?"

"Someone stole my magazine."

He raised his brow, and I heard how stupid the accusation sounded. People in this building didn't steal magazines. If they were set on stealing anything, embezzling millions seemed a more appropriate crime for their tax bracket. But someone had taken my magazine.

"Perhaps it didn't get delivered yet."

But I saw it there earlier. "You're sure no one messed with the mail?"

He straightened the notched lapel of his jacket, the gold trim matching the cuffs and creases of his pants. "You're the only one who had an outside guest in the building this evening. Well, you and Mr. Wolfe."

"Mr. Wolfe?"

Winston grinned. "Your neighbor."

Wolf, lion, thief... Regardless, he was dangerous.

"Oh."

Wait...

Trying not to appear overly curious in my neighbor's life, I casually asked, "He had company tonight?" Was his guest male or female?

"Just a supper delivery, but I watched the cameras the entire time the man was in the building, and he didn't go near the mailboxes, Ms. Johansson."

My gaze darted to the surveillance screen. Five views captured the front entrance, each floor, and the lobby. "Can you see who did?"

"Uh, I could, but that involves rolling back the tapes and interrupting the feed. I'm not the person to do that. I'm sure it's just a simple misunderstanding, another neighbor mistaking the magazine for their own. How about I give you the four dollars to purchase a new one and from now on I'll ask the mailman to leave any extra items for you at my desk?"

I sounded like an idiot, making a big deal out of a four-dollar magazine. Swallowing my disappointment, I shook my head.

"No, that won't be necessary. It's just a magazine. Thanks anyway."

But it was *my* magazine, and someone took it. Who the fuck steals a *Cosmo*?

Jamming my finger against the elevator button, I stepped inside. There went my big plans for the remainder of the night. I should probably get some sleep anyway.

Tomorrow I had school and tomorrow night I had a date with Josh. Josh was a regular, in his forties, what most women would consider dull, but he had a sweet personality, and I'd come to enjoy his anecdotes.

6

AVERY

After class, I rushed through my routine and had my hair blown out into sexy waves and my makeup done in a matter of thirty minutes. Josh didn't do fancy. He enjoyed ordinary things, but with some guaranteed company.

I never had to load on the makeup or wear more than a pair of trendy jeans and a cute shirt with him. He said he liked my hair down and thought women were prettiest when they looked like they weren't wearing any makeup at all. I couldn't do zero makeup, but I made it look like I could.

We had dinner at a trendy sports bar and played some games in the game room afterward. Josh kept quiet around outsiders, but once in a while, he'd find the courage to cradle my hips at a pinball machine. He seemed harmless, so I let him. I liked Josh, and one day I hoped he found his Mrs. Right and fell in love.

Josh needed confidence, and I wanted to give it to him. So when he cupped my hips, I leaned in just enough to let him know harmless flirting worked when on a date. His tameness kept our dates worry free. I selfishly used his need to practice physical displays of affection to feed my need for mild contact.

After our date, he drove me home and watched me walk to the

door. It had been one of my easier nights. Our ease together kept him penciled in, even when I could be making a bigger profit with a more affluent client.

I let myself into my apartment and kicked off my shoes. Not two seconds after I walked through the door did someone knock. A partial chill chased over my arms as I worried Josh might have gotten the wrong impression and found the nerve to finally ask for more. Sighing, I walked to the door and opened it. Not Josh, but Noah, holding my *Cosmo* magazine in his hand.

"The mailman accidentally put this in my mailbox."

Liar, liar, pants on fire...

My brows slowly lifted. "Is that so?"

He smiled, and I bet that smile got him everything his little heart desired, which was probably why he thought it was okay to run around stealing people's mail.

"The post office is always screwing up."

Now, he was blaming the post office? Outraged on behalf of mail carriers everywhere, I arched a brow.

"Well, thanks." I took my magazine, and his gaze lifted over my shoulder.

I turned, wondering what he saw, trying to see my home for the first time with fresh eyes. Sometimes it still got me in the chest when I stepped back and appraised how far I'd come. But now was not the time to get nostalgic and emotional.

When he made no move to go back to his door, I gave a tight-lipped smile. "Thanks for returning it."

I'll be sure to collect my mail more promptly in the future.

"Do you have plans Friday night?"

I frowned, wondering why he wanted to know. "Um..." Did I have plans? No, not yet. "I'd have to check my schedule."

"I'm having a party. Just a small get together with a few work friends."

His gaze drifted over my shoulder again, and I did a double take. He seemed to be searching for something in my apartment.

His attention snapped back to me. "Sorry, am I interrupting? Do you have company?"

Well, wasn't he nosy? I angled the door for privacy, bracing my body between him and the opening.

My upbringing embedded the need for maintaining the upper hand in all things and left little room to trust outsiders. He obviously thought I had someone there, and I strangely enjoyed his unanswered suspicions. Mystique could serve as a powerful aphrodisiac, and I'd accidentally stumbled into teasing him again.

I lowered my lashes and smiled. "I don't think I have plans."

His eyes flashed to mine, and this time, I didn't buckle under the intensity of his stare. "Everyone's coming over around eight. Just some drinks and hors d'oeuvres. Nothing fancy."

Where I came from, anything with a dollar store tablecloth and chips was fancy, but he wouldn't know that. "If I'm free I'll stop by."

I *was* going to stop by because we were playing a metaphorical game of doctor—show me yours and I'll show you mine. He saw my apartment now I needed to see his. Tit for tat. I might even steal something while there to even the score for my *Cosmo*.

"Great. I'll see you then."

"See you then."

As I closed the door, I smiled, but quickly rolled my eyes. "You know better, Avery. Don't waste your time."

The rest of the week passed in a blur of dates and studying. Friday morning I received a text from a sporadic client who paid well but got under my skin. He wanted to meet downtown for a few drinks after work. I hesitated, curious to see Noah's apartment and meet his friends, but then common sense kicked in, and I accepted the date.

It was good money, and next semester's tuition would be due soon. I needed to cover all my bases so I could get my books and replace the money I'd sent my mother.

The polite thing would have been to tell Noah I wasn't going to make it to his party, but he'd gone and stolen my mail, so I didn't think normal rules of social etiquette applied.

Although I didn't particularly care for Friday night's client, my appearance served as my moneymaker, so I put the same care into my outfit that I would with any date. My navy blue dress fit like a glove, accentuating all the right curves. And my hair celebrated one of those amazing days where it settled into perfect flowing waves.

My date, an obnoxious prick I only saw on occasion, rattled on about himself and all the ways he saved the day at work this week. I knew his sort well, type-A personality, little dick, terrible in bed because they couldn't stop blowing themselves long enough to take care of the girl. My fake smile cemented on my face for a solid three hours before my cheeks went numb.

Finally, I couldn't take it anymore. "You know what, Richard, I suddenly don't feel so good. I'm so sorry to do this to you, but do you think you might be able to drive me home?"

An easy excuse, being that germaphobia trumped the reasons why Richard remained single. He arched back as far as his stool would allow.

"Is it your stomach or chest? Maybe you should take a cab?"

Was he fucking kidding? "It's just a headache."

His shoulders sagged. "Oh. Sure. I'll have the valet grab my car."

The ride home passed in a tribute to himself and by the time I stepped out of the car, I considered the night worth every penny I'd earned, regardless of cutting it short. When the elevator opened to my floor, bass pounded through the walls, and muffled voices carried. My steps slowed as I eyed Noah's door, open a crack.

No. I should just go to bed.

Sliding my key into the lock, I pressed into my dark, silent apartment and looked back over my shoulder at my neighbor's apartment longingly.

It was a losing battle and my curiosity—the same curiosity that killed the stupid cat—won. "Damn it."

I adjusted my dress and drew back my shoulders before crossing the hall. My fingers tapped lightly on the door, and it eased open.

Couples gathered in every corner and perched on every free surface of furniture. This was just a few friends from work? Wow, his job certainly looked different than mine.

Cheerful conversations and laughter emphasized the easy mood of the living room. Noah was nowhere in sight. I scanned the crowd and made eye contact with a few men dressed in high-end suits and wearing an edge of class. No one wore jeans, and the appetizers Noah mentioned consisted of an omelet station in his den and a gourmet crepe station by the dining room. What kind of party was this?

"Hi. I'm Steve. Are you a friend of Noah's?" Steve looked to be in his late twenties, not wealthy enough to afford me and too handsome and personable to require my services.

"I'm his neighbor."

"Oh. Can I get you a drink? I didn't catch your name."

"It's—"

"Avery. Johansson." Noah's voice stole my attention and a few others' as he spoke my name as if tasting each syllable. "Didn't your mother teach you it's bad manners to arrive late to a party and not let the host know?"

My mother taught me how to shoplift and fix a shoe with duct tape. She also taught me what drunk looked like, which I was pretty sure Noah was.

He sauntered clumsily across the room and pressed an empty glass into Steve's chest, then draped a heavy arm over my shoulder, depositing enough of his weight to make my legs stiffen.

"You're late, Ms. Johansson." His breath, warm and alcohol scented, fanned over my cheek. An inappropriate chill raced down my spine.

I carefully extricated my body out from under his arm. "Sorry. I had an appointment."

His eyes narrowed, one more than the other as if trying to see through a monocle lens that wasn't there. "An appointment? Or a *date*?"

Wouldn't you like to know?

I took his glass from Steve and sniffed it. "Mmm. A honey bourbon man. Steve, I'll take that drink now. Why don't you show me where the bar is?"

Noah frowned as I walked away with his friend.

Steve seemed like a nice guy. Interesting and full of trivial knowledge. We fell into a game of *Fuck, Marry, Kill* with a few other guests while I finished my brown derby cocktail. Several women drank mint juleps, and there seemed a sort of Connecticut class underplayed in the room.

I prided myself in adapting quickly to the setting. Being a sugar baby meant possessing an apt skill to reading a room and sometimes acting as a chameleon, switching roles at a moment's notice. I fit in fine with Noah's friends, and that seemed to confuse Noah all the more, which I loved.

By the time I reached the bottom of my glass, I'd seen enough. Three martinis with Richard and one brown derby put me over my limit. Plus, my feet were killing me in these heels.

I excused myself to find the kitchen and deposited my glass in the sink. Noah's apartment appeared a mirror image of mine, so it didn't take long. However, his kitchen was prettier, and that pissed me off.

Distracted by the cathedral moldings and glazed cabinetry, I didn't hear him come in behind me.

"Enjoying yourself?"

Slowing my breathing, I drew back my shoulders and turned. "Your kitchen's nicer than mine."

"Your bedroom's bigger."

"Excuse me?"

He chuckled. "I checked yours out before you signed the lease. If it was nicer, I'd have switched."

Well, he certainly had an unapologetic thing going for him. I didn't know how to process that comment as it somehow dropped my incredible home down a notch. I reminded myself that I had the bigger bedroom, which made sense since I likely had more clothing.

"I'd love to see what you've done with it." The look in his eyes held full-on challenge.

My chest lifted as I held his stare. "I bet you would. But I think your prior appraisal's going to have to last." There was no way he was getting an invite.

"Don't be sour."

"I'm not. I don't spend a lot of time in the kitchen, so these amenities would be wasted on me." *Damn, was that a wine fridge?*

He edged closer. "Turns out I love to cook as much as I love to fuck, but I've yet to master some culinary arts so I figured I'd keep the apartment with the best space to improve my less honed ... skills."

"Charming." Every guy thought they had the map to the G-spot, but most were more likely to find the Holy Grail first.

He rounded the granite island and glanced into the sink, arching a brow at the empty glass. "Leaving so soon?"

"It's late. I appreciate the invite but—"

"Why were you late?"

"I... I told you. I had an appointment."

"You could've gotten out of it."

I frowned at his arrogant assumption. "How would you know?"

"Because I don't think it was business." He glanced down at my dress. "I think it was personal."

Ahh. "You know, I think I hear my phone ringing."

I turned, and he caught my arm, tugging me back with enough force that my hands braced against his chest, my head tipping back to look into his eyes.

"Have dinner with me, Avery Johansson."

"No."

"Why not?"

"Because we're neighbors and we both like living here and I don't want it to get weird."

"Maybe it'll get good weird."

"It won't."

He leaned his long body into the counter, his thumb sliding slowly over my bare arm where he held me as we faced off. My breath hitched, and I held it so not to give any clue of the effect he had on me.

"Come on. One dinner. I'll treat."

I laughed. "I know you would, but my answer's still no."

"Afraid you'll actually enjoy yourself?" His gentle grip glided to my wrist, reminding me that my hands still rested on his chest.

My frown deepened. "What's that supposed to mean?"

"I see you going out on dates, a different guy every other night. None of them are right for you. Why would you date someone so much older? You're young, beautiful, and I bet you're incredible in bed."

I yanked my hands away from him but kept my position, his body pinning mine between the sink and his. "Wouldn't you like to know what earns them my time? It's a shame you never will."

"A thousand bucks says you're wrong."

I gave a humorless laugh. "Only a thousand?" That was no small bet.

He brazenly caught a piece of my hair between two fingers and gently tugged. "You'd like it. I'd make sure of that. First, it would be gentle, and then it would get frantic. I'd make you wait, for your own good, letting the torture build into an intense burn until you begged, *Please, Noah, please...*" His voice took on a falsetto tone as he did an impression of a woman who sounded nothing like me.

I rolled my eyes. If anyone begged it'd be him.

He leaned closer as if imparting a dark secret. "By the time I'm inside of you, you'd be gasping out my name, and when I hold your arms behind your back and dig my teeth into your shoulder, pounding every hard inch of my cock into your hot little pussy, you'll be wondering why you ever considered dating those losers when everything you wanted, waited right across the hall."

My jaw literally unhinged. What. A. Douchebag.

That wasn't how it would go down—which it wouldn't—but if it did, it would be Noah pleading. Eyeing him from head to toe, I eased closer, letting my assets brush against his front as I moved my mouth only a kiss away from his.

"Do you know what I like to do with men like you, Noah Wolfe?"

His lashes lowered as he stared at my mouth. "What?"

"I like to strip them down, unburden them, remove every touch of ego, and leave them utterly bare. The things I could do to you... You wouldn't be able to handle it. So let's pretend you didn't just share all those fantasies and it won't be weird the next time I sense you watching me in the hall. Because no matter how much you wish you could fuck me, that's not how I operate."

I glanced around his hundred-thousand-dollar kitchen, still pissed it was nicer than mine. "This little game of cat and mouse we've been playing... I think you've got the roles mixed up. Poor, little Noah. You're not the cat. I am. I eat men like you for breakfast." Rising on my toes, I slowly dragged my tongue over the stubble of his jaw and bit his earlobe until he let out a guttural moan. "And I know you stole my fucking magazine."

With a smile cocky enough to rival any arrogant, penis-toting prick at the party, I lifted my chin and sauntered out of the kitchen. And, yes, he watched me go.

7

NOAH

I gripped the granite lip of the cabinet as she sauntered out of the kitchen, my cock fully engorged and pressing noticeably against the zipper of my pants. Jesus Fucking Christ, she was a thousand times better than I'd imagined.

So. Many. Fantasies.

After her clumsy little fall in the hall, I'd entertained some nice damsel in distress scenarios where I'd come to her rescue, and she'd act shy and skittish in my presence, but this outranked all those fantasies. She had a fierceness about her I'd never come across before, a fucking killer queen bee, a perfect blend of adventure and hauteur. Getting close to her meant I'd likely get stung, but I didn't care.

My mother had friends in Rhode Island, women my father referred to as WASPs, white Anglo-Saxon Protestants. They were the well-bred New England women with a lineage dating back to British Ancestry and money old enough to be linked to household patents. Maybe Avery hailed from upstate New York.

She had class, a sweet ass, and her sexy little mouth just got a serious upgrade when she called me out for stealing her *fucking* magazine. I scratched shy off the list.

That woman had grit, and spice, not at all sweet and zero interest in playing nice. Assertive as hell, I needed to know what motivated her, what made her tick, and what she sounded like when she came —preferably on my dick.

"There you are."

Lucy entered the kitchen, and the sexual tension evaporated. Lacking the height of the bombshell that just left, my assistant stared across the island at me.

"Why are you in here all alone?"

Her round eyeglasses swallowed her face, reminding me of a cartoon owl. With a small, pointed nose and those thick, dark bangs and big eyes.

I rested my forearms on the countertop, waiting for my semi to go down. "I ... lost my drink. I needed to get a new glass."

She smiled as if I'd said something clever. "I can make you a new cocktail."

She opened the cabinet with perfect familiarity. Of course, she knew the location of items. She'd been the one to purchase my dishes and supervise the deliveries of everything down to my throw pillows. When I couldn't find something, I called Lucy, and she knew exactly where to find whatever it was I needed.

As she leaned up to reach for a tumbler, my gaze drifted to her skirt. Pleated wool hid what appeared to be a flat ass, and her shoes were adult T-strap Mary Janes. I paid her well enough to afford a decent wardrobe, but her style remained that of a frumpy librarian. Sort of nerdy hot, but not my type.

"While I have you here alone," I said, thinking this the perfect time to thank her for putting this party together, even if Avery only stopped by for thirty minutes. "I've been meaning to tell you, you're getting a raise."

Surprise skittered across her face as it angled up at me. "I am?"

She remained a puzzle, so capable yet sometimes seeming so unsure, a total contradiction within herself.

"You've earned it. I'd be lost without you, Luce."

Her smile beamed, and she tugged on her mauve cardigan, which had pulls and pilling at the seams. “Wow, Noah. Thank you.”

I stilled as her hand rested on my arm, still draped on the counter. We both stared at it for a split second, and when my gaze returned to hers, her smile fell. The touch disappeared.

“I’ll get you that drink.”

She hustled out of the kitchen in a cloud of mauve wool and bad shoes.

Returning to the party, I played the happy host slash cool boss. The party improved when the guests discovered the karaoke streaming setting on the television.

As the alcohol poured and inhibitions faded, the music grew louder, and the talent took a serious hit. Through it all, my gaze kept returning to the front door, my thoughts wondering what my neighbor was doing.

A silent laugh churned through my chest. Was that ego talk a challenge, because if so, I was game.

We’d see who couldn’t handle it. I caught her nipples hardening in the kitchen. God, she was so fucking mouth watering.

You wish you could fuck me...

It was more than a wish. It was a goal. And I had every intention of succeeding.

Tracing where she’d scraped her tongue, I smiled. Challenge accepted.

The next time I saw Avery Johansson’s nipples, I intended to sink my teeth into them.

8

AVERY

The following few weeks passed in a whirlwind of projects, dates, and cramming for upcoming finals. Although I heard Noah in the hall at times, I made sure to avoid crossing his path, and he seemed to do the same.

Late November, my mother called crying. It had finally happened. She'd lost her job at the mill and wasn't sure she'd qualify for the subsidies her neighbors were receiving, because I'd been sending her additional income.

"Why does Sheryl Pinkerton know I'm sending you anything, Momma? It's nobody's business."

"She saw the check stubs and said the IRS would see it as income and it'll mess up my welfare."

Although educated about a lot of things, income tax and subsidized programs were outside of my knowledge. "Sheryl isn't an accountant. And why are you leaving your banking around for the neighbors to see?"

"Don't you get it, Avery Dean? The checks are drawing suspicions. You're gonna have to get me cash."

"How am I going to do that? No one mails cash."

"You could come home."

"No."

Momma scoffed. "Ain't you ever comin' back? You know Bobby Pritcher's been askin' about you."

I frowned. Bobby Pritcher wasn't going anywhere in life, and I doubted he had rotting teeth left in his sneering, perverted mouth. When he spoke, never saying nice things, it looked like a slithery snake tongue slipping past his lips.

"That's not the way to get me home." All the things that made home a tolerable place weren't there anymore.

"Then what will it take? You've been gone three years. It's enough already."

"I thought you wanted me to make something of myself. That's what I'm doin'."

"By hooking? That ain't what I meant, Avery Dean. I don't know what's become of you. You ain't even a Mudd anymore. Got yourself a fancy name for all those fancy Johns."

My jaw locked, but that didn't stop the sharp prickle of tears burning my eyes. "That's *not* what I do, Momma. I have to go."

"Don't you blow me off, young lady. I raised you better."

She'd always been the one person capable of cutting me down. No matter how much I said her opinions didn't matter to me, they still stung. And now, with her out of work, she'd become more dependent on me for help, more entwined in my life, more toxicity eating away at my goals to be normal.

Unable to draw in enough air, my lungs burned as if I were drowning. "Goodbye, Momma."

After I got off the phone, my mood and focus were shot. In no state of mind to study, I cleaned my apartment.

Within an hour, I had an enormous pile of designer clothes on my bed mixed with shoes, purses, and jewelry that were hardly worn. One by one, I took pictures of each item and uploaded them onto an online auction site. Once I made it halfway through the pile, my tears had gotten the better of me, and I needed to find a tissue.

I was *not* a hooker. I'd never have sex with someone for money, and certainly not with any of my clients. Though there were a few I enjoyed spending time with, like Micah and Josh, there wasn't any real attraction there.

As I reorganized my closet, I thought about how empty my life remained. I had company almost every night, but no one to really call a friend.

Even on campus, when other students spoke about their weekends, I longed to chime in and relate, but I couldn't because I had nothing relevant to add. My life remained different, shrouded in secrets typical twenty-somethings didn't keep.

"Fuck this." I shoved the rest of the shoes into a laundry basket and went to the kitchen in search of something to make me feel better.

As I rummaged through the fridge, shoving away various high-protein, low-carb snacks, my frustration grew.

"Goddamn it!" I slammed the refrigerator door.

My back hit the stainless steel as I slid slowly to the floor and wept. I was pathetic, giving into shame that shouldn't be there.

There was no shame in what I did. Prostitution was a different animal entirely.

If she wanted more money, I'd send her more—enough that she'd never be able to make a comment like that again. But I had to send something fast. Without a paycheck, her calls would turn relentless, and I had too much going on to battle her criticisms on a daily basis. Her words would distract me from my goals, and the guilt for hating her would eat me alive.

Avery Johansson didn't do guilt.

I also didn't easily accept the hatred my mother spurred. Such negativity grew from bitterness. Little comments and digs that cut deep and failed to heal over the years, seeping pain into my dreams for an ordinary life until nothing but mirrored resentment between us remained.

I wanted her to love me but accepted she never would, so I paid her to leave me alone. She wanted to be paid. End of story. I honestly don't think she cared about me as a daughter and the older I got, the less I cared that she might have never loved any of us, which was why we all left the second we finished high school.

Reaching into the pocket of my hoodie, I withdrew my phone and scrolled through my contacts. My sole purpose became finding the money to shut her up as fast as humanly possible.

My thumb hovered over a name I hated above all others. It wasn't because of his bad hair or unpleasant breath. His personality grated on my every nerve. But he paid amazingly well, and I wanted to make a point. I hit send.

His heavy breathing preceded his words. "Well, well, well. It's been a long time, Avery."

"Hi, Don. How have you been?"

"The same. And you, my little doll?"

I rolled my eyes. "The same. I was wondering if you were looking for company?"

He grunted, and I could hear him shifting his position over the phone, his breathing that of a man carrying an extra hundred pounds. "I'm always up for *your* company, sugar. What do you say to tomorrow night at seven?"

I hesitated and shut my eyes. "How should I dress?"

"Mmm. I want a skirt short enough that I can tell the color of your panties and a shirt low enough that it's a guessing game when your little nipples are going to show. And put in some pigtails."

And this was why he paid well. "How long and where?"

"I'll pick a nice place. Say, four hours?"

A second longer and I wouldn't be able to take it. "That'll be two."

"Your price went up."

"Inflation. Did you still want to meet?"

"Four hours, two grand? You better hope I see your nipples. I'll pick you up at seven tomorrow. Don't make me wait."

Do I ever? "I'll see you then."

I ended the call and dropped my head back to the fridge. Four hours and I'd send my mom enough money to shut her up for at least a few months. And then I'd just have to get through my last semester and never have to do this again.

It was all about assuming control. So long as it remained my choice, outside judgment couldn't hurt me. I was in command of my future, and I was doing what needed to be done. Fuck anyone who didn't understand that.

Feeling a bit more grounded, now that I had a plan in place, I went to my desk and stacked my school stuff to the side. My bills weren't overdue, but they were piling up, and they were high. I hated debt, hated owing anyone anything. My profession allowed me to finance my own education so I could graduate without a single loan, and that pleased me more than anything.

One by one, I signed off on checks and slowly emptied my savings until there was only enough for a few meals and most of next semester's tuition. Once school was paid, there would hardly be enough to buy anything else, but I'd get by. I always got by.

The next day was one of those off days that started on the wrong foot and never straightened out. First, it was the machines at the gym. Did no one know how to clean up after themselves?

Then it was a red sock someone left in the laundry room. I didn't think anyone used the facility except me, but apparently, there was another person too poor to hire a service. And now they were running around with one red sock while half my white wardrobe looked like an Easter peep costume.

On top of that, my Lit professor, who apparently hated me for some reason and refused to give me anything more than a C+, put another massive dent in my GPA. My last paper should have earned at least a B. Part of me questioned if she even read the papers. Maybe she had a TA grading them, and that person just randomly threw out any old grade he or she felt like assigning.

If that wasn't enough, my conditioner ran out, leaving my hair a disaster of tangles that wouldn't cooperate. And the bra I intended to wear tonight was nowhere to be found.

Suffice it to say, by six fifty-four I still wasn't ready, and Don was going to be there any minute. I couldn't keep him waiting, or I wouldn't earn my full rate. He had very strict rules about these things.

Hustling out the door, my ass practically hanging past my short miniskirt and my tits bursting from the top of my skintight blouse, I quickly locked up.

"Costume party?"

My back stiffened. Of *course,* he'd see me dressed like this.

I played it off. "Ha. Ha. Sad you're not invited?" The second I turned to face him, I regretted it.

Noah's lips parted as his eyes dropped down to my hips and back up to my chest. "Damn."

I fidgeted, shoving my arms into my coat and covering myself as quickly as possible. "Stare much?"

"Sorry... I just... You look..."

"Whatever. I'm late."

"Hey, Avery, I'm sorry if we got off on the wrong foot." His eyes continued to scan me from pigtails to patent leather school shoes. "I can see you're used to a more sophisticated—"

"Now, you can see?" My attire proved his sarcastic claim a blatant lie, and I hated him for seeing me this way. "Just get out of my way."

"Jesus, are you always such a bitch?"

I drew back. "Excuse me?"

"I'm trying to apologize, and you're twisting everything—"

"You're trying to bait me. Besides, I don't need an apology. I need you to get out of my way before I'm late for my appointment. And I need my neighbors to stop stealing my mail and basically leave me the fuck alone."

His brow lowered. "Are you okay?"

"I'm fine!" Just then the elevator pinged and I wanted to cry. *God fucking damn it with this day!*

Without turning around, Noah's gaze narrowed. "Let me guess... Your *appointment.*"

If I could vanish into thin air that would be fantastic, but my life would never be that easy. Fuck!

"Please just go into your apartment."

His frown deepened, his natural easy going expression tightening with a much more severe look and something else I couldn't quite name. "Why?"

It was too late. The elevator was opening.

Noah quickly whispered, "Tell him to go home. Tell him you changed your mind."

I couldn't see over his shoulder, but I heard the doors open and Don's heavy breathing. I braced for the brutal skid of judgment. He didn't know my reasoning for going out with such a man, and I hated the urge to justify my logic, which there wasn't time to do anyway.

Blinking up at Noah, I gave him a pleading look, silently begging him not to be another person that judged me. I didn't know why it mattered what he thought of me.

"I have to go."

He did a double take of the man now hogging the hall, and I turned, shutting out all distractions and putting myself on the clock. I forced a smile.

Don wore a lecherous smirk, his ruddy coloring coated in a glaze of sweat and his greasy hair combed over his scalp so severely, each strand lay like a black wax strip of dried licorice. There was no way Noah wasn't judging me.

"You ready, my little doll?" His hand slipped under my coat and around my hip, and I cringed. He tugged one of my pigtails. "My pretty little doll." As if just noticing Noah, Don tipped his chin. "How ya doin'?"

Noah didn't move. He didn't blink. He stood stiffly, watching me with a blank expression.

Part of me wanted to say *fuck you* and *mind your own business*! But another part wanted to explain that this was just a job, conversation and cocktails, nothing more—except maybe a few uncomfortable pictures this one liked to save as keepsakes—all for four hours and two grand. Who would turn that down? Maybe a normal girl, but I'd never been normal. Probably never would be either.

I lowered my gaze and accompanied Don to the elevator, nudging his hand away when it lowered to grip my ass. He chuckled as if grab ass was a game we both enjoyed.

I didn't look at Noah. This time it wasn't about playing coy or keeping the upper hand. It was about plain old cowardice and shame. My gaze remained on the ground until we reached the first floor, far away from my neighbor's judgment. And then the clock was ticking. Eight dollars and change per minute.

9

NOAH

My gut knotted as I watched the elevator close to carry them down. All my instincts came to a screeching halt and the excitement to tease her shriveled to nothing. What the hell was she doing with a guy like that?

It made no sense. That man was at least twice her age and was so out of shape his skin seemed made of wax. The way his beady eyes watched her wasn't right. She knew it wasn't right. Yet ... off they went.

Frowning, I headed into my apartment, replaying what just happened and trying to make a lick of sense of it. Sure, I fully intended to break her balls. I enjoyed the banter, especially with a woman who never seemed to flinched.

But tonight she didn't seem in the mood for games. And why did she call her dates "appointments"? These guys were obviously interested in her—though I couldn't see what she was getting out of the deal.

I cringed at the thought of the man who took her out tonight, once again wondering what the hell she could possibly see in him. The longer I thought about it, the closer my confusion turned to revulsion and anger. She could go out with that greasy, pinky ring wearing car salesman but not me?

The little game between Avery and me stopped being fun the instant that guy showed up. If I had to nail down a specific moment, I'd say the game ended the moment I saw something akin to shame flash in her eyes, just before the elevator pinged and her guest arrived.

For a week, I'd been waiting for an opportunity to bait her, tease her, and ask her out again. I also wanted to apologize.

I preferred her with her claws out. Even when I riled her and she showed her bitchy sides I wasn't deterred. What I didn't like was the look in her eyes when that guy put his arm around her. She should never be the type of woman who backs out of a room with her tail between her legs.

Please just go into your apartment...

When she made the request too much vulnerability showed in her big eyes. From minx to field mouse on the run, I couldn't make sense of her.

Every time she went on a date, I saw a side of her I didn't recognize. And why did she date so many men? Not only were the men showing up in droves, they were all wrong for her—too old, too fat, too boring, too ... not me.

I had to have her. And I wanted the real her. The longer she put me off, the more intent I became. My instincts never misled me. Everything inside of me demanded she and I would eventually wind up in a sweat-drenched tangle of sheets. I couldn't wait.

My nose twitched. The other man's cologne still saturated the air. My stomach turned at the thought of Avery wearing such a scent on her skin. That guy would suffocate her.

Maybe it was a blind date, the sort one wanted to escape the second it started. Even if she did call it an appointment, the way he looked at her clarified it as a date. But she flinched when he touched her.

Fuck. I should have done something. She didn't want to go out with that guy. I saw it in her eyes.

I have to go...

She didn't *have to* do anything. Now, I was pissed. Have to go... Why the hell did she have to do anything when it obviously made her uncomfortable? Irritated, I tried to think about something else, but my thoughts quickly returned to her.

I needed to know more about her. I needed a glimpse beyond her front door and an explanation for why she insisted on dating so many obviously wrong men. But none of that was happening tonight, so I needed a distraction.

Pulling out my phone, I Facetimed my sister. The line buffered and her smiling face appeared.

"What's up?" By the wobbling screen and dusky sky, I assumed she was out for a walk.

"Nothing. Just figured I'd check in."

"I just spoke to you this afternoon. Did something happen since then?"

I forgot I already talked to her today. Laurel and I typically touched base about once every three days. Anything more than that signaled something was wrong.

"No, nothing happened. I'm just bored."

"Bullshit, Noah. This afternoon you told me how busy you were. You don't go from that to bored in four hours. Something's bothering you if you call and I—"

"Fine." Jesus, she could be annoying when she wanted to, particularly because she knew me better than anyone else. "I need a distraction."

"From?"

"Some girl. My neighbor."

Her gaze, which had been mostly focused on her path, flashed to the screen, and she raised a brow. "Really? Did she just move in? This is the first I'm hearing about..."

"Avery."

"Pretty name. What's she like?"

Sexy as fuck. Legs that went on for days. Hair that smelled so good it could get you high. Lips meant for my cock, and tits meant for my mouth. "She's difficult to read."

"But she's caught your attention."

Brakes squealed in my head. "Hold on, Laurel, this isn't like that. She isn't someone I plan on getting serious with."

"Why, because you might actually stumble on something with substance? How tragic!"

"While your sarcasm's appreciated, it's unnecessary. She's not the monogamous type." Not according to her fucking merry-go-round doorway of dates. "I just want to get to know her."

"You mean sleep with her."

"Well ... yeah. That too."

"God, Noah, if it's all just sex, who cares what she's like."

"I do."

"But why? I mean, if it's over by morning, what difference does it make."

She had a point. "I don't know. It's the way the game's played."

She growled, and the sky shifted to interior ceilings. I recognized the crown molding from her place and waited as she took a guzzling sip of water and blotted the sweat off her brow. When she was refreshed, she looked at the screen, the sternness of her stare reminding me of our mother's serious look saved only for threats of grounding and loss of privileges when we were children.

"Margaux cheated on you four years ago. How much longer are you going to let someone else's actions control you?"

And there it was. The stinging truth I still hated to face.

"This has nothing to do with Margaux. Why would you even bring her into this?"

"This has *everything* to do with her, Noah. Come on! You've spent years getting over what she did. Enough wasting time."

"I'm not wasting time." But now I regretted calling my sister. "Look, I didn't call for a lecture."

"No, you called because a woman caught your eye and you want to know how to keep it superficial when your nature insists you find something with depth. You're not some philandering bachelor. Once you accept that, you'll be happy again."

"Laurel," I spoke slowly so there could be no misunderstanding. "I'm not looking for a relationship."

"Why not?" Her sharp tone gave me pause.

"Because I'm not." My debating skills were taking a hit today.

She rolled her eyes. "Fine. But I can't help you."

Irritated I brought Laurel into this, I quickly shut it down. "I don't want help. I just wanted a distraction—"

"Well, keep looking for one, Noah. If you find one big enough to get this girl out of your head, I'll believe it was just a casual sex thing. But if you can't, then you have to admit it might be time you move on and put the past behind you. You've always been a serial monogamist. Sleeping around isn't your style. *That's* why you're bored."

When I got off the phone, I made dinner. My sister's final warning lingered in my thoughts. We were close in age, but she always seemed so much wiser when it came to relationship things. Maybe she was right.

No, I knew she was right. Random hook-ups had always bored me, but the thought of trusting someone again deterred me from anything long term.

One-night stands were fun but redundant. The same old meaningless conversations, the getting to know you and knowing there was never going to be more than a few frisky fucks...

After a year it got tiresome. I'd fucked my way through several women, obliterating all traces of the girl I was supposed to marry.

Once I could hardly remember Margaux's scent or the sounds she made when she came, I kept going, working to erase her face and laughter from my memory. I still knew what she looked like, but there were several other women stacked on top of my memories of her now, so it kept her away from my surface thoughts.

There was only one memory I couldn't erase. Margaux and Shane, my ex-best friend. They were married now. She finally got the spring wedding she'd always dreamed of. Who the fuck knew who

Shane's best man was? We always assumed we'd be up there with each other. But I also assumed he would never be the sort of guy to stab me in the back. Lesson learned.

And why was I still thinking of this?

After a quick shower, I shoved all thoughts of my past away and hit the sac. I needed to focus on the future, not the past.

Even if Laurel was right, and I was ready to move on and start dating again, I highly doubted Avery was the girl. Something about her struck me as unattainable, purposely out of reach. She didn't seem like the dating type. Or maybe she was still playing the field. She was definitely a few years younger, so that made sense.

The fact that she didn't seem into anything serious worked to my advantage. We could have something casual and fun. No need for things to get awkward.

And despite her objections, there was something there, something that made her breathing shift in my presence and her cheeks flush. We had chemistry, and I'd make sure she couldn't ignore it.

We were neighbors. There were certain neighborly rules I could use to my advantage. Even if I had to borrow a cup of sugar to get her to open that door, I'd do it. And eventually, she'd open up as well.

My sister was wrong. I could do casual. Casual was fun. The hunt was fun. And Avery was a competitor.

Staring at my ceiling, I imagined all the ways I could have her. And as I closed my eyes, my sleepy brain filled with visions of Avery.

The longer I pictured her, the easier it became to note subtle details I'd overlooked, such as the cheap jewelry. The few times I'd spotted her began to add up. Was she a student? Students didn't live in this section of the city, at least not in this building.

Her age, I decided, had to be around twenty-two, so I likely had her beat in life experience. Remembering her vulnerable eyes, my fantasy shifted from seducing her to simply comforting her.

These men were way too old for her. She should know better. I imagined kissing her and holding her, and never once would she look to me with such uncertainty because I had nothing but decent intentions. Okay, I had filthy intentions, but I'd make sure she had fun too. With all those other men, there didn't seem to be any balance. The scales were tipped in their favor, and I wasn't sure how, but with me, Avery would understand how dating could be fun.

10

AVERY

"Would you like insurance?"

"Yes, on all six, please." The limit for postal insurance was four hundred dollars, so I was shipping my mother six tightly taped boxes of cold, hard-earned cash. All for the price of letting some fat pig breathe into my ear at an uptown bar and stare down my cleavage while taking faceless pictures of my body for four hours.

It was worth it. I had to keep telling myself that until I believed it to be true. But my dignity took a hit this week no amount of money could compensate. It wasn't about what others saw, but what I endured privately. I might have escaped guilt, proving I'd do more than most women would, but I'd never actually sell my body for sex. But shame was a sticky thing.

The following night I had a gala with Micah scheduled. My dress was recycled couture, and my jewels were the same paste garbage I always wore, but they looked excellent. I wore my hair slicked into a smart ponytail, and my makeup was extreme, giving me the devastating look of a woman on the catwalk in Milan.

Not wanting any drama, I decided to wait in the lobby for Micah to arrive, but Noah caught me locking up, and there was something different about the way he watched me.

His eyes were too watchful, his usual nonchalance gone. His focus unapologetically followed my every move and I hated it. I wanted the old Noah stare back, but I knew our last encounter spoiled any chance of that happening.

"Another *appointment?*"

My molars locked, my mood shifting from regretful to downright pissed. "Why don't we do each other a favor and keep to our own sides of the building?"

Hands deep in his suit pockets, he held my gaze and dramatically stepped into my half of the hallway. Then he took another step. And another until he had me backed against my door.

I didn't understand his game. Did he actually think this sort of taunting would get me into bed with him?

My chin tipped up to hold his stare. "If this is flirting, it's not working. Excuse me, I have an appointment."

He glanced at my dress. "You're a busy girl, Avery."

And you're a dick. "Excuse—"

"Why a different date every night?" Something flashed in his eyes. Beneath the purposeful intimidation hid a spark of curiosity and possibly a hint of jealousy. "Let's call it what it is. You're not off to a business meeting dressed like that."

I didn't have time for this—whatever it was.

His lashes lowered as his gaze traveled down the front of my dress, held at my nails, my purse, and lifted to the rhinestone necklace at my throat and then to my glossy lips leaving me feeling all too exposed.

Something in his stare shook my confidence, and I couldn't afford to be off my game tonight. What did he see when he looked at me? Why did I care? What was this weird hold he had over me, this instant jumble of uncertainty I suffered every time I entered his presence?

It seemed a contradicting sensation that taunted me and tempted me. His eyes, missing nothing, seemed to silently call to me as if promising the truth might set me free. I had the strangest sense that I could tell him secrets and he'd listen without judgment, which either made him incredibly transparent or me a complete idiot.

But what if this teasing persona was merely an act meant to frustrate me enough to let him in? Playground taunting to get a peek up the new girl's dress...

I shook my head, almost believing it. It used to be my nature to believe everyone hid a little good inside, but I wasn't that girl anymore. He might be trying to get into my pants, but he was just my nosey neighbor. He wasn't my friend.

I hardened my stare. "Back off."

The side of his mouth quirked. "I think you like me this close."

"I think you're delusional."

My heart rattled behind my ribs as my body pressed against the support of the door. What the hell was wrong with me? He was cornering me, goading me, and I was allowing it—maybe even enjoying it on some twisted level.

Enough.

I lifted my chin, hiding any sense that he might be intimidating me. "One of these days you're going to push your luck with me, and it won't end well for you."

"Oh, I disagree."

The clear vision of my hand slapping across his beautiful face flashed through my mind, and my body warmed, liquid heat pulling slowly through my veins the way it absolutely shouldn't. Oh, I'd love to hurt him just enough to prove a point.

"Don't pretend to be indifferent to me, Avery. You're getting aroused. I can see it in the way your breath just quickened, and your cheeks are pinker than usual. Your eyes are darker, too, and your tits are pressing so hard against your dress my fingers are itching to touch them. A hundred bucks say your panties are wet."

"I think you have a gambling problem."

"I think you should admit I turn you on."

I might have been slightly aroused, but he'd be whimpering if he saw into my head, saw the ways I imagined punishing him for being such a colossal shithead.

He had no clue what really turned me on. "Not for the reason you think."

His half smile stretched into an even grin, and he leaned closer. "No?"

"No," I rasped.

I could see it so clearly, his body stretched beneath mine in all its glory. Taut muscle and sinew wearing a sheen of sweat as I teased him into a needy frenzy. His body pulsing with desire while I denied him every pleasure and inflicted little nips of pain.

I'd track my nails down his chest, leaving slightly raised trails as he arched into my touch. My breath would tease his cock, but I wouldn't touch him. Torment, blow, scrape… He'd beg so prettily. I bet I could make him come without ever using more than my words.

Then, when he was just about to cry out, I'd grip him hard enough to force it back. He'd jerk at the repudiation, fight it, try to hide the struggle, and fail. And then he'd beg for forgiveness, accepting I was the one in total control.

My gaze lifted to his mouth, and I fought the urge to drag my tongue over his lips. I wanted to wrench his head back, my fist gripping tightly in his beautiful hair. If he was a good boy, I might let him fuck me, but *my* way, on my terms.

He'd do everything I commanded and make me come as many times as I wanted. He'd worship me, beg for me, and never once think he could outmaneuver me like he thought he was doing now.

"You don't know a thing about me, Noah, and I doubt you have the patience or stamina to figure me out."

"All I need is one night. Let me take you out, prove I'm better than the rest."

"So persistent."

"Always, especially when I see something I want."

No mention of what I might want. God, he was selfish. Yet, I humored him anyway. "And what is it you want?"

He lifted a brow. "Are we being honest?"

I held his stare, unflinching. "Why not?"

"Fine. I want to strip you naked and lick every gorgeous curve of your body. I want to hold you by your hair as you swallow my cock. And when your shoulders tense and your eyes water, I want you to look up at me with that determined look I see now, and I want you to show me you can handle every last inch of me. I want to fuck your tits, your cunt, and your tight little asshole. I want to make it so good for you, there's never a doubt in your mind that I'm the best you'll ever have. And then, I want to sleep with you, naked and soft, worn out from everything I did to you, everything you begged me to do. Then we'll wake up and do it all over again until my skin smells like yours and you're wearing a rosy glow of whisker burn, come, and me."

Keeping my expression blank, I glanced toward the elevator as if the political correctness police were going to storm the hall at any second after that little speech. My breath shook as it filled my lungs. No one had *ever* said anything so graphic and arrogant to me. I wanted to smile at his boldness, then punish him.

It was not only improbable, it was also the exact opposite of what I liked, so why the hell was I breathing so fast? He was rattling me.

This game had to end. I moved my mouth to speak, but my voice had dried up. Clearing my throat, I straightened my shoulders and looked him directly in the eye, whittling all my excuses down to the sharpest point.

It was time he understood how impossible his fantasies were. "Poor Noah. You can't afford me."

His brow furrowed. "Afford you?"

His glance took another perusal of my attire, and he cocked his head as if something occurred to him. I endured his inspection, awaiting and dreading the moment the light bulb flickered on. As a private person, my career choices had always been personal. After my mother's latest episode, I hardly felt like shouting my profession details from the rooftops.

His posture relaxed, and his hands burrowed back in his pockets, a knowing smirk now teasing his lips. "I think you underestimate the size of my ... bank account."

An unexpected ache formed in my chest. On some level, he comprehended my confession when I'd hoped his first response would be disbelief or denial. But he seemed to understand what I'd admitted and hadn't batted an eye.

His acceptance that I came with a rather large price tag withered something inside of me. My confidence staggered and my pride flinched. His cocky assumption that he *would* have me—no matter the price—released an unpredicted pain in my chest I wasn't prepared to process. He didn't realize some things were *not* for sale, but damn the assumption in his eyes for hurting me so.

I guess I looked like a whore to him. It shouldn't matter how he saw me. Hiding my disappointment, I swallowed the lump in my throat and forced my emotions out of the way.

Keep it light... "I'm pretty sure your *account* is much smaller than what I'm used to." If he wanted to treat me like an object, I'd treat him like the chauvinist dickhead I believed him to be.

He arched a brow. "Name your price."

Why did this keep backfiring on me? Time to be firm. "You'll never be my client."

"Is that what you call them?"

I shrugged, trying to situate my indifference and gracefully escape the conversation in one piece. But something was off, and I had about as much grace as Cinderella's sisters trying to casually slip into a glass slipper.

Irritated that he'd knocked me off balance so easily, my words became terse. "It's business. And I'm the one with the final say. Now, if you'll get out of my way—"

"Wait." He frowned and caught my arm. "Are you serious? Are you..."

My breath held. Thank God he didn't finish his question. My self-esteem might not survive the hit today. We needed to wrap this up, and I couldn't afford to waste time explaining my life to him.

"I'm not a prostitute, jerk. Sex isn't on the table. That's not what I do. I really have to go."

His brow knit as uncertainty flashed in his glacial stare. While my job was uncommon, living as a sugar baby remained a very real business—not to be confused with prostitution. Every client needed to fully understand that.

Although Noah would never be my client. *Never*.

"Avery..." His focus pulled from my body for a split second, but when it returned, his eyes were more challenging than ever. "I'm not looking to be your client or whatever you call it."

His voice sounded so genuine I instantly relaxed and then he said, "But I'm also not giving up. And trust me, I never have to pay a woman for her time."

"I don't have time for charity cases, Noah."

He laughed. "Avery, you misunderstand. I'll be the one doing *you* a favor. Maybe one good, hard fuck would get you out of this bad mood you've been in since we met."

My lips twitched, but I hid a smile. As great as fucking Noah would probably be, it was a can of worms I couldn't open. My little thrill died as fast as a lone breeze on a still day.

Maybe he thought I was bluffing about actually coming with a price tag. That was better than him not questioning the possibility. But the truth remained, I needed to ruin whatever this was for my own good.

"That's not going to happen," I said, priding myself for not allowing my voice to waver. "I told you how it works. You're not listening—"

"Oh, I heard you. You want me to believe they pay to play. Maybe they do, but I don't. I'm not buying what you're selling, so stop with the act. I see you lugging your little backpack up and down the hall as you scurry off to class, looking like an average twenty-something trying to make a future for herself. This..." He brushed a finger over my fake diamond bracelet. "This isn't you. It's an act, and I bet you play the part damn well. But you aren't going to play with me, Avery—not in that way. Maybe you'd smile a little easier if you dated someone for more than their wallet."

"Maybe I'm only miserable around you."

"If that's what you have to tell yourself."

I wanted to growl and shove him out of my way. "You know what? You don't know a thing about me or the men I go out with."

He didn't have to live a secret life to afford his home. He was almost too upfront, too raw and unfiltered.

He thought my appearance was an act. But he didn't realize *all of it* was an act. Avery Johansson wasn't a college student living a few miles from home. She didn't exist before I arrived.

"So let me get to know you."

Noah was the sort of man who wouldn't rest until he had a puzzle mastered, and I wasn't going to be a game he played. "No."

"Why not? Scared?"

I'd never admit that to him. Avery Dean Mudd might have earned a scholarship, but Avery Johansson had been paying her tuition since. The girl I left behind was a piece of trash, and the woman I became didn't know any more about social graces than she could learn online and by emulating others. It was enough to fool the men I spent a few hours with at a time. I wasn't sure if I could fool Noah.

"I said no."

The elevator pinged and my focus pulled to the dial climbing toward our floor. Micah. Time to squelch his little crush once and for all and focus on what mattered, what kept my apartment warm, and my name on the enrollment list.

"Here's all you need to know. In five seconds, that elevator's going to open, and a man's going to step out. He's sixteen years older than me. He's going to open doors for me and take me to a fancy party, and I'm going to let him because he pays my rent every month so I can live in this gorgeous building that's probably a dump compared to where you grew up. He bought my clothes and my jewelry—"

"The jewelry's fake. He's ripping you off."

"I know it's fake," I hissed. "But I paid for it with *his* money. I'd rather keep as much as I can for tuition and other bills. My point is, *this* is who I am, whether you accept it or not. This is how I afford to live here. If you saw where I came from, you'd run. Trust me, Noah, you don't know me, and if you did, we wouldn't be having this conversation."

The elevator pinged, and Noah took a step back just as the doors parted. Micah's familiar leather soled footfalls broke the silence.

Micah's eyes held nothing but polite patience. "Avery?"

I blinked away from Noah and gave Micah a shaky smile. "I'm ready."

His assessing gaze traveled to my neighbor and back to me. He approached and held out an arm. Dressed in black tie as he was, he should've easily been the most intimidating person in the hall, but Noah didn't flinch. Micah gave him a stiff nod and escorted me toward the elevator.

"I'll talk to you later, Avery. We're not finished."

My eyes continued to blink as we stepped into the elevator and Micah keyed in the first floor. He didn't say a word, but I knew his mind was full of thoughts and opinions.

Noah unapologetically watched us as the doors slowly closed.

"He's just—"

Micah's hand tightened on mine. "No need, love. I see you're upset. Let me take your mind off whatever that was and treat you to a pleasant evening."

Strangely, his nonjudgmental response relieved me. I knew it was a cop-out, and that I was running from some emotional baggage I didn't feel like carrying, but that was the perk of being a sugar baby. I didn't need to think beyond my own personal safety. All I needed to do was let my clients pamper me.

I had the luxury of pretending to be someone else for the evening. Tonight, like most nights, that was exactly what I wanted to do.

11

NOAH

"Gin and tonic." I put my back to the bar at the club, doing a quick scan of the room.

Women in white tennis skirts and men in sports jackets crowded the well-appointed tables of the country club. It was all so monochromatically mundane and redundant. But the Florida weather offered a nice break from the Philadelphia fall, and I was glad for the distraction.

After my last run in with Avery, I put all plans on hold. The things she said about going out with so many men really stuck in my brain and left an unsavory aftertaste. It was starting to make sense. She lived in an upscale apartment, wore Valentino and Oscar De La Renta, and went out with men who drove cars retailing over the hundred thousand dollar mark.

Avery was a user. She used men to get what she wanted. She blatantly admitted that the one guy was paying her rent. Her rent was the same as mine, so that guy was either wealthy enough to throw money away or was getting a substantial trade-off in his deal with Avery.

I couldn't stomach the thought of her hooking up with that guy or any of the others. Yet, like clockwork, a new date showed up each night. So flying down to the Keys for Thanksgiving with my family seemed like a welcome reprieve and great change of scenery from my neighbor and her revolving door of bachelors.

"Having fun?" Laurel slid onto the barstool, and the bartender slipped a cocktail napkin under her chardonnay before it hit the countertop.

"A blast. Where's Stanley?"

Stanley was Laurel's on again-off again date who often crashed Florida holidays but passed on the Pennsylvania ones. Lately, he seemed to enjoy the spoils that came from our family's situation more than he enjoyed passing one on one time with my sister. And it was starting to piss me off.

"He's changing into his bathing suit. Said he wants to digest by the pool."

My sister had the complexion of a porcelain doll, so she rarely spent time poolside. "And what will you do?"

She lifted her wineglass and clanked it to my tumbler. "Get drunk with my little brother."

"Sounds ambitious."

She shrugged and settled in beside me. "Any progress with your neighbor?"

"No, and I'm over it. She's ... baggage."

"Married?"

"No."

"Kids?"

"Not that I know of."

"Gay?"

"Definitely not."

"So what sort of baggage does she have?"

I shrugged and sipped my cocktail. "It's hard to explain. She's busy."

"Ah, too busy to date?"

Hardly. "Sort of."

"Maybe if you proved you were worth her time she'd find time to fit you in."

I leveled my sister with a look that said I wasn't in the mood for her snark. The entire situation with Avery was riddled with complications. It threw the idea of a one-night-stand with her into the high maintenance category. I wanted to sleep with her, not marry her.

"I changed my mind about her. That's all."

Scanning the room again, I looked for someone to get my mind off ... other things. No one appealed. They were all either too tall or too short or too fair or too dark. It pissed me off that Avery had become the measuring stick to all other women. It didn't make sense. I needed to get off this Goldilocks sort of thinking.

I finished my drink and shifted away from the bar. Maybe Stanley had it right. All the hot women were at the pool. God, why the hell was my sister still with him?

"I'm going to change and go for a swim."

"I thought we were hanging out."

I hesitated for a second. If I hung with Laurel people would assume we were together and I needed to get my mind off Avery by taking a shot with someone else. "Sorry, sis. Not tonight."

"Thanks a lot, Noah."

I stilled at the hurt tone of her voice and turned back to the bar. Her wounded expression hardened as her eyes narrowed.

"What's going on with you?"

"Nothing. Go find some faceless woman to distract you—"

"Hey. This isn't you, Laurel. What's with the attitude?"

She shrugged. "I'm just sick of men. You all want something meaningless over something substantial."

I returned to the bar and lowered my voice. "I'm not trying to put my nose where it doesn't belong, but all men aren't Stanley, Laurel. Maybe stop going out with a guy who clearly doesn't want the same relationship you need."

Her gaze drifted to the bar. "It's easier being with him than being alone."

"Is it? Because right now it doesn't look like you're having such an easy time."

Her lashes lowered. "I don't know why I invited him. I'm not even sure what we are anymore. For all I know, he's hitting on women and then coming back to my bed."

"Fuck him. Want me to send him home? He's your guest, using our family's club membership. Rescind your invitation, and he has no right to be here."

"I don't need my little brother cleaning up my messes."

"I know you don't, but I will. Believe me, I don't mind."

It was more than a hunch that Stanley was hitting on other women. I'd seen him getting too close a few times and finally said something to him, but the guy excused his behavior by claiming he and my sister had a sort of understanding, which seemed true, but not at all what Laurel wanted.

Laurel gave a sad smile. "You're a good brother, Noah."

"You're a good sister."

As much as I wanted to get my mind off Avery by getting inside another woman, those plans would need to be postponed. Laurel needed a friend, and since Shane had screwed me over with Margaux, my sister had stepped in as my best friend, always there whenever I needed a distraction. Tonight I needed to be hers.

Waving a hand at the bartender, I said, "Another chardonnay for the lady, and I'll take a refill as well."

"You're staying?"

I sat on the stool beside her. "Maybe that whole getting drunk thing is exactly what we both need."

"Cheers to that."

12

AVERY

It had been nine quiet days without a peep from my mother or my neighbor. I took a few nights off of work to focus on school. I needed to get my Lit grade up to a B, and my professor wasn't making that easy. I also needed to reassess some things that were keeping me up at night.

Thanksgiving was a quiet day in the building and a much-needed chance to think. The halls remained silent through the weekend. It was as if everyone disappeared, which was probably what normal people did—home to visit families that actually enjoyed each other.

Noah claimed our conversation wasn't over, yet he hadn't tried to contact me in any way. I knew his schedule, but nothing about his occupation. He left around seven-thirty each morning in a suit, and I could smell his soap in the hall every day when I returned from the gym.

Then, I could sense his presence when he returned from work around six each night. I wasn't sure if he had a commute or worked in the city, but I wanted to know these things, and that had to make me the stupidest girl on the planet.

Finished with my final English paper, I packed up my books. The close of the semester left me wanting to celebrate, but I had no one to share in my personal accomplishment, no one that really cared.

Wandering around my apartment, I debated if I should call a client—maybe Micah. He'd celebrate with me in his own Micah way. I had nothing better to do, but the idea of making a date didn't sit right.

I nosed around in the fridge for a few minutes and snagged a bottle of wine off the shelf. I wasn't a big drinker, so I'd been saving this for a special occasion. Cocktails were nice, but I only indulged when someone else was making them or paying. This bottle of wine had been in my fridge for over three months, and I wasn't sure if there was some sort of expiration date I was missing.

Rummaging through my drawers, I searched for a corkscrew, unsure if I owned one. About to give up my search, I stilled when I heard a door close. My gaze drifted to the front of my apartment and then down the front of my body for an inspection of my appearance.

I wore sweats, slippers, and my hair twisted into a messy bun. There was nothing sexy about my outfit, so maybe this was the best time to see what had caught my neighbor's tongue. Grabbing the wine bottle and my apartment key, I crossed the hall and knocked.

His footsteps shuffled, and the door opened. His eyes did a double take of my outfit, and then he grinned. "Do I know you?"

Funny guy. I held up the wine. "I need a screw."

He laughed and gave the door a nudge, so it opened wide. "You guessed my magic password. Come on in."

I followed him inside, immediately noting how different his apartment appeared when not full of fifty drunken guests and gourmet food stations. We headed into the kitchen where an open box of pizza sat on the island, one slice removed and sitting on a plate.

"Did you eat?"

The scent of garlic and basil filled the air, and my stomach stirred at the opportunity. "Not since lunch."

He brought down another plate from his nicer-than-mine cabinets. "One slice or two."

"One."

He pursed his lips. "Really?"

"Really."

Appearing unimpressed, he dropped a slice on the plate and went to a drawer. Holding up a corkscrew, he took the bottle of wine from me, pausing to frown at the label. "What is this?"

I slid onto a wooden stool and pulled the pizza slice closer. "I don't know. I bought it when I moved in."

"And you never opened it?"

I shrugged. "I'm not much of a drinker."

"Yet you like bourbon."

Surprised he remembered what I drank, I smiled. "Honey bourbon. It's whiskey with training wheels."

He scoffed. "Whiskey's whiskey. You drink. You just don't know how to open bottles."

I pulled the cheese off my slice as he twisted the cork free.

"What the hell are you doing? You're ruining the pizza."

"I don't eat cheese."

He narrowed his eyes. "Is that some girly bullshit to do with your body?"

"No. I have a dairy allergy. Cheese doesn't do nice things to me."

"I could order something else." He filled two glasses and slid one to me.

"It's fine. This is how I've always eaten pizza."

"Okay." He took a sip and grimaced. "This is terrible wine."

"You don't have one of those little voices in your head that tells you not to vocalize every single thought that crosses your mind, do you?"

"Like a Jiminy Cricket? No. I'm a real boy."

I laughed. He certainly was.

We settled in and quietly ate. Noah finished off three slices before calling it quits. He nudged the box toward me. "Have another one."

"I can't."

"Why?"

I hesitated. "Because I'm still a girl and I still follow some rules. I had a big lunch."

His eyes studied me for a long minute. Reaching into the box, he plucked the cheese off a slice and dropped it onto the wax paper, then plopped the piece on my plate. "Eat."

"I'm full."

"Liar. Eat."

I had no intention of eating that slice. "Where do you work?"

"I own a company that does media marketing for extreme sports."

"Like cliff diving?"

"That, and skateboarding, wakeboarding, mountain biking. You name it I've probably videoed it."

"How did you get into that?"

"I'm a guy. I love anything dangerous."

"Do you *do* those things?"

"I'll try anything once."

"Have you ever jumped out of a plane?"

"Twice. I'm going again in a few months when the weather breaks."

"So you're insane." I took a bite of pizza.

"I like the rush. It's fun. You should try it sometime."

"No, thank you. I prefer to stay on the ground and leave the flying to the birds."

"Chicken."

I waved a finger. "Yes, a perfect example of a flightless bird. Like me."

"You don't fly at all?"

"Nope."

"Why? Don't you like to travel?"

I shrugged. "I never gave it much thought."

His brow tightened as he sipped his wine. "Have you ever been out of the country?"

"Nope." Truly full now, I picked at the crust of my half-eaten slice.

"Those guys that take you out, I've seen the cars they drive. Any of them ever offer to fly you anywhere?"

I'd wondered if we were going to talk about that. "Some, but travel requires overnight accommodations, and that's not included in my services."

"Your services... What exactly *do* your services include?"

"Are you looking to hire me?" That would never happen.

"Let's presume you're not selling sex and I don't need to buy it. Deal?"

"Deal." I pushed the plate away. "I let them take me out, buy me delicious food from fancy restaurants, pretend I'm whoever they need me to be for a few hours, so they feel good about themselves. I listen to them when they need to vent—sort of like a therapist, but totally underqualified. But we share a sort of confidentiality, so there's no drama. They take me to concerts, operas, museums, art showings, private galas, weddings, all sorts of things."

"And they ... they pay you for this?"

I blushed, not used to openly discussing my services with anyone other than my clients. "Yes, they pay me. It's all legit. I started with a service, but now I book my own clients. It's not a secret. I'm not doing anything illegal."

"So ... you signed up for a service, men contact you, you agree to see them, they take you on extravagant dates, and then they pay you at the end of the night, but you never fuck them?"

I didn't flinch at his question. It was blunt and to the point which I appreciated. I'd rather cut out all the bullshit from the start to avoid any future confusion. Because the truth was, I thought about Noah way more than I should, but I still couldn't cross certain lines with him. Maybe we could form a sort of understanding and truce and somehow form a friendship.

"They buy me clothes and jewelry, too. But no, I never touch them."

"I saw one guy kiss you."

I laughed nervously. "You're quite the stalker. I have two clients who are permitted to give me pecks on the cheek, but that's only because I fully trust both of them not to get carried away."

"The guy from the other night, the one who picked you up when we were talking...?"

"Which, the comb-over or the tall, dark, and—"

"Not the pig."

Micah. "He was my first."

"Your first...?"

"Daddy."

A slight V formed between his brows. "Please tell me you mean sugar Daddy."

I laughed. "Yes. It's nothing perverted. They enjoy taking care of me, and I enjoy being taken care of."

"How did you start? Did he come up to you and just offer you money for a date?"

"Pretty much. I was studying at a café, and he sent over a cup of coffee. I was new to the city and short on friends, so I approached him to say thank you. We ended up talking, and then we ran into each other again a week later, and he asked me out. I didn't feel any attraction, so I turned him down."

"Then he named a price."

I gave him an unimpressed look. "If you're trying to offend me, you won't. I'm not cheap."

"How much did he offer?"

I smiled. "Two thousand dollars."

"*For a date?*"

I laughed at his shock. "Yep. And it wasn't a crappy date."

"No way," he laughed. "Where'd he take you?"

"To a private concert with Elton John and only about twenty other couples."

"Get the hell out of here! And he never tried anything?"

"Nope. He was an absolute gentleman."

"So unfair."

"Are you kidding? You're a guy. No one looks at you and says, *hmm, I wonder how much it would take to buy that*. Women have always been pared down to buyable commodities. I'm not a prostitute, but...

Never mind." I looked at my half-eaten slice and felt sick. Maybe it was the shitty wine.

Noah's hand closed over mine and squeezed. My gaze jumped to his as he offered what I hoped was a friendly grin.

"You're nothing like a prostitute. I have a friend who paid her way through college by selling her eggs. Another friend of mine got college loans to pay for a boob job, never taking a single course. She's up to her tits in debt, but she got what she wanted. People do all sorts of things to reach their goals. I think it's sort of fascinating that you go on all those interesting dates and make money. They *should* pay you. I bet you're a ton of fun when you're not playing the bitchy neighbor. Sort of like now, your guard's down, and we haven't bickered once."

I pulled my hand free. "You've called me a bitch a few times now."

"I said bitchy."

"And before?"

"I was drunk and out of line."

"No, this was when you were trying to apologize in the hall. You were sober."

He smiled, and something shifted as if a veil came down. "I'm sorry."

And I *had* been a bitch to him, so really, I shouldn't expect more than the apology I already received. "I'm sorry I was a bitch to you."

"I get why you're not interested."

"You do?"

"Sure. You want to focus on school and *work*—"

"Please don't use finger quotes."

"Whatever. You have a job, and I was distracting you from that, getting you all hot and bothered before your *business appointments.*"

I laughed, refusing to acknowledge his arrogant assumption. "Again, the finger quotes aren't necessary."

"I know, but I like using them. They make conversation more fun. Like let's say you had an *appointment*, but I stopped by your place ten minutes before you had to go. Let's assume we start talking and, of course, it turns into bickering, and I suddenly—" Finger quotes.

"—*kiss you.* That can't be conducive to the sort of—" Finger quotes. "—*work environment* you're trying to create."

"You're a jerk."

He laughed. "Why? I'm just laying out a hypothetical situation."

"Hypothetical because it'll never happen?"

"Oh, it'll happen."

I rolled my eyes. "Does anyone ever tell you no?"

"All the time, but eventually, I get a yes. Especially from women. It starts out slow. *Mmm, yesss...* Then it gets a little more enthusiastic. *Yes... Yes!*" He used finger quotes to emphasize each impersonated female cry. "And then it's all about giving her what I knew she wanted from the beginning."

"Which is?"

"To be taken away. Life's stressful. Sex is an escape. I can be that for ... people."

"You have problems." He thought he could be that for me, but that wasn't how I operated. I found escape in other ways—surrender wasn't one of them. "And you've reached your finger quote quota for the year."

"But you're curious."

"About what?" I laughed. "Sleeping with you? God, no!"

He grumbled and refilled his wine glass, then grimaced as he took a long swallow. "We gotta get you some better wine."

"Leave my wine selection alone. I think it's good." I refilled my glass, finishing off the bottle.

"It tastes like my grandmother's perfume."

"And you drank that?"

"No, but when she walks into a room after Sunday mass, it's strong enough to choke a horse. It sticks in your throat until Monday."

"You know, at first I imagined you were charming. I don't think I've ever been more wrong about a guy."

He raised his glass. "That'll teach you to make assumptions. So, what do you say we watch a movie? I have a great one about this girl who's house sitting, and something goes wrong with the alarm system, so she calls the company. When the rep gets there, they figure it out, but then the boiler breaks, and she takes off all her—"

"Are you describing porn?"

"I believe the appropriate term is *adult film*."

"I'm surprised you didn't say *that* with finger quotes."

"I wanted to, but I was afraid you'd bitch at me again. And I'm told I have to work on my charm, so I'm trying to not piss you off."

I suddenly realized I'd been smiling since the moment I walked into his home. It was strange to be so at ease with someone I mostly didn't like. In the beginning, his attention had rattled me, but now... Something changed. We had ... chemistry. I was having fun joking around with him, and in a way, I didn't want it to end.

With only a few sips of wine left, I glanced at the clock. "If you really want to watch a movie, we can. But I have to go home after that."

"Why, you got a hot date?"

"Do I look like I'm going anywhere tonight?"

He eyed my sweats and sloppy hair. "You'd look hot in a sack. How would I know what you have planned?"

"I'm off tonight, but I do have to get up early tomorrow."

"Tomorrow's Saturday."

"So?"

"So, do you have class?"

"No, but you made me eat that second piece of pizza, and there's no way I'm missing my workout."

His eyes rolled dramatically. "I can't talk to you for the next three minutes. Come on. Let's pick out a movie."

I followed him into the den. "Why can't you talk to me?"

"Because you won't like what I say. Thriller or action?"

"Neither. Romantic comedy or drama. What were you going to say?"

He tossed some pillows around and searched for the remote. "I'm not watching a drama. I'll do a comedy, but not a romantic one. And I can't say it, because your whole gym comment proved you have screwed up girl thinking and that means I might upset you and you might start to do other girly things like cry or get all bitchy again."

I grabbed the remote off the cushion as he lifted another pillow. "I won't cry. Say it."

"No." He snatched the remote.

I scoffed. "Pussy."

His head whipped around and he smiled. "Did you just call me a pussy?"

"Yeah. I don't use girly terms like—" Finger quotes. "*chicken.*"

"Oh, you *are* a bitch. Fine. I was going to say how stupid it is that girls can't eat two slices of pizza without developing some big guilt complex. Like that's going to make you fat. You're a twig. I hate that shit and most guys feel the same way. Just eat and shut up about it."

I had plenty to say, but my lips wouldn't move.

"Ah, fuck. Are you going to cry?"

"No." But I did want to punch him in the dick.

"Don't get all sensitive. I prefer you bitchy."

Oh, I could be a bitch. If he only knew how much...

"First of all, I'm not going to cry. I just needed a second to process everything you said. Second, I don't work out for anyone but myself. It's a great stress reliever, and I use it as an outlet when I'm tense. And third, I ate the second piece, so shut the fuck up about my eating habits."

"You know, there are other outlets for stress relief—"

"Oh, my God! Do you ever think of anything but sex?"

"I'm just saying, my door's closer than the gym."

"If you're such a sex god, why don't I ever see any women at your place?"

"Maybe I take my business elsewhere."

I snatched the remote back and plopped on the couch. "I'm sure you do."

He sat beside me and stole the remote again. "I have plenty of sex. Way more than you."

"Well, I don't doubt that."

He turned and gave me a questioning glance. "When's the last time someone gave you something worth thinking about?"

"I got flowers yester—"

"No, I mean something that made you scream in a good way."

The last time I ordered someone to make me scream. "It's been a while."

"Why, though? You're beautiful, sort of fun. Are you going through some kind of celibacy thing on purpose?"

"Maybe I'm trying to graduate from 'sort of fun' to something that's actually flattering. Let's just say I'm picky and it's not worth my time if it's not done my way."

"So you haven't had good sex."

I twisted to face him. "I've had incredible sex, but if everyone did it that good, it wouldn't be incredible. Trust me, I've had good sex."

"How good?"

"Great."

His eyes narrowed. "Meh, I don't believe you."

I scoffed, and folded my arms, then scoffed again. "Well, lucky for you, I don't give a dirty fuck if you believe me or not."

"You sure about that?"

"Put on a damn movie."

He chuckled. "One day you'll give a dirty fuck. And I'll give it right back." He shut off the lamp and hit play.

"What the hell is this?"

"Shh... You don't want to miss the backstory, that's what makes it hot."

"Oh. My. God. I'm not watching porn with you!"

"Just a few minutes."

I reached for the remote, and he jerked his hand out of reach.

"Give it."

"Five minutes, then we can watch whatever you want."

"Noah!" I stretched over him, but his damn long arms were like telephone poles. "Change it!"

"It's a good one. Chicks like the ones with a plot."

That was it. I locked in on his nipple with my thumb and knuckle and pinched hard. "Shut it off!"

"*Ow!* Fuck! Okay! Okay!"

The remote fell to the floor, and I let go. Bad acting and crappy lines played on the surround system as I tried to change the movie. "How the hell do you work this thing?"

"I think you dislocated my areola."

"You'll live." I finally found the source button, and the screen switched to something appropriate.

"I really think you did some damage."

I glanced over my shoulder to find him peeking under the collar of his T-shirt. My lips twitched. There was something so adorable about him in that moment. I pictured myself straddling his thighs, removing his shirt, and kissing his nipple all better.

Good God! I needed to get the hell out of there.

I placed the remote on the coffee table. "Seeing as you're busy with other things, I think I'll just head home."

He dropped his shirt and grabbed my arm, taking me off guard as he yanked me to the sofa and pinned me there.

"What the hell are you doing?"

"You pinched mine, now I get to pinch yours."

"Uh, no. That's not how this works."

"Chicken."

"Yeah, that'll convince me."

"Pussy?"

"You wish. Get off."

"Fair is fair, Avery."

"You stole the remote, hijacked the television and put on pornography, so I pinched your nipple. *That's* fair."

His weight settled over me, silently warning he wasn't going to let me up until I gave in. "Fine. Over the shirt for ten seconds. That's it. And I'll be sure not to whine like a baby, the way you did."

He took my wrists and yanked them over my head, pressing them into the couch pillows. I became hyper-aware of the span of flesh now showing just above the waistband of my pants.

"Don't move."

I rolled my eyes, so not used to being bossed around when it came to this. "Oh, okay."

He sat up and stared at my chest, but didn't touch me.

"Are you gonna do it?"

"I will. Be patient."

I huffed and rolled my eyes again. "Don't forget, I have to be at the gym in the morning. Aaaannnny day now. Whenever you're ready."

"You talk too much."

"Well, what's the hold-up?"

"I'm waiting for your nipples to get hard."

I snorted. "What do you think you have, magic laser beam eyes? Sorry to disappoint, but they're not going to get—"

"Shh..." He rocked his hips into mine.

"Hey! That's not what we agreed to."

"Quiet." He rocked again, and the base of my spine tightened. His gaze lifted to mine, and he smirked. "Fucking bingo."

"Someone notify the press."

He leaned over me. "This sweatshirt's ridiculously thick."

"So?"

"So your nipples must be really hard if I can see them."

"You're a twelve-year-old."

"Don't scream." His hands moved so fast I wasn't prepared as his long fingers pinched down harder than clamps.

I sucked a sharp breath through my nose and gave into the pain. The slow burn transcended into pleasure, and my body reflexively arched into his. My eyes threatened to close, but I forced them to stay open, holding his challenging glare, pretending what he was doing had no effect on me.

"Nine..." he counted, giving me a smile that would destroy a less disciplined woman. "Ten." He released my nipples and sat back.

Damn him. The second he let go I felt his touch all over again, the sharp twinge of sensation traveling to the tips of my breasts, making me itchy for more. If he were anyone else I'd make him strip and eat my pussy wearing only butterfly clamps until I came, but he was Noah, and that wasn't how this worked.

"Happy now? Can you please get off?"

"Sure, but maybe I should get you off first. Cheeks are awfully flushed, Avery."

I shoved his chest and pulled my legs out from under him. "I'm going home. Thanks for dinner."

"I thought we were going to watch a movie."

"Turns out your taste sucks." I walked to the door.

"Not true," he called, still sitting on the couch. "I like *you*."

"Well, find another girl to like."

"Nope! Soon we're gonna be more than friends. I'm gonna have you, Avery Johansson. Just wait."

I let myself out and smiled as I crossed the hall. He wouldn't get his wish, but that didn't mean I couldn't enjoy his perseverance while it lasted.

As it turned out, Noah Wolfe was also "sort of fun".

Before climbing into bed, I stood in front of my dresser mirror and stripped off my sweatshirt. My nipples, puckered and deliciously sore, tightened in the cool air. God, I missed sex.

Visions of past experiences mingled with moments from tonight, and again, I was reminded of how unfitting Noah was for me. Yanking open a drawer, I grabbed a T-shirt and changed for bed.

That metaphorical shelf, the cluttered one with old memories I rarely examined, seemed to call to me, and soon enough I was picking through dusty recollections that were better left alone.

Meandering thoughts wandered through my mind, taking me back to where I used to live and how my life used to be. The musty scent of our trailer seemed so embedded in my head that my nose twitched as the walls of my present home fell away, replaced by dingy wallpaper and dirt smeared windows. I could feel the crusty shag carpeting against my knees and taste the faded cigarette smoke lacing the air. And suddenly I was home again.

. . .

I COWERED *in the corner as my mother waled on Kenny with a book in the next room. We were all teenagers, and in my mom's head that made us each fair game for her belligerent drunken tirades, which usually ended with someone getting struck.*

Kenny, although closest in age to me, was bigger and could take a wallop. He often took the brunt of her abuse to protect me. If I kept quiet, she might forget I was still home.

"I told you it was gettin' late and now look what you've done!"

"The bus was early!" my brother screamed. "I left the same time I always do."

"I ain't got no way to take you to school, Kenneth! The truant officer's gonna be back."

"Let him come! I ain't ever gonna graduate anyway!"

The book hit the wall, and I flinched.

"Get outside! Avery Dean, I gotta get the neighbor to drive your brother to school. Do not *miss your bus. You hear?"*

"Y—yes, Momma." The front door slammed, and I quickly gathered my backpack, rushing out the door the moment they were out of sight. But I didn't go to no bus stop. I had bigger, more important things to do.

I rushed down the back path and hopped the fence, moving quick, so the neighbor's pit bull didn't cause a fuss. My heart raced faster with each yard I cut through until I finally made it.

The sight of the rusted trailer with its siding held on by dry rotted strips of duct tape calmed my racing heart. He said he kept it that way, so people didn't suspect he had anything nice enough to steal inside, which made him smart.

I knocked on the rickety screen door, and it rattled against the frame.

"Who is it?"

"Avery."

The door flung open, and Gavin looked down at me. My gaze traveled up his body to his bare, muscled chest. He was so strong yet so delicate. "Come in."

I quickly slipped inside and tossed my books on the cluttered bench seat. "I have the form, and I forged my mom's signature."

"It's seven-thirty in the morning, Avery Dean."

Wringing my hands, I gave him a pleading look. "Please, Gavin. The deadline's Friday and this is my only hope of ever getting out of here. I'll do whatever you want. I just have to get it turned in."

His scowl softened. "If this doesn't work, you have other options."

This had to work. He was leaving, and I'd never survive this place alone. "Please."

He sighed. "Go ahead. The computer's on. Just wiggle the mouse."

Relieved, I smiled and rushed to the back bedroom where he kept his desktop. Gavin was the only one in Blackwater who had such technology. He was also the only one I trusted, being that he'd always been tight with my oldest brother, Drew—the only sibling to ever show me kindness.

I jostled the mouse and the screen lit. There it was, the scholarship essay that was going to get me the hell out of this shithole town once and for all.

When I'd first shown Gavin my scribbled draft, he tried not to be too critical, but we were never able to hide things from each other.

"You can't send this. Let me toy with it for a while, and it has to be typed." He'd spent weeks helping me polish my essay until we were both confident it might win.

Most guys wouldn't offer such help, but Gavin was different. He didn't make me blow him or fuck him for his assistance either. He was a little more complicated than that. In exchange for his help on that essay and many other things, I let him touch me, put his mouth on me, fondle and pleasure me.

I gave Gavin what he needed, and he gave me things I never expected to want. In his home, I was free. I was powerful. I was wanted.

I scrolled through the document, noting the various improvements he'd made. Not only was his vocabulary better than mine, he had everything formatted with proper headings and all the required important information.

The essay—How My Family Changed the Way I See the World—was perfect. It was raw and honest and almost painful to read at parts, boasting the right amount of drive with plenty of hardship. Portrayed in a manner that a person would have to be a monster not to empathize with my plight. It was a beautiful explanation of hope and adversity.

"What do you think?"

I blinked up at him and smiled. "I think every time I read it, it gets better. This might actually work, and I'll have you to thank."

He smiled, his dimple flashing with a good amount of boyish charm. "You need my credit card?"

"You're sure about this?" This was my only option, and I'd never be able to pay back the money.

His fingers softly brushed a strand of hair away from my face. "I'm sure."

Gavin had become my one sanctuary. He knew what my life was like at home, had seen enough when Drew still lived here to know there was a reason each one of us counted down the days until we could leave.

Now, with just Kenny and me left, things were getting unbearable. Momma was drinkin' all the time, and dinner was hardly ever defrosted, let alone hot.

Gavin fed me, watched TV with me, helped me with homework, he even ... loved me. But neither of us ever breathed a word of such feelings out loud. I just knew it like I knew I'd never survive this place alone once he enlisted.

We filled out the application and attached the scholarship essay. He hesitated just before hitting send and glanced over his shoulder at me.

"You want to do the honors?"

I leaned over his arm and clicked. A swarm of hornets teased my insides as the computer made a little whoosh sound and the application was sent.

"Now, we wait."

His head tilted, his cheek resting on my hip as we both stared at the "message sent" note on the screen. My fingers grazed the stubble of his jaw, and he sighed.

"You'll get it. I feel it in my gut."

I looked down at his face wondering where he found so much faith in me. I wasn't anyone special. But for some reason, he always believed I was capable of great things, sometimes before I even knew I wanted them.

Sliding off the chair, he dropped to the floor and kneeled. I stepped back and looked down at him, noting the swollen bulge in his pants. He was the only one I'd ever been with, the only one I could imagine being with. And come April he'd be gone.

"What do you want?" I'd give him anything, but he didn't want to know that. He liked to work for every concession, earn every ounce of praise. He'd make a great soldier.

His gaze remained cast toward the floor, his posture rigid, his arms behind his back and his shoulders lifting with labored breaths. "I want to touch you. Please you."

I wasn't sure what other people did, but this was all I knew. It was everything Gavin confessed to wanting, and his fantasies spoke to me the moment I first heard them. "Get on the bed."

He climbed onto the mattress and rolled to his back, crossing his hands over his head where a pair of leather studded cuffs draped. He never touched me first. Everything was my choice, and he only put his hands on me if I commanded it. I went to the drawer where he kept his other toys.

He was, without a doubt, the safest person I had in my life, and it pained me to imagine him leaving, which was why I had to get the hell out of there, too. "Do you want pain?"

He sucked in a sharp breath, the sound full of palpable anticipation. "Yes, please."

I wasn't gentle with him, and he preferred I not be. Gavin had his own difficult demons to overcome. He sometimes said the only way to numb the pain of his past was to create pain in the present. I got that. For me, the only way to escape the uncertainty of my present was to take control of the now. Gavin gave me control, and I was addicted to the rush that came with his surrender.

If there was something broken in us, we fixed it for each other. "Spread your legs."

MY GAZE LIFTED to the ceiling as a tear rolled from my eye, the memories fading the way precious love letters become more tattered each time they're reread. Gavin died in action the November after he enlisted and I rarely let myself think of him.

We made a promise the day he left. We were both getting out of Blackwater, and neither of us ever wanted to look back, not even for each other. It was survival of the fittest and holding on to the past would be an anchor keeping us there.

Nothing about me and Gavin's relationship was ever meant to be permanent, but he released something inside of me that wouldn't go away. He helped me find a piece of me I hadn't known was there and after losing him, that piece remained.

I had no regrets for the short yet defining time he was a part of my life. He was the one person I wished could watch me graduate in the spring, but that was impossible.

I rolled to my side and wiped my eyes. There was a reason I didn't let people in. Friends were wonderful—while they lasted. But when they disappeared, the pain was unbearable. I wasn't sure if I was ready to take that kind of risk again.

But part of me wanted Noah as a friend. There was something different about him, something I struggled to resist. Finding him attractive complicated matters. But what attracted me most of all was the thought that I might be ready to try to make friends. Was my life finally reaching that point of normal? God, I hoped so.

13

AVERY

Barely awake, I took the elevator to the bottom floor. Last night I'd tossed and turned until I was certain I wouldn't sleep. Around three in the morning, I decided to release some tension, so I pulled out some heavy artillery.

There I was, having a nice old time with myself, picturing God knows what, when Noah's face suddenly popped into my head. He was looking down at me, eyes heavy, mouth crooked in a half grin, strong hands touching my breasts, pinching me, pinning me...

I shoved away the images but my body responded too soon. Legs quivering, heart racing, the memory of those visions sent my sex into overdrive. *Fuck!*

I'm supposed to be in command here! Could I not even maintain control when I fingered myself?

"Damn it." I blew out a frustrated breath. *Not* what I had in mind.

I passed out for a couple of hours until my alarm went off at dawn, and now I was zombie-walking my exhausted ass to the gym. Damn Noah. He wasn't supposed to be in my head, and he certainly wasn't supposed to be in my fantasies. He was ruining everything.

Thinking we could be friends was a mistake. From now on, I was not going to think about him. If I saw him, fine, I'd be polite. But there would be no downtime *Noah thoughts*. I should have never let him touch me last night.

Swiping my card through the keypad, I pushed into the gym and froze. Was someone here? No one ever used the gym this early besides me. Great. I hated working out around other people, and I didn't bring anything to cover up. Hopefully, it was a woman, because my sports bra and booty shorts weren't exactly concealing and I wasn't going back upstairs.

Heavy footfalls pounded as the motor of a treadmill hummed. I turned the corner and came up short.

Him.

"Morning, neighbor!" he shouted, face all chipper like he'd already gotten in his Wheaties and knocked out a decent warm up.

"What are you doing here?"

"Girl, last night I killed half a bottle of wine and, after my company left, I annihilated an entire pizza. From lips to hips, I swear."

He was making fun of me, and I sort of liked it. Hiding a smile, I climbed onto the other treadmill.

The gym was nothing fancy, but it was private, for residents only, and had all the basic necessities. Two treadmills, a step machine, free weights, mats, yoga balls, and a few press machines. Except now, there was a wolf in my den.

I adjusted the incline and set my track for eight miles. My gaze skittered to his settings and saw he'd already been at it for thirty minutes. It didn't matter. This wasn't Noah time. It was me time. I plugged my headphones into my ears and hit play.

Florence + the Machine's *Shake It Out* came on, and my body fell into a steady rhythm as I shut out everything else. The drums kicked in, and she sang about burying regrets and pushing through challenges, and my heart rate picked up the pace. By the time her voice careened into the first climax, my speed was up, and I was going full throttle.

I loved to run, the freedom of it, the results, the endorphins. It was exhilarating, and it was mine. Faster, I raced to a goal I couldn't see but felt deep in my bones. There was a better me out there, and if I ran hard enough, I'd eventually find her.

All of my issues peeled away as sweat broke over my skin and my mind cleared. The chorus kicked in, and I was lost, going hard and fast toward everything I wanted and—

My steps faltered as my earbud was yanked out and Florence cut off.

Noah ran at a rapid pace, his head angled in my direction. "Hey."

I quickly lowered my speed and scowled at him. "Do you mind?"

"No, not at all. What are you listening to?"

He was like a child that needed constant attention. Adorable, but draining. "Music." I plugged my earbud back in only to have it yanked out again. "Hey!"

"Talk to me."

It was too early for conversation. "I don't talk when I workout. I clear my head and listen to music."

He pursed his lips. A second later, he jumped off his machine and was fiddling with his phone and the sound system by the door. I wasn't sure if we were allowed to touch that. I always brought my own music.

"I think that belongs to someone."

"Yeah, me." He plugged his phone into the AUX outlet. "Now, we can both listen."

I had a rapid two-second guessing game of what song he might choose. I wasn't even close.

The quick bass came on, and Robin Thicke's sexy voice filled the gym, talking about good girls getting nasty and wanting dirty sex with blurred lines. Noah bounced back to his machine, cranked up the pace, and tossed me a defiant smile.

Oh, was this some sort of challenge? Okay. I increased my stride and ran full speed ahead. Impressively, he kept pace. His longer legs meant he wasn't working as hard, but whatever. I'd outrun him any day.

I was in a full body sweat when Rhianna yelled *Na, na, na, na, come on* and started singing about whips and chains in *S&M.* His music wasn't my type, but I was picking up on a theme in his playlist. When the chorus belted out about the scent of sex in the air, my body started to stir.

At seven miles, my heart was thundering, and my legs were throbbing. The music dropped to a thrumming pulse as Nine Inch Nails' *Closer* echoed through the gym, and I laughed. The guy truly had a one-track mind.

I dropped my speed, and he dropped his, but we didn't talk. We dialed back and glanced at each other every two and a half seconds as we cooled down for the last mile.

But I didn't feel cool. I felt tight and burning hot and ready to launch myself at him. This was absolutely not how my morning was supposed to go.

I clicked off my machine, more concerned about getting a head start to safety than conquering that last tenth of a mile.

"You quitting?" He punched his speed down to a slow crawl.

"I'm done. See you later."

He frowned, but I pretended not to notice as I wiped off my machine and made a quick escape.

The elevator was busy during this time of the morning, so I impatiently poked the button like a Morse code, as if that might get it here sooner. My gaze shot to the stairs, and I debated.

A fight or flight sense of urgency buffeted me from all angles, yet I was alone in the hall. I heard the door open behind me just as the elevator arrived.

I stepped in and turned. Noah paused at the door to the gym, breathing heavily, gaze fastened to mine. Sweat marked every muscle under his fitted T, delineating his six-pack and pecs. His arms were swollen, and his fists were clenched.

Close the door... Close!

No matter how much I willed the elevator to shut, time seemed to stand still. The door finally started to move, but Noah crossed the distance in two strides, pivoting and sliding into the elevator at the last second.

I didn't hit the floor button, and we didn't move. We stared at each other in the cramped space, smelling like sweat and lust and sucking all the oxygen out of the air as we panted.

The damp hair at the back of my neck prickled. He wasn't blinking, and he wasn't giving me much room. I was cornered.

"Noah—"

"Shut up." He ducked down and caught my bare hips, lifting my back against the wall as he slammed his mouth over mine, his tongue plunging deep and demanding I kiss him back.

"*Mmph!*" I shoved at his shoulders, but he anchored his hard body against mine forcefully, holding me prisoner and taking what he wanted.

His hot mouth and talented tongue instantly lured me into the kiss. But I didn't ask to be kissed, so I didn't make it easy. I rammed my elbow into his ribs, but in the confined space it hardly drew a grunt out of him.

"Kiss me back, Avery. Give in."

"No." I bit at his lips, but that only seemed to encourage him.

He growled and groped my breast through my damp sports bra, squeezing and tugging the unyielding fabric. "I want this off."

"Tough." I ground my lips into his, pushing him off but never letting my mouth leave his. He took over, plunging his tongue deep and locking his fingers in my tangled ponytail.

His hard cock gouged through his gym shorts into my hip, seeking my center as his fingers curled around my ponytail and tugged, exposing my throat to his mouth. It had been so long since a man kissed me with such desire. For a moment, I was lost, falling into a dark abyss of need as my limbs curled around his strength, my muscles humming, and my blood purring.

My eyes went wide as the sheer size of him became evident. This was all wrong. This wasn't the way I operated. He completely dominated me in bulk and strength, but I refused to allow him to dominate me in other ways. And how dare he knock me off balance like this!

Reaching down, I grabbed hold of his bulging erection and curled my fingers like a talon around his cock and balls, demanding his attention. He sucked in a breath and jerked back.

"That's a little tight—"

My grip intensified, my fingernails pressing through the loose fabric and delicate skin, as I leveled him with a look that told him my hold was intentional. "Put. Me. Down."

Uncertainty flashed in his eyes, and he lowered me to the floor. I didn't release my grip as I stared up at him.

He clutched my wrist. "Avery, you're crushing my—"

"Is this what you want? To fuck me in an elevator? Against a wall? Maybe on our way down the hall and on your granite countertops?"

He groaned, the sound half pained, half excited. "If you could just loosen—"

"*Quiet.*" I was done getting passively blindsided by this guy. "I warned you. I told you one day you'd try your luck with me and not like the result." My grip tightened, his shorts, hard cock, and full balls fisted firmly in my hold. "I don't do gentle, Noah. And I'm never a bottom. Understand?"

"If you want to be on top—"

"No. It's not about the physical position. It's about the mental one. I'm in charge. Always. And I don't think you'd like that very much."

"Maybe I would."

I arched a brow, wishing that was true, but certain it wasn't. "Have you ever had a woman fuck you, Noah? Ever experienced true helplessness and surrendered your will, your choice, and your body for her pleasure?"

His hungry eyes darkened. "Holy shit."

I loosened my hold but held his full attention. He could have stepped back, but he didn't move an inch.

My mouth curled into a slow, satisfied smile. I fucking loved achieving control. Especially when the man didn't realize he was already under my spell, already submitting to my authority. But eventually, Noah would snap out of it and run.

"You don't want what I want, Mr. Wolfe, so maybe it's best we just remain ... friends." A friend was what I needed more than anything else.

He didn't move, didn't answer.

"Push the button, Noah."

He blinked and turned, and we were suddenly moving. The short ride seemed a year long as his gaze kept shooting to me. My expression was a mask over secrets he'd never know.

The doors parted, and I stepped out, leaving him staring. I didn't have to look back to know he watched me until the moment I disappeared inside my apartment. Let him figure it out, jerk off a few loads, and find a passive plaything. I wasn't that girl, and he wasn't my guy. The sooner that sank in for the both of us, the sooner our lives would find balance again.

I toed off my tennis shoes and flinched as a fist pounded on my door. "Open the door, Avery."

What. The. Fuck?

Couldn't he take a hint?

He pounded again. "Avery."

My heart jerked. This never happened before. I never had a guy literally refuse to accept *no* for an answer. I slowly crept to the entrance, standing where my feet wouldn't cast shadows.

He banged his fist again, and I flinched again. "I know you're in there. You're *hiding*."

I wasn't hiding. Was I? I forced myself to say something.

"Go home, Noah."

Silence.

I lifted to my toes and peeked through the peephole, only to find him hunched around my doorframe, shoulders taut, as he bore down on my only escape. My heart did a cartwheel in my chest as I sagged back against the wall. Why wouldn't he give up?

Hiding my uncertainty, I took on a somewhat cocky, unaffected tone, thinking indifference might be my greatest weapon in this war. "Go rub one out, and you'll be fine."

His chuckle scraped along my every nerve like gravel. "Why don't you give me a hand?"

I rolled my eyes but took another step back. He was wearing me down, and I wasn't used to making excuses.

Disappointed in my wavering, I lifted my chin. "That's never going to happen. Go home. I have things to do, and I'm not letting you in."

"Pussy."

He was using my word, yet the way he let it roll off his tongue... It curled around me and tangled up my insides.

Knots of confusion throbbed with need and curiosity. "That's not going to work this time. Go home."

"Fine. But you can't hide forever, Avery. Eventually, I'll find you, and you'll regret every minute you made me wait."

He didn't deliver the promise as a threat. It hit my chest like an absolute guarantee, a punishment issued in a vow before delivery, and I shivered, wondering if he had the balls to dare to kiss me again.

Next time, I wouldn't be so gentle. Flirting seemed harmless and fun, but in the end, it was dangerous and a little too tense where Noah was concerned.

No one said anything for a few seconds. Creeping back to the door, I peered through the peephole again, only to find the hallway empty. I should have been satisfied, but my gut tightened with disappointment. Part of me enjoyed the torment a little too much. The ease of chasing him away instantly diminished part of my interest. That was the moment I realized I wanted Noah to like me, even if I couldn't like him back.

14

AVERY

Signing up for classes was always a hassle, but there was a quiet satisfaction in seeing the light at the end of the tunnel. Almost finished and then I could go where I wanted, be what I wanted, and never think of the girl I left behind. Avery Dean Mudd would finally be a forgotten memory.

As I printed out my spring roster, there was a knock at the door. I frowned because it was the middle of the workday, and the building was usually empty at this time.

Peeking through the peephole, I smiled at the sight of flowers. They must be from Micah. He usually sent flowers at the end of each semester and on other special occasions.

Opening the door, I greeted the deliveryman with a smile.

"Ms. Johansson?"

"Yes."

"These are for you."

They were gorgeous. Sprays of vibrant lilies mixed with enormous sunflowers and eucalyptus sprigs and full bloom roses. "Thank you."

I tipped him and shut the door, carrying the heavy arrangement to my dining room table. He'd really outdone himself this time.

Pulling out my phone, I sent Micah an email.

They're BEAUTIFUL. Thank you!

A minute later, my phone rang, Micah's name flashing on the screen. I answered with a smile. "You're so sweet."

"I'm flattered but confused. Mind filling me in, sweetheart?"

I frowned. "The flowers. They're lovely."

"Avery, I didn't send you flowers. Do they not have a card?"

My smile fell. I searched the large arrangement for a card and found one stuffed deep in the back—*not* from Micah. I majorly screwed up. "Oh, no..."

"Did you find one?"

"I'm so sorry, Micah. I made a mistake."

He was silent for a beat. "Apparently, I have some competition. I'll have to send something more impressive than flowers next time. I assume you have another call to make."

"I'm sorry, Micah. I just thought—"

"No need to apologize. It was an honest mistake. Enjoy your day, love."

"Thanks. Bye."

How embarrassing. I should have identified the sender before assuming. Now, Micah... *Ugh.* I lowered my phone and stared at the card.

Dinner tonight.

This time open the door.

~Noah

I wasn't going.

Of course, I wasn't going.

This was crazy. Noah's persistence had very little to do with me, and *everything* to do with not getting what he wanted when he wanted it.

He left a phone number on the card, so I texted him because, yes, I was too chicken to call.

Thank you for the flowers.

I hit send, sat my phone on the table, and stared at it, waiting for a response. My heart jerked the second the screen flashed.

You're welcome. We're going out tonight. Be ready.

Ready for what? It didn't matter. I texted him back.

I appreciate the invitation, but I can't. I have plans.

Cancel them.

I scowled at the phone. This was the problem with arrogant men. They constantly wanted their way, and they didn't bend easily. Every ego had a price, and I was tired of paying it.

The men in my life who wanted to tell me where to be and how to dress also understood the expectation of paying me handsomely for every demand I let them get away with. They were jobs, and I didn't want Noah to be a job. I wasn't sure what I wanted him to be. Everything was getting messed up.

I couldn't let him bark out orders and assume I owed him

anything. That wasn't how real relationships worked—not that we were in one—especially the sort of relationship I gravitated toward.

No. I wouldn't ask you to call out of work, so don't ask me to miss an appointment. Thank you for the flowers.

THAT WAS ALL I intended to say, and while the flowers were lovely, they changed nothing. End of story.

He texted a few more times, but once I stopped responding, he gave up. So long as we had to continue living across from each other, we had to figure out a way to be civil and respect each other's boundaries. But part of me feared the short friendship we found would get destroyed in the process of building necessary walls.

That night I met with Josh, and the next evening was Christopher. Micah had kept his word and sent a beautiful Louis Vuitton bag to my apartment. It was gorgeous and smelled of fine leather, but I hardly enjoyed it.

Carefully keeping the custom wrapping intact, I took a few pictures and uploaded them to the auction site. Regardless, it was an incredible gift, and I graciously thanked him.

He took me out to dinner on Thursday, to celebrate the end of the semester. It was a lovely evening full of champagne and oysters and chocolate desserts that were rich enough to make any woman's toes curl.

"Thank you for tonight, Micah."

"It was my pleasure." He walked me to my door and smiled, tucking a strand of hair behind my ear. "You'll be graduating soon."

I couldn't hide the pride that bloomed in my chest at the thought. "Can you believe it?"

"Yes. I always knew you'd succeed. There's something special about you, Avery. Something that doesn't know how to walk away without a fight."

I thought of the various people I met through Micah, the social circles he introduced me to. Every ounce of class I owned resulted from our association and his gentle guidance. "I never would have made it this far without your help."

"Nonsense. There's always a way." He leaned down and brushed a kiss on my cheek. "Get some sleep. It's a school night."

"Goodnight."

Once I had the door locked behind me, I heard his steps drift away. I refused to accept money for tonight, and that actually made me happier than getting paid.

Micah was crossing into tricky territory. I didn't want to let him go. He was my mentor, and I liked having him in the background of my life. I think he sensed my fear that we would soon part ways and, for his own reasons, objected to not paying me.

Maybe in his mind, the money guaranteed my time. Money secured our association, sure. But so did our friendship, I hoped.

A soft knock sounded, and I peeked through the peephole, not prepared for the ragged face on the other side.

"Oh, my God."

I pulled open the door, and Noah looked at me from under low brows and glassy eyes.

"Your doorknob *does* work."

"What happened to you?" He looked like death, pallid skin wearing a glaze of pasty sweat, clothed in too many layers for the temperature of the building, bloodshot eyes, and his blonde hair shooting every which way.

"I'm fine."

He was *not* fine. "Are you sick?"

I pressed my fingers to his scalding cheek. "You're burning up."

His eyes closed, his face leaning into my touch. "Mmm. Feels good."

"Come in." I pulled him into my apartment, and he dutifully followed. "Sit down. I'll make you some soup."

He collapsed on my couch and groaned. "Your pillows smell like you."

I opened a can of basic broth because I wasn't much of a chef. "Is that a good thing or a bad thing?"

"You smell like ... cookies ... and sunshine. A breeze ... on the beach ... on a hot August afternoon... Christmas morning..."

My brow quirked at his ramblings. Though he wasn't making much sense, he definitely wasn't sticking to the friend zone with those sorts of compliments. Playing it safe, I ignored his description. "This'll only take a few minutes to heat up. Sorry, I don't have anything better than broth."

He didn't answer.

Once the broth was hot, I added some parsley, because that was always good for the immune system, and poured it into a mug. I carried the steaming cup into the den only to find him out cold, sleeping with his lips slightly parted and his hand curled under his cheek like a little boy.

"Look at you. You're not a lion or a wolf. You're just a sick little lamb."

A glassy, blue eye opened and shut. "Tired."

I placed the mug on the coffee table and sat in the crook of his hips. My hand pressed to his brow again. He was really hot. "Maybe you should take some aspirin."

"I'm fine. I don't get sick."

"You're such a man."

Despite his weak demeanor and exhausted state, he flexed his hips. "Damn right."

I sighed. This subdued patient was not the Noah I was used to.

"Get some sleep. I have things to do." I stood.

"Do you love him?" His softly mumbled question stopped me in my tracks, exposing my secrets in a moment of silence.

I frowned, always uncomfortable with the word love. "Who?"

"The guy you were with tonight. He kisses you. I don't think he's just business."

"Noah..." Did I love Micah? He was my confidant and closest ... client. But at the end of any day, our association remained defined by business. So why was I dreading the end of said association?

"Don't love him, Avery." His words were quiet and slightly slurred. His face was blank, eyes closed and lips hardly moving. "Love me." Those last two words came out on an almost inaudible breath.

My head tipped. "Do you even know what you're saying right now?"

"Lay with me."

"No."

"Please."

"Noah."

His silence told me I'd lost him for the night. Stepping away, I removed my earrings.

"I could love you," he mumbled. "Better than any of them."

My heart snagged just as I prepared to escape his presence. "You're delirious. Try to sleep for a little bit."

I quickly moved out of the living room to a place where I'd no longer be able to hear his fever induced mumblings. I changed into pajamas, but couldn't avoid him forever. He needed to get some fluids in his system. Luckily, he mostly slept.

By the end of the night, I got him to drink the broth and finish a bottle of water, but he wasn't much for conversation, so I suggested he crash on my couch.

Closing the door to my bedroom, I paused, eyeing his still form and suffering a strange sense of awareness. It had been years since anyone slept under the same roof as me. I turned the lock and told myself this was just simple charity, nothing meaningful.

The next morning I was up at dawn and on my way out the door to hit the gym after briefly checking on my sleeping patient. Noah slept in a twisted mess of blankets, one bony foot peeking over the arm of the sofa. I figured it was fine to leave him there.

When I returned from my workout, he was awake and sitting up, drinking something out of a mug.

"You're awake."

He watched me but didn't say anything.

"How do you feel?"

"Better. I barely remember coming here last night. Sorry for passing out on your couch."

I smiled. "It's fine." Leaning in, I placed my hand on his head, and he stilled, his sapphire eyes watching me closely. "Your fever's gone."

"I think this is the most you've ever touched me. I'm pissed I was too out of it last night to appreciate it."

I sat on the coffee table across from him. "Last night you were mumbling some pretty weird stuff."

"Sorry."

We suffered through an awkward silence. "Noah, I want us to be friends."

"I want more."

"I know, but all I can be is your friend right now."

The arrogant mask was gone, and he looked at me with honest curiosity. "Why?"

"It's not about you. I don't date. I work and go to school, and I just want to finish my degree and move on. Dating complicates things."

"It doesn't have to be complicated. I don't date either."

"I don't do meaningless sex either."

"Who says it has to be meaningless," he challenged. "We're both single, and I'm almost certain the attraction's mutual, Avery. It's only complicated if you let it be."

But it *was* complicated. He was bossy, and I was bossy, both of us gunning for the upper hand. I tried that before, after Gavin. I couldn't take it. I needed to be in control, or I couldn't enjoy myself.

We bickered like children and, eventually, he'd object to the way I earned a living. He thought he just wanted a shot at sleeping with me, but due to our shared address, if we did it once we'd likely do it again—even if only out of convenience.

We were too on top of each other here, and there would be no hiding my clients from him. I couldn't deal with living under a microscope. My life was mine, and I was in the last mile of a marathon. He would only trip me up.

"I like the way I manage my life. I only have to think about myself and take care of me. I don't want to change that."

Something shifted in his eyes, a flash of hurt or vulnerability. "But you'll date them."

"That's different, Noah. There's no emotional attachment."

"I don't believe you. I see the way that guy treats you. I've seen you with him before. There's something there, Avery, and it's more than business."

It was already starting. He was already watching me too closely. "Micah's special. He takes care of me."

"Aren't you afraid he might stop? Where's the security in that?"

"I'd survive."

And Micah wouldn't just vanish out of my life. He wouldn't abandon me like that.

He laughed with little humor. "The irony is, if I paid you, like them, I'd get to date you."

I shook my head. "I wouldn't accept you as a client."

"Why not?"

"Because..." I don't sleep with clients. I wasn't sure if that truth stopped me because I wanted to fuck Noah or because I wouldn't. With Noah, there was emotion, and with my clients, it was strictly business. "Because we're friends."

"You're scared. You don't know how to give up control. Every little part of your world is orchestrated from the second you wake up to the moment you go to sleep. That's not living, Avery."

"And fucking you is the answer? You think that's going to make me seem somehow more alive?"

"Why not? Maybe you need to get laid."

"What I need is for you to leave." Why had I ever let him in? He saw my place and now thought he had me all figured out. "You don't even know me, Noah, so don't pretend you're the solution to my problems."

Right now, my biggest problem was him and the fact that he was suggesting things I didn't want to hear. I stood, hoping he'd do the same and walk his ass out the door.

"I know you're uptight. You pretend to be calm and indifferent, but you're wound so tight you need to run in place for an hour a day just to unwind enough to function."

"So what? You jump out of planes to feel alive!"

"I jump to feel detached. You should try letting go some time. You might like it."

"I've done the uncertainty thing. I don't need to fling myself out of a plane to know I'm alive and temporary. And I don't need to have meaningless sex with random men to prove I can. I like balance and security—"

"You date a different guy every night! That's structure, not security."

"That's how I prefer to live. I choose the boundaries, and I determine how long they stay."

"None of it's real."

"That's how I want it." Real was complicated.

"Don't you get lonely?"

My lips pressed tight. The loneliness was the hardest part, but I was too much of a control freak to rely on others when it came to my happiness. Even in marriages, people walked away, people changed, people died.

"I manage."

"Let go, Avery. Just for one night. If we're really friends, trust me and let me take the reins."

"I can't."

"You can."

"No, Noah, I can't. I have a system and—"

"Fine. But in my mind, friends go places and hang out together. And sometimes, friendships evolve." He stood. "I'm sorry I crashed here last night."

Something tightened in my chest. "You're mad."

"I'm annoyed."

"Noah, I said we could be friends—"

"I'm not your buddy, Avery. I'm a guy who's painfully attracted to you, and no matter what I do or say, it changes nothing. Every time I hear your door open it's another man taking out the woman I want. I can't do this anymore. You won't even give me a chance."

"The reason I won't go anywhere with you is because to you it would be a date, when to me it would be nothing more than friendship."

"I told you I don't date, Avery. Why can't we just have fun and leave the labels out of it."

"I don't know you, but I know that's a lie. You wouldn't care this much if you were just after sex. You want something more than that and I can't give it to you. It wouldn't work between us."

"How do you know?"

I drew in a deep breath, hiding my emotions far below the surface. I didn't know, but I also didn't want to be so forgettable that a man could fuck me and forget me. "I just know."

His eyes narrowed. "If life's so damn predictable, then why do you need so much control?" He shook his head. "You won't even admit you're attracted to me and I know you are. We have chemistry, and I'm not buying that it's one-sided. We might work as a couple, and that's what scares you. At least I'm open-minded enough to consider the possibility."

"Open minded? You just went from claiming you don't date to talking about us as a possible couple. Which is it?"

"I don't know! But the unknown excites the fuck out of me, especially when it has to do with you." He ran a hand through his hair and shifted his glare away as if regretting his words. "You're under my skin, and I can't get you out. Maybe if we just tried…"

"Noah, please. I'm not going to date you, and I'm not going to fuck you. We're friends, and that's it."

His jaw locked hard enough that the muscles bulged under the stubble. His nostrils flared. "This…" He waved a finger between us. "This can't go on. I hate it."

I never meant to cause him this much stress. "If you got to know me better, you'd see I'm not right for you. If we could just try being friends—"

His glare returned to me, penetrating and cutting off my words.

"You have plenty of empty relationships with—" *air quotes* "—friends."

"What are you saying?" I'd assumed this was a game to him, but the stress showed in his eyes. Maybe he still didn't feel well enough for this conversation.

"I… I don't know." He forked his fingers through his hair again. "I don't want to be one more meaningless relationship in your life, Avery. I want to be the one who gets all your attention, at least until we figure out what this is between us."

My head shook. Keeping up with his Jekyll and Hyde desires gave me whiplash. In a small voice, I said, "Two minutes ago you said it was just—"

His hand cut through the air. "That was then. This is now." His gaze locked with mine, sharp and challenging. "I'm laying it all on the table. I want you—as more than a friend and possibly for more than one night. I don't know how to shut it off, and I'm tired of acting like it's some passing phase." His arms spread, exposing his palms. "I'm putting it all out there, Avery. No more games. Just say yes, and we can figure out what this is once and for all."

My heart raced, and I felt myself shrinking inside. He was too forward, too attractive, and too self-assured. I'd never have control of him and the thought of giving up my neatly controlled life terrified me. He lived twenty feet from my fragile world, and too much tampering could leave everything in pieces.

Folding my arms around my waist, I dropped my gaze to the floor. "We're just neighbors, Noah. I'm just a temporary piece of furniture in your world, and in a minute I'll be gone."

He shook his head. "No, Avery, you're this accidental shift I didn't expect, and no matter how much I try to ignore your presence in the fray of my day to day life, you've totally consumed my thoughts. There's a reason for that. There's a reason I find myself zoning out in business meetings trying to picture the exact shade of your eyes."

His words surprised and delighted me, but they also scared me. "I thought I was just some conquest to you."

"I guess I was lying to myself. I *like* you, Avery. I want to know you better. I want to be everything that makes you nervous and unsure, everything that scares and excites you, everything that makes you sigh and moan. But you have to let me."

He was all of that. He was the nervous energy that made my heart race for no apparent reason. He was the thrill of a narrow hall shrinking around us. He was unpredictable and intense, and occasionally sweet. He could also be a total dick, which I strangely enjoyed as well. He was ... *Noah.*

My chin lowered, as did my voice. "It's not you. It's me. I literally can't date *anyone.* I just ... don't. I'm sorry. If we could just—"

My breath hitched as he walked toward the door.

"Noah, wait."

He paused at the door but didn't turn around to face me.

"You're right. You scare me. I don't know what you're going to say or do, and I like that, but I also hate it, because I like the order in my life and I don't want anyone or anything to interfere with my goals."

Scowling over his shoulder, his gaze narrowed on me. "News flash, a good guy doesn't fuck with his girl's goals. He supports them and encourages her."

"In a perfect world. Think about my job, Noah. Think about how you'd feel if we were involved."

"There's other work—"

"Nothing that pays like that. I'm not some genius. I struggle to make B's, and I wish I had twice as many hours in the week to study, but I don't. I work less than part-time and can clear enough to live comfortably—if I play my cards right."

And if my mother stopped draining me dry. But that was none of his business.

"It's a good job. There's no other work like that. Not for my skill set."

Come next September I would hopefully be teaching in a classroom with a respectable career, a new *legal* name, and a modest paycheck. But most of all, I'd have no college debt tying me to my unsavory past.

Everything from this part of my life and the stuff that came before would be nothing more than a memory. I'd be free to be whomever I wanted, and I wanted that freedom more than anything else.

I didn't have a wealthy spouse or established parents to give me a leg up. I needed to build my own foundation, and I was running out of time. The next eight months were my last shot at earning enough money for a down payment on my own home, somewhere that matched my future income.

No. I couldn't let him interfere with my plan. I couldn't let my heart do my head's thinking when things were so close to the dream I'd been chasing for years. Survival first, before everything else. Always.

"I'm sorry. I need the money. I'm good at what I do. And it's worth every penny."

He turned and scowled. "You're more than a tight ass and pretty face, Avery. Those things shouldn't be your *skill set.*"

"You're angry because I'm putting work before you."

"No, I'm angry because you call it *work*. What exactly are you selling?"

I stiffened. "You know it's not like that."

"All I know is I'm done negotiating. I'm out. I can't do this with you anymore."

"Do what?"

"This nit-picking. I'm a good guy, Avery—a hell of a lot better than any of those guys picking you up."

"You don't know them."

"I know there's gotta be something wrong with a guy if he has to pay for a woman's company."

My fingers twitched with the urge to slap him when he spat out the word *company* like it dirtied his mouth.

"Don't blame me for your feelings. I didn't put them there. And if you're so disgusted by what I do, then stop knocking on my door!"

His laughter filled the tense conversation with awkwardness. "You're right. It's all me. This is totally one-sided, and you'll lose nothing when I walk away,"

His sarcasm stung, but I couldn't bend, not on this. Calling his bluff, I whispered. "We're just neighbors, Noah. I'm sorry."

He nodded and blanked his expression. "My mistake."

He opened the door, and my heart jackhammered against my ribs. It wasn't fair that the sight of him walking away had the emotional finality of a lowering coffin. This was nuts. I didn't need his friendship, and I certainly didn't react to ultimatums, but...

Damn him!

He admitted to feeling the chemistry, too. What if this was a once in a lifetime connection and I was blowing it? I didn't want that sort of connection with anyone now, but I might want it later. Wait. No. My occupation was only part of the problem. Noah would never bend the way I needed a man to bend. He wasn't the right guy for me.

Or was he? *Fuck!*

Our words from the other night echoed in my mind.

I'm in charge. Always. And I don't think you'd like that very much.

Maybe I would.

Damn him for making me second-guess my first instincts. Torn, and none too happy that my feet were now moving after him, I rushed into the hallway.

"One date."

He paused, and I caught my breath. He didn't jump with joy or gloat or anything that I expected. More unpredictability from the curious Noah Wolfe.

I kept my distance and tried to remain firm, even though I was conceding in a big way. "I'll give you one date. I can't... You're my friend, Noah."

I laughed at how pathetic I sounded, but I had to see if there was something special here, seeing as he was being so damn persistent.

"You have plenty of friends, Avery. Let me be something more."

"Don't you get it? You're my *only* friend. The others... They don't know me at all."

"Well, you don't make it easy."

"They don't know me because I don't want them to. None of them see inside my apartment, and they don't know where I go to school or what I do in my free time. You think I don't open up with you, but you've seen more of my personal business than anyone else has in years. I'll go out with you on *one date*, but if it doesn't work out, you have to promise we can still be friends."

A slow smile curled his lips. "Deal."

That seemed too easy. "Really?"

"Really. But Avery, this isn't business. It's pleasure. There are no ground rules, so prepare for anything."

I swallowed, fearful he'd do something terrifying like take me skydiving or bungee jumping or convince me to sleep with him. "Okay, but—"

"No buts and no rules, Avery. That's the only rule. No rules." He grinned as he shut the door behind him.

What did I just agree to?

15

AVERY

"Come on..." I fussed with my uncooperative hair. Up, down, half-up, sloppy bun, nothing looked right.

I growled and threw my comb at the mirror. "Damn it, Avery. Focus!"

It was just a date. A stupid date. I went on four to five dates a week. This was no different.

"I have too much makeup on." Returning to the bathroom, I scrubbed my face clean and started over.

Halfway through lining my eyes, my phone pinged with a text from Noah.

You ready?

Shit. It was almost seven.

Not yet. fifteen minutes.

. . .

I STARED at my phone as text bubbles bounced, disappeared, bounced, and disappeared again. Then I waited another minute, but nothing came.

I didn't have time to sit there and wait for his response, so I went back to my makeup. The text came through a few minutes later, when I was just finishing up my eyes.

TIME'S UP. I'm coming over.

MY GAZE SHOT to the mirror. My hair wasn't done. If it was staying down, I had to curl the ends or at least add a braid. A knock sounded at the door.

I rushed into the hall. "I'm not ready. Come back in twenty minutes!"

"We agreed on seven." His voice was muffled through the door.

I took several slow steps to the door but didn't touch it. "I'm not dressed."

"Perfect. Let me in."

I rolled my eyes. "Five minutes."

"*Avery*."

"Please..."

He sighed. "Fine, but your ass better be ready in five. Hurry up."

I shook my head, not used to that sort of talk from a date. Rushing back into the bedroom, I flipped over my head and roughly brushed out my hair, spritzing it with some product meant to give it a beach look.

I applied a light layer of gloss to my lips and jerked on a pair of boyfriend jeans with an intentional tear at the knee. My cropped, off the shoulder, cream sweater paired with cream stilettos took the look from casual to sassy. I just needed to find earrings.

He knocked again. "Time's up."

"I'm coming!" Distractedly, I yanked open the door.

"You're not supposed to come until the *end* of the date," he greeted with a cocky grin. And damn, he looked good.

I rolled my eyes. "I just need to find my earrings."

"Wait." He caught my hand and pulled me back to face him. "You look great. I love your hair like that."

"Th—thanks." I disentangled my hand and searched the living room for my little gold hoops.

"Are these them?"

Turning, I came up short as he held up the earrings, not ten inches away from me. Why the hell was I so out of breath? I needed to calm the fuck down. "Yes, thank you."

"You look great. Let's go."

As his hand slipped into mine, my brain blanked, and I nearly forgot my purse and coat. "Where are we going?"

"To a tap house."

"A brewery?"

"Yeah." His arm curled around my hips as soon as we were inside the elevator, and my breathing suddenly seemed unnatural and out of sync. I had to chill.

My sweater was cropped, and my coat was still in my arms. As his thumb brushed the bare skin of my back, I shivered.

He glanced down at me and smiled. "Ticklish?"

"Not usually." Nothing about this was usual.

We stepped into the lobby, and he helped me with my coat. "Button up." He carefully slid each button into its hole. "It's chilly out there."

I wasn't used to him touching me so much or with such casual entitlement, as if we had done this a thousand times before. The instinct to pull away remained out of habit, but as if he sensed my tension, he held tighter each time I thought to put a little space between us.

Winston greeted us at the front door. "I have your car, Mr. Wolfe."

"Thank you."

"We're driving?"

"Yup."

He drove a beautiful, black BMW 328i hardtop convertible. He held my door, and I was pleased to find the seats already warmed. "This is a nice car."

"Thanks. Buckle up. We've got a thirty-minute drive."

"We're leaving the city?"

"Heading to the suburbs. I want you all to myself tonight, so I figured I'd take you somewhere we wouldn't run into anyone from the city."

He focused on the congested roads as he navigated his way to the interstate, but once we were cruising down 95 North, he appeared totally at ease. "Are you warm? We can turn down the heat."

"I'm always cold. How did you hear about the place we're going?"

"It's near where I grew up."

"And where's that?"

"Bucks County. How about you?"

Not a good topic. I adjusted the dial for the heat. "It is a little warm. How long have you had this car?"

"Wow." He laughed. "You're really going to completely ignore my question?"

"What did you ask?"

He turned and gave me a look that said he was positive I knew. "Where did you grow up?"

"A little nowhere town out west."

"What's it called?"

"Um, Blackwater."

"How far is it from Philly?"

"What, are you writing a book?"

He laughed again. "No, just trying to get to know my date. The fact that you're getting defensive only intrigues me more. Why don't you like talking about where you're from?"

"I didn't say that."

"You didn't have to."

I fidgeted, getting cold again. Adjusting the dial, I turned up the heat. "My life three years ago was nothing like it is now. Trust me, there's nothing intriguing about where I'm from."

"I highly doubt that. Do you have a big family?"

"Four brothers and one sister."

He frowned. "Did you visit them for Thanksgiving?"

"No. We don't do holidays. They all have ... other obligations."

He glanced at me and back to the road. "You guys don't get along?"

Growing up as we had, it was survival of the fittest. Aside from Drew, I didn't get along with any of them. And Drew was still active military, so the most I saw from him was his handwriting on a postcard since Gavin died.

"We're not really close. We're only half-siblings."

"Oh. Did you grow up in the same house?"

House... Trailer... "Yes, but I'm the baby, so they were mostly gone by the time I graduated high school. We don't really keep in touch."

Kenny should have graduated the same year as me, but he'd run away that spring and last I'd heard he was in jail. I needed to turn the conversation back to him.

Before I had the chance to think of a distraction, the interrogation continued, and he asked, "What about your parents?"

"My mom's still there. I talk to her every couple of weeks."

"And your dad?"

I sighed. "Can we not do this?"

His eyes strayed from the road, but only briefly. "Sure. Sorry."

I was terrible at this. No wonder I preferred dating people who didn't give a shit about the real details of my life. I had no experience with sharing.

"Sorry, I just don't like talking about my family."

"No problem."

A drawn-out silence consumed the car until even our quiet breathing sounded awkward. "Um, what about you? Are you close to your family?"

"Yeah. I only have one sister, and my parents are awesome. They're living in Florida for the winter—snowbirds—so I haven't seen them since Thanksgiving."

"Oh."

"No one's at the house tonight. I could show you where I grew up."

Equally intrigued and frightened to see his childhood home, I agreed, "Okay."

We reached a small town in less than thirty minutes. Charming stores dotted the old street, and I suddenly felt like I'd stepped onto the set of *Gilmore Girls*.

"You grew up here?"

"Right down that road."

"It's so pretty."

"It's a nice area. They filmed the movie *Signs* in the next town over."

It looked like a movie set. He parked in a half-full lot filled with expensive cars. As I waited for him to get my door, it occurred to me he hadn't taken me anywhere over the top, but somewhere that would teach me a little bit about him. It was personal and intimate, in a way my other dates weren't.

The taproom was a restored historic building with exposed stone masonry and glass walls and vaulted ceilings. The menu was New York inspired but simple—gourmet pizzas and samples of exotically seasoned lamb skewers and bacon wrapped scallops.

Between the delicious food and laid-back atmosphere, my anxiety slowly dissipated. The beer also helped.

The waiter supplied narrow trays of tiny beer glasses, each one a different shade of amber and some tastier than the rest. "I don't usually drink beer, but this is fun. I like learning the different flavors."

The more I sampled, the more at ease I became. Conversation soon flowed effortlessly between us, and I stopped worrying if he was out to unravel all my secrets.

"What's your major?"

"Education."

"Really?"

"Does that surprise you?"

"No, I think there's a nurturer hidden in you somewhere, the sort who makes her neighbor chicken soup when he's sick."

"Well, it was broth—"

"It was sweet." His hand closed over mine, his thumb tracing the back of my fingers. "What grade do you want to teach?"

"Kindergarten or sixth grade. They're not as cute in between."

"I'm glad you didn't say high school. You'd have a class full of hard-ons and no volunteers to go to the board."

"I doubt that."

"No, you don't. You know boys better than most, and you're well aware of how sexy you are."

When he called me out like that it made me nervous. "Did you go to college in the city?"

"No, I did a two year school down south that specialized in media, arts, and technology."

"So you always knew what you wanted to do?"

"Didn't you?"

"No."

I just knew I wanted something different, something useful and respectable. I wanted something I could count on that wouldn't become obsolete and something that would make others believe I was decent and good—two things I very much wanted to be.

He nudged the last glass toward me. "Drink up. I'm driving."

I chuckled, my tension now transformed by tipsiness. "Are you trying to get me drunk on the first date?"

"It's only a first if there's going to be a second."

"True."

The word left my lips before my common sense weighed in. The agreement was one date. One. Yet, the idea of doing this or something like this with Noah again held more appeal than I wanted to admit. I was enjoying myself more than I had on a date in ... years. Or ... *ever*.

I raised the glass and sipped, finishing off the tray of sample brews. "This one's good. Probably one of the best I've had tonight."

He smiled. "After you've had that many samples, everything starts to taste good."

I waved a playful finger at him. "Ah, is that your strategy with dates?"

"Yeah, but don't tell my date."

I laughed. "Your secret's safe with me."

He glanced over his shoulder, but there was no one left in the dining room but us. "Do you wanna get out of here?"

"And go where?"

He shrugged. "Walk around? Drive?"

"Two seconds ago you said I knew boys. That carries over to men. If leaving here meant driving back to the city and saying goodnight you wouldn't be rushing us out the door."

His blue stare met mine, and he smiled. "Touché. Will you let me show you where I grew up?"

"Noah..."

"Night's not over, Avery. Have you been enjoying yourself so far?"

"Yes, but..."

He tossed several twenties on the table and stood. "Come on. It'll be fun. I'll show you where my mom keeps the embarrassing pictures of me."

Unsure if this was a mistake, I followed him. What choice did I have? He was my ride home. But more than that, I wanted to pretend for a few hours—see how the other half lived.

As I slipped on my coat, he helped me with the buttons again, this time holding my stare. Our breathing seemed suspended, as if holding onto an unspoken promise about to be released.

He held my hand as we walked to the car and opened my door, making sure I had plenty of opportunities to notice his manners. As we drove, the streets were uncongested, and the night was clear.

"Do you live far?"

"Just another few miles up the road."

Tension twisted with anticipation, forming a delicious potion in my belly. It was enough to keep me on the verge of punch drunk, yet sober enough to maintain my wits. I wanted to tip over to the drunk side and let go, but that wasn't my nature.

His house was enormous, the sort of home featured in magazines with Martha Stewart baking muffins in the kitchen and Pottery Barn furniture in every room.

"I'll hang up your coat."

He left me standing in a gaping foyer feeling well outside of my comfort zone.

"Want a tour?"

"Sure." The contrast in our backgrounds had never been as evident as they were the moment he flipped on the lights.

The kitchen was incredible. He took my hand and escorted me into what could only be the living room. It was twice the size of my mom's trailer. There was an entire game room in the basement, furnished with cinema chairs, a big screen television, and numerous arcade games.

"I can't believe you grew up here. It's a suburban palace." And completely intimidating.

"Wanna see upstairs?"

I hesitated, knowing full well what *upstairs* would lead to and unsure why I was still fighting what now seemed an inevitable outcome. I was in a losing battle, and it wasn't like me to surrender without a fight.

There were consequences. I knew my answer would come at a price, but standing here in his beautiful—*normal*—childhood home made me want to pretend I belonged, pretend I was worthy.

Tomorrow we would be back home, and I'd be a sugar baby, and he'd be the out of my league man I fucked. He had to realize the consequences wouldn't change.

Was it just about tonight for him? Was that how he could overlook all the ways we were unsuited? Was this about sharing his background or fucking me on a neutral playing field?

"Why did you bring me here, Noah?"

He cocked his head. "I wanted to show you who I was."

And he had. He wasn't playing the douche bag, nor was he trying to impress me with over the top treatment. He was just being himself, and it wasn't fair that the real him was more irresistible than the handsome stranger who lived across the hall.

Everything was normal here. My phone hadn't rung. The costumes I wore in the city were out of sight and out of mind. I didn't know who I was when I stood in his home, so many miles from my own. I didn't know how to act or be with him.

But I wanted him, and I didn't want to think about the consequences for once in my life. I wanted to live in the now and experience the fantasy because he made the possibility of normal seem so tangible I could reach out and grab it. I just had to find the balls to give in.

I glanced around the empty house. "No one's coming here?"

"They're all in Florida. We have the house to ourselves."

"You want to stay here tonight?" I inwardly winced, not used to asking. I kept waiting for my assertive self to take the lead, but for some reason, it wanted Noah to call the shots. Maybe that way I could blame him in the morning.

"Only if you want to stay."

I shrugged—more shy bullshit I wasn't used to—my fingers tracing over the polished banister that led to the second floor.

"I'm not sure what I want. You confuse me." The honest vulnerability kept leaking out. *Damn it, Avery. Where are you?*

"Maybe that's not a bad thing."

"Maybe it is." It definitely wasn't good.

"Care to find out?"

My gaze lifted to his and a shiver shot through my system. This was so different from everything I thought I wanted, everything I *knew* I needed. Despite my wishy-washy words, I had to be clear on the outcome.

"What happens tomorrow?"

"We go home and see how things play out."

So this could still be just one night. I could live with one night. It was the thought of more that scared me.

When would I have another opportunity like this with him, alone and isolated from the stresses of the world, away from the city and the life it represented for me? If we both treated this as a one-time thing, we might be able to stay friends. He'd have it out of his system, and I'd prove that—in the long run—he wasn't the right man for me.

Glancing down at my feet, I slipped off my heels and set them on the first step. "Show me your room."

"Really?"

I nodded, too afraid to talk.

His fingers slid alongside mine as he took my hand and led me upstairs. The quiet seemed to echo through the empty, immaculate home. We stopped outside of a closed door, and he faced me.

"I... I don't expect anything, Avery. Don't think just because we're here, I assume..."

Why did he have to be sweet now? I needed him to be transparent as much as I needed him to be unwavering and sure of what he was asking. Otherwise, we couldn't do this. It was now or never.

"I know why you brought me here."

"Do you ... expect...?"

Yes, and so did he. Talking was only jumbling matters. "Let's not decide what this is and just let it happen." I reached for the knob and opened the door.

Grays and dark wood, uncluttered by items a teenage boy might have left behind, presented a clean space with subtle personal touches. For some reason, the maturity of the room made me like him more. It spoke of his good relationship with his family and testified he still slept here on occasion, even as an adult.

"This is nice." I scanned the room and stared down at the bed.

His hands rested on my shoulders as he approached. Slowly, he swept my hair aside and pressed a kiss to my neck, causing my nipples to tighten.

My eyes closed as I drew in a deep breath. His fingers trailed down my arms, over my hips, and across my midriff, teasing the skin of my belly.

"I'm not going to lie, Avery. I want you more than my next breath."

I leaned into him, passively resting my arms at my side, wondering how long I could let someone else take the lead. Eventually, I'd take over, but this was nice. His fingers trailed up my stomach, teasing soft circles on my skin.

He was like a magic snake charmer or some sort of wizard. No one else settled me the way he did, and it was strange that he somehow subdued my usual instinct to take the lead. His teeth scraped along my throat, and I sucked in a sharp breath that exhaled as a moan.

"I think you like when I'm a little bit rough, don't you?"

Mmm... Rough was the only way. "Yes..."

"I can do that." His hand slid under my loose sweater and cupped my breast, his thumb dragging slowly over the tight tip. "You liked when I pinched your nipples, too, didn't you?"

"Mmm..." I had been a mess after leaving his apartment that night.

"What is it you want, Avery? To be loved or fucked?"

Love? My mind shied away from that sticky word.

Love was uncomfortable, a source of guilt and obligation that led to grief. No matter how much I might want to be loved, it wasn't what I wanted tonight.

I wanted something I could count on and judge at face value, without accidentally mistaking it for more.

"I want you to fuck me."

His hands yanked my sweater over my head, and in the next second, I was facing him, his fingers buried in my hair, angling my head back as his lips sealed over mine.

He backed me toward the bed, his tongue devastating my mouth as it plunged deep, silently delivering promises of what was to come.

Noah was a man who kissed with his whole body. When his mouth was on me, so were his hands. His front pressed to mine as if we were melded into one and I savored every inch of warm, hard contact.

"I love that you're not fragile." He tugged the straps of my bra down my arms, and I pulled free.

If only he knew how breakable I was. How broken. Grasping at his broad shoulders, I deepened the kiss.

"You're a greedy little thing, aren't you?" His fingers shoved into the front of my jeans, tugging my hips closer to his as his erection pressed between us. "I can't wait to get in your pussy."

I gasped as he shoved me onto the bed, his tall body towering over mine. Holding my gaze, he reached behind his head and stripped off his shirt in one forward yank.

My mouth went dry. How was he so built when he hardly worked out? Or did he, just not at the same times I used the gym? He flicked open the button of his jeans but left the zipper intact.

"God, you're fucking sexy." His mouth devoured the sensitive curve of my neck as he lifted my arms. "Keep them up."

I stiffened, his command grating against my nature and calling up all my usual instincts. "I don't bottom."

There she is. Finally, the Avery I knew and loved was getting into the game.

Noah chuckled, dragging his hand up my spine to flick open the first hook of my bra. "What does that even mean?"

"It means I don't play the submissive in bed."

He laughed and yanked my knees forward until I was flat on my back. "We'll see."

No, we wouldn't, because I wasn't going to lie there like some fuck doll for him to boss around. I didn't follow directions from men off the clock. And if this was truly going to be a one-time thing I had only this one chance to show him what it meant to fuck me.

"Freeze." I held up a hand, and he stilled. Holding eye contact, I untwisted my bra and tossed it on the floor. Next came my jeans. As I slid them down my legs, revealing a deep violet thong, I watched his color rise.

"Jesus."

Shifting onto my knees, I reached for his pants, tugging him closer, much like he'd tugged me. "On your back." The command followed a hard yank, and he tumbled to the mattress.

I didn't give him a chance to contemplate how the roles had changed. I straddled his hips, rocking my body over the bulge beneath his waist and finding the position that was most pleasurable to *me.*

His hands caught my hips, his grip tight, almost bruising. Just as momma was finding her groove, he flung me off of him, and I landed on my back again, under him.

"Don't be selfish." He flashed a cocky grin and dropped his head to my breasts.

I gasped as his mouth closed over one nipple, teeth scraping and lips pulling tight. My body arched into his, my nails scaling down his muscular arms.

My fist closed around his wavy hair, anchoring him to my chest. "Harder."

He ground his erection into me, rocking us like two teenagers on the brink of disaster. His mouth tightened while his other hand teased and pulled. I could come if he did this a while longer.

"*Ah...*" The bite to my nipple pinched on the cusp of too hard, but then my body adjusted to the pain and I moaned. My taut muscles relaxed as my lashes lowered, giving in to the pleasure.

"You *really* like it rough, don't you?"

"You have no idea." I grabbed the back of his neck and yanked him closer, shoving his mouth to my other breast.

He sucked and bit and I was pretty sure he was leaving a few hickies. His free hand curled around my wrist and brought my hand to his crotch. I twisted out of his grip and caught *his* hand, pressing it to my pussy.

"Finger me."

"Bossy."

"Do it."

My panties were shoved aside as his finger drove into me. I arched beneath him, bucking against his touch, riding his palm as I still held his arm.

"Harder."

"Demanding little thing."

"Just *do* it."

He wedged another finger into my cunt and fucked them deep. "More?"

"Yes. Faster."

"Christ."

His fingers pumped hard, and my eyes rolled back as he hit that magical nerve where heaven and earth met inside of a woman's body. I screamed, trembling as my first climax rushed through me, bathing his fingers. We both were out of breath, but he was far from finished.

I met his stare and gave a satisfied smile. "Now, clean it up."

He drew back and arched a brow.

Recalling he would still be my neighbor tomorrow, I wavered between the girl he knew, the submissive woman men wanted me to be, the dominant control freak I was, and the class act *I* wanted to achieve. Fuck. *Fuck!* I shouldn't be thinking this hard.

I pleased men most of the time. This was *my* time. Mine and Noah's. What if he didn't like this side of me? What if no one would ever like me aside from Gavin? Did this part of me have to disappear with the rest of Avery Dean Mudd?

Realizing he was no longer touching me and still looking at me with that confused expression, I suddenly wanted to crawl out of my skin and be someone else.

"Forget it." I shoved him off.

"Wait a second!" He leveled his body over mine, refusing to let me up. "What's happening here? Is this... Are you, like ... one of those women who..."

Oh, my God, I couldn't do this. I searched for my bra. "This was a mistake."

"No, it wasn't." He yanked me back to the bed when I tried to escape again, this time pinning me in place. "Talk to me, Avery."

My lips pressed tight. I wasn't going to spell it out. Or maybe I was because I still wanted to fuck him. "I like control."

He laughed. "No shit."

"No, I mean I *really* like it. I ... get off on telling you what to do."

He sat back on his heels. "All the time?"

I shrugged. "In bed."

"And what do I get?"

I flashed him a cocky smirk. "You get to fuck me."

"But on *your* terms."

"Yes."

"What if I don't like your terms?"

I shrugged again. "That's the only way this can work."

"Why? Did something happen to you?"

"No, nothing fucking happened to me." His question riled my defensiveness, and I silently told myself to calm down. "It's just ... how I am." I huffed and looked away. "I can be nice, you know! It's not like I'm going to strap on a leather skin suit, gag you and shove a ten-inch dildo up your ass." *Not without asking...*

"Oh, *I know* you're not fucking doing *that.*"

This was getting awkward. He was thinking and taking too long to make up his mind. The moment was rapidly dissolving, and the longer he contemplated the situation, the more I wanted to rewind and erase the whole night.

"Forget it." This time when I tried to get up, he shoved me back down—hard—and moved so fast my thread of authority snapped.

His hands pinned mine to the pillows, and his knees trapped my legs immobile. "Don't move."

Trying to play it cool, I kept my tone dry. "I think you misunderstood the dynamic."

"I think you misunderstand me. You basically want me to do whatever you say. I'm not used to that. I need a second to think."

"Look, I get it if it's not your thing. That's why I told you this wouldn't work—" His hand closed over my mouth, and my eyes bulged.

Oh, he did not just shut me up! I bit him.

"Ouch!" He jerked his hand back and examined his palm where teeth tracks left little divots. "You bitch."

"Give me my shirt."

"No."

"Noah."

"We're not finished."

"I think we are."

He tipped his head back and glanced at the ceiling, mumbling something I couldn't make out.

"What?"

"I *said,* I can't believe I'm about to do this. Tell me what you want."

Was he serious? I didn't expect him to actually agree. Figuring this was some sort of trick, I started small. "Kiss me."

He leaned down, and I turned my face away.

"Not there."

He paused, mouth a few inches from my cheek and chuckled. "I'll get to that—"

"*Start* there."

"This is hot to you?" His frustration was palpable.

"No. This is a waste of my time. I knew you couldn't take orders from a girl."

"Yes, I can, but I want to be *with* you, not just service you like some..."

I rolled my eyes to fight off any sting of tears. I didn't do well with criticism. Who knew why I was the way I was. This whole exchange was to prove a point about how mismatched we were as any sort of couple, so I kept up the cold, selfish act.

My manicured fingernail pointed toward the apex of my thighs. "Either put your face between my legs or get off of me so I can get dressed."

"You're such a bitch." He scooted lower and I blinked hard, wondering why being called a bitch didn't feel like teasing this time. Maybe because I was being one.

"Call me bitch one more time, and I'll redefine the word for you."

He dropped to his elbows, and I spread my thighs, his warm frustrated breath bathing my soft skin.

"Do you want me to take your panties off? This is so fucking weird."

"That's it." I swung my leg over his shoulders and sat up. "I'm done."

"No!" He tackled me to the bed and had me stripped in one second flat. "I'll do it. Just..." He scooted low again. "Open your legs."

My thighs parted, and the room went utterly silent. "Fuck. That might be the prettiest view I've ever seen."

I pursed my lips and stared at the ceiling. This had gone on for far too long, and I was pretty sure I wouldn't be coming again.

A reluctant breath filled my lungs and gasped out as his fingers stabbed deep, and his mouth closed over my clit.

"Yes." Maybe the night could be salvaged after all...

He shoved his shoulders under my knees, using the bulk of his arms to spread my thighs. Burying his tongue in my cunt, he fingered me and fucked me with his mouth. I didn't even have to tell him what to do. It was like he knew every magical spot, and I was suddenly careening into an ocean of ecstasy.

"Yes, yes... Don't stop." My body trembled as a wave of pleasure crashed over me.

Warm breath teased over my wet folds as he lifted his head. "Again?"

Panting, I nodded. He fed his fingers into me, stuffing me full and pumping hard as his mouth nibbled and sucked. His other hand teased lower, and the second his finger breached the tight tissue there I came hard against his tongue.

Throat dry, I swallowed huge gulps of air as my entire body thrummed. My mind was spinning. Either I hadn't had sex in so long I'd forgotten how good foreplay was, or he was extremely gifted.

"Again," he growled. He didn't hesitate, nor did he wait for permission to sink his fingers back inside of me.

His touch filled me every possible way, his tongue twisting as his teeth scraped over-sensitized flesh. My body was a red-hot ember that never had a chance to cool. The more he pleasured me, the less effort it took to orgasm.

"Fuck!" My legs trembled as I came almost violently, but he didn't relent. On and on, he penetrated every opening, tasted every exposed inch of secret flesh. One release blurred into the next until I was sure I was losing my mind.

"Enough." I panted. "No more."

"Bullshit. One more. Give it to me, Avery. Give me one more good one." His fingers rubbed rapidly over my swollen clit, and I couldn't take it.

My hand grabbed for his, but he was faster, pinning my wrist to the bed.

"It's too much!"

"You can take it."

"Noah, I can't!"

He pressed a finger deep, and I wriggled back, but there was no escaping him. He was everywhere, using his larger body to trap me beneath him, gripping my limbs with his heavier ones.

"Let go, Avery. I've got you."

Something was happening. It was too overwhelming, too intense. I was scared. I wanted it, yet I didn't. The sheer vacillation of my thoughts was terrifying. "No, stop!"

"You're there. Just let go."

I was there, but the drop seemed too far, deadly and life-altering. I couldn't do it. I wasn't reckless like him. Something inside of me, something insecure and vulnerable whimpered at the unknown. And then it was too late.

All pretexts that separated my many façades shattered, obliterating my thoughts. My grip on reality slipped through my fingers as my voice echoed around the room as if shouting from someone else.

I was hot and cold. Sweating and shivering. My mouth was parched, and my vision unclear. I fell into a dark place where there was no pain. There was fear, but I was too far away for it to reach me, yet I was aware of its presence.

Floating. Buzzing. I was high as a fucking kite on endorphins, as hot-blooded and hungry as an injected addict, too gone to do more than let numbing pleasure swallow me whole.

What the fuck did he do to me? Pressure welled behind my eyes as something painful bloomed in my chest. My demons exorcised by the flick of his hand, I shivered with drenched thighs on the bed, pleasure racing up my spine in the aftermath of an orgasm unlike any other.

I couldn't stop shaking, even as he wrapped me in his arms and pulled me to his lap. I went without a struggle, curling into the shelter of his strength like a scared little girl unsure of who to trust.

"Shh... I have you."

His lips pressed against my hair, as his fingers curled around the back of my neck and held me close. His heart beat steadily beneath my ear, warm moisture seeping from my eyes.

Was I crying? I wiped my face, mortified and confused by my tears.

"It's okay. You were beautiful."

Then it hit me. He'd tricked me. He acted like I was in charge, made me believe I had his devoted surrender, but he held the upper hand all along. He stole the authority right out from under me, and now I was the fool crying in his lap getting fucking aftercare for something I wasn't sure I consented to do.

We hadn't even had sex, yet he absconded with part of my soul and hid it someplace no one would ever find it again. Gone forever, and more valuable than a hundred virgins' innocence. Whatever he took, he stole it. It was my *Cosmo* all over again, but so much more. I shoved at his chest.

"Don't. You're going to let me hold you."

My jaw locked as I blinked against my infuriating tears. "You tricked me."

"I *worshipped* you."

I was angry and confused and relieved in a way I didn't understand. It was too much. Too intimate. Too open. Too ... real.

No matter how many times I tried to break the hold he had over me, both emotionally and physically, he wouldn't let go. And somehow I knew there was no going back to the way things were.

"I hate you."

He sighed and pressed his lips to the top of my head, keeping them there as he whispered, "No, you don't."

Didn't I? Every feeling toward him was now tarnished with this moment I'd never be able to erase. I wasn't the sort of girl who found comfort in exposing the soft underbelly of her soul. I needed the upper hand at all times. I foolishly trusted him. I *believed* him when he said he'd try it my way. But that was all a lie.

I didn't hate him for lying. I hated him for tricking me into something I didn't want to feel. He made me vulnerable. He made me weak.

Maybe I didn't hate him, but I was certain I couldn't trust him.

Tonight wasn't supposed to change anything, yet after he stole the control, it changed everything. "I want to go home."

"We're staying."

Yeah. I hated him.

16

NOAH

My mind blanked as I rocked her in my arms, tucking her head under my chin to keep my startled stare hidden from her view. Jesus, what the hell just happened?

I got that she liked to play Little Miss Bossy Boots in bed, but this was more than that. I wondered if she ever had an orgasm that wasn't manufactured in her own puppeteering way. Had every guy she'd ever been with let her call the shots—one hundred percent of the time? No way.

I was outside of my jurisdiction, but now I was involved. As I rocked her, I tried to decide if I pushed us into a better, more honest territory or if I majorly crossed a line. Fuck me, because I didn't know.

She sniffled, breathing settled as I rocked her, and her limbs slowly relaxed. The tension in her spine curling as she settled more onto my lap.

Avery was an ongoing contradiction. One minute she was assertive and self-assured, and the next minute, she was vulnerable and insecure. How had I ever thought her to be tough? But she was tough, just not now as her tears chilled my chest and her shoulders gently shook under her soft, jagged breaths.

She reminded me of a dam. Chip one hole in the wall and from a tiny leak, sprung a tsunami. Maybe only an insane man would pick at such a barricade. She'd been closed off for a reason, and I arrogantly assumed I could handle whatever was on the other side. Now, I wasn't so sure.

Easing onto the pillows, I pulled her into my side. She tensed the moment we shifted positions, but a quick tightening of my grip showed her I wasn't letting go and she didn't waste her time arguing.

"Let's just lie here together."

She made no comment or objection. Every once in a while she'd blink, and I'd feel the flick of her long lashes against my bare chest.

Her full breasts pressed like warm pillows against my ribs, and I loved the weight of her in my arms. Every breath filled my lungs with her scent, and I found nothing but tranquility in the tease of her hair. Some strands clung to my five o'clock shadow, and for some reason, this turned me on. It made me want to drag kisses over her front and leave her skin rosy with whisker burn. But not tonight.

She was emotionally wrung, and I was a little out of my element. I had the sense that she'd fall asleep if I held her here long enough. My phone was on the nightstand. If she passed out, I could look a few things up, find out more about all this topping business.

I loved sex and got a rush out of a good, rough fuck, the same as I got a rush out of playful foreplay, and intimate lovemaking. Sex was sex. It was good even when it was just okay. But maybe for Avery, it was only good when it was a certain way.

I knew about BDSM. I'd overheard water cooler talk from the girls in the office when the whole *Fifty Shades* thing happened, but I'd never actually met a real person who was into that scene—that I knew of.

How into it was Avery? Who had she slept with before and what had they done? I wanted to know everything about her and her past, but first, I needed to bone up on my knowledge. I meant it when I'd said I'd try. It wasn't my fault I naturally took the lead. She couldn't blame me for that. Could she?

Fuck, I needed to do an internet search.

Her breathing tapered into soft, even breaths. How far would I be willing to take this? We hadn't even had sex, and this already seemed more intense than any other hook-up. How was that possible?

The longer I considered my history with women and the big question mark that was Avery's past, the more I felt like an uninformed virgin. Nine times out of ten, I was doing it missionary. I'd had anal, but only that one time on my birthday and Margaux never wanted to try it again after that. She hated it so much I never asked for it again—with anyone.

Come to think of it, I hardly ever asked for anything. If a girl went down on me, it was a bonus, never an expectation. My head was so fucked from finding out my best friend had fucked my long term girlfriend, I just wanted to be with women who were glad to be with me. And I bailed long before they ever had the chance to reject me.

My sister was right. I was still a mess from Margaux. She and Shane were married, yet here I was, holding my naked neighbor and thinking about the bitch who fucked me over with my best friend.

I dragged a hand over my face, trying to scrub away all the uncomfortable memories. I had to get over this. And maybe I was ready. Maybe that's why I wanted a shot with Avery so badly, to prove I was ready to move on. But what if Avery was more than I could handle?

I glanced down at her sleeping face. Dried tear tracks marked her perfect skin, and my breath caught at how fragile she suddenly appeared. It was so different from the hard ass she usually pretended to be, yet I recognized this side of her too. I'd spotted some of this vulnerability in her the night she went out with that grease ball. I still couldn't figure out why she'd go out with someone like that. Money or not, she was way too good for that guy.

Reaching for my phone, I tried not to jostle her. Turning the volume on low, I started my search. If I could just understand what the end goal was, I might have an easier time agreeing to her terms.

Within the first five minutes of searching, I knew I wouldn't find what I was looking for. There was no forum out there with notes specifically tailored to Avery Johansson's kinks. And that was what I wanted. I wanted to know her every fantasy, and I wanted to be the one in the driver seat, taking her places she'd never been before. It seemed those places would be new to me as well, but I was game if she was.

The longer I read about it online, the more intrigued I became. I definitely saw the appeal of such a delineated, dominant role. But I worried Avery and I were both attracted to the same side of the coin, which might be why she claimed we would never work as more than friends.

17

AVERY

My body tensed as I opened my eyes. Nothing about waking up in Noah's arms felt right. Not this place, not this room, and certainly not the shit he pulled last night.

Glancing to the side, I noted the way his chest rose and fell with each even breath. Silently sliding the covers off my body, I slipped one foot to the edge of the mattress and carefully eased—

A large hand closed around my bare arm. "Where are you going?"

I scowled at the fingers gripping my forearm, memories of last night rushing to the surface and warming my cooled rage. I wasn't falling for his tricks today.

I yanked my arm free. "You're awfully grabby."

"You're awfully sneaky. Where are you slinking off to?"

"I have to pee." Not a lie. I couldn't help that my internal clock woke me up every morning at dawn. A rigorous trip to the gym each morning instilled such habits in a person.

"Fine." He released my arm. "But you're coming back to bed when you're done."

After using the bathroom, I washed my face and nosed through his cabinets, glad to find an unopened toothbrush still in the package. I brushed my teeth, eyeing every corner of the immaculate room for clues about Noah, yelping when the door swung open.

"Do you mind?" I mumbled, spitting out a mouth full of minty foam, and rinsing my teeth clean.

His fist rubbed the socket of his eye as he groggily stumbled toward the toilet. "It's your fault for waking me up stupid early."

My eyes widened as a trickle echoed through the tile room. "Oh, my fucking God! Are you taking a leak?"

He shrugged, his bare back thick with muscle and his naked, toned ass emphasizing his tapered hips. He was fucking pissing while I was in the middle of brushing my teeth!

"You're disgusting." I dried my hands and returned to the bedroom.

"Sorry..."

I searched the floor for my clothes, gathering items against my naked chest. The toilet flushed, and water ran. Just as I was reaching for my discarded thong, strong arms banded around me, tugging my clothing out of my grip and tossing it back on the rug.

He laced his fingers with mine and towed me back to the bed. "No, no, no, no, *no*. It's too early."

"My clothes..." I wasn't even sure if his eyes were open.

He collapsed on the mattress, face down, and groaned. "You don't need clothes."

I hesitated.

"Come back to bed, Avery. There's no need to wake up with Jesus and the chickens."

My gaze trailed over his toned thighs, dusted with masculine hair, and held at the perfect cleft separating his biteable ass cheeks. My handprint would look divine on his flesh. My inner Mistress purred at the sight of him, face down, ass up. I had to get out of there.

I shifted away from the bed. "I'm wide awake."

He shoved a pillow over his head. "Haven't you ever heard of a Sunday? I'm not leaving this bed for at least another two hours."

I pulled the blanket to my chest and sat. Waiting. Was I supposed to just sit there while he slept the day away? Like I had nothing better to do with my time. I was his guest. He should be making me breakfast or something. At least pointing me in the direction of a coffee pot. "You're a terrible host."

"Avery."

"What?"

"Lay down and shut the fuck up. It's five thirty in the morning. The sun isn't even awake."

Pursing my lips, I eased my back to the mattress and stared at the ceiling. "Can I take a shower?"

He flopped onto his back and glared at me. "There's something wrong with you."

"I'm sorry. I'm used to waking up at dawn." I was usually thirty minutes into cardio by this time. He knew I had a routine.

"Well ... go run around the block a few times and chill out."

"I can't. I only brought heels."

He chuckled. "You actually thought about it, didn't you?"

I shrugged. "I don't like missing a day. It makes me lazy."

"You're a freak of nature."

I wasn't a freak, but I didn't like straying too far outside the lines. Noah, on the other hand... He was a haphazard disaster. A rule breaker. A risk taker. And someone I had no business waking up next to.

Last night was a mistake. What the hell even happened?

You know...

I winced at the memory and then scowled at my snoring bed partner. This was all his fault. He turned me into an idiot whenever he came around. I should never have agreed to go on a date with him.

I groaned. I was attracted to him. But sometimes we liked the wrong people. And I needed him more as a friend. He was pretty much the only friend I had that didn't pay me for my time.

Whatever happened last night couldn't happen again. Period.

I poked him in the ribs, and he growled. "Can you wake up and take me home?"

"Maybe I'll wake up and strangle you. Go back to sleep, Avery!"

I'd take a cab, but we weren't in the city. I wasn't even sure if they had taxis in neighborhoods like this. Every driveway seemed adequately supplied with fully loaded SUVs and sports cars. The cost of Ubering back to Philly would be astronomical. I hated not having control.

"Come on, Noah. You brought me here. I wanna go home."

His blue eyes narrowed and his scowl curved to a wounded frown. "Why are you in such a rush to leave?"

"You know why."

He shifted to his side, propping his body up on one elbow. "No, I'm serious. What's going on?"

This was what he did. He was a dick, and then he turned all nice and concerned. Mixed signals everywhere. "Never mind."

I wasn't spelling it out. Last night went totally wrong.

It had been amazing and mind-blowing, and I actually thought for a minute I'd hit the cunnilingus jackpot. But he'd taken it too far. I needed control, and I told him that, but he wouldn't listen.

Words like *stop, enough, don't,* and *no* didn't register in his vocabulary, or if they did, he cajoled his way around them. That's why there were safe words, but usually the safe words were for the other person, not me. Would I have safe worded?

He hadn't hurt me but pushed me miles outside of my comfort zone. He made me believe I was in control, but I never was. And I fell for it, like some stupid girl who knew absolutely nothing about men.

I knew men. I had plenty of them in my life. That's what being a sugar baby was all about. But none of them—well, hardly any of them—meant anything to me. Noah wasn't a client, and he meant something. He was my friend, and he knew I had loads of reservations about going out with him. Last night he broke my trust and—

Why was I even debating this—even with myself? He broke my trust. Fuck him. I flung the blanket off and grabbed my thong, hiking it up my legs. "Where are your keys?"

"What?"

"Your keys. The things you use to start a car. I'm going home, and if you're not going to drive me, I'll drive myself." Let him pay for a cab or take a train back.

He sat up, eyes glaring under his disheveled bedhead. "What the hell is your problem? I'll take you home. It's early—"

"*Now*, Noah! I want to go home *now.*"

His hands lifted, fingers splayed. "All right. Jesus. You don't have to be a—"

"Call me a bitch and I swear to God I'll punch you in the dick."

He climbed out of bed and shoved his legs into his wrinkled jeans. "Good morning to you, too."

By the time I was dressed, I was trembling and on the verge of tears, but I didn't know why, nor did I want him to see me upset—again. "I'll meet you downstairs."

"I'm coming," he huffed.

I waited at the front door, wondering where the hell he hung my coat. He was there a few minutes later, opening a closet and handing me my jacket. I avoided eye contact as I stuffed my arms into the sleeves. "I'll meet you in the car."

"It's locked."

"Then I'll wait outside."

The lights on his BMW flashed, and I climbed in. The car started, scaring the bejesus out of me. Of course, he had an automatic starter. I adjusted the heat and waited for the interior to warm. What the hell was taking him so long?

Several minutes later, the driver's door opened, and he slid in, wearing a scowl and holding two travel cups of coffee. "Here."

I took one of the hot cups. "Thank you."

He backed out of the single home driveway and sped down the empty roads of suburbia, not uttering a single word and holding the wheel in a white-knuckle grip.

Since he provided coffee, I felt the need to send an olive branch back. He was, after all, taking me home.

"Thanks for leaving so early."

"Like I had a choice."

Okay. He was pissed. Well, so was I. And confused. And a whole bunch of other crap I didn't have names for.

"Well, it's probably best we get back to reality. Put this whole mistake behind us." The car veered right, and I screamed, "*Jesus! Watch out!*"

He peeled off the road, careening onto the shoulder fast enough that I nearly dropped my coffee. He slammed it into park and twisted in his seat, arm braced on the wheel as he glared at me.

"What the hell was that last part?"

"You maniac! I almost burned the shit out of my hand!"

"Repeat what you said."

Rolling my eyes, I secured the hot tumbler in a cup holder. "Come on, Noah. This was a mistake. I told you—"

"Last night was not a *mistake*, Avery. You cried, and I fucking held you. Shit like that isn't meaningless."

My jaw locked. I cried because he pushed me past my comfort zone and stole my control. "I disagree." And damn my voice for wavering. "We can't do anything like that again. We're better off as friends."

"Bullshit! I knew you were going to pull this crap!"

This wasn't my fault. "I told you to stop, and you didn't!"

"I was giving you an orgasm!"

"It was too much! I said *enough*."

"Don't twist it around like I'm some sort of predator who made you do something terrible. I didn't hurt you. You know I'd never hurt you. Tell me you know that."

"That doesn't matter. I ... didn't like it."

"Bullshit. I was there, Avery."

This was getting far too personal. "Well, we're not doing anything like that again."

His eyes narrowed. "There's something here, and I'm not letting you run from it."

"You don't control me!"

"Yeah, well ... neither do you. *Fear* controls you. Stop acting like you're some badass chick who doesn't need anyone. It's obnoxious—"

His words cut off as my hand slapped across his cheek. Everything silenced.

"Sorry..." I never actually slapped a man out of frustration. I didn't know what to say, and he looked ready to strangle me. "My hand slipped."

His jaw ticked and time stood still, the energy of the car tightening like a slingshot about to spring. He dove across the interior and jerked back when his seatbelt stopped him. I laughed because it was funny, but he didn't appear to think so.

The buckle clicked and flung toward the door. He was free. The strap of my seatbelt whisked off my chest, and he grabbed my wrist, tugging me over the center console.

"Hey!" I yanked back, but he had a tight grip. "Get off of me!"

He tugged my arms over his lap, and my hand shot out to protect my face from hitting the steering wheel. The back of his arm weighed me down, and I squirmed to get back to my seat.

"What the hell are you doing?"

I nearly swallowed my tongue as heat exploded through my jeans, and the sound of his hand smacking down on my jeans reverberated in the car. It took me a minute to process that he just spanked me.

My heavy breathing challenged the sound of heat pumping from the vents. The moment I processed his actions, I committed to a reflexive reaction.

"You fucker!" I went for his nipples.

Twisting to my side, my back hit the wheel, and the horn honked. I went for his nipples, twisting hard enough to change the color of his face.

"No!"

I pinched as hard as I could through the layers of his clothes.

"You fucking bitch!" He shoved me aside and walloped my ass again.

"Stop!"

"You stop!"

"No! You started it!"

"You slapped me!"

"It was an accident!" I scrabbled away as his palm peppered my ass.

He was going to leave bruises! My jeans did nothing to spare me pain.

"*Stupid dick!*"

I twisted and tried to punch him in the crotch, but there wasn't enough room with me wedged between his chest and the wheel. The horn blared as I squirmed to save my butt another smack.

His palm landed on my hip. "*Enough!*"

I jerked free and panted, my hair falling in my face and my coat slipping off my shoulders. My throbbing butt sent a pulse through my veins. Furious, I glared, gritting my teeth.

"Jesus, you're fucking sexy."

Sexy? I wanted to kill him, and he was thinking about sex? "There's something seriously wrong with you—"

His lips smashed to mine, his fingers locking in my hair and holding me still as his tongue plunged into my mouth. Something unraveled inside of me, and before I turned into a puddle of brainless hormones, I slapped the thigh of his jeans.

A satisfying *smack* filled the car.

Our mouths broke apart, and his arm flung out with surprising speed, and pain exploded in my boob.

Cradling my chest, I gaped at him. "Did you just tit-slap me?"

"You hit me first."

I lost it. My hand swatted at his face, shoulders, arms, anywhere I could reach. He wasn't holding back either. My ass was burning hot, and when his seat slid back, I panicked and reached for the door handle.

"No, you don't." Strong hands wrenched me back, my fingernails scraping on the metal handle as it slipped out of my grip.

"No!" There was no way he was spanking me again.

I squirmed and struggled, but he was faster and stronger. My hand shot out to the door, the scent of pristine leather filling my nose as his palm landed on my upturned ass with a sharp sting sending fire into my veins.

This wasn't happening!

I bit his side, tasting the cotton of his shirt and not letting up until he let go of me. Jerking my body off his lap, I made a fist and aimed for his dick.

"Avery, *no!*" He caught my hands and glared. "You don't hit a man in the crotch!"

I struggled to break out of his hold, but he was too damn strong. "You. Spanked. Me."

"You slapped me in the face."

Damn it! He had a death grip on my fists. "Let go of me."

"No."

The warm interior of the tiny hardtop convertible spiked toward a hundred degrees and my knee was jammed between the gearshift and the console. I met his glare and narrowed my eyes. His nostrils flared. Those sharp blue eyes held me prisoner as much as his hands. Such Nordic beauty stripped away my resolve.

As far as physical strength went, I would never be stronger than him. I jerked my arms and slid into my seat. "I hate you."

He finally let go. "No, you don't."

No. I didn't. That was the problem. My shoulders sagged. If I hated him, it would be so much easier to stay mad at him. But even now, ass burning and one sore boob, I couldn't bring myself to dislike him.

What was wrong with me? This was not how people our age were supposed to act.

"Noah..."

His fingers brushed a snarled clump of hair from my eyes and his arms wrapped around me, pulling me into a hug but leaving me the dignity of allowing me to stay in my seat. This was not where I wanted to be. His lips pressed against my hair, my temple, my eyes.

"You need to stop fighting this."

I looked up at him, unsure what was happening between us, terrified I was losing my only friend a little more each time we hung out. We didn't work as a couple. He wanted more. I didn't. I knew more would only end in disaster, and we'd end up losing everything. Why couldn't he see this wasn't worth that?

His lips traced mine, smooth yet firm, and my eyes closed. That mouth. It wasn't fair for anyone to kiss so well.

His hand cupped the back of my head, and I let him, because I, apparently, was a weak moron who thought with her vagina. His other hand slid inside the back pocket of my jeans, massaging the area he'd smacked.

I gave in to the kiss, too exhausted to fight him off. It wasn't supposed to be like this. We were caught in the *frienemy* zone, in a traffic jam of sexual tension, sarcasm, and explosive chemistry. It was the unhealthiest relationship imaginable. When his lips pulled away from mine, I forgot why we were fighting in the first place.

He looked at me through gold-fringed lashes. "Are you done?"

"Yeah." I slid my feet to the floor and buckled up. "You're a jerk. My butt hurts."

"So do my balls. I'll take you to Fourth Street for breakfast."

And that was that. Nothing resolved. Nothing changed. Just stuck in this weird, little, maybe relationship of *I don't know what the fuck is going on.*

But the label didn't matter. All that mattered was I still wasn't ready to sacrifice our friendship for something sexual. Nor was I ready to sacrifice my control. So we were basically back where we started.

18

NOAH

I should have known better than to assume this would be easy. Nothing with Avery was fucking easy. The morning we returned to the city I kissed her goodbye and paused at my door. Something told me I should take a long hard look at her, but when I turned around, she was already gone.

The following day I didn't see her on my way into work. Nor did I spot her in the building that night. I texted her, but she didn't respond.

On Tuesday I texted her again, but she still wasn't answering. I was growing concerned until a familiar man picked her up. She seemed to open the door just fine for him. I paced a trench in my floor the entire time they were gone, and when he walked her to her door, I pathetically watched through the peephole.

Seeing another man kiss her—even if it was only on the cheek—filled me with so much rage, I worried for my sanity. What kind of hold did she have on me to incite this much emotion? We hadn't even had sex yet.

I tried to do the healthy thing and let her go. She claimed she wasn't interested anyway. But she was. We both knew she felt something. This was just some bullshit game we had to play until she couldn't take the distance anymore. We'd played it before. Sooner or later she'd show up in her sweatpants with a bottle of wine and an excuse.

I hadn't decided if I'd forgive her. I shouldn't care this much. I should be in a place where casual was just fine. No expectations, no problem. But I wasn't. I was eye fucking my peephole every night and stalking my text messages for any response from her.

By Wednesday, I was pounding on her door. She was home—I could hear her phone ringing when I called—and yet she wouldn't fucking answer.

"Avery! This is childish."

Fury bubbled out of helplessness. What the hell sort of woman was I dealing with? It was like dating a child.

"Answer the fucking door—please."

By the end of the week, my pride was a pile of mush, and I was embarrassed for myself. This wasn't me. Women never affected me like this. I needed to get control of my senses.

I spent the remainder of the week working through my emotions and convincing myself that I was rejecting her before she ever rejected me. It was bullshit, but it was also the only way I could move on. And I would move on. There was no way I'd start the new year like a pussy whipped little boy pining over his crazy bitch of a neighbor. I had better things to do.

And she was a bitch. Only a bitch could act so cold and warm at the drop of a dollar. Infuriated and at my wit's end, I decided if she wanted to ghost out of my life, I'd beat her to it. She might be a cold-hearted bitch when she wanted to be, but I could be a callous prick if that's what she wanted.

19

AVERY

I was a big, fat coward—and turning into a bit of a recluse. After our date, Noah assumed all was good and he'd won, but we both lost. I just couldn't give him what he wanted. And that meant he couldn't give me the one thing I needed—a friend.

The following week, I hid in my apartment, binging on Christmas classics and eating things I had no business putting in my mouth. Being that Noah and I shared a floor, a building, an elevator, and the common areas, I had to change my usual routine to make sure we didn't cross paths.

I stopped going to the gym at dawn and started going at seven-forty-five after Noah disappeared for the day. I also started studying on campus so I didn't have to be around when he was home on the weekends. As far as my clients... I broke my usual rules and asked them to come up to my door. That way if I did have to use the hall, I was never alone.

I knew Noah watched me in the past. He'd admitted as much. He knew what clients were closest to me, who I allowed to kiss my cheek, and which ones took me out the most. These men were my only source of income and while I still had nothing sexual going on with any of them, I had a business relationship with each. Noah wouldn't dare interfere with that because whether he approved or not, it was my job.

He called and texted and even banged on my door a few times, but I never answered. We weren't going to be romantically involved. Once he understood I wasn't budging, he could have settled for being my friend, but he didn't. His texts crossed a line, turning nasty before they stopped altogether.

Avery, please call me.

Why won't you answer your texts?

I know you're home!

Fine, you want to be a fucking coward, enjoy passing time with your Johns and fulfilling an empty life! We could've had something real!

Tapping my pencil on my textbook, I pursed my lips, ignoring the pinch of rejection that accompanied his silence. I should be used to having no friends. I'd written off everyone I left in Blackwater. And living the secret life of a sugar baby didn't really create genuine relationships.

Some of my clients confided in me. I listened and comforted and tried to offer advice as much as I could. But that wasn't a reciprocated dynamic.

Sugar babies were meant to be low drama and soothing company, pretty sources of confidence-boosting companionship. It was very one-sided, but that's why I got paid. I couldn't show up at a job with baggage. I had to smile and laugh at all the right moments. Dish out compliments and flatter men the way they liked their egos stroked. So, as much as I knew their problems, I couldn't share mine.

I shut my textbook and slouched in my chair. "This sucks."

Snatching my phone off my desk, I scrolled through my recent texts. It had been four days since Noah knocked on my door and his texts had grown increasingly nasty toward the end. But the last one hurt the most.

My thumb swiped over my messages, opening up his texts as a painful reminder of where things stood. It should have cemented the accomplishment and taken Noah off my to-do list but, instead, reading his texts again only left me wallowing in doubts that his accusations were right on the money—maybe fear did control me more than anything else.

I DON'T KNOW why I ever wanted someone who doesn't even have the basic manners to answer the phone. Have a nice fucking life.

I RUINED IT. Or he did. Maybe we both did. Did the autopsy really matter? Our relationship was pronounced dead the moment I said goodbye to him the morning after our date and I needed to wrap up the wake.

But his angry words remained on my phone, a lingering reminder of how I could manage to fuck up just about anything if I tried hard enough. A reminder that I wasn't worth the work, as he eventually gave up and moved on.

It was a new year and I had nothing better to do than bathe in my own self-pity. Since I'd spent the holidays alone again, and only interacted with men who believed I was someone else, no one suspected how down I could get this time of year.

There was so much confusion on top of my usual holiday depression I felt drunk on a toxic cocktail. I needed something to cheer me up. The new semester had just started and wasn't filling the void in my life the way it usually did. I didn't have any appointments until tomorrow night. I'd go insane by then if I didn't get the hell out of this apartment.

I scrolled through my contacts, my thumb pressing down on the only other person who might cheer me up. He answered on the second ring.

"Avery. I wasn't expecting to hear from you today."

"I miss you."

Micah made a noise that said he didn't mind hearing that he was in my thoughts. "You sound … down."

"Am I interrupting you?" Maybe I had seasonal depression.

"Interruptions tend to be unpleasant. I never mind hearing from you. Is there something you need?"

And that was the perk of being a sugar baby. Some of my Daddies made it their business to take care of me. Their role in my life made them feel necessary, powerful, and satisfied, while I felt momentarily adored in a world of make-believe.

They achieved real emotions from the fake role I played. But with Micah, it wasn't always fake. He was my first and he knew me better than all the others.

"Can we go somewhere? Do something?"

"Are you free tonight?"

"Yes."

"It's still early. Why don't I set an appointment for you at the spa? I'll spoil you and take you to dinner around seven."

"Thank you, Micah."

He was so generous. He helped me get my apartment, bought me clothes, and pampered me. It had been three and a half years since meeting him, and once school was finished my business as a sugar baby would conclude. I wasn't sure I wanted to let him go when that happened and those feelings had been confusing our arrangement lately—at least on my end.

"Tonight's on me, Micah."

"Avery." His deep voice was thick with objection. "That's not how this works. You know better. The moment you start doing favors it stops being a job and starts being a hobby. Hobbies don't pay the bills."

"I still have…" It was bad form to discuss one Daddy with another. The game was to make them feel like the only man that mattered. Micah knew I had multiple clients. He's the one who started me in this line of work. "Sorry."

"We'll discuss this over dinner tonight. We'll set normal rules aside and meet as friends—but just for tonight."

"Thank you."

"I'll pick you up at seven."

As soon as I hung up the phone I received an email notifying me of an electronic transfer into my account. Micah might agree to put the rules aside, but he was never going to stop honoring our original arrangement. He promised to take care of me and it meant something to him that he kept his word.

In a way, it meant something to me, too. He was dependable, trustworthy—unlike some other people I knew.

20

AVERY

Micah was the perfect solution to my mood. An evening with him affirmed everything I already knew but had started to doubt.

I chose to be a sugar baby the moment I realized I wouldn't be able to afford a degree without serious financial help. It was scary and exciting and he guided me along the way, teaching me how to run a legit business that covered the cost of a life I never dreamed of having. He advised me on how to handle myself and made sure I knew how to avoid men who took advantage. It was a smart choice then and a smart choice now.

"Don't forget, the last mile's always the longest," he said, brushing a strand of hair behind my ear as we said goodnight at my door.

"Thank you—for everything."

He pressed a kiss to my cheek and hugged me, his long arms bundling me in a supportive hold that, for a minute, I wished would never end. Then the elevator pinged.

I drew back just as Noah stepped into the hall carrying a box of items in his arms. The elevator shut behind him and there was a painful second when no one said a word and all the tension of the past few weeks pummeled my chest like cannon fire.

His mouth flattened as he walked to his door, silently unlocking his apartment and stepping inside. I flinched as the door slammed behind him. Micah's arms still held me and I had no doubt he felt me tense.

"Did you sleep with him?"

I drew back and looked up at Micah in surprise. He never asked about my personal life or other relationships. I wasn't sure how to answer. Honesty seemed best. "No."

"But you were involved."

He wasn't asking, but I answered anyway. "We had a date. It didn't end well."

"Do you need me to get involved?"

"No."

He glanced at Noah's door, and then mine. "There are only five months until graduation. How do you want to proceed, Avery?"

He was asking if I wanted to move. I loved my building, my home. "I'll tough it out."

"If he's a problem—"

"He's not. He'll get over it." *But would I?*

Micah nodded. "If you change your mind let me know."

"I will." That was a lie. I'd never ask him to find me a new apartment or involve himself in my personal drama just because my neighbor was a jerk who hurt my feelings. "I'm fine. Really."

There was a silent moment where I wasn't quite sure if we made a mistake discussing my reservations tonight. I told Micah I still liked my job, but there was a strange fear associated with letting it go and stepping into the real world after college.

I also tried to confess how much I worried about losing my connection to him, but he never truly allowed me to get the words out. I wasn't sure why that was, but I sensed he knew what I wanted to say and had a reason for deterring me from saying it.

"Goodnight." He kissed my cheek again, but this time his mouth lingered near the corner of my lips—different from his usual goodbye.

A tingle of heat radiated in my chest. The placement of his kiss seemed intentional as if meant to tell me something. Something I wasn't sure I wanted to know.

"I'll see you in a few days."

That night I couldn't sleep. I kept picturing Noah's face and hearing the echo of his slamming door. He was either a juvenile prick or he hated me for being one. Neither was what I wanted.

Tossing and turning, I tried to think of other things, but my mind always went back to him. We weren't friends. We were nothing. If I could somehow channel my sadness about that into anger, maybe I could hate him, too. But I couldn't. Losing Noah just made me sad.

It was stupid. We barely knew each other. In a few months, I'd be moving out of the building and taking my degree to start a brand new life. For all I knew, I could end up in California or Oregon or Minnesota. He was a blip in time and I was giving myself an ulcer worrying about the minuscule significance he held in the grand scheme of things.

He. Was. Nothing.

The following night when Josh walked me to my door and thanked me for a nice evening while casually placing a thin envelope in my hand I felt a little better. This was normal. This was good.

"I'll see you next week?"

"Of course," I reassured. He was a regular and one of my sweeter clients.

"Goodnight, Avery."

As he called up the elevator I stepped into my apartment but paused at the sound of voices. Noah's laugh filled the hall followed by a distinctively female giggle.

"That's what I said!" The female voice seeped into the air like noxious gas and my shoulders tensed.

"Pardon me," Josh said, stepping into the elevator after they stepped out.

I peeked through the cracked door, remaining hidden by the frame. After seeing Josh, he'd know I was home. But he was clearly too preoccupied to care.

Noah laughed again. "I wish I could have been there."

"It was so funny. You would have loved it."

They approached his door as he reached for his key. My stomach pinched at the sight of the woman. She looked a couple of years older than me, closer to Noah's age. She was undeniably pretty, with long dark hair and the height I wanted. We looked nothing alike.

Her body brushed against his arm and something sharp stabbed in my chest. It was late, almost midnight. Were they on a date?

He turned, smiling at whatever she'd said, and stilled. His blue gaze snagged with mine, expectant and satisfied to find me watching him. I couldn't hide the hurt tightening my expression. His mouth flattened and he looked down at the other woman.

"Tonight was great. It's so refreshing to go out with a mature woman."

My chin trembled. He knew exactly where to stick his knife.

"Same. You should see some of the guys out there. I'm so glad Laurel set us up." Her body pivoted, angling her best assets toward his front. Her fingers trailed over the sleeve of his coat. "I don't have any early plans for tomorrow. I could stay the night."

I stopped breathing. Everything inside of me twisted airtight as I waited for him to turn her down. His eyes lifted, his gaze shooting to my door and back to her.

Don't. Please don't...

His hand lifted as his head lowered. Bile rose in my throat as his lashes slowly drifted lower and his mouth pressed against hers. I couldn't watch. Quietly shutting my door with a shaky hand, I stepped backward until I'd walked myself all the way into my den and stumbled onto the couch.

He was a jerk. I hated him. He wasn't my friend and he'd never be my friend again. I didn't want someone like that in my life. So why was I crying?

21

NOAH

The moment I heard her door shut, I broke the kiss. Unsure if Avery still watched through the peephole, I kept my voice low.

"Let's not rush things. How about a cup of coffee, though?"

"Sure."

I unlocked my door and slipped an arm around Morgan's slender waist, nuzzling her neck for good measure. We mustn't disappoint the audience.

Her hair didn't smell especially nice, and her lips were too thin for the sort of kissing I enjoyed. Though she'd been a fun date and an indisputably attractive woman, there was zero chemistry.

It pissed me off that I seemed to measure every quality against Avery. I was going out with Morgan to get over Avery. It should be good that they were so different. But I was the fool who kept looking for a clone.

I made two cups of coffee and hardly paid attention to how she took hers. What was the point?

I could probably go to bed with her. She'd said something about having an open morning. But the desire just wasn't there. What the hell was wrong with me? Maybe I should just do it, force myself to get into it so I could get over my damn neighbor.

"You don't talk much."

"Sorry?" I stopped staring at my coffee and glanced at her, her words taking a moment to register. "Oh. I guess I'm more tired than I thought."

She studied me for a moment then put her cup on the counter and stood. "I should go."

"You don't have to..." What was I doing? I only wanted to keep her here long enough for Avery to think we were fooling around. Good God, I was pathetic. "I'm sorry if this isn't ending the way you hoped. I have a lot on my mind."

She smiled and pressed her fingers to the back of my hand. "Hey, tonight was fun, and I got a free meal. At least we'll know each other the next time we're out for your sister's birthday."

I appreciated her letting me off the hook. "It has nothing to do with you. I'm sort of hung up on—"

"Your neighbor?"

Startled she'd guessed so accurately, I drew back. "Please tell me Laurel told you that."

Morgan laughed. "She warned me you were getting over a girl who lived in your building. *And* I sensed we had an audience in the hall. It was the first time you got affectionate all night."

"Sorry. That was a total dick move."

"No, I'd call it an extremely human response. How about this? If I ever need to make an ex jealous and you happen to be single, you help me out the way I helped you tonight. Deal?"

Now that the pressure was off, Morgan actually seemed like a pretty cool woman. "Deal."

"Should we kiss goodnight in the hall or are we good?"

"I think we're good." If anything, this was a reality check to how pathetic I'd become. Thank God Morgan was cool, or I'd be totally humiliated. "Thanks again for tonight."

"My pleasure." She kissed my cheek and pulled on her coat. "For what it's worth, Noah, I think you're a pretty great guy. If she doesn't see that she probably doesn't deserve you."

I don't know what she sees. "Thanks."

Walking her to the door, I noted that Avery's apartment appeared dark. Though she looked hurt to see me with another woman, she probably didn't care all that much. I needed to nail this coffin shut once and for all.

"Goodnight, Noah."

"Goodnight. Be safe getting home."

As I shut the door, I let out a breath. It was a New Year. I'd spent most of Christmas moping into my beer and making my sister's ears bleed. This had gone on long enough. Even if Morgan wasn't the answer, she was a step in the right direction.

I was ready to be in a relationship again, but the last thing I needed was a relationship with another woman who didn't want to be with me. And that truth seemed to shake some sense into me more than anything else.

22

AVERY

Sometimes I was grateful I wasn't some above-average, off the charts prodigy. My classes were never easy, and I struggled to keep my GPA above a 2.5. The goal had always been to make Dean's List and graduate with honors, but I lived in the real world, where I was lucky to get accepted at a top-tier university and invited back each year. The beauty of my struggle was that it kept my mind occupied for most hours of the day.

But there were moments when my syllabus was handled, and my clients were scheduled, and boring, normal tasks had to get done. Hence the joy of lugging groceries from the corner market all the way back to my place on Society Hill in the middle of January.

Slipping on a sheet of ice and catching my balance just as Winston caught the door, I huffed and blew a stray hair out of my face from under my wool cap.

"Can I help you with that, Ms. Johansson?"

Before I could vocalize an answer, he relieved me of my bags. "Thank you, Winston."

"You gotta watch getting around in those shoes. I'll salt the walk again soon as I'm done helping you to the elevator."

Plucking my hat off my head, I caught my breath. My boots

weren't rubber soled or the sort any sane person would wear in the snow. Stretching my fingers to get the blood circulating under my mittens, I accepted the bags again.

"It's supposed to snow quite a bit tonight," Winston said, as he followed me to the lobby and called the elevator.

"Great."

Philadelphia and snow were a catastrophe. Cars had to be moved so plow trucks could fit down the narrow streets. Then, once the plows came through, the drifts piled up in the usual parking spaces, giving pedestrians the claustrophobic pleasure of feeling like they were walking through a luge shaft to get where they needed to go.

The cold, northern temperatures ensured the snow piles took forever to melt, leaving hundreds of cars displaced, and the walks slicked with frozen black slush. Yes, I definitely needed to invest in new winter boots.

Lugging my groceries into the lift, I thanked Winston again and keyed in my floor number.

"Hold the door." A hand slipped through the cracked opening just before it sealed shut and my heart stopped. Noah, holding his own bags, stared across the threshold.

"Hey." He broke eye contact and turned away.

Were we speaking? To each other? "Hey."

Lips pressed tight, I stepped to the far side and stared at the buttons. The doors closed again, and I could swear the elevator was moving extra slow today.

His natural scent mixed with the metallic trace of winter air on his clothes. From the corner of my eye, I noted he was wearing a new coat, this one wool with a duffel hood and wooden hoop buttons. Men really shouldn't wear such nice clothes. It gave the impression they were trying too hard to be attractive, which he'd succeeded in doing. The man could honestly wear a poncho and bring sexy back.

"It's supposed to snow tonight."

Was he talking to me? Of course, he was. No one else was here. "Yup."

"The stores are all picked over. I got the last loaf of bread."

"Congratulations."

For some reason, people in this area bombarded grocery stores, stocking up on obscene amounts of bread, milk, and shovels at the first sight of a flurry. Where did all the shovels go from last year, I often wondered.

"Did you get a backup charger for your phone? Sometimes the power goes out in the building when we get a blizzard."

I frowned. Was he actually trying to be nice to me? Like a friend? "No, but I'm sure I'll be fine."

"Well, I have one if you need to use it."

"I said I'll be fine."

"I'm just being neighborly."

"Well, don't hurt yourself."

For some reason, his gentle tone only reminded me of how awful his last few texts had hurt, and the sight of him plunging his tongue into some other woman's mouth when he knew I watched. I couldn't help the nasty tone in my own voice. It was the only way to keep from crying or apologizing.

The doors finally opened to our floor and I stepped out, walking quickly to my door. Fumbling with my purse, I dug out my key just as my bag split at the seam and my groceries clattered to the floor, scattering everywhere.

With a huff, I dropped my purse and other bags in the hall and went to collect my crap. Noah put his stuff down and bent to pick up a runaway can of soup.

"Here."

"I've got it. Thanks." I shoved the closest spilled items into my other bags.

"You dropped these, too."

I stilled, my attention zeroing in on the box of tampons filling his hand. I snatched the box and shoved it deep into my purse. "I said I got it." I scrambled to gather the rest of my items, but they were all over the place.

"Avery."

This was so embarrassing. Couldn't I just live a peaceful life without humiliating myself every time he showed up?

"Avery..."

He'd obviously moved on to greener, more brunette pastures and gotten over our little whatever the hell it was. No need to pretend we were still friends.

"Avery, look at me."

"*What?*" My vision shimmered as my chin hardened.

"Hey. I'm sorry."

"For what? You didn't bag my groceries."

His head tilted, and his brows drew together. "You know this isn't what I wanted."

"Oh, I know. I know all about what you want. You made sure of that." I shoved the last of my frozen veggies into my bags and stood.

I couldn't look at him. I could barely stop my hand from shaking long enough to get my key in the goddamn door.

"I didn't sleep with her."

Come on with this fucking key!

"The woman from the other night ... she didn't stay."

Finally, the lock turned. I kicked my bags and purse over the threshold and went inside, turning to face him.

"It's none of my business what you do, Noah. Excuse me. I have groceries to put away."

I shut the door, and his hand caught the wood, stopping me from closing it tight. My heart jolted as the muscles of his forearm bunched and flexed.

The door pushed open against my protest, and he met my stare. "It matters to me."

I couldn't do this dance with him anymore. It hurt too much to watch him move on, and I couldn't do anything with him long term. "Get out of my home."

He shoved his way into my apartment, and I took a startled step back. "No. I want to talk to you."

"Well, I have nothing to say to you. You're breaking and entering."

He shut the door behind him and stepped over the pile of bags on the floor. I took another step backward. And another, but he intruded deeper and deeper into my personal space.

"You're the one who refused to answer my calls or the door. What was I supposed to do, wait around forever?"

"I don't know. Why don't you stick your dick in a few randoms while you figure it out?"

"You're angry because you care."

"I'm angry because you won't get out of my fucking apartment!" The back of my thighs bumped the arm of the sofa.

He stopped walking when he was only a few inches in front of me. His eyes, pinched at the corners, stared down at me, his mouth flat. "Why does it have to be like this?"

I looked away, unable to hold his stare. "*You* said it did."

"I said I didn't want to be your friend."

"Well ... your texts proved that to be true."

"I was angry. I don't like feeling ignored."

"I told you all I could offer was friendship and you refused to listen."

"Why? Why is that all you can offer?"

"We've been through this, Noah."

"Walk me through it again."

My eyes closed. Why did my chest suddenly hurt? "You're too much."

"Too much what?"

Everything. He was too intense, too real, too attractive, sometimes too sweet. Always too dangerous. I closed my eyes, forcing myself to restate the facts.

"I'm moving in five months. I just need to finish the semester and graduate."

Warm fingers slid into my hair, and I flinched, pressing my eyes tighter, so they remained shut.

"Where will you go?"

"Anywhere I want."

"Why are you always running? Maybe just stop for a second and appreciate where you are."

His thumb dragged over my lips, and I swallowed the urge to whimper. He stepped closer, and I stopped breathing.

"You're so beautiful. Avery. So strong yet fragile. I want to rattle you and protect you. Just let me in. Please."

Warm breath teased my cheek as his voice lowered, and his head angled closer. I let out a whimper as he rasped, "Don't move." Soft lips traced delicately over mine, and I didn't pull back. His mouth firmed, and I shamefully leaned into him. Slowly, he tipped his head, and his tongue pressed past my lips, swiping softly over mine.

I turned my face away. "Don't."

He turned my lips back to his. "Stop telling me *no*." His long body pressed warmly against my front as my hands caught the side of the sofa.

There was no escaping him, not because he held me down or had me cornered, but because only half of my brain wanted him to go away. The other half very much wanted him to keep kissing me.

My hand lifted to his chest, riding over the curve of his broad shoulder and pulling him closer. I was tired of fighting the attraction, and when he touched me like this, it seemed impossible to push him away and so natural to give him everything he wanted.

My muscles loosened as my grip tightened on his shoulders, and he eased me back. My mouth opened, and he groaned with satisfaction.

"I've missed kissing you," he whispered, taking it deeper and sliding his hands around my back. "I've missed hearing your voice."

My bottom shifted to the sofa, and his legs filled the narrow space between my knees. His hands massaged my ass, strong, groping clasps sending little shockwaves to my pussy.

My fingers tugged at the collar of his coat, seeking the heat of his skin. He moaned at the first brush of contact and pressed his erection further into the cradle of my thighs. Then we were falling.

The couch cushions caught my back as his body blanketed mine, our legs tangling as he pressed into me, kissing, rocking, tormenting. I stopped pretending I had any sort of objection and gave in to the pleasure he offered. My hands pulled at his coat, wanting to get it off, see his body, touch him with nothing in between.

"Take this off," I demanded, tugging at his layers of clothing, wanting it all gone.

He sat up and quickly removed the garment. I did the same. He tossed his to the floor, but mine wasn't so easy. I twisted and yanked my arms, wrenching the material away. By the time I wrestled it off, I was out of breath.

He looked down at me, his gorgeous chest shifting above me with each breath. "What about this?" His fingers pulled at my shirt, and I nodded.

He lifted my head and pulled the shirt away. His mouth crashed into mine, and I tugged him closer, my fingers forking through his blond hair as my other hand dragged down his muscular back toward his ass.

Strong fingers pulled at my bra, stripping away the cups, and cold air hit my nipples as they puckered tightly. His mouth ripped from mine, working quickly down my throat to my chest.

"God, Avery..."

The way he touched me... It was the closest form of worship I'd felt in years. I wanted him to deliver a thousand licks of pleasure at my command, beg to satisfy my needs, heed my warnings, and obey my every command.

"Put your mouth on my nipples. I want it hard."

The first hot lick had me arching into him. His hips rocked as he sucked and nibbled. He plumped my tits, squeezed, and held me to his mouth like a sacred offering.

"Keep going."

The button of my jeans was yanked open, long fingers stealing into the front of my panties, and reality crashed over me like a bucket of ice water.

"Wait!"

Knowing he wasn't good at minding the word no, I panicked and bucked my hips, knocking him right onto the floor. He landed with a grunt, and I sprang after him, rolling to my side, but he was already on the ground.

"Shit!" I hadn't meant to hurt him. "I'm sorry! That was an accident."

He rubbed the side of his head, his hair standing on end. "How did I know that was going to happen?"

But it wasn't what he thought. "I..."

I glanced at the box of tampons, preferring to embarrass myself one way to the truthful option, which involved me explaining that I was emotionally unprepared for this. It wasn't technically a lie if I didn't say it out loud. He followed my gaze to the box on the floor and understanding dawned. He'd made the assumption on his own.

"Oh," he said, mouth twisting with disappointment.

"I didn't mean to throw you on the ground so hard."

"It's cool."

"We can still ... do other stuff."

He sprang off the floor and tackled me back to the couch. I grunted as he kissed me hard.

I turned my face away. "Do what you were doing."

"Give me a chance to get there, bossy." His hands cupped my breasts, his thumbs and fingers teasing.

I *was* bossy. The question was, could he be obedient?

I had yet to see his goodies, so I reached for his fly. My fingers wrenched the zipper until his jeans opened. Shoving my hand into his briefs, I was welcomed by thick, hot flesh. He was hard as a rock, and the second my grip closed around him he sucked in an audible breath and stilled.

But this wasn't right. "I need you under me."

It was comical how fast he rolled to his back, taking me with him. The side of my mouth curled into a smile as I straddled his legs. There was nothing sexier than a man who could follow directions. He was finally getting it.

"Take these off." I nudged his pants and lifted to the arm of the sofa to give him room. "All of it."

He kicked off his shoes, toed off his socks, and stripped in two seconds flat. My God, he was beautiful. His cock stood, tall and proud, like the first flag of a Fourth of July parade. Thick, muscular legs, cut abs, chiseled chest … perfection. Oh, this was going to be fun.

I slid onto the couch cushion, filling the space between his knees. "Arms above your head."

His jaw ticked, but he slowly obeyed, raising his hands to grip the sofa and revealing twin tufts of blond hair under his arms. I let my stare crawl over him, purposely trying to unnerve him.

Where to begin?

Creeping forward, I let the ends of my hair tease his six-pack, enjoying the way he sucked in a breath the moment my nipple grazed his hard cock. My tongue traced the flat circle of his nipple, and he groaned. Smiling, my teeth teased the hard tip.

A hand closed over my ass, and I sat up, cutting off all contact. "No touching."

"What?"

"I told you to keep your hands above your head."

He opened his mouth to object but snapped it shut when I raised a challenging brow. His arms lifted back to the cushion and he let out a heavy breath. My mouth returned to his nipple, this time closing around the tight tip and biting the way he bit and teased mine.

He grunted. Most men weren't used to having their nipples toyed with, and I never understood why. They could actually draw quite a bit of pleasure from nipple play. My body shivered thinking of all the sexy things I could do to him there.

I gently closed my teeth over the rigid point and pulled until I heard him hiss in a breath.

"Avery. Careful."

I smirked, remembering how sensitive he was the last time I pinched him. "You can take it."

My hand dragged over his stomach until my fingers circled his other areola, my tongue tormenting and playing a game of *will it be pleasure or pain*. I pinched the tip and pulled.

"Fuck, that hurts!"

"Should I stop?" My tongue swirled to ease the pain, and he shivered.

"I thought we were going to do something else."

"We will." I released his nipple, blew over the damp flesh, and moved my mouth to his other one. "Once you've earned it."

He groaned but kept his hands in place above his head.

I played with him for a good ten minutes, really making him wait for more. The longer I teased, switching from one nipple to the other, the more he found pleasure in the slight pain. By the time I was ready to move on, his chest was heaving, lifting his swollen nipples toward my mouth, and arching his back off the couch as if silently begging for more.

"Good boy."

I petted a hand down his flat stomach and sat on my heels. His arms were still resting behind his head, cheeks flushed, and his cock dark with arousal, a thick vein embossed along the side.

I tilted my head, considering how I wanted to proceed. His eyes darkened to the deep blue of a midnight sky, and his breathing grew labored.

"You're torturing me."

"I know. But you're being very good. I think you earned a reward."

Curling my fingers, I scratched my fingernails up his thighs and released a slow breath along the length of his cock. His body twitched, and I grinned. My hand slid over his hips, and I cupped his balls.

"Somebody's been manscaping."

He shut his eyes, a dark flush working across his neck and chest.

"You have a beautiful cock, Noah. Should I put it in my mouth?"

"Yes."

He forgot the magic word.

I massaged his balls, still not touching his dick, I waited. Pre-come seeped from the tip, and I blew warm air over his length. My mouth brushed the smooth crown, moisture transferring from his hot skin to my mouth, and he groaned.

Looking up so he could see my eyes, I slowly licked my lips. "Mmm."

"Fuck, Avery, you're killing me."

I almost had him saying the words I needed to hear. This was exactly how it was meant to be. Me in charge, him at my mercy. "Tell me what you want."

"Suck my cock."

I tsked. "You have to ask."

"Will you suck my cock?"

"Nicely."

His eyes narrowed as the word pressed through his teeth. "*Please.*"

"Please, what, Noah?"

His lips tightened, his jaw noticeably locking as muscles in his face twitched. "Will you *please* suck my cock, Avery?"

"I love it when a man begs." My mouth closed over his flesh, taking him deep to the back of my throat.

He arched, his body bowing with the elegance of a musical instrument as he groaned in pleasure. My fist stroked with every pull of my lips and glided down with every mouthful.

His knees drew up, and he let out a string of curse words. I worked quickly, driving him to the point of near explosion, showing him how nice I could be when he did as I said. And then I sat up.

He looked ready to scream, his stormy eyes wide and his face tight. "Why'd you stop?"

I held the silence, treasuring the anticipation, bathing in his needy desire as it swaddled me like a hot blanket. I wished I could fuck him, but that was too intimate, too personal. This was exactly what I'd been needing, exactly what had been missing the last time we hooked up.

"Tell me how much you want me to keep going."

"Avery."

"Noah."

We faced off for several seconds, and then he huffed out a frustrated breath. "I *need* you to keep going. *Please*. I wanna come."

I bet he did. Lowering my mouth, I opened my jaw, rewarding him for being so compliant and straightforward, and letting me take the reins.

With a few tugs of my fist, his dick pulsed heavily over my tongue and his balls tightened in my hand. My eyes watered, his thick cock pressing deeper still.

A hand closed over the back of my head as he groaned and my concentration faltered. His fingers tangled in my hair, and my mind screamed. He was doing it again! Stealing my control!

I jerked my head back, glaring down at him. "Your hands are supposed to be up there."

"What? Sorry. Don't stop."

Breathing heavily, my jaw locked. He returned one arm behind his head and held his cock with his free hand, stroking to keep himself rolling toward the climax that *I* was giving him.

I smacked his arm, shoving his hand off his dick. "Do you want to do it yourself?"

He frowned. "No, I want you to keep doing what you were doing. It felt amazing."

"I know it did. I was doing fine without your help. Why did you have to touch me?"

He scoffed. "Because I like touching you. Don't ruin this."

I wasn't ruining it.

"I bet you'd just love to hold a fistful of my hair and fuck my mouth. Maybe pin me against a wall, so I have nowhere to go but down on you."

"Now, we're talking."

"Well, that's not how I do it! If you want that, go find a different girl. If you want me, get your hand out of the way and let me finish what I started."

"Why do you have so many rules?"

I drew in a slow breath. "You know what, you ruined it. Make yourself come. I'm out."

"*What?*" His shoulders shot off the couch.

I folded my arms in front of my chest and raised a brow. "Make yourself come."

"Are you fucking serious? Avery—"

"Haven't you ever jerked off in front of anyone?" This could actually be more fun than the blowjob.

He scowled. "If I wanted to jerk off I'd be home doing it right now. I want your mouth back on my dick."

"Well, you should have followed directions better. I want to see you come and I want you to say my name when you do. I wonder which one of us is going to get what we want?"

His eyes narrowed in challenge. I unlatched my bra and tossed it onto the floor, waiting him out. I had all night.

"I'll need my hands."

That little hint of seeking approval tightened my nipples, and I sighed. "You have my permission to touch yourself."

His gaze held mine as his hand gripped his cock, stroking as if every slow glide of his fist was somehow meant to reach my skin. "This is what does it for you?"

"No talking."

"Only when I say your name as I come."

"Exactly."

His mouth twitched as if he was hiding a smile. He groaned and stroked harder. "Oh, Avery…"

He was such a smart ass. Whatever. I was getting my way.

"*Avery…*"

I rolled my eyes. "Are you enjoying yourself?"

"A—ver—y…"

"You're ruining it."

His hand tightened and jerked faster. "Avery's mouth…" His chest flexed, his hips digging into the sofa. "Avery's pretty tits…" He cupped his sack. "Avery's tight little ass … squeezing my dick."

The sound of his hand stroking along smooth, hard flesh matched his fast breathing.

"Avery's pink little cunt…"

His eyelids lowered, the blue irises rolling back under the fringe of gold lashes. "Avery's tight cunt wrapped around my cock … milking every last drop…"

I shifted my weight as I kneeled between his legs, pressure forming in my lower abdomen.

"Avery's long, blonde hair teasing my skin, fisted in my hand..."

My eyes narrowed. He knew I didn't like that.

"Avery's back arched as I pound into her sopping pussy and she screams my name..."

"You wish."

His eyes opened, thin slits of promise watching my response too acutely. I held my breath, willing my skin to cool.

"Avery's body trembling as I make her come again, and again, and again."

"Maybe one of these days *you'll* come."

His grip slid faster, his free hand shooting out and snatching my fingers, curling them around his. He double fisted his cock, jerking rapidly, my fingers now tangled in the mix.

I flexed my fingers, trying not to appreciate his engorged size and intensity. "This wasn't the deal."

"Avery's pleas and moans as she *begs* me to..." His lips parted. "Never..." His head angled back. "Stop..." His spine bowed as he grunted, all of his muscles rippling under his flawless skin. Liquid heat spurted from his throbbing cock, coating our entwined fingers. "...fucking her!"

My mouth hung open as I stared down at his slack face, his sated blue eyes, and his heaving chest. My gaze shifted to his erection, still pulsing in our hands as pearly come dribbled to the base of his balls.

He sucked his lower lip between his teeth and grinned. "Is that what you had in mind?"

Turned on against my will, I swallowed and cleared my throat. "Something like that."

His thumb rubbed slowly over the back of my knuckle, the gesture incredibly intimate and full of implication. His stare held mine, our fingers sticky with his come. I pulled my hand, but he tightened his grip, holding me to him.

"Noah..."

"When do I get to see *you* masturbate?"

"Never."

"So, sometime next week when the little red devil's gone?"

Or every night while I had my own private Noah show in the shadows of my bedroom. "I don't think so. Give me my hand back."

"First, tell me something."

I pursed my lips, never quite sure what was going to come out of his mouth. "What?"

"This thing you do ... when you want to be in charge, is that like a kink thing or a permanent thing?"

"It's a me thing. It's what I like."

His head tipped as his eyes continued to study me. "Have you ever just had normal sex with someone?"

"Yes, but even then I prefer my vanilla with a little topping."

"My God, your porn collection must be fascinating."

"I think if you saw it, you'd get scared."

"I think you underestimate my curiosity and infatuation with your pussy—and all the things I can do to make it wet."

I glance down at his softening cock. "My hand."

He let go. I slid off his lap and washed my hands. He lounged on the couch, stretching out in all his naked glory.

"Don't get come on my pillows."

"You're a little bit of a tight ass."

"I thought you liked my tight ass."

"I do. But, as far as your control freak issues go, every time you tell me not to do something it makes me want to do it even more, totally disrupt your perfect order and watch you get all flustered and bitchy."

I shut off the faucet. "You get come on my cushions, and you're paying to have them reupholstered. Is that bitchy enough for you?"

"Don't be ridiculous. A little steam cleaning would get it out. You're so extreme sometimes."

I snatched a dishtowel off the counter and tossed it at his chest. Grabbing my shirt off the floor, I slid it back on while he wiped himself clean. Still sprawled on his back, his gaze never left me, the soiled dishtowel now on the floor.

"You can put your clothes back on."

"Nope. If I put them on, you'll make me leave, and who knows how long it'll take for me to convince you to let me in again."

"You think I won't throw your ass out in the hall naked? And I didn't *let* you in. You shoved your way in and wouldn't leave." He was more intrusive than a termite.

"You regret it?"

I paused, not wanting to answer that question right now, even in my own head. "I have to put my groceries away. And someone probably stole yours by now—it *was* the last loaf of bread in Philadelphia after all."

"Nobody's stealing my stuff."

"That's right. You're the only thief in the building. I forgot."

My magazines now went right to the front desk, out of reach of men with sticky fingers. Speaking of which... "You should really wash your hands. Touch your face, and you might wind up with pink eye."

"That's not how you get pink eye."

I went to collect my bags by the door. "Yes, it is."

"No, it's not. It's from shit."

This had to be the most unsexy, post-orgasmic conversation in the history of human existence. "It's from bacterial secretions. What do you think come is? And can we talk about something else?"

"You're the one who brought it up."

I emptied my bags on the counter, frowning, as he just laid there —naked—on my couch. "Are you really not going to get dressed?"

"Depends."

"On?"

"Are you going to make me leave if I do?"

I turned my back to him, stacking soup cans in the cupboard. A little smile pulled at my lips. I honestly didn't want him to leave. I'd missed him, and this was the first time I actually felt settled in the last week.

"I guess you can stay for a little bit."

When I turned back around, he was sliding into his jeans. "What do you want me to do with this towel?"

"There's a hamper in the bathroom." He headed down the hall, and I shouted, "Wash your hands while you're in there!"

I heard the water running and smiled. He returned a few minutes later. "Hey, did you know your faucet's leaking?"

"I know. I told Winston, and he said he'd get a plumber out sometime next week."

"A plumber? I can fix it in a few minutes. It's a simple washer replacement."

"I don't know what a washer is."

"It's a… You know what? I'll just go grab one. The hardware store on Pine doesn't close until eight."

I frowned, not expecting him to actually leave the building in order to fix my sink. "You don't have to do that. The plumber will be here on…" He was already putting on his coat.

"It'll take ten minutes." He kissed my cheek, and I stiffened. "I'll be right back."

What was happening here? "O—okay."

The door closed behind him, and I stared at my empty apartment. Were we playing house or something? Was I supposed to feed him now? This was definitely not the way I did things.

23

AVERY

As Noah messed around in my bathroom, I scrambled to put together a nice meal. I didn't do meals. I was used to only feeding myself or dining at fancy restaurants while my clients picked up the bill. Extremely unprepared for a two-person dinner party, I felt every bit of my inadequate upbringing.

"How's it going in there?" I called as I dumped a box of whole grain macaroni into a pot of boiling water and searched the cabinets.

"Good. Almost finished."

He'd returned from the hardware store, tracking a decent amount of melted snow through the door with him, and carrying a little bag with the washer thing he needed. The ground outside already wore a dusting of white, and my wood floors now wore damp towels to mop up the puddles from the ice chips melting off his boots.

I opened a can of tuna and let the liquid drain into the sink. I didn't cook. I grazed on things like veggies and Greek yogurt and granola, filling up only when a client handled the bill. My culinary skills weren't honed beyond my mother's four regular dishes, and those recipes weren't what anyone would call tasty.

Forking through the tuna, I fluffed it in a bowl and squirted some mayo on top. Salt, pepper, and some chopped green olives and there you had it. Mom's signature dish for funerals around the trailer park.

Fuck. He was going to hate this.

Noah appeared as the noodles were about ready to strain. "You're sink's all fixed up."

"Thank you. You didn't have to do that."

"No problem. What are you making?"

"Um ... pasta." That sounded better than tuna noodle surprise or whatever the hell this was called.

"Need help?"

"No, you did enough. Just relax, and dinner will be done in a few minutes." No idea where this Suzie Homemaker talk was spouting from. My mother certainly never used words like that.

I carried the pasta to the sink and drained the water. While it rested in the colander, I searched for a serving bowl. I didn't own one.

In my bedroom, there was a ceramic dish I used to hold my scarves, and I briefly debated using that but feared it might look stupid. Resigned to nothing but a saucepan, I brought down two plates.

I dressed the table with folded paper napkins—diagonally because that seemed nicer—and silverware I bought at the dollar store. Shit. I had nothing but water or coffee to drink.

Noah was quiet as he waited in the living room, his head tilted down as he paged through something. I rounded the sofa. "Do you have anything to drink at your—"

The blood drained from my face.

I snatched the photo album out of his hands. "Where did you get this?"

"Hey, I was looking at that!"

I clutched the photo album to my chest. "This... This isn't for sharing."

"You still look like you did in high school. Do you still have that cheerleader uniform?"

My face burned. "No."

"What's wrong?"

Maybe he only got as far as the high school pictures. My mind rapidly tried to recall if there were any incriminating photos—Shit! Prom! We'd taken pictures in front of my mom's tacky Precious Moments collection, the battered wood paneling and green carpet probably showing behind me and Bobby Pritcher.

"Please don't go through my stuff."

He frowned. "Okay. Sorry."

"Do you have anything to drink at your place? I just have water." And now I was in need of something much stronger.

"Yeah." He stood, and the second he left my apartment I flipped open the album and winced.

Me with pimples and horribly frizzy, mousey brown hair. Me with my belly hanging out of a shirt two sizes too small when I was going through my chubby stage. Me holding up a bedazzled denim jacket that had *never* been in style, even when I traded all my bracelets for it. Our shithole home, my dirty room, the parched, dusty lawn in front of our trailer. I slammed the book shut and stuffed it under the couch.

Maybe he didn't see past the first few pages. Maybe he just opened to the picture of me and the cheer squad and that was as far as he got.

The door opened, and I returned to the kitchen. Noah placed a bottle of honey bourbon with four lemons and a jar of honey on the counter. "Where's your shaker?"

Who did he think I was, James Bond? "I don't own one."

"I forgot you're the girl who doesn't have a corkscrew."

That wasn't true. I bought one a few weeks ago after I couldn't get my wine open.

"How about two plastic cups? I can improvise."

He was turning into a real MacGyver. I handed him two plastic cups and watched as he expertly squeezed the lemons, added some water, a scoop of honey, ice, and the bourbon. Then he sealed the cups together and shook.

"Where did you learn to do that?"

"I bartended in college one semester."

Was there anything he hadn't done? And done well? "Oh." I handed him two glasses, and he poured.

"Taste."

It smelled delicious. I took a small sip. "Wow. What's this called?"

"Honey bourbon lemonade. You like it?"

"It's delicious."

"Good. Is dinner ready?"

His cocktail was amazing, and I was about to ruin it with my crappy two-dollar dinner. "Yeah. I'll bring the plates into the dining room."

We sat next to each other, and I fidgeted with my fork, waiting for him to take the first bite. "If you don't like it we could order pizza or something."

"It smells good." He took a big bite and chewed. "Interesting."

My shoulders sagged. "You don't have to eat it. I wasn't expecting company."

"No, I like it. It's different."

I was pretty sure he was lying, but I let it go, nibbling a bite of my own.

"So how come I never knew you were a cheerleader?"

"There are a lot of things you don't know about me."

"Such as?"

He didn't have the code to my vault yet. Chances were he never would. "I don't know."

"Were you involved in any other sports?"

"Not really."

I only cheered for one year. After that my mom couldn't afford to drive me to the meets or get me a new uniform.

As if sensing how much I hated talking about my past, he changed the subject. "They're saying we might get a foot of snow by midnight."

"I thought we were only supposed to get five inches."

"I overheard the guys at the hardware store talking. They updated the forecast. Now they're predicting as much as two feet."

"Ew. Seriously?"

He laughed. "Don't you like snow?"

"What's to like about it?"

He shrugged. "You're a student. You might get a snow day."

I also might lose some appointments next week if the roads were bad. "I'd rather be in school."

"I've never met someone who didn't like a blizzard. They're the best kind of snowstorms because everything shuts down. You have no choice but to be lazy and enjoy it."

"Snow sucks. It's messy and dirty and turns people into idiots. Everyone's running around like it's Black Friday and there's a mad rush on shovels."

"I think you missed a major defining moment growing up."

"Probably."

He went to the kitchen and returned with another helping of noodles. Maybe he actually did like it.

"You know what we're going to do tonight?"

"What?" Apparently, we weren't just having dinner.

"We're gonna build a snowman."

"Um, no."

"Yup. As soon as the ground's covered enough, we're going to bundle up and play in the snow."

"I hate the snow."

"That's because you're playing in it wrong. Trust me. You'll have fun."

I didn't play in snow. It ruined my shoes. And I certainly didn't trust him. All I could picture were wet socks and cold cheeks and freezing fingers.

"Can't wait."

24

AVERY

After finishing the dishes, we watched a comedian do standup on Netflix. I was getting tired, but every time I shut my eyes, Noah nudged me, reminding me not to fall asleep because we had a date at midnight.

Outside, the sky wore a gossamer mask of powder, and the glass on the windows was starting to crystallize with frost. It was a white nightmare, and he was going to make me go out there and do things in the cold.

The show ended, and he shut off the TV. As he stood and stretched, a delicious slice of his smooth belly showed.

"Okay, time to get bundled."

I groaned, totally content snuggled under a blanket on my couch. "Are you really going to make me go out there?"

"Yes. Go put on warm clothes. I'll meet you back here in five minutes."

"I don't wanna."

He was already walking out the door.

A few minutes later he was back, wearing flannel pajama pants and a thick hoodie. I also wore a hoodie but paired mine with a frown.

"Give me your feet," he said, coming over to the couch.

"Why?"

"Just do it."

I rolled my eyes and lifted up my foot. He covered my wool sock with a plastic bag.

"Now, the other one."

"I do believe serial killers are supposed to dice up their victims before they start the bagging process."

He covered my other foot. "That'll keep your socks dry."

I raised a brow. "Impressive."

He reached into his pocket and pulled out a handful of teabags. "Put these in your mittens."

"Are we having a tea party?"

"They're hand warmers." He shook them as if activating something.

The second he placed them in my palm heat warmed my hand. Okay, this wasn't starting out so bad.

"Come here." He held up a jar of Vaseline, and I drew back.

"What are you doing with that?"

"It's for your cheeks. It'll keep them from getting chapped."

I grimaced as he slathered a thin layer over my face. Next, he gave me lip balm and wrapped my neck in a long scarf.

"Where did you get this?"

"My nana made it."

Aww, he has a nana. I don't know what was cuter, his grandmother knitting him a scarf or the fact that he called her Nana without blushing.

"Where are your boots?"

I frowned at my bagged feet. "I don't have any without heels."

"What about those wooly things girls are always wearing?"

"UGGs? They aren't meant to get wet."

He shook his head. "I'll never understand women's clothing. We better double bag your feet."

Once my sneakers were on, and my coat was buttoned. I felt like the little brother who couldn't put his arms down in *A Christmas*

Story. As much as I was dreading the cold, I was starting to sweat under all these layers and wanted to get someplace cooler.

Noah faced me and shoved my wool hat on my head. "You're adorable."

"You're not so bad yourself."

Actually, he looked hot as fuck in his hoodie and PJs with his duffel coat overtop. He pulled on a black beanie hat and enhanced the look to SWAT team sexy. He was SW*awt!*

"Let's go."

"Wait, I gotta lock up."

"We're going right out front. It's fine."

I glanced back at my apartment, scanning all my valuable possessions I worked my ass off to own. What if someone broke in when we weren't looking? What if they stole my laptop—?

A sharp whistle echoed down the hall. *"Avery, let's go!"*

I twisted and shut my door, swishing like a fat penguin waddling down the hall as he held the elevator open. Our clothes rustled as we walked through the lobby and I felt like an idiot as we passed the doorman.

"Evening, Winston."

"Evening, Mr. Wolfe." He jumped up to grab the door. "Evening, Ms. Johansson."

I sighed at the doorman, silently informing him that I was being abducted on a midnight, snowy play date against my will. "If we're not back inside in twenty minutes, send out a search party." The door opened, and icy snowflakes pelted me in the face. "Oh, yuck."

The walks were covered with a good six inches of snow. It caked on the front of buildings and street signs and covered the mailbox and the road. A small path was cleared in front of the door, but that was it.

Fat, white flakes mixed with a misting of frozen rain. The damn shit was everywhere, sticking in my hair, flicking me in the eye. Who liked this? And it was eerily quiet for the city.

"This way." Noah walked to the corner of Delancey, and I waddled after him, our footprints the only proof of human life anywhere. "We'll start over here and roll it toward the door."

I wasn't rolling shit. I stood off to the side while he formed a boulder of snow. With my arms crossed over my chest, I bounced to stay warm, He packed the snow into a tight ball and rolled it down the walk, each turn increasing the size.

"Are you going to help?"

"Nope."

I squinted up at the light from my apartment, snowflakes catching in my lashes, noticeably dancing in the glow of the streetlamps. A snowball pelted my shoulder, exploding on impact, getting my cheek wet.

"Hey!"

"Help me. This is a team effort."

Grumbling, I marched over to where he'd rolled the ball, which I supposed formed the body of our snowman. He fumbled with his phone.

"What are you doing?"

"Just wait."

He pressed a few buttons and looked up. I followed his gaze but didn't see anything. Suddenly a flute trilled, and Bing Crosby started to sing *White Christmas.*

"A little ambiance..." He pocketed his phone and put his glove back on.

He'd thought of everything, even had the foresight to set a stereo in his window. His apartment was going to be freezing. I couldn't help it. I smiled.

"I see that smirk." He took my hand, tugging me into the empty road.

Just as the backup chorus began to sing, he spun me to his chest and wrapped his arms around me. "What are you doing?"

"Dancing with you."

"Um..."

"Humor me, Avery."

I went with it, my pants swishing with every step as he turned me in a slow circle. We were literally dancing, in the center of Delancey Street, under the glow of antique streetlamps, as snow fell around us.

"Relax, Avery. Embrace the moment."

I let him lead, mostly because I didn't know how to dance like people were supposed to in real life. I only knew how to do the freshman mixer hold, where I wreathed my arms around a guy's neck and swayed from side to side. Noah knew how to *dance.* It was unexpected and romantic. When the song ended, I was a little sad it didn't last longer.

But Noah didn't let go. He held me and continued to turn as our feet made tracks in the snow and Nat King Cole took over singing *The Christmas Song.*

A lump formed in my throat. I loved Christmas carols. They were like fables of perfect lives, where families didn't fight during the holidays, and the turkey was never dry, and people decorated with real greenery instead of cheap metallic garland and flea market, felt placemats.

His arms tightened around me, and I rested my head on his chest, blinking as the music echoed from his apartment window down to the vacant street. I didn't know how to process this magical moment, but I wanted to keep it forever.

I bet Noah had a lifetime of beautiful holidays at his picturesque family home. I found myself trying very hard to imagine what childhood might have been like for him. How different it probably was from the holidays I had as a kid.

My chest tightened as Judy Garland's *Have Yourself a Merry Little Christmas* played next. This was my *favorite* carol of all. The hope of a better year ahead and troubles being left behind, miles away. The thought of real friends and togetherness. My eyes closed as she belted out the need to *muddle through,* and my lashes were suddenly wet with something other than snow.

Enough. That was enough.

I pulled away and turned so I could wipe my eyes without him seeing how ridiculous I was. "So..." Stupid mittens getting in my way. "How do we do this snowman thing?"

Once I had my face under control, I turned, and he kissed me deeply, wrapping me in a tight grip I never wanted to loosen. I gave in, because, in that moment, it was exactly what I needed.

The music suddenly switched to Mariah Carey's *All I want for Christmas is You.* I was such a sucker because those bells made my mouth smile against his and my indifferent, tough girl façade took a major hit.

"You like this song?" He smiled into my eyes, his teeth flashing behind a puff of breath as he smiled.

"I love all carols."

Our breath formed a cloud of vapor between us, and I realized this was one of those unforgettable moments that make the word *nostalgia* so beautiful. I wanted to dip it in gold and seal it in time. I wanted to tell him I loved him.

The proverbial record skidded to a stop in my head.

I didn't love Noah. Did I? No. Of course not. And my feelings didn't matter anyway. I couldn't love anyone. *Especially* Noah, because I hated him six hours ago and I was clearly suffering some sort of honey bourbon, yuletide, snow-induced acid trip brought on by too much stress.

But, for a second, I pretended I could love him, and he could maybe love me. I imagined being in an actual relationship with him and dancing in the snow like this every year. My brain was casting its own romantic comedy, the sort where Hugh Grant narrated, and *I* was the girl the great guy wanted most of all.

I was definitely tripping, but wow. It was an incredible fantasy.

"You're smiling."

Of course, I was. I mean, who had nights like this with men like him? This was insane and perfect and… "You're amazing."

His grin stretched across his handsome face. "Why, Ms. Johansson, I do believe that's the first compliment you've ever paid me. My, my, I'm all atwitter."

"That's not true. I said I liked your cocktail earlier."

He cupped a gloved hand around his ear. "I'm sorry, did you say you liked my cock earlier?"

"Way to ruin it."

But he hadn't ruined anything. He was so outrageously adorable I couldn't take it.

"You know, you're prettiest when you laugh. It's a great sound."

Something trembled in my chest and, before I realized I was moving, I threw my arms around his shoulders and kissed him, lifting my feet off the ground and making him hold me whether he wanted to or not.

He laughed and stumbled back. "Oh, shit!"

And we fell. So not *quite* like the movies.

Luckily, we were wearing enough layers that we didn't get hurt on impact. We rolled to our backs and groaned, staring up at the swirling wind, coated in what appeared the sweetest sugar God had ever made. Under the quiet moonlight, it was ... majestic.

My mitten covered hand closed around his, and I smiled, my legs stretching. I tipped my face into the cool flurries and hummed happily.

"Let's make snow angels."

Swiping our arms and legs from side to side, we lay in the middle of the street, laughing, making angels in the snow. Maybe I liked snow after all. It had to be a dream because it was too perfect to be real.

25

AVERY

I stomped my feet, waiting for them to warm as chips of ice and drips of slush melted onto the hardwood. Noah pulled down pots and mugs as he measured out powdered cocoa and milk. Seriously, what other guy had the ingredients for hot chocolate on hand?

I peeled off my hat, my hair a mix of chilled waves and sweaty kinks. It was nearly two in the morning, and I was too wound up to go to bed. Luckily, Noah wasn't tired either.

I feared if I shut my eyes this feeling might end and I'd never be able to find it again. So, I decided sleep wasn't really that necessary.

I glanced at his expensive barstools. "I'm going to go change my pants. These are all wet."

He shot a smile over his shoulder. "Just take them off."

I paused, considering it. "Okay."

He did a double take, and I laughed, stripping until I was in nothing but my T-shirt, thong, and thick wool socks. Noah rounded the island so fast he slipped on a puddle of slush, catching himself before he hit the ground. I gasped, but he seemed fine, and then he was staring at my lower body. No, not staring. Gawking.

"Fuck. You're so fucking... Fuck."

I laughed. "You wanna take off yours?"

He yanked down his plaid pants and stomped them into the floor. His briefs were looking a little snug with all that pressure building between his hips. I took a mental picture, never wanting to forget the sight of his exposed thighs and knobby boy knees, pants bunched around unlaced boots and that look of enchantment in his eyes. He was adorable.

"Your milk's boiling over."

He frowned, then cursed and grabbed the pan off the burner as it hissed and steamed. I laughed as he carefully transferred the hot milk into mugs and stirred in the cocoa, topping it off with mini marshmallows.

"Cheers."

We clanked our mugs and—oh, my *gawd!*—it was the best damn hot chocolate I'd ever tasted. "This is exceptional."

"Thanks. So many compliments tonight. I can't wait to write them all down in my diary."

"You can be such a guy and such a girl at the same time."

"Guys can be sensitive."

"I think it's more of a deep-rooted sarcasm. I don't buy for one minute that you keep a journal or even have a book in this apartment."

"I have an old Playboy from the sixties that my dad gave me. Does that count?"

"No."

I had a slight dairy allergy, but the hot chocolate was so damn good I pretended my allergies weren't real for a minute. Halfway through my cup, I forced myself to put it down, but it wasn't easy.

We sat on the kitchen stools, the carols still playing from his den, the world's greatest snowman guarding the door with Winston downstairs.

I grinned and stole another sip of cocoa. "This is probably the best Christmas I've ever had."

"It's January."

"Shh. Don't spoil it."

When everyone else disappeared a few weeks ago, I sat in my apartment eating a vat of gingerbread cookie dough with a spoon and crying over *Home Alone*. It wasn't even one of the sad Christmas movies, but I always cried on Christmas. And somehow I knew crying alone on one of the happiest days of the year was better than going home.

Enough thinking about things that made me feel bad. I pushed my mug aside and scooted up on the counter. Noah watched closely as I placed my feet on either side of his stool, my legs dangling off the edge of the granite countertop.

"What are you doing?" He eyed me carefully and placed his mug next to mine.

"I want you."

His gaze lifted to my face and dropped back to the satin crotch of my panties. "I thought you couldn't."

My cheeks flushed. "I need a wax."

"*That's all?* I thought you had—"

"I know. I will in a few days."

He scoffed. "You lied to me?"

"Technically, I didn't. You just assumed."

He frowned. "You think you should have the final say on everything, don't you?"

"Do you really want to waste time being mad about a misunderstanding, or do you want to take the opportunity in front of you?" I slowly parted my thighs.

His fingers trailed up my knee and his mouth curved as he slid a finger under the seam of my panties. His stare lifted to my face, and a meaningful smirk curved the corner of his mouth.

"May I?"

Oh, my God, he was actually asking. And now I was soaked. "You may."

He slipped his fingers between my thighs, and I moaned, stretching back on the counter, opening for him. He intently fingered me, shifting onto his feet to get a better angle. My weight balanced on my elbows and my head angled back.

His thumb nudged my clit and my breath hitched. His other hand gripped my hip as his mouth worked up my thigh.

Warm breath teased my folds as my panties were nudged aside. "I wanna eat your pussy."

"How do you ask?"

"I don't."

"Noah."

"Let me eat your pussy." He drilled a finger deep and teased my G-spot until I moaned.

"That's not asking." I gasped as he continued to make me arch.

"How about this... Do you want me to make you come, Avery?"

Fair enough. It was a question if not a request. "Yes—make me come."

His hot lips closed over my clit, and I sighed, my eyes shutting in absolute bliss. His free hand slipped under my shirt and pulled down the cups of my bra, his fingers pulling hard at the tip of my nipple.

He wrenched me closer, his mouth making a meal out of me, and my breathing accelerated. He released my nipple, and his hand closed over mine.

Pulling my arm lower, he pressed my fingers between my thighs. My eyes flashed open at the touch of his tongue. He smiled, licking along the length of my middle finger, trying to penetrate my slit with his tongue.

"Your turn, Avery. Make yourself come, and I want to hear *my* name when you do."

Did he think I wouldn't do it? "Put your fingers back inside of me."

His teeth flashed as he shoved two fingers deep and started pumping. My hand rubbed over my clit as my eyes shut again. Pleasure knotted and tightened beneath our touch, his driving strokes pushing me faster than I could ever get there alone.

I didn't have to think about whose name I said. It was always his name. Every night I touched myself, it was his face I pictured. Peeking through my lashes, I watched him watch me, his breath coming fast as his fingers slid in and out of my body.

"Noah..." It was starting. "Noah..." Almost there. "*No*—" My back arched as every muscle pulled tight and my pussy pulsed around his penetrating fingers. "*—ahhhhhh...*"

My arm dropped to the countertop as I panted and then gasped. His mouth took the place of my touch, devouring my folds, licking, and tasting. His hands gripped my hips as he scraped his teeth over my tender flesh, stabbing his tongue deep. My legs draped over his shoulders as he lifted me higher, pulling me off the countertop and against his devastating mouth.

The next orgasm came out of nowhere, crashing through me like a tidal wave and I screamed his name. I barely had a chance to process what happened as he lifted me in his arms and rushed me through his apartment.

Soft pillows surrounded me as I bounced down onto his mattress. My panties were gone. Next went my shirt, and then my bra. I was cold, then burning hot as his body blanketed mine, flesh to flesh. He reached between us and I watched him fit a condom over his straining cock.

He lifted a brow. "Open."

My eyes narrowed. "Ask."

"Avery, if I don't get inside of you I'm going to go insane. Open your fucking legs."

I twitched at his command, but my legs parted of their own volition. His hips wedged between my thighs as if they belonged there. He thrust in, and my back bowed, my fingers twisting in the covers.

His hips snapped forward, hard and fast, his hands groping my tits as his mouth kissed and licked my neck, biting at the sharp angle of my upturned jaw. I reached for his back, and he caught my hand, pressing it into the mattress.

"Noah—"

His mouth slammed over mine, and I moaned. He caught my other hand and pinned it in the pillows.

"Look at me, Avery."

My attention jerked from his clamped hand holding mine, to his face, a frisson of discomfort spiking through me.

"I'm not hurting you. I'm taking you. Give yourself to me."

My heart tripped out of rhythm as he leaned over me, filling me with his pumping cock, my hands totally useless as he held them over my head.

"Let go of my hands."

"I don't want to. I like pinning you down, same as you like having control."

My pussy tightened, and I didn't know why. This wasn't right. He wasn't supposed to restrain me.

"Noah, I'm not kidding. Let go."

His hips slowed. "What if I promised—"

"I don't want your promise. I want you to let go." My hands were suddenly free.

He withdrew and rolled onto his back. "There."

I frowned at him. "What are you doing?"

"You want control? Take it."

My eyes narrowed. Was this some sort of trick? I watched him, once again not trusting his motives.

But we couldn't stop now. I wanted to fuck him. My way.

Straddling his hips, I rose above his body and fit him against my slit. "Don't grab my hands again."

"One day, you'll beg me to hold you like that."

My jaw locked, and I sank onto him. "Not today." *Never.*

My clit rubbed along his pelvis bone as I rode fast and hard.

His head tipped back in the pillows, his eyes shut, mouth tight. I frowned when I noticed his arms braced above his head as if tied there. Did he think his submission would upset me? Yeah, right.

So why was this less exciting than it had been a minute ago? "Look at me."

His eyes flashed open, his expression blank as pools of blue watched me rock over him. His body stretched beneath mine, his ribs pressing against his skin as he breathed fast, but made no show of enjoyment otherwise. He wore a mask of indifference, and I hated it.

"Stop looking at me like that."

He shut his eyes.

Damn it. What was he doing? Why wasn't this getting me off? I climbed off of him and stood, circling in place, unsure how to make this better.

"Get up."

He stood, and my mind blanked. I needed him to do as I asked and do more than just lie there.

"Fuck me against the wall." I faced the wall and braced my hands against the surface, angling my ass out and bending my body at a sharp angle.

His thighs brushed mine, but he didn't touch me with his hands. His cock nudged my entrance, and then he was in, fucking at such a sedate pace it was a wonder he stayed hard.

"What the hell are you doing?"

"You tell me! You're the one calling the shots."

"Fuck me like you mean it!"

His hands clapped onto my hips, and he plunged deep. My head yanked back as he fisted my hair, my throat stretched at a vulnerable angle as his breath was suddenly at my ear. "Like this, *Mistress*?"

I sucked in a breath as my arousal slid down the length of his cock, his palm flattening on my belly and holding me to him. He sank deeper.

He was mocking me, giving me what I wanted but making sure it was on his terms. I grunted and tried to shift my hips away, but his hand groped my breast, squeezing hard and forcing me to stay put.

"My turn, Avery. Stay still."

I sucked in a breath as he thrust hard and fast, giving me no time to adjust or think. My head fell forward as he released my hair, but then his hand closed around the front of my throat, drawing me back to his chest and pressing my front into the wall.

"Tell me to fuck off, and I'll stop." He shoved his dick as deep as it could fit and I gasped. "Say *no,* and I'll listen. Tell me to *get off,* and your wish is my command. Or just enjoy it for once."

He bit my shoulder, and I whimpered, my fingers holding his as they wrapped around my neck. I could breathe fine. He wasn't cutting off my air, but he was holding me in such a vulnerable position.

I couldn't slow my heart from racing out of control. His other hand pressed against my lower abdomen, his splayed fingers seeking my clit.

"Spread your fucking legs."

My feet stepped wide, balancing precariously on my toes, and I started at my compliance. It was as if I moved out of panic, but I wasn't scared. Not really. Not of anything he could do to me physically. But I was terrified of the things he was doing to me on the inside.

He rubbed my pussy, his dick pistoning in rapid strokes and I was suddenly screaming as my body clamped around his, pulsing until my legs gave out. His arm banded around my midsection, lifting me to my toes as he pinned me to the wall and continued to fuck me harder than I'd ever been fucked.

My body was thrumming with pleasure, replete, and satisfied, but he wasn't done, and it became perfectly clear that he wasn't going to stop until he was good and satisfied.

He suddenly withdrew, and I whimpered. I groaned as he hauled me from the wall and tossed me on the bed. He gripped his cock, guiding it back inside of me, his hands holding my legs wide.

Outside, he'd been an angel in the snow, but here he was the devil in the dark. How could one man possess so many different sides?

Why was I letting him do this to me, fuck me like I belonged to him, like he owned me? I should be fighting him.

I lifted a hand to scratch his chest, and he caught my wrist before I even made contact, squeezing in warning, and pinning it to the bed. My legs bent back as he leaned forward, folding me against the mattress as his rapid thrusts slowed. The room quieted, as we held each other's stare and panted.

"Do you want me to stop, Avery?"

Maybe it was because I didn't want him to think I was weak. Or maybe it was because I wanted to be nothing in that moment but the source of his pleasure. I didn't know why, but not knowing made me want to scream.

Swallowing tightly, I glared into his eyes, accepting his challenge, and rasped, "If you can't go on..."

He slammed his hips forward, the blunt intrusion shutting me up and exemplifying his strength over me. Maybe it was because I wanted to see how far he'd go. How much it would take for him to actually break me, but the pain only added to my pleasure.

He fucked me for days, years, and centuries. Time didn't exist where we were, because the way he fucked me, it ensured the only thing that existed in my thoughts was him. And the longer he controlled the moment, the lighter my burdens weighed, shrinking into nothingness. Just Noah. Only Noah. Noah.

He was my god and master, my lord and savior. My only one, my everything. I didn't know how he did it or if it was even real, but nothing inside of me had the nerve or the will to tell him to stop. And in a twisted way, I envied him because he so easily consumed all the power I wished belonged to me.

When he pulled out, he ripped the condom off and crawled over my fatigued body. His hand cupped the back of my neck, lifting my head off the pillows.

"Open your mouth."

My mouth parted like a puppet, as if he held every string. He pressed his cock deep into my mouth, and my eyes watered. His grip on my neck tightened, and he smiled.

"Look at those full lips wrapped around my cock. No getting out of it this time. I wish you could see how beautiful you are right now."

My shoulders tensed as he pressed deeper. He slowly wiped a tear from the corner of my eye, pulling back ever so slightly and angling in again. The crown of his cock pressed against the back of my throat and I moaned, the sound garbled and semi-panicked.

He withdrew. "Should I stop?"

I caught my breath, staring up at him, confused and curious, scared and excited. Fuck him. I could take whatever he could dish out. I opened.

"Good girl." He fed his cock over my tongue, his legs shifting as he moved closer, thrusting his hips downward, into the bed, into my face.

His knees shifted, and my arms were suddenly trapped between his thighs at my sides. I shouted around his cock, and it was gone.

"*Look at me, Avery.*" His voice snapped through my hysteria, and I blinked up at him. "Say the word, and I stop."

I couldn't catch my breath. Time seemed to be moving twice as fast, and I was slipping into the dark and dangerous place I hated. Hated, but wanted to overcome. I wasn't weak. My mouth opened again.

"There's my good girl." But he didn't shove his cock down my throat this time.

He teased my spread lips, painting them with his arousal as he straddled my arms and shoulders. I just laid there, mouth open, panting for him.

"Keep your mouth open wide for me, beautiful."

I blinked, so outside of myself, all sense of shame disappeared. My jaw loosened, and he rose above me, stroking his cock, his eyes staring into mine.

"I've dreamed of coming in your pretty mouth... And you've teased me enough that I earned the pleasure." He tugged his flesh hard and grunted as hot come splashed across my lips and tongue. "*Averyyyyyy...*" he hissed, jerking every last drop over my lips and tongue.

My chin trembled as he looked down at me. My lips closed and tasted him. His finger trailed softly down the side of my face as he watched me swallow his release.

"So beautiful." His weight lifted off of me, and I remembered what it was to take a full breath.

He pulled me to him, his body stretched beside mine, his mouth kissing my swollen lips, definitely tasting his own come.

"You were very brave, Avery." He cradled me to his chest, his hands petting over my hair and shoulders, rubbing soothing strokes down the length of my arms. "Very, very brave."

I didn't have words or thoughts. All I had was Noah. Noah wanted to hold me, and I wanted to let him because Avery had gone somewhere else and I couldn't find her right now.

His lips pressed against my temple, his breathing deep and steady. My dazed mind followed the rhythm like a metronome, counting off time in little Noah beats.

His kiss moved to the side of my face, his hands gently cupping my breasts as his body curled tighter around mine. I'd never been held so firmly in all my life. I wasn't sure I could breathe like this, but he seemed to be breathing for the both of us.

"Avery?"

My thoughts scattered like frightened little woodland creatures at the sound of an approaching predator. "Hmm?"

"Don't run from me when I let you go."

My eyes flashed open, forced wide by a new emotion I didn't recognize. Terror? Euphoria? Panic? Anxiety? Love? I didn't know what it was. I was too exhausted to think. "Okay."

His mouth curved against my cheek. "Good girl."

"But Noah..."

"Hmm?"

"I'm going to hate you tomorrow."

"All right. But just for one day."

26

AVERY

I tiptoed back to my apartment before the sun came up. Noah was out cold, and the email announcing that classes were canceled due to the storm had already hit my inbox. The streets were a sheet of white, trapping me on Delancey Street with my instinct to avoid and nowhere to hide.

Unsure what the day would bring, and honestly frightened about any awkward moments that might address last night, I escaped to the gym. I worked out as long as I could, hitting every possible machine, spending an extra thirty minutes on stretching, and then wasting as much time as I could doing yoga poses.

It sucked that it was only quarter to eight when I returned upstairs. This day was going to take forever.

After I showered, I received an email from Micah. We had to postpone our plans for tonight, but he said he wanted to talk to me. As I toweled off my damp hair, I called him.

"You're up early," he answered.

"My classes were canceled."

"Everything's closed."

My stomach twisted with anticipation that could be good or bad. "You said you wanted to talk to me."

"Yes." The slightest pause made me nervous. "I've been thinking about our arrangement, love. I know you've been thinking about it as well."

"I have." Mostly because it no longer seemed right to charge for time spent with someone I wanted to keep in my life after graduation.

"How would you feel about continuing our association?"

"I don't understand. Are you saying you want to keep seeing me after I graduate?"

"Yes, but I'd like to renegotiate our terms."

I folded the damp towel on my lap and frowned. I always made time for Micah, so I couldn't imagine what more he wanted. Maybe specific days of my week.

"What were you thinking?"

"I really wanted to have this conversation face to face, but I know your future finances have been weighing on you. I'd like to stay on as your Daddy once you're finished school. It would be different, Avery. The others would go away. You would work as a teacher during the day, and your nights would be open. I would take care of you."

He already took better care of me than anyone else in the world. "But what if I found a job somewhere else?" I wasn't sure I wanted to teach in the city.

"I have connections to some nearby private schools you might want to consider. I could help you find a respectable position nearby."

I silently deliberated. After a certain point, it all became about debt. "Would I continue to live here?"

"There or somewhere else if you prefer. Your finances would improve—notably." He paused for a moment then said, "This would be different, Avery. Our arrangement would be better defined as a closer relationship. You would teach as you planned, and never have to worry about finding a date for social functions. We would keep each other company—dependably there for one and other. No fuss, no drama, two satisfied parties."

My first thought was of Noah, but I shoved it away, keeping my head on business. "Would we see each other more frequently?" I'd have a real job and my time would be divided. More so than now, even if I dropped all my other clients.

"I would want us to see each other at least three nights a week, but I'd also like you to accompany me when I travel—depending on your teaching schedule, of course. This would be a more ... permanent arrangement, Avery. To others, we would seem a typical couple. However, I'd insist on seeing you were taken care of in all matters."

"Where would we go?"

"Anywhere I'm needed. Next month I'll be in Berlin. A few weeks after that, I'm visiting Mumbai. My schedule's always changing."

I didn't even know where Mumbai was. "And if I went with you... We would...?"

"I'd expect you to stay with me in my suite."

A jumble of nerves let loose in my stomach like a school of minnows. What was he saying, that we would actually have an intimate relationship as well as a sugar one? "You want a ... relationship?"

"I want simplicity, Avery. I enjoy your company. I think you're beautiful. You're always graceful when we attend functions together. And I like taking care of you. But you're growing up, and I'm not going to keep you from the future you worked so hard to achieve. What I'm suggesting is a clearly defined association where I take care of you, and you take care of me. It would be very different from what we have now, but it would also be similar."

"So ... not through the system?"

"No, this would be a private agreement. I would take care of you financially. Anything you wanted you'd only need to ask. If you preferred to live in a house, we could meet with a realtor. If you needed a car for your commute, I would supply one. You could compile a list of assets you might require, and I'll take each one into consideration."

"And what would you get in return?"

"You're a smart woman, Avery. You know how this would work. I wouldn't want anyone else interfering with a woman others come to identify as mine. Reputation is important to me."

I'd be a kept woman. Letting anyone keep me to that degree might feel like I was owned. At what point would Avery the sugar baby end and Avery the person begin?

"This is a lot to think about." I couldn't wrap my brain around his offer. Being a sugar baby had always been a temporary solution, a means to an end. Micah was proposing much more.

"Think of it this way, love, you would continue on the same path, hold a respectable job, but you would be taken. It *would* be a relationship, but unlike a traditional courtship, ours would have specific guidelines and expectations to assure we both remained equally satisfied."

"Like a business agreement."

"A contract." He paused then softly explained, "In today's world, such agreements are not unheard of, Avery. If you're uncomfortable with those terms, it won't happen. But the offer is there. Think about it."

I believed him. With the rate of divorce and the amount of money some people accumulated these days, having an agreement seemed smart, but I had nothing. I wasn't sure I wanted more if it was contingent on someone else. I looked forward to an honest paycheck with taxes removed and a 401K. Those things were normal. Contracted relationships were not. Or maybe they were, but no one talked about them.

This was a lot to digest. "When do I need to make up my mind?"

"When's graduation?"

"May twelfth." If I said no, that would be the day our current association would end.

"I'd hope to have your answer before then."

"I'll have to think about this."

"You will. And you'll let me know once you've made up your mind."

"Yes."

"Until then," he said, voice casual. "We'll continue as usual. The roads should be clear by tomorrow. How about dinner tomorrow?"

Our current situation suddenly seemed much more manageable. Familiar. "I'll be ready."

"Have a good day off, love. I'll see you tomorrow night."

"See you then." My hand slid into my lap with my phone.

It took a few minutes to mentally step back and understand the proposition I'd just received. I wanted to keep Micah in my life, and he didn't seem ready to let me go. But... While I wanted to stay friends, he wanted to take our relationship to the next level. I'd been hoping to dial back the formalities, and he just added a shit load of complexities to the arrangement.

I pictured his flawless, dark skin and tall, lean build. He was a sharp man with a sleek manner. He was always calm and collected, but he was so different from, say, Noah.

Noah was fun and juvenile, overbearing, and sexy. Micah was sexy, too, in a quiet, unapproachable way. He said the others would go away. I assumed that meant *all* men, including Noah.

Why are you even factoring him into the equation? He knows you're moving after graduation. This is business.

But it wasn't. What Micah was proposing might be a financial arrangement, but it was way beyond business. This was smack dab in the G-spot of personal. We would have sex.

Micah and I would have sex. Would it be his way? I mean, he would be the one paying for my life. And what was *his way* anyway? For all I knew he could be into some crazy fetishes or horribly vanilla. Sex suddenly seemed insanely intimate.

I wasn't stupid. I knew some women had arrangements like this, but I was a newborn as far as sugar babies went. I didn't kiss my Daddies, and I never slept with any of them. For me, it was all about keeping company, getting paid, and making them feel like big strong men.

But there were sugar daddies out there who kept the same babies for years. Men who didn't want marriage or complications or children. I wasn't sure I wanted those things either—at least not yet.

And then there were those who didn't bother with contracts. Of course, they were called paramours. All my lines were blurring, and I needed to step away from the situation to gain perspective. I wasn't a paramour. I was going to be a teacher. But would I be alone? I didn't want to be alone.

This was a lot to think about. I wouldn't have to do it forever. But it might be worth pursuing for a time. Who knew if I would get hired right out of college? I needed to make an income if I wanted to support myself. And maybe it would be exciting traveling around the world with a wealthy, sexy man like Micah.

I wouldn't have to juggle a schedule full of dates. I wouldn't have to spend time with so many men. To outsiders, it just might look like a respectable relationship. And it would be. Teacher and businessman, the picture of respectability. He said he'd respect my schedule and teachers managed to get holidays and summers off. It was complicated but also simple.

Micah had never treated me with anything but the utmost respect. He made me feel good about myself, confident. He showed me the joy of empowerment by teaching me how to take advantage of my assets and become an independent, self-reliant woman. This would be—

There was a knock at the door, and I knew who it was without checking. It was my complication. My distraction. My weakness. No longer merely my friend. And suddenly the simple offer of Micah taking care of me turned into an insane idea I'd be crazy to accept. Right? Or was it crazy to turn down such an offer for a hot neighbor I hardly knew and who might only hold interest in me for a few weeks?

I was so confused.

I went to the door, leaving my private debate behind to simmer. Taking a deep breath, I turned the knob and—yup—he was still gorgeous. Damp, tousled blond hair flipped over his brow as his smile highlighted his cleanly shaven jaw. My ovaries took an immediate hit.

With his arm braced against the door frame, he looked down at me and smiled. "You ran." His voice still held the gruff rasp of morning, the scrape of his un-caffeinated vocal cords having a direct link to my nipples.

"Actually, I tiptoed." I left the door open as an invitation for him to follow me inside.

"No school?"

"Everything's closed."

He hovered by my hall table, not quite entering the den as I took a seat on the couch.

He cleared his throat, the sound almost unsure and totally incongruent with the greedy lover I met six hours ago. "So, last night..." He really was a Jekyll and Hyde.

"Yeah." We endured several awkward seconds of silence. I picked at a hangnail and Noah watched me carefully.

"You're not mad?"

I didn't know what I was. "I'm not sure."

"You're not being bitchy. Is this like the calm before the storm?"

"I don't know."

He took a hesitant step closer. "I ... I'm sorry if I took it too far."

"No, you're not." Giving him the impression I wanted things PC in the bedroom would be my worst mistake.

He smirked, meeting my eyes and showing zero regret but plenty of satisfaction. "No. I'm not."

"Good. I prefer to keep things honest where sex is involved. Fewer misunderstandings that way."

"So you're okay with what happened? Your feelings matter to me, Avery."

Why did he have to be a nice guy when it would be so much more convenient if he were a jerk at the moment? It made it impossible to hate the shithead who occupied the other half of his soul.

"I'm okay." The words didn't feel like a lie.

He took another step closer. "Did you like it?"

"N—I... Some."

He smiled and lowered to the coffee table, so we were sitting across from each other. Our knees brushed as he gently took my hand. "Which parts?"

I wasn't sure. I sort of liked the way he touched me now. I liked when he was nice to me. "I'm not sure."

I also kind of liked when he wasn't so nice, which probably made me fucked in the head.

"You can tell me."

"I honestly don't know. Last night was weird. Different from what I'm used to. If you were anyone else, I would have ripped your nuts off. But you're not anyone else. You're my *frienemy* neighbor who slow dances with me in the snow to Christmas carols. The guy who cooks me hot cocoa and makes sure I have a backup phone charger available in a blizzard. I want to be mad at you for last night, and I should, but I'm not."

His head tipped away from my full view, toward the floor as his smile widened. "I think, if we can manage not to kill each other, we can have something great, Avery. I know you like things a certain way, but last night I proved my way wasn't so bad either."

I scoffed and rolled my eyes at his arrogance. "Because your way *has* to be better, right? I mean, it's *yours*."

"I'm just saying we could try some things—"

"Okay. Let's try it *my* way. What are your soft and hard limits?"

"Don't get all dominatrix woman on me." He smirked. "I mean, if you want to put on a tight leather corset, you might get my attention, but otherwise the bossy stuff doesn't do it for me."

"And you know this because you're so experienced as a bottom?"

"Use normal words, Avery."

"Bottom is submissive. Top is dominant. These aren't advanced terms, especially for someone as deep in the rabbit hole of the porn industry as you claim to be."

His eyes narrowed. "I could be a *bottom*. But I'd rather be in charge."

"So would I."

"But you loved last night."

"Nobody used that word. I said I didn't know how I felt about last night, but it was okay. I'm not going to stroke your ego and basically fake orgasmic praise to make you feel good. You got laid last night. You *should* feel fine."

He dropped my hand. "I didn't ask you to stroke my ego. And I know for a fact no orgasms were faked."

"But you're fishing for praise."

He glared at me. "I want to figure you out."

"Well, where did you put your morning newsletter of Freud's theories? That will have all the main bullet points of how women are innately masochistic and passive. Being that you have a penis, and therefore a bigger brain, it should be easy enough for you to figure me out."

"Don't make me out like some male chauvinist. I'm trying to be open-minded."

"But that's what you want, isn't it? A woman to be your passive little fuck toy and tell you what a big man you are."

His lips tightened, and I sensed he wanted to call me a bitch. "I just wish I knew why you need so much control."

"Why do *you*? Rather than act like there's something wrong with me, why not do a little research, Noah? There's a great big world out there on that thing the kids call the Internet. You know, the place where you find all your porn. Widen the search for a change."

"Avery, I've done the search. It's a black hole of kink. I want to know where it ends for you."

My smile was slow. "That's the fun of it. I'll let you know when I decide."

"No." He shook his head. "We aren't playing a game, we're having a conversation."

"What do you want to know, Noah? You want answers? I don't know why I'm this way, but I am. It's who I've always been. You might sneak a few nights of male domination in when my radar is down, but in the end, I am who I am."

"But you go out with men who..."

I raised a brow, daring him to judge me based on my occupation. "Consider it my professional persona."

He dragged a hand through his damp hair and let out a breath. "You go out with all these guys who ... buy you things. You make a trade out of letting men dote over you. I think you're lying if you can't admit wanting a man to take care of you on some level."

"I can take care of myself. They're paying my tuition. Everything else is just fluff. And last I checked, fucking is fucking. That has nothing to do with how I make a living because I don't screw my clients."

Oh God... Was I actually considering changing that rule? Could I have sex with Micah?

"That's what I mean, Avery. You have different rules for different situations, but you're the same woman in all those scenarios, so maybe you prefer to live a little bit in both worlds."

Being a sugar baby put me in a subservient role where empathy was key, and my main purpose was to see that my Daddies' needs were met. Part of me liked serving that purpose and nurturing in an emotional sense. I never really thought about it, but it was a complete contradiction to what I wanted in my personal life.

At home, I wanted control, order, and obedience. I wanted my words and desires to be law. Out there, I had no such authority. Or did I? I chose my clients, made the rules, and negotiated my rate.

Was it possible to be a little bit of both? Because I loved having men take care of me, yet... None of their attention was genuine. Nor was my response. It was all bought.

No. I had control. He was confusing things. He looked at things through a novice lens, and there were layers upon layers of rationale behind my choices.

"Domination isn't about sex, Noah. It's about social anxiety, the bending of a strong will, the feeling of outmaneuvering someone who should be stronger. Having submissive traits in public tells nothing about a person's behavior in private. There are countless female CEOs who love to come home and play the submissive. It's the role reversal that gets them off. I might have the occasional tendency to nurture, but at the end of the day I like when men..."

Beg? Squirm? Worship me? Grow frantic with desperate need? Suffer at the brink of a climax that would inevitably be denied? Jeez, maybe there was something wrong with me.

"I just like control," I said, deciding that word summed it up enough. "I like sex when I'm in total control. Last night, you stole that from me—*again.*"

"I'm pretty sure you handed it over. If I recall, your words were, *fuck me like you mean it.* I did exactly what you told me to do."

Huh. Maybe that's why I let him treat me that way. My eyes had watered as he pinned me down and rammed his cock down my throat, choking me… And I fucking loved it.

I fucked up. Where was that precise moment I could feel his will bending under mine?

It hadn't happened.

Noah never ceded control. Yet, he had me bending every humanly way possible last night.

Damn him! What was it with this guy? What was so special about him? I didn't want to keep making these mistakes. I liked sex when I was in control, and the longer he fucked with me and proved otherwise, the more my authority and common sense took a hit.

"Avery," he said my name quietly, drawing my attention back to the conversation. "Could it be possible that you're wrong? Maybe—before—there were certain circumstances that made your life feel out of control, and you were supplementing. Could it be that things are better now? You're almost finished school, and you have a great apartment. Maybe whatever had happened before isn't a threat anymore and you can let go now. Is that such a bad thing?"

My gaze hardened. I didn't like feeling psychoanalyzed. "Gee whiz, Noah, maybe you're right. If I could just pinpoint that moment of my childhood that broke me, you could fix me up." I looked up at him, just a waif with big eyes. "We could try pushing my limits and safe wording when things got too intense. Either way, I'm sure your magic cock can save the day."

His mouth formed a flat line, and his jaw hardened. "I wasn't trying to offend you. You hardly ever open up about your past. It makes sense to think something might have happened—"

"*Nothing happened to me!*" I flung my hands in the air and stood, pacing the floor. "Women went from Victorian gowns and fainting spells to building bridges and sitting on Capitol Hill. Is it so hard to comprehend I might be less sugar and more spice? When will men stop trying to pigeonhole us in these dainty little molds? Nothing fucking happened to me. I'm not broken. I'm strong."

"Okay." He held up his hands, palms out, in surrender. "I never said you weren't strong."

I scoffed, the sound coming from the back of my throat. "I grew up in a normal home with a normal family just like you."

I could hardly believe the lie sprung so easily from my lips but fuck him for acting like the only excuse for my personality might be broken parts of my past. I wasn't broken!

He continued to hold up his hands. "I'm sorry."

Encroaching uncomfortable territory, I redirected the conversation. "I have studying to do and, apparently, so do you."

He frowned. "We're talking."

I moved to the kitchen, putting distance between us. "We're done."

"*That*, right there." He rose from the table and cornered me. Startled, I twisted my back into the cabinets as he towered over me. "See what you're doing? You're grappling for authority. But in bed, you're different, Avery. I've seen you."

"Only because you suck at following directions, Noah."

"Bullshit. Last night I gave you a thousand chances to call it quits. You want to be the boss, but not as much as you want someone else to do it for you. Power can be a burden."

I rolled my eyes. "You have it all figured out." I turned, and he grabbed me from behind, his hands curling around my arms just above the elbows, his body and bulk angling me forward.

"I think I have a little more figured out than you want to admit," he whispered, mouth against my ear.

"And this is what you think *I* want?"

"I think you like when I take you, and you don't have a say in how I do it. I think you like the break from responsibility."

"If this is for me, how come it's *your* dick poking my back."

His arm slid through mine, pulling them tighter at my back as his hand shoved into my pants. "I call your bluff."

His fingers twisted in my panties and I grunted as he inserted a finger into my pussy. A second later, his hand was in front of my face, finger glistening with my arousal.

"You're soaking wet, Avery."

My molars locked as I glared at his finger. I jerked in his hold, but he didn't let go. "Get off."

"Lick them clean."

"Get fucked."

His hand covered my mouth, and I growled a scream, the sound muffled.

"Do you taste yourself?" His breath teased my ear as he turned my body, bending me over the lip of the counter. "You're a little liar."

He removed his hand from my mouth, and I panted. He shoved my pants down, still holding my arms tight at my back. "Look at you. You're drenched."

"I could have you arrested."

"Or you could stop denying that you like having the choice taken from you and let me fuck you in a way I know you'll enjoy." His fingernails scraped over my ass, and I sucked in a breath. "Little Avery, so tough and in charge."

I jerked my body, and he chuckled. The heat of his cock rested on my bare skin. "Noah..."

"Tell me to go home, Avery."

Go home. My lips wouldn't open. My mind playing a game of hide and seek where one second I was *It,* and the next second, I was the prey. I couldn't decide which role I wanted.

He loosened his grip and gathered my wrists in his hand. "Don't move. I have to put on a condom."

Well, he was an idiot. The second he took his hands off me. I bolted and yanked up my pants, running full speed into my bedroom.

"Avery!"

27

NOAH

I caught up to her in only a few long strides. She swung the bedroom door shut, and I caught it before it slammed. My heart raced as I backed her toward the side of the bed. Stroking my dick, now suited in a condom, I stalked her. She claimed she preferred sex to be honest, and I intended to get the truth out of her if it killed me.

"I'm not having sex with you, Noah!"

"Yes, you are." The challenge only got me harder.

"Um, no. I'm not."

"Get on the fucking bed, Avery."

She shook her head.

I crowded closer, and just as her knees bumped the mattress, I gave her one more chance to obey. "On your back."

"Fuck you."

"I'd rather fuck *you*."

"I bet you would."

She could be so fucking hot when she turned feisty. I shoved her shoulder, and her back hit the mattress. There was no time for her to object as I blanketed her with my body, wrenching her pants down and tearing the thin material of her panties. Fucking gorgeous. And I absolutely loved the fight she put up.

"Tell me no, Avery. Tell me to stop."

"Noah!"

The word *stop* or *no* didn't come out.

"You're heavy as hell!" She shoved my chest and grunted, the sound exasperated and adorably feminine.

I wrenched her legs open, and she stilled the moment my dick pressed against her opening. We panted but didn't move.

Not wanting to push her too far, I gave her another chance. "Tell me to go home, Avery. Say no. Any one of those words you love to throw at me will work. You just have to pick one."

Her eyes purposefully turned away. "I hate you."

I knew it. She wasn't like other women. She loved it rough and she needed it a bit out of hand to get off. She was a goddamn treasure and I wanted to bury myself so deep inside of her I was losing my mind.

"I'm not judging you," I said, hoping we could cut all the bullshit.

Keeping her gaze turned away, she pursed her lips. "Men always judge."

Maybe they did. And maybe I was. But I liked everything I suspected she hid. "Just be yourself with me."

Her brow pinched as if she didn't know who I wanted to see.

I needed her attention, so I turned her face back to mine and kissed her full lips with more need than passion. "Give me the real you."

She hesitated a split second then shoved her tongue into my mouth, and I moaned at the delicious force. I loved her greedy, hungry side. Fuck the formalities. Fuck everything else.

I didn't let it build or take any time to make us more comfortable. Every encounter with Avery was a game of King of the Mountain. We both loved the race to the top.

I fucked her hard and fast, my body overpowering hers, pressing her into the bedding as I trapped her wrists. She fought the restraint, yanking her arms free of my grip, but I eventually caught and subdued her struggles—sort of.

There were those forgotten moments, little pockets of time when her body turned nimble and she submitted to my desires. Her gaze softened and her mouth slackened, and everything in her expression screamed how much she liked being taken. But then she'd fight me again, as if some hard headed part of her awakened on fire and needed to take it all back.

Sex had always been good, but with Avery, sex was fun. We wrestled and laughed and gave as good as we got. Her natural setting was somewhere between pissed off and telling me to go fuck myself, but jumbled in all that beauty was a soft woman who just wanted to be held. The victory was feeling her relax in my arms. But, God, was it work.

"Stop fighting it." My balls smacked her bare ass as I drilled into her tight little cunt, her arms now restricted by my grip.

Her body tightened, wrapping my cock in delicious wet, heat. She was going to come but, as always, fought letting go.

I laughed at her determination. She didn't want to give me the satisfaction. We'd see about that.

I switched angles and pumped deep, using quick thrusts to hit all the right places. My mind fragmented as her pussy clenched my dick. Her back bowed, pressing against me, cunt throbbing, as she bared her teeth in protest and screamed.

Fuck, it was incredible. I refused to let her deny what was happening. I groaned. "I feel you coming all over my dick."

"Fuck you." Her words hissed through clenched teeth. "This is the last time we do this."

My hand moved to her throat, holding tightly beneath her jaw. "More lies."

I'd never been into choking—or so I thought. I'd never use bruising force with a woman, but with Avery, there was something so fucking hot about her resilience. I never doubted her ability to fuck me up if I went too far. Nor did I ever want to actually hurt her. She was ... special.

I wrapped the delicate column of her neck in my fingers, seeing the contrast of our skin and watching her anger subdue to calm when I held her like this. There was no pressure, but she knew I had total control.

But she still challenged me. "*Not* a lie," she gritted, chin tipped upward above the cradle of my fingers.

Slowing my strokes and holding her stare, I ground my cock against her swollen folds, and her lashes lowered. She was softening.

"How about we make a deal?" I never wanted to give her up. She was a drug, my greatest addiction.

"I don't negotiate with terrorists."

Her phenomenal wit made me want her all the more. Such a smart, sexy mouth. Releasing her throat, I kissed her, biting her lower lip hard enough that she stopped fidgeting for a moment.

"Noah!" she snapped, possibly pissed because she was enjoying it.

"Avery," I mimicked, smiling.

She huffed. "What are the conditions of the deal?"

She was as curious as a fucking cat.

I met her stare and grinned. "Every time you let me fuck you the way I want, I'll give you one hour to play Little Miss Control Freak with me."

I was curious to see what she'd actually do with all this authority she claimed to need. Part of me still believed it was all an act, sort of like a cute Chihuahua that thinks of itself as a Great Dane. I could survive an hour of that.

She stilled, her expression instantly sobering. "Are you serious?"

I ground into her. "Does it feel like I'm serious? Whatever it will take to keep you from hiding from me, I'm down. We can take turns."

"But you get to fuck me however *you* want in exchange?"

"That's right." Just like I was doing now and like I'd done last night.

It took one second of being inside Avery Johansson to realize she would easily rank as the best sex I'd ever had. With her, there was no shame, no limits, and no modesty. Just unrefined, animal instinct.

I'd never experienced such raw eroticism before. I never felt so free to experiment with my own sexuality, and I planned on taking full advantage of our deal—should she agree.

"What about hard limits?"

"We'll figure them out as we go." I didn't want to be the cliché, but we needed a safe word if we were going to do this. Every forum I read insisted on starting there. "What's a word you hate?"

"What?"

"Something you never talk about or say."

Her expression shifted like a mask falling into place. "Blackwater."

I definitely needed to know about the home she left. And a better man would take the opening now, but I wanted to close the deal first. The story about Blackwater would come in time.

"Okay. You say Blackwater, and we immediately stop whatever we're doing. Same goes for me. Deal?"

She looked suspicious, as if she expected a monster to jump out of the closet at any second. "Deal," she repeated slowly.

Her agreement came so easily I felt slightly played. Yet she did the whole skepticism thing so well. Who exactly was the player here? Maybe there wasn't one. No, there was always a strategizer in every deal.

Sleeping with someone as cool and open-minded as Avery was wild. Maybe she wasn't bluffing, and this was just *cute* to her.

Fuck. Maybe she was used to men striking deals with her.

How was it, the more I got to know her the more she proved a mystery? I laughed to myself. *I'm going to figure you out, Ms. Johansson...*

"Something amusing?" And that snark...

She definitely got hot from rough play, but I was starting to get off on her bitchiness. "Just relishing our negotiations."

She rolled her eyes. "Where would the world be if men didn't take time to stroke themselves after a job well done?"

I stilled, taking her jab as a challenge. "You'll be the one stroking me now."

"Tit for tat. You better stretch before I get my turn."

Oh, it was like that was it? I needed to crank it up. I could tell she expected little from me and that just wouldn't do.

I wanted to be the best she'd ever had. I didn't know my limits yet, because right now, I was solely focused on her. She was the goal. I wanted to live in every crevice of her and leave her wearing my scent like a tattoo. I wanted to be all she thought of, even long after we part ways. I wanted to shock her.

I pulled out and she frowned.

"What are you doing?"

Time to push her. "On your stomach. I want to play with your ass."

"*What?*"

Grabbing her ankle and wrist, I quickly flipped her to her stomach and pried her cheeks apart.

"Wait!" She squirmed out from under me. "We need lube or something!"

I dragged her across the bed. "That's what spit's for."

Her face hardened as she glared over her shoulder. "You fucking spit on my body and I'll rip your eyes out of the sockets. I have some in the drawer next to my bed."

Most women kept magazines in their nightstands, but okay. Convenient.

I reached for the drawer and pulled it open. "Holy fuck."

"Just get the lube and get out of there."

She had a fucking arsenal. "This is just for you? What the hell are you doing with these?" I lifted the box of clothespins.

She chuckled. "You'll find out when it's my turn."

I glanced down at my body. "You're not pinning my dick or my balls."

"Oh, are you scared?"

Slamming the drawer, I made a mental note to do something about her patronizing tone. She could be such a sarcastic smartass sometimes. Speaking of her ass..."Spanking. Yes or no?"

"I'll have to change positions for you to lie across my lap—"

More sarcasm. My hand came down with a crack.

"Fuck!" She scrambled to her knees, but the handprint was already forming. *"You asshole!"*

"That's where I'm headed." I shoved her shoulder to the bed and climbed over her thighs, drizzling lube down her lower back.

Pulling her cheeks apart, I sucked in a breath. Such a tight little rosebud. Every inch of her was perfect.

The mood suddenly shifted and I felt out of place, like I didn't belong there, like I didn't have the right to touch her. What was I doing? Was this about proving something to her or proving something to myself?

I blinked at my surroundings. There couldn't be a more inconvenient time for introspection, but all I could think of was Margaux bitching about how terrible anal was when we tried.

"What are you doing?"

So not to appear distracted, I massaged the oil over her smooth skin, teasing a generous amount into the tight pucker of muscle. Disappointing Avery seemed much worse than disappointing anyone else. But why?

Her arms folded under her head and she shut her eyes as I used the oil the massage her thighs. I needed a moment to catch my breath and think. She remained rather subdued through all of it.

Maybe I was proving something to myself. As much as I enjoyed Avery's body, I didn't want to use her as a pawn in my own personal therapy session. I wanted her to enjoy this.

Teasing my thumb over the oiled crease, I asked, "Do you like anal sex?"

"When it's done right. I doubt you know how."

Maybe I didn't. Fuck. I was having some sort of crisis of doubt and my dick was suffering the brunt. I casually stroked myself. "Has anyone ever done it wrong with you?"

She lifted her head and glanced over her shoulder. "You're big. That could go either way. The trick is making it feel good not painful."

But she liked rough play. "So slow?"

"Not too slow. That's not great either. As long as there's enough oil, and you don't rip into me, it will be fine."

"What if—"

"For the fuck sake, just do it already. God, you can be such a pain in the ass."

I was trying to be the exact opposite, but whatever. "Okay. Stop yelling at me. Just remember our safe word if you want me to stop."

Fuck, I really wanted her to like it. *I* wanted to like it. Maybe then I could put the last bad experience behind me.

I pressed a kiss to her ass cheek. There was something priceless about her adventurous nature and her ball breaking wit. "I can't believe you're letting me do this. You're so confident and sexually self-assured. And you can be so sweet."

"I can't believe you're still talking."

I narrowed my eyes. "Until something bitchy comes out of your mouth."

My finger pressed against her opening, and she grunted, relaxing into it. I held her down as I probed deeper, exploring her limits. She remained quiet, but her breathing turned labored.

I returned to the drawer and dug around. "I know you got a plug in here somewhere, you kinky little thing."

"In the next drawer down."

I stretched, keeping my leg over the back of hers to ensure she didn't try to escape. She was perfectly still.

"Hol—lee—fuck." I laughed at the sheer volume of toys. "I'm not sure which one to use."

"The purple one's nice."

"Not big thunder here?" Did she actually use all of these?

She glanced at me, her cheek resting on her folded arms. "Certainly not. That one's for you."

My eyes widened, recalling our agreement. I dropped the big one back in the drawer. "The small one it is."

Something told me whatever I put in her ass was absolutely going in mine, so I'd better tread carefully. More lube for sure.

Once everything was slick and relaxed, I worked the plug inside of her. She didn't utter a single complaint, which pleased me but also made me nervous. Her submission was a tradeoff for mine. I wasn't sure I'd be as cooperative. It all depended on what she had planned.

"Put your arms behind your back."

She hesitated. "Why?"

"Because we had a deal, Avery."

Her hands twisted, each one cupping the opposite elbow behind her back as she lay flat on the bed.

"Beautiful. Now, spread your legs wider."

I lifted off of her, and her feet shimmied outward, widening to the edges of the mattress. The plug slipped, and I wedged it back in place. Her cheek rested on the comforter.

She was definitely aroused. "I wish you could see what I see right now. Your pink pussy's dripping wet. You like this, Avery, whether you'll admit it or not."

She didn't respond, which was fine.

"Shall we then?"

Aligning my cock to her delightfully wet pussy, I nudged the swollen tip past her glistening folds and sank to the hilt, burying myself deep. That first moment, embedded in her body, was unrefined ecstasy.

The plug made her incredibly tight. Lowering my mouth to her shoulder, I whispered, "I'm going to fuck you every chance I get. Hard, dirty, soft, tender... You can do your worst, Avery, because I intend to have you so often and in so many ways, that you forget every lover that came before. You know what that means, Avery? No more hiding. I'm going to know every part of your body—intimately. And you're going to know mine. I'll finally learn what you're after and we'll both get exactly what we want."

The promise came from a dark, shadowed crevice of my soul. She was introducing me to places within myself I'd never met before.

"I look forward to my turn."

Pulling back, I drove forward, and she let out a cry, her fingers tightening on her elbows. I made sure I was barely putting any weight on her. "Are you comfortable?"

"I'm fine."

Nudging the plug, I tapped it deeper and thrust again. Once I found my rhythm, there was no stopping it. Orgasms tore out of her, milking my cock and my stamina never waned. Her moans fueled my thrusts, driving me deeper and harder.

"You feel that, Avery. I'm all the way in."

"Yes..." Her voice had transcended to a breathy sigh.

I unlaced her arms, massaging her shoulders, and nibbling her jaw. She was getting tired. "Do you want me to come in your pussy or your mouth?"

I loved watching her consider every option and desperately wished I could hear her thoughts. "My mouth."

My stomach turned like a carousel, sending thrilling shockwaves to my dick. Satisfied and surprised, I kissed her cheek. "Turn around. I want your head on the edge of the bed."

Parting from her warmth caused a physical ache in my gut. I helped her into position, carefully gathering her hair behind her head, so it didn't get stuck under her back.

"Rest your head over the edge of the mattress. There you go." I removed the condom and stepped closer, slowly stroking. "You ever do it like this before?"

She shook her head. No sarcastic follow up. Just a clear view into a very small secret of her past. It was progress.

"Show me you want it."

Her lips parted, and I pressed in, not fast or hard, but slow and deep. Upside down, everything was different. I thrusted, and she gripped my hips, guiding my pace and pulling me deeper. It was fucking incredible how easily she adapted to whatever I threw her way.

"Let me see your pussy."

Her legs spread and I reached for her clit, her body arching as I gave the plug a little tap. As I rubbed her swollen flesh, her mouth grew clumsy, but still felt sensational. My hips pumped greedily.

Her face turned away, and she gasped. "It's too much when you touch me too."

It might have been, but it also could have been a power play. We weren't going to play those games anymore, so I stuck to the ground rules. "Did you say something? I didn't hear the magic word."

Her lips firmed, and her eyes narrowed, but she didn't utter a peep. Her tenacity was admirable. Even when having fun, she consistently tried to regain the upper hand.

Not today. "Get your mouth back on my cock, Avery."

"I can't concentrate when your hand's on my clit."

"That's the beauty of it. Stop thinking. Just open yourself up and let me have control."

She debated for a silent second and huffed, directing me back into her mouth. I pushed to the back of her throat, watching her toes curl as my fingers sink into her pussy. She let out a garbled cry, her sex pulsating around my fingers with greedy little pulls as her come bathed my hand. Bending lower, I sucked her hard nipple into my mouth, using my teeth to add a bite of pleasure-pain, which she seemed to love. Not forgetting about the plug, I gave it a nudge, working my fingers over her wet pussy and wringing out another orgasm.

She was panting, unable to keep her concentration as I switched directions again, always keeping her on her toes.

"You know you can suck harder than that."

She growled. It was the cutest sound. But then her mouth tightened with the added bonus of her fingers massaging my balls. My eyes rolled back at the first tug. Fuck. Now *I* was distracted. I zeroed in on her clit, thinking I could get one more good one out of her before I came.

Her dainty finger teased around the puckered skin of my ass, stalling my game and—"Jesus! *Fuck!*"

Her finger shoved all the way in, and my calves locked. I lifted to my toes, toppling forward and catching my weight on my hands at the last moment. "What the fuck, Avery!"

I caught her wrist but didn't pull her free, too afraid she might damage something back there. She giggled, vibrating my dick out of her mouth.

"Problem?"

"Get your finger out of my ass!"

She poked deeper, and sweat broke over my brow. My fucking eyelids were sweating. "*Avery!*"

"Oh, come on, Noah. Stop thinking and just feel. Open up..."

My molars locked. "It's not your turn."

"I know. It's yours. Most men would beg to have a woman do this to them."

"I'm not most men. Get it out."

"Okay. But first..." She did something, twisting her wrist and sharpening her reach as her mouth wrapped around my cock. Another poke and I trembled, a nearly violent release ripping through me with hardly any warning.

"Gah—What the fuck? *Shit!*"

Hot come shot through my veins, as shivers chased down my spine. She withdrew her finger and released my throbbing dick, rolling out from under me just as I collapsed on the bed.

Cocky as ever, she sprang off the mattress and smiled as I panted. Her voice practically sung like a smug canary. "I'll give you a minute to find your bearings."

She disappeared into the bathroom, and I lost track of how long she was gone. What the fuck just happened? Where had she learned to do that? I didn't want to know.

I stared into space, eyes unfocused, my flaccid cock resting against my hip when she returned from the bathroom. "You cheated," I rasped.

She put the toy and lube back in the drawer. "How's it feel?"

I should have known. She *would* be that sort of girl. In hindsight it seemed all too predictable. The moment I let down my guard, she rammed a finger right up my ass.

"You cheated."

She chuckled. "Serves you right. This is actually good. Now, you'll be a little more prepared for when I take my turn. I'm not sure when that will be. I really do have to study at some point today, and tomorrow night I have plans. I guess I'll let you know when the mood strikes and you can just enjoy the sweet anticipation of waiting and wondering when I'm going to knock on your back door again. I wonder which toys I'll have with me that day."

My gaze narrowed. Did she think I was going to back out? Not a chance. She could talk all the smack in the world, she wasn't intimidating me out of the deal.

"Bring it. And when you're done playing Mistress, I look forward to fucking that smug look right off your face."

"I'm sure you will, but I still think I'll have my fun while it's my turn." She tossed my shirt at my chest. "Get dressed. I have homework to do."

I sat up, her earlier comment just registering. "Wait. Where are you going tomorrow night?"

"I have work."

"Oh." Right. Meaning she had a fucking date.

She doesn't kiss them or touch them. Though that one guy always walked her up and hugged her. The fucking lines were blurred, and why did she have to have that job?

I silently stepped into my pants, my blood pressure rising. There was nothing I could do about her job right now, but maybe if things got more serious, we could figure out another option for her to make money, something that didn't require my girlfriend to date other men.

Was she my girlfriend? Not yet. "What are you doing next Saturday?"

She shrugged, brushing out her hair. "I don't know yet. Why?"

I savored the glimpse into her world and loved witnessing her performing personal acts like brushing her hair. She fascinated me.

"Maybe I could take you out."

Putting down the brush, she turned to face the bed. "Are you asking me on another date?"

"Yeah." Whether she realized it or not, I planned to date her. It figured that after all this time as a bachelor, I waited for the most unavailable woman to decide I want a monogamous relationship again. I'd break it to her slowly.

Noting her hesitation, I said, "You're in charge this time. It's your turn."

That seemed to do the trick. "Okay, yeah. Let's go out."

I caught her hand, lacing our fingers loosely and pulling her close for a gentle kiss. "I'll be at your door at seven. Don't be late."

"I thought I was in charge."

"It's not a matter or power, it's a matter of etiquette. Be on time."

"Fine. I'll be ready."

Good girl.

28

AVERY

Micah took my key and unlocked my door as he always did. "Mind if I come in for a few minutes?"

I stilled, not used to him inviting himself into my home, but I couldn't tell him no. It was his name on the lease after all. "Sure, come in."

He followed me inside, and I awkwardly stood by the table, unsure of what to do. This was the moment I usually pried off my heels and put on pajamas, reverting from sexy sugar baby to slouchy college student.

He walked over to my desk and ran a long finger over the edge of my textbook. "Do you like your classes this semester?"

"So far. They're all in my concentrations, so they keep me interested. Next week I find out where I'm student teaching."

He looked at me. "You'll need clothes for that. I can set you up with my personal shopper."

"You don't have to do that."

"I know I don't have to, Avery. I made the offer because I want to."

"Thank you."

He left the desk and took a slow tour of my living room. As beautiful as the renovated mansion was, my apartment was decorated with items that testified to my age. Bright red sofa, fuzzy white shag carpet, brightly colored candleholders. He stuck out like a sore thumb in his exquisite suit that played up his beautiful African complexion. Even his polished dress shoes made me feel unsuitable. I straightened my posture.

"Does it make you nervous having me in your home?"

"Um, no. I just wasn't expecting company."

"Yet you invited me in any way. I can leave."

"No." I was being so rude. "Can I get you something to drink? I have … water."

His dark, chestnut eyes studied me as he stepped closer, his hand trailing along my cheek. "Don't trouble yourself, love. You've made a sweet little home for yourself here. I only wanted to see it."

My head angled back so I could see his face. "I love my apartment, Micah. I'll never be able to say thank you enough for helping me get it."

His mouth curled upward. It wasn't quite a smile, but Micah never smiled, so that might have been it.

His thumb traced over my lips. "Have you given any thought to what we discussed?"

I blinked and lowered my lashes. "A little. I'm—"

A heavy knock rattled the door.

"Are you expecting someone?"

"No. It's probably just my neighbor."

My chest tightened as if I were doing something wrong. Noah would be upset if he found another man in my home, but this was my home, and I could invite whomever I wanted inside. Yet the knock gave me the urge to shut off the lights and hide. What the hell was happening to me?

"The blond man?"

Heart racing I stared at the door and nodded. "Yes."

"Does he often come by at eleven at night?"

"No. He's probably just…" He's being nosy. "…wants to ask me something." The knock sounded again, heavier and harder. "I'll see what he wants."

Micah hung back as I went to open the door. Noah scowled into my apartment.

"Can I help you?"

"I need to borrow a cup of milk."

I frowned at him. He knew I had dairy allergies. Angling the door for privacy, I hissed, "What are you doing?"

He glared over my shoulder.

Micah cleared his throat, pulling the door out of my grip, and held out a hand. "I'm Micah Buchanan. I didn't catch your name."

Noah shook his hand, using evident force. "Noah Wolfe."

Micah's dark eyes slowly took Noah's measure, and then turned to me. "Will you be all right, love?"

I nodded. "You don't have to leave." I turned my attention back to Noah and scowled. "I'm all out of milk."

Noah stepped away from the doorway but didn't leave.

Micah glanced back into the apartment and back to me. "I'll see myself out." He leaned down, and my eyes widened as his mouth pressed to mine. Before it was just the corner of my lips, but this time, he wasn't hiding his intentions. As he pulled away, his fingers pinched my chin. "I'll call you tomorrow, love. Sweet dreams."

I didn't blink until the elevator closed behind him. Noah scowled at me.

"I thought they weren't allowed to kiss you," he snapped the second we were alone.

"I... Micah's..." Why was I explaining myself to him? "Do you even need milk?"

"No, I don't fucking need milk! Why was he inside your apartment, Avery?"

"Because I invited him in, *Noah*." Irritated, I kicked off my shoes and removed my earrings. "If you don't need anything, then get out."

As I plucked the pins from my hair, I flinched at the sound of the door slamming. I slowly turned, finding my apartment empty.

"Noah?" He left? That wasn't like him to just walk away. I frowned. He must be really angry.

I scoffed. Whatever. He had no right interfering with my job. This was *my* life.

I took off my dress and shoved my legs into PJ pants. Taking off my bra, I grabbed the first T-shirt I found and pulled it over my head. Shoving my feet into my slippers, I marched back to the living room and glared at the walls, my irritation amplifying.

"Fuck this."

I marched across the hall and pounded on his door. It flung open, and he scowled at me but said nothing. His eyes did a slow perusal of my body, pausing at my feet, which were stuffed into cow slippers, and returning to my face. Still glaring.

Fine. I'd talk first. "You have no right to—"

My words muffled as his mouth slammed down on mine, his body backing me into the hall and against the wall across from his door. My overstuffed cow feet tripped and lifted off the ground as he shoved me into the hard surface. He wasn't being demanding or grabby, just ... passionate.

My fingers knotted in his hair, and I softened. "Noah..." His name was a whispered caress from my lips to his.

"I don't like when other men are in your apartment," he whispered, his mouth brushing over my lips.

My fingers forked through his hair as I pulled him closer. "It's my job."

His hand pressed into the back of my pants and squeezed. "No, it's not."

He was right—for now—but that might change in the near future. I still hadn't had time to consider Micah's offer.

"You can't do that when I'm with a client." I fed my hand up the back of his shirt, touching hot flesh and muscle.

He lifted me and my legs wrapped around his hips as he carried me into his apartment and kicked the door shut. We tumbled to his leather sofa where he continued to kiss me, stripping off my shirt and groping my tits.

"Don't invite them in," he rasped, dropping his mouth lower and kissing a path down my stomach. "Just me, Avery."

He pulled down my pants, and his mouth was on me the second he had my panties out of the way. I arched and fisted his hair as he ate me with pure determination.

"Just me," he whispered over my wet folds, driving a finger deep. "Tell me what you want. I'll please you however you need."

What he was doing was rather nice… "That. Keep doing that."

He licked and kissed and teased. "Let me make you come."

Was he asking? What kind of question was that? "Yes."

He pressed another finger deep, striking a tender nerve as he thrust faster. His tongue swirled over my clit, sucking, nibbling. And then I was crying out as I came against his mouth.

His eyes found mine as I slowly came down. "Wow."

"Should I lick it up?"

Oh, my God… "Yes…"

He spread my folds and slowly dragged his tongue up my slit, licking and cleaning me like a cat, his eyes on me the entire time. I moaned and caught my breath, savoring his delicate attention.

"And here?" His mouth lowered, his breath teasing my soft skin as his tongue slid in a slow circle. Lower.

"Mmm, yes…"

He spent days down there, asking and then doing everything I said he could do. Eventually, he moved to my legs, kissing the backs of my knees, massaging up my calves and thighs and coming back to kiss my clit with the softest little caresses. I wasn't sure what his motivation was, but I was never one to object to being worshipped.

His hands fondled my breasts as he worked his way around my body. There was no groping or grabbing. Just delicate caresses that had my mind lulling in the sweetest place. He kissed my lips, and I peeked through my lashes and smiled. Damn, he was good.

Lowering off the couch, he slid to the floor, to his knees. I wanted to pull him back to me, but maybe he was tired of being the giver. He folded his hands behind his back and lowered his weight onto his heels. Then he looked at me as if waiting for instructions.

Oh, my fucking God, he was kneeling for me. My heart tripped, and I eased up on one elbow.

"Noah?"

"Should I do more or would you like something else?"

I blinked, noting the sizable bulge in his pants. Dear lord, this must be killing him! "Come here. Take off your pants."

He rose and stripped, then stood next to the couch. "Where do you want my hands?"

This wasn't how I expected this to go, but I wasn't about to complain. "Sit down. Lift your hands behind your head and hold them there."

He complied without a single objection. I slid between his legs, resting my knees on the floor. Watching him carefully, I slowly stroked. His nostrils flared, and his chest lifted on a deep inhalation, but he didn't reach for me.

I took my time blowing him, my hands sliding over his smooth flesh as my mouth played and explored.

He was incredibly still, watching my every move. Always watching me.

When I took him deep and looked up at him, the black of his pupils swallowed the blue of his irises. But his hands remained obediently clamped behind his head.

His breathing labored as I toyed with his balls and dragged my tongue slowly up his shaft. Sucking a finger deep into my mouth, I watched him as I brought it down to his taint.

"Spread your legs, Noah. And scoot forward."

His jaw ticked, but he did as I said, his body easing to the edge of the couch and his knees gradually widening. His hesitation was notable, which made his compliance all the more rewarding. I teased his puckered flesh, and his lips parted as he drew in a breath.

"Do you want my finger inside of you?"

I saw the emotional debate in his eyes, unsure if this might be the moment he stole back the control or gave a breathtaking show of submission. There was nothing I wanted more than his surrender in that moment.

"Yes. Please."

His words tickled through me like shards of a tiny orgasm. I pressed, and his jaw locked, his Adam's apple shifting as he swallowed.

A vulnerable sound escaped his throat as I penetrated. Smiling up at him, so he felt my praise, I took his cock into my mouth and sucked him for several minutes, my finger leisurely exploring.

He was panting and sweating, his cock twitching and his ass clenching. The dark color of his swollen erection told me he could come at any second. "Do you need to come, Noah?"

"Yes..."

"Do you think I should let you come?"

He blinked rapidly, a flash of panic showing in his eyes. "Please ... Avery."

I withdrew my finger, and he hissed. "Where are your condoms?"

"There's one in my pants."

"Such a boy scout."

I found the condom and rolled it onto his straining cock. Moving with excruciating slowness, I stood over his knees, not lowering close enough to touch him.

His eyes shifted, his gaze traveling over every inch of my body as I watched him, my feet apart, hands on my hips, holding everything he wanted within arm's reach but outside of his control. "What do you say?"

"Please."

I smiled. "I love when you beg." I bent forward, angling my ass out behind me, dangling my tits over his thighs and rubbing up against his body like a cat. It seemed more than he could take, so I stroked him.

"Don't come."

His thighs bunched with muscles and his arms flexed behind his head. "Please, Avery..." He was breathing fast, jaw twitching. "Shit..."

I squeezed the base of his cock, and he grunted. "Not yet. Not until you're inside of me."

His head tipped back, and he groaned. "Fuck." A bead of sweat worked its way down his chest, and I caught it with my tongue, slowly licking my way to his mouth.

"You're being very good, Noah." I kissed him slowly, the tremble of his jaw evident under the soft pressure of my lips. "I think you've earned an orgasm."

His eyes closed and my body lowered until his cock touched my pussy, but didn't penetrate.

"Look at me."

His eyes, wearing lines of tension, full of desire, found mine, and I sank onto him. He let out a held breath with enough force to blow hot air across my nipples.

"Do you like being inside of me?" I asked, pinching the tips of my breasts while riding him.

"Fuck, Avery." He gritted his teeth. "I'm not going to last."

Of course, he wasn't. "Do you know why that is, Noah?"

"Because your pussy feels incredible."

"True, but that's not why." I reached behind me and cupped his balls, closing my grip and giving a sharp tug before sliding back down and impaling myself on his hard cock. "It's because you like being dominated. *Now, come.*"

I saw his attempt to fight ejaculating at the precise moment I gave the command, those accusing words still ringing in the air, but he failed.

His hips bucked as he let out a garbled string of nonsensical slurs. Every muscle in his body tightened as if he was receiving an electric shock.

I took my pleasure, riding him hard even when he begged me to stop, hissed it was too much. He arched and growled, but never moved his hands. He took it. Every last bit of my commanded authority over him. He took it with striking submission.

29

NOAH

The faucet shut off, and I heard her bare feet approach the couch where I lay comatose, my veins still trembling from my last release. When Avery made me come, she did so with the calculated force of a Scud missile. I moaned, arms limp at my sides, head back, eyes shut.

"Are you alive?"

"*Mmm…*" Words took too much effort.

She giggled and peeled the condom off my flaccid cock, causing me to suck in a sharp breath, but I didn't open my eyes. Only when I heard her dressing did I peek through my lashes.

Her shirt said *Hugs Not Drugs* and her pants were covered in a fuzzy ladybug print. But the cow slippers were my favorite.

"It's late. I should go."

I forced my eyes fully open, taking a mental picture of her full appearance. "I can't believe you're the woman who just put me through hell."

"I'm sorry, did you not enjoy yourself?"

So sassy. "Don't gloat."

"A polite submissive says *thank you* when he's permitted to come."

"Don't ever call me that."

My clothes were scattered, and I didn't give a fuck. Stuck to my couch in all my naked glory, I simply stared at her. "Don't go."

She sighed. Sliding onto my lap, she cradled my face and kissed me slowly. It wasn't bad letting her take the lead. She definitely knew a thing or two about pleasure. Her full lips pulled back slowly, and she stared into my eyes.

"Now, Momma's gotta get her biscuits. You sleep while I'm across the hall calling your name until I come and I pass out."

As she pushed off my lap, my hand snaked around her waist, halting her sly escape. "Why go across the hall for that?"

"Uh, uh, uh..." She waved a finger. "It's still my night. My rules. I decide when you get to touch me."

"I'm too tired, anyway." My grip fell away. I had a feeling she didn't realize what she gave up tonight. "Tomorrow night's our date."

"I know."

"I want you to sleep over."

She stood. "We'll see."

"Avery." I leveled her with a glare that said it wasn't up for negotiation. "You took tonight, so that means tomorrow your ass is mine—literally, if I want it that way."

Her lips pursed. "Fine. But I'm leaving early in the morning. You don't get to hijack my day."

"As long as I have you all night, you can do whatever you want with your morning. But expect to be tired."

"I'm opening the door. Do you want to cover up?"

"Why bother? The neighbor already sampled the goods."

She rolled her eyes. "I like you much better when you're sweet, but you seem to do annoying arrogance so effortlessly. Bye."

She breezed into the hall, leaving the door to my apartment wide open. "Avery," I yelled after her. "You forgot to shut the door!"

"Sorry," she sang but never came back.

Shoving off the couch, I dragged my exhausted ass to the door and peeked into the hall. She was gone. I'd count down the hours until I'd get to spend time with her again. As much as I enjoyed this kinky quid pro quo thing we had going, I was equally, if not more excited to just take her out and have the chance to know her better.

Shutting the door, I locked it and grabbed a towel from the closet before heading to the shower. Things weren't perfect, but I was having fun. She was having fun. Despite the rough start, this seemed to take a turn in the right direction, and I couldn't be more pleased.

Avery was ... sweet and complicated and so much more than I originally expected. Beneath the layers of sarcasm, there hid a gentle-hearted girl, who—if my instincts were right—had been overdue for some unconditional kindness. I honestly believed that if she realized she could be herself and still earn a guy's attention, she'd stop pretending to be someone else for all those guys paying for her time.

I didn't want to pay for the perfect woman. I wanted the real Avery, someone I wasn't sure Avery even knew all that well. But I sensed her goodness as much as I sensed her wild side. I loved the fact that no one else realized how much she kept hidden under the surface, but every day I chipped away at her barriers, and I didn't plan to stop until I found the real her.

30

AVERY

I might have a boyfriend. Maybe.

Noah was such a versatile guy. Sometimes he was growly and demanding, other times he was romantic and sweet. And then there were times, like last night, when he was everything I ever dreamed of wanting.

It didn't escape me on the way back to our building that he was going to shift the second we walked through the door. I could already feel the tension building as we stepped into the elevator. I wasn't nervous, but I also wasn't going to make this easy on him.

The elevator doors parted, and I stepped into the hall. "Well, tonight was fun. I really liked that toffee dessert thing. Goodnight—"

He caught my arm and pulled me back to him, wrapping an arm around my shoulders and tucking my body into his side. "Do you think I was born yesterday?"

"I'm pretty sure you're older than me."

"And I'm pretty sure we had a deal." He held me close as he unlocked his door. "Go into the bedroom. I left a surprise for you."

"A strap-on?"

"You wish."

I took off my coat and hung it over the back of a chair. He slowly unbuttoned his coat and watched as I walked toward the bedroom. My hand reached for the switch and… Oh, my God.

Roses. Rose petals. Champagne on ice. Music kicked on, and I turned. He watched me from just outside the door. This was not what I was expecting.

I licked my lips and glanced back at the beautiful display. His bedroom looked like a honeymoon suite at an upscale resort. A bottle of Cristal rested in the silver ice bucket.

"I … don't know what to say."

"Don't say anything."

I nodded because silence wasn't really a choice. I was literally speechless.

He could have done any number of perverted things to knock me off balance. I anticipated that, mentally prepared for it. But this… I had no pre-calculated response for this sort of … romance.

He stepped closer and traced a finger down the side of my arm. His mouth lowered, and I met his lips before they needed to find mine. He backed me toward the bed.

Lana Del Ray's gritty voice echoed through the apartment, singing a familiar song. *Love* was possibly one of my favorites on her album, but he couldn't know that. How was he doing this?

As she sang about being young and getting all dressed up to go nowhere in particular—to get the blues—the lyrics hit me right in the moneymaker, ricocheted around in my cold heart, and took a nip out of some tender part I'd never felt before. My palm pressed into my chest as if that could somehow subside the ache.

It was my song. My anthem. It was my life she sang about. It was the hollow void I felt in a crowded room, but somehow forgot when Noah was near. Damn him for taking a nip out of my heart when I preferred it safely packed in ice.

My arms wrapped around his shoulder as he walked me backward toward the bed. His fingers caught the hem of my dress and lifted, leaving me in four-inch heels, my panties, and bra. His fingers laced with mine as he lowered me to the mattress. He unbuttoned his shirt and tossed it aside and covered me like a blanket.

"Do you want champagne?"

"I want you." The words fell out without thought, so unguarded I nearly flinched at their accuracy.

As he lifted my arms over my head and kissed down my front, I stretched beneath him, not protesting the pose. His fingers pulled at the hip of my panties but didn't lower them.

The soft churn of ice caught my ear, and I hissed as cool water trailed over my breasts and down my stomach. His mouth licked as thin rivulets formed tributaries at my ribs and I shivered.

He dampened the front of my bra, the ice chip melting between the heat of his fingers, rolling over my skin. His teeth closed over the hard point, and I pressed against his mouth, silently begging for more.

He reached into the ice bucket again, this time swirling a puddle at my belly button. Lower and lower he teased, over the silk of my panties until my chilled clit was swollen and begging for more.

He sat up and unbuckled his belt, sliding it slowly through his belt loops and letting it coil on the bed beside my hip. The cork popped, and sweet-scented mist fizzed into the air. He took a sip from the bottle, and I gasped as he trickled some over my hips, soaking my panties and thighs.

He knelt with his knees outside of my calves, his hands at each hip as his mouth sipped through the silk covering my pussy. I moaned and rocked into him.

Pulling both sides lower, he slipped my panties off my hips, dragging them down to my knees. His hand twisted, pulling the wet silk tight and binding my thighs.

More champagne spilled across my hips, gently fizzing and tickling as it touched my skin. He drank from the puddle at the V of my clamped thighs and pussy.

His mouth lowered and he pulled back my folds, exposing my clit, his blue eyes watching mine as he teased me with only the tip of his tongue. My body throbbed, and I wiggled, but he twisted the panties tighter around my knees. His lips curled as a warm breath ghosted over my pulsing sex.

He squeezed a finger between my folds, not penetrating, but teasing. The upward glide had me moaning and, when he slid that tapered digit down again, I was begging. "Please..."

"Patience."

He reached for the belt and wrapped it around my thighs, cinching it tight and locking it in place. My legs were sandwiched together so tight he'd never get his finger in there, let alone his dick. I frowned because it all seemed rather counterintuitive.

With my legs locked in some sort of mermaid bondage, he slid my panties off and reached for my hands.

Balling the fabric up, he folded the red silk into my palm, closing my fingers tightly around it. "Hold that. Don't let go."

My fist tightened around the panties as he stood and removed the rest of his clothes. Here I was, holding my panties, tied up with a belt around my thighs, wound tight enough for my skin to plump around the leather, and my bra still on. Oh, and I was soaked and shivering from a champagne tongue bath. Definitely a first.

His arms slid under my knees and my back as he adjusted me and then moved me again. He seemed to have a plan in his head and wanted to get it just right.

"Should I keep my hands up here?"

"Yes. I want to be able to see them." He crawled over my body, pulling down the cups of my bra, so my tits were semi-held in place. He brushed the tip of his dick to my nipple, a smear of pre-come trailing behind.

"I'm going to fuck your mouth, and you're going to drop your panties if it's too much. Understand? If I see the red of your panties, I stop."

My thighs, although locked together, pressed tighter. "I understand."

"Open your mouth."

I opened, and he didn't hesitate, sliding to the back of my throat until my shoulders tensed.

"Relax your throat. Don't fight it."

I tried to relax, and he sank in again, his hand catching his weight on the bed. I moaned around his length.

His hips cocked back and thrust deep, gagging me, but there wasn't time to pause. He moved like a professional dancer, pressing into my mouth with rapid strokes and panting at the strenuous way he held his body over me.

"Goddamn, your mouth feels incredible." His strokes slowed as he savored the delicate curling motion of my tongue. "Moan. I want to hear you."

I let out a small sound that took on the pattern of his thrusts. That only egged him on. The faster he moved, the less he penetrated, but it was a lot to manage. My eyes were watering, and my nose inhaled his intense scent with each rapid breath. Saliva built and there was no time to swallow.

I should have felt dehumanized, meaningless. But the sounds streaming from him kept those ugly feelings at bay. He gasped and panted, plunging over my tongue as I clenched those red panties tight in my fist.

"Look at me."

I forced my stare upward, eyes wide.

"So fucking sexy. I can smell your pussy. Sucking my cock makes you wet, and I love it. You're gonna be soaked when I finally work my way down there."

I moaned, and he slowed, taking careful strokes over my tongue.

"Tighten your lips, Avery. Suck me hard. The tighter your lips, the more I know you want me."

Lifting my head, I pulled my lips tight, and he shivered, his body shifting his weight to his legs as he cupped the back of my head.

"Keep looking at me."

My eyes watered and my lashes fluttered, but I held his stare, certain my face was flushed, and my lips were swollen.

"So fucking sexy."

His fingers sifted through my tangled hair as he pulled my face to him, stuffing my mouth with his cock until my shoulders tensed. He slid free, and I gasped for air.

"Do you want to stop? Is it too much?"

I blinked up at him, unsure why or how I was so turned on by this, but I was. I was sopping wet. Jesus, no one ever did this to me before—not the way he was doing it. I wasn't blowing him. He was fucking my mouth. And I liked it. It was as if I wasn't there. Or I was, but he needed me like this in this moment, for his pleasure. And dear God, did I want to please him.

Perhaps there was a zip of panic that my dominant nature had gone dormant, but it was so small and slight I hardly felt anything beyond the dark desire to please. What the hell was happening to me? A stranger was suddenly running the show in my head, controlling my body. And I liked the way she drove.

Blinking up at him, I rasped, "More."

His hand tightened in my hair, and he impaled me, holding my face tight to his pelvic bone as he groaned.

"I think you have a dirty side I like. I think you like it, too." The fist in my hair tightened, jerking me back. "Can I call you my dirty little slut, Avery?"

Fuck. Never agree to anything in the throes of passion. That was rule number one about sex. "Yes."

"Tell me who you are."

"I'm your dirty little slut."

"Show me."

I angled forward, mouth open wide and his fist tightened, preventing me from closing the distance. I whimpered, delirious with wanting him.

"What does my dirty little slut want?"

"Your cock."

"Beg me for it."

"Please give me your cock, Noah. I want you to fuck my mouth like a dirty slut."

"Goddamn." He shoved his dick in my mouth and jerked my head up and down, grinding into my lips and growling out a stream of filthy words. It was ... strangely empowering.

My fingers tightened around the panties, and my lips formed an airtight seal as he plunged in and out of my mouth. My scalp tingled as he pumped my mouth over his drilling cock. My arms moved, but I held the panties, sure to not let any red show.

"I need to see your hand, Avery."

I extended my arm, so it rested in his view. My other hand curled around his hip, my fingernails digging into his skin. He ripped his dick from my mouth, and I gasped, catching my breath. I looked up at him, unsure why he stopped.

"Lick your fingers."

I frowned but did as he asked—what he *told* me to do...

He shoved his dick back into my mouth, holding my hair tightly as he pressed to the back of my throat and stilled. My wet fingers tightened on his hip as my eyes leaked. He caught my hand on his hip and dragged it to his ass.

Suddenly, he released my hair. My head dropped back to the bed, and I panted. He didn't give me much time to catch my breath.

Back in, fucking deep to the back of my throat, he moved my hand again, this time to his crack.

"Do it."

My eyes flashed wide, my breath coming so quickly I wasn't sure I heard him correctly. He rose up on his knees, his cock still in my mouth, his hand braced on the headboard.

"I said, do it."

He *wanted* me to finger him? My touch slipped down the seam of his ass and pressed on his puckered flesh.

He grunted and slowed his thrusts. "All the way in."

Seemed there were two dirty sluts here tonight.

I pressed, and he let out a guttural moan, his body trembling as he sank his cock deep. I withdrew by the slightest degree and pressed in again. His thrusts slowed, and his moans intensified the longer I fingered him. It was evident how much pleasure he drew from my touch there, but also how new this experience was for him.

His motions turned jerky, and he withdrew his cock from my mouth. "Enough."

I removed my finger and waited, unsure if something was wrong. "Noah?"

"Just a second."

He climbed off the bed and reached into a drawer. He tossed a few condoms on the sheets and a bottle of lube.

"Lift up your legs."

I lifted my bound legs, and he rested my ankles on one shoulder. The sound of foil tearing mingled with his heavy breathing. Then he was pressing my legs back until my knees were at my chest, and his cock was seeking the slightest entrance between my clamped thighs. He nudged my pussy, wet with arousal and glided home.

The fit was incredibly tight. I wasn't sure how he was managing, but he made it work, squeezing in and out in quick, deep strokes. He used my body like a toy for his pleasure, and I let him. I wasn't Avery Johansson tonight. I was Noah Wolfe's dirty little slut.

Our cries of pleasure beat against the silence, dominating every other sense. It was all pleasure. Raw, unrefined pleasure.

His hips bucked faster, and his body shook. His spine jerked, and his eyes rolled shut in a magnificent show of male ecstasy. I knew I'd given him everything he wanted. Somehow that equated to me getting what I wanted, too. But I wasn't sure how.

The belt loosened, and my legs fanned apart. My pussy was swollen and throbbing, and my heart pounded in an erratic beat. He stripped away the condom and rolled to his back, cupping my head and pulling me to rest my cheek on his abs.

I let go of the panties, not sure I needed to hold them anymore, and kissed his stomach. He groaned and ran a hand through my hair. I kissed the top of his softening cock and shifted lower, my hands gently massaging and cupping his balls.

I thought about how he took care of me the other night, worshipped my body, laving kisses all over my tender flesh long after I came. I wanted to give him the same satisfaction, so I crawled between his legs and licked every curve of him.

He watched me without saying a word. I tended to his body, and then I came back to what he'd wanted earlier, realizing the lube might have been for him.

"Can I see that bottle?"

His gaze lifted to my face, held, and then he nudged the bottle within my reach, not saying a word. I massaged the oil into my hands, coated my fingers, and looked at him.

"Do you want me to?"

His feet parted, and his knees lifted. I reached beneath his heavy sack and massaged, stroking, and gently probing. The lube made a huge difference, and the moment I sank into him, he moaned.

His cock twitched and started to swell as I slowly pumped my finger in and out. The edge was off, and our pace had slowed substantially. I tried for another finger, and he tensed.

"It's okay. I won't hurt you."

He nodded tightly, and his body visibly relaxed. My mouth lowered to the root of his cock, kissing, licking, and whispering words of praise.

He was thick and swollen by the time I was pumping my fingers easily. I stroked him slowly with my fist, watching him come to terms with the visible pleasure he was deriving from this.

There seemed a silent handoff of power, as graceful as Olympian athletes pass a torch. This time, there was no struggle or argument, only acceptance. I surrendered to him, thereby earning some of his trust, and he proved he could surrender to me in return. It was a breathtaking give and take, one I'd never experienced before.

"Come for me, Noah."

My fingers teased deep, and he arched and moaned, come erupting over my fingers in ribbons of pearl as his body bowed beneath my touch.

His weight dropped to the bed, and I removed my hand, nestling alongside him and smiling against his ribs. A few nights ago, he flipped out when I touched him there. Now, he was practically begging for it and coming on command.

Somehow, we figured out a way to both get exactly what we

wanted. And while I'd had previous lovers who allowed me to play to my proclivities' delight, this was the first time I felt this sort of intimacy with a man.

I ... liked it. I could even come to ... love it. *Be still my cold, twisted heart. Be still.*

31

AVERY

I *definitely* had a boyfriend.

Sort of.

Maybe.

Every day that I got home from class, there was a surprise waiting at my door. Sometimes it was something as sweet as a single, long stem rose, but other times it was something clever, like the copy of the Kama Sutra with highlighted passages and notes telling me to pencil him into my schedule and to stretch.

My favorite surprise was a burned CD. Inside the case, he drew a picture of a house with two hearts. In marker, the CD simply said, *PLAY ME.*

I popped it into my laptop and smiled as Harry Styles *Sweet Creature* played. It immediately became my favorite song. *Our* song.

I loved the lyrics. Two hearts in one home, arguing and making it hard. Being drawn to a place by another person...

Every day I left campus, my steps quickened at the thought of Noah. My apartment no longer seemed like a place I leased. It felt like a home. It was a strange notion, being that even Blackwater hadn't felt like more than a shelter after a lifetime of living there.

Blackwater would always be a mistake I'd been born into. It would never be my home.

At night, before my appointments, we'd share a quick meal, usually at his place because I didn't cook. Then, as soon as I wrapped up with my clients, he was there, carrying me to his bed or mine.

There was no balance, no structure. There was no decided bottom or a top. It was whatever it had to be in that moment, whatever one of us needed. And whoever needed it most usually got their way. Strangely, that seemed to work for us.

It had only been a week since the tension broke and we could be ourselves without wanting to freak out on the other, but it was an incredible week, the sort of week that made you lose sight of reality and wonder if you ever had to live in the real world again.

I wanted to stay tucked away in our cozy world forever, where the snow kept us in, and Winston kept others out. But life still found a way to intrude.

My mother was out of money again, and that meant my phone was ringing nonstop. When I finally got back to her, she was impatient for an excuse as to why I'd been avoiding her.

"I've been busy, Mom."

"Do you think I was born under the stupid tree, Avery Dean? You're shirkin' your responsibilities and I ain't had heat since the boiler went last Tuesday."

"Did you have someone come look at it? Maybe you're just out of fuel."

"It ain't the fuel. I had a man out yesterday. He says the whole thing's shot and I need a new one."

"How much does that cost?"

"Two grand."

"*What?* Mom, I don't have that kind of money. I just paid my tuition, and I need to save for student teaching."

"School before family?"

"It's my internship. I have a commute now, and I need a ton of supplies, including an iPad—"

"Oh, well, don't let my need for heat and hot water get in the way of your fancy techy needs."

"These are requirements. I can't help what they tell me to get."

"Avery Dean, you figure out a way to get me that money before my toes fall off and my hair catches a squirrel because it's so filthy. Or so help me Jesus, I'll take a bus to Philadelphia and come stay with you until the weather breaks."

"No, don't do that." My mother absolutely could *not* come here. "I'll figure out a way to get the money. I just need a few days. I'll get it."

"I can't go another week like this, Avery. I'm lucky the pipes haven't burst."

"I'll figure something out."

After the conversation with my mother, I was so distracted I could barely focus on my studies. I was supposed to be writing up my first lesson plans and researching the staff at the school so I'd remember everyone's names, but I was consumed by anxious worry that my mother might show up on my doorstep uninvited.

I wasn't a terrible person. But my mother had a way of making everything about her and nothing about me. If she came here...

I just couldn't let that happen. She'd see how I was living and feel entitled to everything I owned. She'd never return to Blackwater and having her close would feel like an albatross around my neck.

She embarrassed me too many times for me to trust her in the vicinity of my clients. Micah wouldn't know what to make of her. And Noah... I couldn't bear the thought of him seeing anything or anyone associated with my past in Blackwater.

I needed to get that money, and I needed it in as soon as possible. Hating that I had to dig to the bottom of the barrel for a solution, I called my least favorite client, Don, but he didn't answer.

"Hey, Don, it's Avery. I haven't heard from you in a few weeks. I was wondering if you had plans tomorrow night. Call me."

When he didn't call, I left another message. He usually got right back to me. He was the only client that I could wheedle a few grand out of in a matter of hours and not feel guilty for taking advantage of him because he was a gross, old pervert. Exactly why he wasn't one of my regulars.

By Friday, when Don still hadn't called back, I started to panic. I wasted so much time banking on the fastest solution and blew my chances to earn money in other ways. The weekend was here, and I had nothing.

"Fuck!" I tossed my phone onto my lesson plans as I got Don's voicemail again. Why wasn't he returning my calls?

My mom had left six more messages that day, each one promising that she'd be on a bus to Philly if the money wasn't on its way by Monday. I called Don again.

"Hello?"

Caught off guard by the female voice, I stilled.

"Hello? Who is this?" the voice repeated.

"Is ... Don there?"

There was a strange pause. "How did you know my dad?"

My stomach twisted as too many realizations bombarded me at once. One, I never wanted to picture Don's children or speak to them. Two, why was this woman speaking in the past tense? I knew why. On our last date, Don could barely cross a room without getting winded.

Oh God... He was dead, and I couldn't do more than sit there in silence.

"Hello? I know you're there. I can hear you breathing."

I hung up the phone.

Should I cry? Was there something wrong with me for not crying? My only regret was the loss of income his death caused. What kind of fucked up person thought like that?

Me. I thought like that. Don was my last resort, the one person I always felt better than even when things were at the worst, and I shamefully posed like a teenage girl as his fat, sausage figures snapped pictures and he panted.

God, I knew he masturbated to those pictures, and I didn't care. I just wanted his money. Even Micah didn't know how low I'd go when in a pinch and now I was out of options and probably crossing a line into that of a sociopath because I felt no grief over his actual death.

How could I when I was still panicked my mom would show up? I needed to do something.

Rubbing my head, I reached for my phone and dialed the only other person who might give me that kind of money, but it wasn't the same as asking for it from Don. Don was gross. With him, I knew I earned every nasty penny. But asking Micah…

Micah already did so much for me. My debt to him was becoming top heavy, and my simple services no longer felt reciprocal to the many luxuries he provided. It was wrong to ask for more than he already offered, and I hated taking advantage of his generosity.

I sent him an email asking for him to call me when he had a free minute. My phone rang ten minutes later.

"Avery? You sounded upset in your email."

"I'm in trouble."

"What kind of trouble?"

"Financial trouble. I didn't know who else to go to, and I need a lot of money fast."

"How much?"

"Two thousand dollars. Maybe more. I'm not really sure."

"That's nothing to get upset over, love." My phone pinged. "I've just sent twenty-five hundred to your account."

My eyes closed, but the relief was bitter. "I'll pay you back. We can work out a trade or—"

"Stop. That's not how this works. I'm sure you need the money, and I hate to hear you upset. Is it family?"

He had a very sketchy picture of my background but knew enough about my circumstances to discern I was running away from something. "Yes."

"Is everyone okay?"

"They will be now."

"Take care of things, Avery. See that they get what they need, but perhaps tell them this is the last time. You work too hard to take responsibility for those who aren't there for you."

"I know. But it's … complicated."

"You have such an empathetic streak." If only he knew the real me, the side that didn't show emotion over death and acted like an absolute sociopath. "It's your nature to want to take care of others."

Was it? Or was that who Micah thought I was? The role I played for him?

I wanted *someone* to know the real me but still believed anyone would be repulsed by what they found. There was simply too much truth in my past, and I didn't want those secrets tarnishing my future. It would always be better to keep the carefully fabricated illusion in place instead of facing reality when it came to my background. Believing that allowed me to fall into my usual role.

"You always take care of me," I whispered, realizing I couldn't risk losing him right now.

"Until the day you no longer let me, Avery. That's a promise. Let's have dinner tonight."

I was supposed to watch a movie with Noah, but after Micah bailed me out, I didn't have the heart to tell him no. "I'd love to."

After thanking Micah again, I made a call to alert my mother that I had the money. A few more calls and an appointment was set to replace her old boiler. Unfortunate didn't begin to explain my disappointment that someone needed to be present for the installation, and a clear path was required to deliver the appliance and remove the old one. Despite all my efforts to resolve this and keep my hands clean, I was going to have to go home this weekend.

By the time Noah got home from work, I was drained and fighting a headache, but I forced myself to go to his place and break our plans in person.

When I told him I had to cancel our plans, he was pissed. I figured he would be, but not to such an extent.

"It's Friday. We had a date."

"We were watching a movie in your living room."

"It's still a date."

"Well, I have to work."

He scowled. "So you're breaking our date to go out with someone else."

"Noah."

He held out his hands. "What's going on, Avery?"

I didn't want to explain all the details of my shitty family life to him and the hoops I had to jump through just to pretend my situation was normal. "Nothing. God, can you just give me one night to myself without making it about you." Okay, that might have been too far. "I'm sorry—"

He held up his hands and took a step back, literally backing off. "Go. Go do your *job*, Avery. It is what it is." He loosened his tie and tossed it on the counter.

"Don't say it like that. I need money, Noah. I have to live."

He reached into his pocket and pulled out a wad of cash, flicking bills onto the granite countertop. Glaring at me, he snapped, "How much do I have to pay to get a Friday night with you? One hundred? Two?"

I drew back as if he'd slapped me. The pile accumulated. Twenties. Fifties. Each one a filthy insult that cut like a razor blade into my heart.

I shoved the money off the counter. *"Fuck you!"*

"Like that's ever going to happen when you pass your weekends with other men!"

"Oh, like you never get a shot at me on any other day of the week! What the hell is wrong with you tonight?"

"I don't want you going out with other men!"

"Well, it's my fucking job, so too bad!"

His eyes darkened, his breath quickening. That familiar predatory gleam flashed in his eye, and he reached for me.

I lurched back. "Don't even try it."

The jerk just threw money at me and made me feel like a common whore. There was no way he was touching me. I pivoted and marched out of his kitchen.

"Avery, wait!"

"Screw you, asshole." I kept walking, and he didn't cross the hall after me.

My fury didn't subside as I put on my makeup to get ready for my date with Micah. Then I had to do it all over again because my rage somehow morphed into tears. All I could picture was Noah tossing money at me. How could he insult me like that? Judge me?

When Micah arrived, I did my best to hide my emotions, but he always watched me a little too closely. The best I could do was lie and make him think my mood had to do with my family problems.

We had a quiet dinner on the Moshulu and then caught a winter concert in Penn's Landing. By the time we made it back to my building, I was frozen to the bone and ready to curl into bed until Sunday.

Micah walked me up while Winston kept an eye on his car. I was glad he hadn't parked because I couldn't deal with any decision-making or pressure tonight.

When we reached my door, he took my key and opened the lock. "I think you need a weekend to yourself, love. Some time to think about your situation and where you want to be in a few months."

I definitely needed to start thinking about that. It was almost February, and it would be May before I knew it.

"I think you're right."

He smiled, and I stilled, not used to seeing his face wearing any sort of telling expression. "Sweet dreams, Avery."

"Goodnight, Micah."

He leaned down, and I assumed he would press a kiss to my cheek or brush one across my mouth, but as his full lips closed over mine, I sucked in a sharp breath, and he took my surprise as an invitation to deepen the kiss, pulling my body into his and pressing a hand to my lower back.

The door across the hall crashed open, and I flinched, jerking out of Micah's arms.

"What. The. Fuck?"

"Noah," I gasped, wanted to explain that I hadn't asked him to kiss me, but unable to find the words.

He seethed in his doorway, shoulders heaving and fists clenched at his sides. "She say you could fucking touch her?"

Micah faced him and adjusted his cufflinks, his face a composed mask of indifference. "I think you should go back where you came from, boy."

"I'm not your fucking boy, and she's not your fucking girl."

"Noah, stop!"

"Avery, shut up!"

Micah stepped in front of me, and his voice boomed, "You'll want to apologize to her right now."

"How about I call the cops and have your ass thrown out of here."

Micah chuckled. "That might be interesting. Give them a call."

"You think I won't?"

"No, I believe you're ignorant enough to do something like that. Not much they can do, being as it's my building."

My gaze jerked to Micah, but he wasn't looking at me. He owned the building? I thought he just rented my apartment.

This new information didn't appear to deter Noah's anger. "Then maybe I'll drag you out of here myself."

Micah took a quick step forward. "Go ahead and try. I'll have you on the ground before you get one hand on me."

Noah roared and barreled forward.

I screamed, jumping back and covering my mouth as Micah moved so fast I heard the clash of their bodies. The terrible smash of flesh hitting flesh and pained grunts filled the hall.

"Stop it!"

Noah's body flung against the wall hard enough that the lights in the antique sconces flickered, his eyes unfocused as he slid to the ground.

Oh, my God, he went down like a sack of rocks.

"What did you do?" I ran to Noah, trying to get his eyes to focus on me. I cupped his jaw and glared at Micah. "Why did you do that?"

"I warned him." He gave his sleeve a negligent tug.

Disappointment welled in my chest, competing with the ache of concern for Noah. The Micah I knew would *never* overreact like that. I brushed a shaky hand across Noah's brow, lifting his hair so I could see his eyes.

"Noah, look at me. Open your eyes."

Blood coated his teeth as he blinked up at me. "You ... kissed him."

I shook my head, but I couldn't deny the accusations. I knew I didn't start it, but that was a stupid technicality, and I could have stopped it the second I realized what was happening. Instead, I let it happen.

"I'm sorry."

"Avery, you should go inside," Micah's voice was cold and absolute.

I turned and scowled. "No. You can leave."

He stilled and raised a brow. "Think before you speak, Avery."

I suddenly felt like a child with absolutely no power. I looked down at Noah. His gaze heavy, a blood vessel bursting into the white of his eye.

Shifting to sit up, he winced and cradled his ribs. "Don't listen to him, Avery. Don't let him tell you what to do."

"*Avery*." Micah's tone grew impatient.

"I just want to get him away from you," I whispered. "Then I'll come back."

"If you go with him, he wins."

He'd already won. Noah was on the floor. How had things taken such a turn so fast? My vision blurred as I blinked down at him, truly regretting that he was on the floor after trying to defend my honor. I had no honor.

"I'm sorry."

He shut his eyes, his face pinching in obvious pain. He grabbed my wrist as I moved to stand. "Make him leave."

I glanced back at Micah, who wore a look of displeasure. "Get off the floor, Avery."

Micah wouldn't leave until he saw me safely in my apartment, and Noah gone. Everything inside of me wanted to stay with Noah and make sure he was okay. His eye was bleeding, and he might have a concussion. This was all my fault.

I looked back at Micah again and wondered what he would do if I told him to go. He was angry and the longer I crouched in front of the man who just tried to attack him, the more his irritation showed.

He'd bailed me out today. I lived in his apartment, his building.

My entire wardrobe was his doing, from the pins in my hair to the designer shoes on my feet. It was supposed to be for my independence, but I never felt more indebted to someone in my life.

I shut my eyes, forcing my tears away. "Noah… I have to go with him. I'll come take care of you as soon as he—"

A pained chuckle rumbled in his chest where his arm cradled his ribs. "Do you know the story of the scorpion and the frog?"

"What?" He was delirious.

"The scorpion and the frog. The scorpion asks the frog for a ride across the river and promises not to sting the frog. Halfway there the scorpion stings the frog, and the frog begins to drown. Just before he draws his last breath, he looks up at the scorpion he trusted and asks *why*. The scorpion replies, *it's my nature*."

"Why are you telling me this?"

"Because I should have known better." He gave up trying to sit up and slouched against the wall.

Chills crawled over my limbs. Was I the scorpion? Some horrible little creature that couldn't be trusted?

He shut his eyes. "Your *date's* waiting."

Noah rolled to his feet and grunted, taking three unsteady steps to his door and leaving me confused, on my knees. He didn't look back, and Micah didn't help me up.

When Noah's door closed, I just stared at it. So many men in my life, yet I never felt more unloved or unlovable.

"Avery, get up off the floor and come inside."

I shook my head, my heart hardening and cracking like ice. "I can't … be around you right now, Micah. I need you to leave."

"Avery, this isn't how we behave. This isn't how *you* behave. Get up off the floor."

I blinked up at him, and a tear fell from my lashes. "You beat up my friend."

"That man is not your friend." He stepped closer and held out a hand. "Come on, love. I'll take you inside."

But Noah *was* my friend. He cared about me. He left me funny little love notes and flowers. We danced in the snow and made love on a bed of roses. He understood me. Maybe a little too well.

And then he called me a scorpion.

I shut my eyes and slid my hand into Micah's as he pulled me off the ground. Was that what I was? Poisonous? Toxic? Was that why I had no friends and why my siblings all left and never called to see if I was okay?

Maybe Noah was right, and this was my nature. Maybe that's why Micah seemed so certain people like me were better off contracting their relationships rather than trying to form organic ones.

I couldn't afford to burn another bridge. I stood and brushed the dust off the hem of my dress. I glanced at the floor. "My purse?"

"I have it." Micah put an arm around me and escorted me inside.

It seemed natural to simply shut off. The reality was too sharp and could only bear a dull throb right now, or I'd crack. Lowering my gaze to the floor, I followed him inside.

32

AVERY

I stared at my lap as Micah ran water in my kitchen. My stomach swirled with a nasty mix of fear and self-loathing. Noah was across the hall, bloody and furious. And I was here—with Micah.

He called me a scorpion, one of the most duplicitous creatures on this earth. A venomous, arachnid predator, so married to its nature, it was doomed to live a life barren of friendship.

I glanced up as Micah's tailored pants filled my view. Dressed in a designer suit, dark skin pampered to perfection, he did not look like the lethal weapon that emerged only minutes ago when Noah charged at him. The man didn't have a scratch on him, yet Noah could barely open his eyes.

He settled across from me, lowering his weight onto the coffee table. "Your makeup's running."

I blinked as he gently angled my chin and traced a warm, wet washcloth across my cheek. His touch was tender, nurturing, and so contrary to the man he was a few minutes ago.

"There are people in our lives, Avery..." He tucked a strand of hair behind my ear and continued to wash away my ruined makeup. "... who we feel an attachment to, but need to cut off for our own good."

He could be referring to Noah or my mother. Both had drained my emotional reservoir. My mother's demand for money was infuriating, mostly because I went through hell to help her so many times and she couldn't even spare a thank you.

But Noah … that look in his eyes as he turned away from me five minutes ago… It depleted something inside of me, something I was already low on and needed very much.

Micah's dark eyes looked into mine, always so patient and guiding. They were wise eyes.

"I know it's hard to cut people out, Avery. I have friends from the Badlands, friends I've known since childhood and loved very much, but it's for my own good that I don't see them anymore."

The Badlands were in North Philly, between Kensington and Broad and not a place anyone wanted to get stranded. An open-air drug market, segmented by dingy buildings, streets covered in litter, and abandoned lots people now overlooked like birthmarks. Even sunlight was sparse on the Badlands, as the rails ran overhead casting shadows in the day and whining with the constant rattle and screech of trains.

Micah didn't look like a person who belonged there. He looked like the shiny politician that promised to clean up the community. But no politician had made that failing vow in a long time. Many believed the Badlands were unsalvageable. It seemed Micah felt the same, lumping the people and the place into one.

"Did you live there?"

"Until I was seventeen. One day, I woke up and decided I could leave and find a better life or stay and die in a place where life seems impossible, and death is so common it's often overlooked. I wanted to mean something in this world, so I packed a bag and got as far as I could. I had a few dollars on me, but not enough to rent a room or take a cab. I slept on the streets for a bit. I did some unsavory things to make money. But by the time I was twenty-four, that kid I left behind was gone. I don't think about him much. I no longer resemble him or recognize him as me. And I certainly have no desire to revisit the world he left behind. But I didn't just abandon my home. I lost some people I loved. I had no choice. If I wanted to get out permanently, I had to make that the final goodbye."

"Are you telling me this because of the money I borrowed?"

Micah knew very little about my upbringing in Blackwater, but he knew enough to recognize the similarities in our backgrounds.

"You didn't borrow that money, Avery. I gave it to you, and I don't want you bringing it up again. Understand?"

I nodded even if I didn't fully agree. That money went beyond our agreement. But that had been a situation I couldn't resolve on my own. It humiliated me to ask him, but, as always, he was a gentleman.

"I'm telling you this because you have a good heart. That's going to get you in trouble if you don't stick to your plan. You have less than one semester left. The world is about to open up to you. I've watched you recreate yourself for three years. You're not that mousey girl from Blackwater anymore. Avery Mudd is gone. You're Avery Johansson now, a woman who knows the taste of fine champagne, the feel of Egyptian sheets, and all the luxuries she deserves. Look around. *This* is who you are. Don't tie yourself to those who can't fathom how far you've come."

My brow pinched as my gaze skated over the crown moldings and granite countertops. Yes, Avery Johansson earned all of this. But Avery Dean Mudd lived here too.

She was the uncultured, little girl who dressed up in high heels and fancy clothes and pretended to be someone better when no one important was looking. Avery Mudd wasn't a woman at all, just a scared little girl wishing to be loved.

Noah didn't love me. He liked fucking me. I liked fucking him, too, so it worked. But he was my friend—*had* been. As much as I didn't want him to see who I was hiding inside, a part of me wished for the courage to show him. The fear of losing him held me back. But that wasn't an issue anymore.

Just like I warned, he drew a line in the sand and made me choose between him and work. He didn't realize how much I was indebted and that I couldn't simply walk away. Maybe I was the fool for thinking I was in control of my life.

Every thought of him hurt my heart until the pressure in my chest became unbearable. "If you mean Noah, I don't think he'll be interfering in my life after what just happened."

"He'll be back—once his ego heals. But this time don't be so quick to let him in, Avery. Sometimes detours only lead to trouble."

I had some decisions to make. Micah had been patient since making his offer, but he wouldn't tolerate being put off for another man, especially one I had an emotional involvement with. And if Noah was right and I was just a scorpion, maybe the wisest thing I could do would be to take Micah up on his offer.

I suddenly felt exhausted and defeated. All of this time, I kept telling myself a respectable career, and honest income would change who I was, but maybe nothing could. Switching my name from Mudd to Johansson certainly hadn't erased any secrets. It merely hid them.

Micah knew me better than most, and he was willing to overlook my past, perhaps because he had a tarnished history as well. Maybe we were better suited for each other than we realized, two hardened scorpions pretending to be civilized. At least with him, I'd know I was safe. I trusted our agreement, and if I took up his offer, I never had to fear being alone.

He took my hands in his, and I braced for the hard truth I sensed coming. "To him, you're a plaything, a hobby. When you give away something of value for free, it becomes a little less precious each day. He's young and handsome, and I'm sure charming on some level, but he's temporary, Avery. Don't let one transient relationship derail your path when you've come this far. Stay focused on the goal, and you'll get everything you ever wanted."

My chest constricted. Everything Noah and I shared turned to ash the moment he looked up at me with blood in his eye and called me a scorpion.

My head lowered as I blinked back tears, refusing to let them fall in Micah's presence. "You're right. I need to concentrate on graduating and start thinking about where I go from here."

"There's the smart woman I know." He lifted my chin, his eyes watchful. "The ache's temporary, love. You'll see." He kissed my fingertips and stood. "I'm going to say goodnight now."

I stood and followed him to the door. I wasn't going back in the hall, but there was a sort of protocol Micah, and I shared. I still had to honor that.

I walked him to the door. "Good night, Micah."

He brushed a finger down my cheek and stared into my eyes. "We were interrupted earlier, so I'm going to give this another try. Stay still." His head lowered and breath held in my lungs as his warm lips pressed into mine.

It was a soft kiss, sensual and slow, his full lips teasing in a way that differed from what I was used to. This was a new side to us, something that started after he mentioned renegotiating our association post-graduation—something I still struggled to accept.

He pulled away, and my eyes blinked open, too preoccupied with other thoughts to notice any flutters or chills such a kiss should have created.

"Good night, Avery." He let himself out, and I hung by the door.

When I heard the elevator come and go, I peeked into the hallway. Noah's door was shut, no light shining from beneath.

33

AVERY

The bitter wind cut through my clothes as I stood outside of the place I'd grown up—the place that never fit the word *home*. The ransacked yard wore a dusty scruff of brown grass and frosted leaves. Faded, broken lanterns hung like ghosts of merrier times, relics that were once colorful, now a bleak reminder that nothing exciting happened here anymore.

I tightened my arms, not ready to go inside. Cars filled every sanded drive like blemished trophies that no longer served a purpose. The majority of folks in Blackwater were unemployed with nowhere to go.

Bare trees curled like talons, reaching as if they, too, wanted to get out. But people from Blackwater rarely escaped. I was one of the few exceptions.

Breath formed a cloud of vapor in front of my face as I proceeded to the door. The rattle of daytime television penetrated the thin windows. My worn key turned in the lock, and I shut my eyes, bracing for the unwelcome reality on the other side.

The rancid scent of unwashed laundry battled the stale stench of cigarette smoke. My mother, buried in a mix of laundry and blankets, snored on the couch. Plates and paperwork covered the coffee table.

The carpet had a few new stains, but the old ones were mostly covered by boxes of God knows what.

A talk show played on the dated television set, the screen scrambling every other second. Not finding the chill I expected, I moved toward the kitchen.

"Jesus." My disgust cranked another notch higher.

Dried macaroni, crumbs, and other grime coated the small counter. Unwashed pots and pans were pushed to the back of the stove, a different color film on the inside of each one. I tried not to look in the corners, certain I'd find mouse shit mixing with crumbs.

Shaking my head, I shut the oven door, which was where the heat was coming from and turned the dial to OFF. She was going to burn the place down.

Dropping my bag on the only chair that wasn't covered with crap, I scanned the trailer, knowing I couldn't let anyone see her living this way—not even the fuel company scheduled to come out with the replacement boiler. I had a little over two hours to clean this place up and about four years of filth to disinfect.

I searched the cabinets for trash bags and any cleaning products I could find. The sink was overflowing with crusty dishes, the stench of rotting food so thick it burned my sinuses and turned my stomach. I dumped several plates of rotting food, wrappers, brimming ashtrays, and soiled tissues into the bag, which was soon full.

I feared what I might find in the bathroom and bedrooms. This was never going to get clean in two hours. Tying off the garbage, I tossed it out the front door and didn't care when it slammed shut.

My mother stirred and grunted. "Avery Dean? What are you doin' here?"

"I came to see that your boiler was installed."

She sat up, her hair so thin I could see her scalp and her clothing wrinkled and stained. "You got me a boiler?"

"I told you I did." It wasn't like I had a choice. Now if I could just tell her this was the end of my taking care of her. But something held my tongue.

I didn't have thousands of dollars lying around, and I couldn't keep doing this. Asking Micah for help was more than I could stomach. I hated debt, especially the sort people wouldn't let you pay back, the sort of debt you could never quite calculate in terms of a loan.

I grimaced as she leaned forward and sipped from a random cup on the table. "They're coming in two hours, Momma. We need to clean up this pigsty."

She rubbed her eyes and yawned, showing a gaping hole of stained teeth and gums. "Let me find my teeth."

The sight of her fishing dentures out of a coffee mug and popping them into her mouth was enough to make me gag. I looked away in disgust, swamped by the overwhelming urge to run out of there.

"How are you living in this filth, Mom?"

She scoffed. "Don't you come home—first time in almost four years—and judge me. I don't got no one here to help with things."

"It's just you. How can one person make such a mess? You can't keep bringing junk home."

"Avery Dean, if you think I'm gonna be criticized in my own house, you got another think coming." She reached under the coffee table and lifted what looked like a dead rodent, placing the ratty, old wig on her head. "How long's this gonna take? I didn't get much sleep last night."

"Cleaning or the installation? One should only take an hour or so." I counted nine overflowing boxes of crap in the living room alone. "Cleaning could take weeks."

She stood and grumbled something about needing coffee.

I followed her to the kitchen and watched in disgust as coffee grounds spilled onto the counter. She made no move to clean them up. Not like it mattered.

When she went to use the bathroom, I got to work. I shoved everything out of the way and set out—what I hoped was—a clean dishtowel and started washing. As I heard her return, I said, "Start bringing me dishes."

"I haven't had my coffee yet."

"Well, you can bring me dishes while it's brewing. We don't have a lot of time."

"Lord knows you probably gotta rush out of here soon as they're done," she grumbled, collecting plates and cups off the counter.

The cabinets were mostly empty, so, once I dusted out the crumbs, I started stacking clean dishes in there. More trash bags filled and I expected to see a notable difference, but there really wasn't one.

"We have to crack a window. It reeks in here."

Several ashtrays overflowed, and I resented the sight, not for health reasons, but because this woman cried poverty and *poor me* but threw away six or more dollars a day to support yet *another* bad habit.

"It's too cold to open a window. And why'd you shut my oven off."

"You'll start a fire that way. And if you move around you won't be as cold." I shut off the television, hoping she'd finish her coffee, snuff out her morning smoke, and get up off her ass.

"I was watching that—"

"Enough!" I snapped. "I came here to help you, and you aren't the least bit appreciative. I'm not cleaning your house alone. Get up, grab a laundry basket, and start doing something with all these clothes!"

Her level stare burned into me as she swept the smoking filter of her cigarette against the bottom of the ashtray. "Well."

I didn't linger to hear what else she had to say. There was too much to do, and we only had an hour until the boiler people showed up.

34

NOAH

The floor had been quiet all day, which seemed unusual, but under the circumstances probably made perfect sense. I wandered downstairs and checked the mail.

"How's it going, Winston?"

"Can't complain," the doorman nodded his usual greeting.

"Quiet here today."

Winston cocked his head. "Seems like a normal Saturday."

"Maybe it's just my floor."

"Ah, well that's probably due to Ms. Johansson running out of here early this morning."

Bingo. "Huh. Probably. Did she say where she was heading?"

Winston raised a brow. I didn't think he got a copy of Avery's itinerary, but I understood he wouldn't share those details even if he knew where she went.

"Right. Okay then. Guess I'll just head back upstairs and watch some TV."

"You do that. Seeing as she took a bus and not a fancy car, I imagine she was traveling someplace far."

I turned and grinned. "Thanks, Winston."

He nodded as if no thanks was necessary, but I was grateful for the information. My stomach was grateful.

If Avery took a bus, she probably wasn't out with that asshole or some other asshole. And she wasn't on campus. So where was she?

I had time to kill before any big decisions needed to be made. Thank God, because I wasn't ready to face her yet. Maybe I'd never be. Last night she chose him over me.

"Fuck that guy," I grumbled, picking up the remote.

This wasn't how it was supposed to go. I was supposed to defend her honor and knock him out, but the fucking ox had me on my back in two seconds flat.

Bullshit.

I checked my phone. Still no texts from Avery.

What did she have to be angry about? No one punched her. Her life was still the same revolving door of insignificant men it had always been. And here I was, the fool wearing a black eye for a girl who chose the other man. What was wrong with this picture?

I was getting a little sick and tired of calling my sister. I was on cloud nine, then I was down in the dumps. Then everything was great again, and then I was icing a black eye. She was getting whiplash from my social life, and hers wasn't much better.

How much longer did I intend to let this go on? This woman was derailing my life, and I was letting it happen. I was the fucking frog, and she was the fucking scorpion. She'd probably never change.

That jerkoff kissed her, and she let him. She was kidding herself if she thought she'd graduate and leave this part of her life behind. Life didn't work like that. People's pasts didn't just disappear.

And I wasn't a fucking idiot. That guy's intentions were clear. He was looking for more than her company. Why couldn't she see that? Or maybe she did and just wanted to keep her options open.

It couldn't be a money thing. I had enough to live more than comfortably. Was she attracted to the guy? Could that be it? There had to be something more than work keeping her loyal to him.

I growled and tossed the remote away. "Fuck!"

Scrubbing my hands over my face, I winced as I applied too much pressure, forgetting about my black eye. "What's he offering her that I'm not?"

If I knew his full name, I could look into his situation. Lucy was great at research. She could get me his social security number and blood type by five if I just knew his last name. Maybe she didn't need a last name. Micah wasn't too common of a first name. Maybe that was enough of a start.

I dialed my assistant, completely overlooking the fact that it was the weekend.

"Noah?"

"Lucy, hey. I need you to do me a favor."

"Sure. Is everything all right?"

"Where are you?"

"At my nephew's first birthday, but I can leave if you need something."

Children's voices registered in the background, and I couldn't think.

"Noah? Do you need me to run to the office or drop something off to you at home?"

What was I doing? She was with her family, and I was behaving like a lunatic. "No. Everything's fine, Lucy. Enjoy your day with your nephew."

"Are you sure? I don't mind—"

"Positive. I'll see you on Monday." I hung up the phone and threw it out of reach.

The concern in Lucy's voice was the wake-up call I needed. Shoving off the couch, I went to my room, stripped my bed, and carried the sheets down to the laundry facility in the basement. I needed every trace of her gone. I couldn't do this anymore.

While I waited for the wash, I toyed with my phone settings and put a block on Avery's number. If she didn't have the guts to face this thing head on she didn't have what it takes to be in a relationship. I needed a mature woman, not a child.

If she wanted the same things I wanted, she'd be here. But she wasn't. She was God knew where doing God knew what and I needed to let her go.

35

AVERY

As the service van pulled away, I stood in the cold, holding a receipt for my last good deed. My mother's trailer wasn't clean, but it was in much better shape than it had been that morning.

I checked my phone for the time, and an unwelcome pain cinched around my heart when I also noticed Noah hadn't called or texted. My finger pressed against his number and after half a ring it dumped—purposely—into voicemail.

"Hey. It's me. I ... wanted to check if you were okay. I'm not home right now, but I'm thinking about you."

A pathetic laugh slipped past my lips.

"I'm always thinking about you when I shouldn't be." I stared into the wind, and a tear gathered in the corner of my eye. "You must think I'm horrible for going with him last night. It's complicated. Life has gotten so much more complicated. Anyway... I just wanted to say I'm sorry."

I ended the call. I couldn't think about him in this place. I couldn't think of anything beyond getting the fuck out of here and washing the residue of grime away. I needed to get back to the train station by dusk, or I'd end up sleeping here, something I swore I'd never do again.

Lingering on the front lawn, I stared at the empty road. My feet carried me down familiar paths, and I was rounding the block before having the sense to grab my coat.

Everything looked the same or worse. The pen where the mean old pit-bull lived was now empty. A metal chain and empty bowl sat in a collection of fallen leaves. I hated that dog, as it tried to bite me on more than a few occasions, but I was sad to think he was dead. What a sorry life, trapped in a pen in Blackwater with nothing but sorry lives to bark at.

Even the dogs here deserved better. The people here could at least try to leave, but most chose to settle for shit. That dog didn't have a choice. Poor thing.

I knew where I was heading, but I wasn't prepared to find the rusted shell of my past sitting untouched, eerie, as if I was just here yesterday. I'd assumed Gavin's lot would have been sold to someone else by now, but there his home sat, frozen in time, a forgotten husk of life corroded by seasons and memories no one cared about enough to put away.

I cared. I cared, and I still couldn't bring myself to come home for his funeral.

A faded pink slip was taped over the door where the screen met the frame. I walked the perimeter and picked up a rock. When I reached the back of the trailer where the bedroom was, I whacked the rock against the rusted lock and shimmied the window open.

Hoisting myself over the frame, I tumbled inside. The air was cold, about ten degrees lower than outside. His furniture was empty and free of clutter, but his blankets were still on the bed.

Lowering to the mattress, my hands rested at my sides, curling into the cold comforter as I stared. This room used to be my sanctuary, the one safe place I could go to escape the madness at home.

My vision blurred as I recalled how many days I'd spent here, learning who I was and realizing I needed more than Blackwater could ever offer.

. . .

Gavin's fingers combed through my hair as I sucked in a shuddered breath, my face pressing to the tear-dampened front of his shirt. My brother Drew was gone, and I'd never felt so abandoned.

"He'll visit, Avery Dean."

Maybe we both had to tell ourselves such lies to cope with the finality of his goodbye. Gavin had been Drew's best friend, and I knew he was as sad as I was, but guys hid their emotions better than girls.

There was an old nursery rhyme that said boys were made of frogs, snails, and puppy-dog tails but young men were made of sighs, leers, and crocodile tears. Where were his tears now? I needed to see his emotions to believe they were real.

I sniffled, trying to get ahold of myself. I was being a baby. "Why don't guys cry?"

"We do. In private."

"What happens when the pain is too much and there are people around?" Didn't they ever just ... break?

"We figure out a way to swallow back the pain and save it for later."

That old rhyme also claimed little girls were made of sugar, spice, and everything nice, but I was more along the lines of an unsweetened tea that attracted flies. And I'd never fit the bill of a young lady made of ribbons, lace, and a sweet, pretty face. Puberty had really botched that deal for me.

Pretty people got pretty things. I was awkward, poor, and a victim of my upbringing in the worst possible way. If I could just look like the pretty girls, the ones on the cheer squad who caught the attention of all the boys, maybe I could get somewhere better than this.

As it stood, I was finding very little to look forward to. "Do you think I'll ever be pretty?"

Gavin leaned back and studied my face. "You're pretty now, Avery Dean."

"No, I'm not. I'm chubby, and my clothes are ugly and I can't even French braid my own hair."

He laughed. "What the hell does any of that have to do with being pretty?"

"Everything."

"Avery, you are *pretty. You have beautiful eyes, a smile that lights up a room when you laugh, and..."*

Hanging on every word as if it were a lifeline leading to a better place, I blinked up at him. "And what?"

"How old are you?"

"Seventeen and a half."

"Well, you're built like a twenty-year-old. You're not chubby. You're curvaceous. Trust me. You're pretty."

No one ever called me more than all right.

I was suddenly very aware of how I was sitting on his lap, the way his face wore a shadow of hair along his jaw, and the intense way his eyes stared into mine. "Why don't you have a girlfriend, Gavin?"

"I don't want one. Not yet."

"How come?"

"Because I'm leaving in a few years and I don't need anything or anyone making me want to stay."

"You're leaving?" *I pulled back, furious he would announce this only an hour after I watched my brother drive away.*

"I can't stay here, Avery Dean. I'm better than this place. So are you. I'll work for a little longer, but then I'm enlisting. I want to see the world. There's so much more to it than Blackwater. I want to live in a city and experience other cultures. There's no culture here, just poverty, pollution, and cynicism. This place is a cancer."

I'd never heard it put that way, but he was right. Something happened to a person when they spent more than a decade here. Their standards dropped to irretrievable depths and a sort of hardness formed around them like a callous.

"I don't want to stay here either."

"You won't. You'll go to college and—"

"College is for rich people."

"College is for smart *people. All you need to do is figure out a way to escape, and then you'll figure out a way to survive."*

I never knew he thought so highly of me. No one else did. I began calculating his age. Drew was nineteen. Gavin had to be around the same. He didn't graduate because he got his GED and had a job when everyone else was still in school. Maybe he was nineteen. My gaze roamed his face, marking all the signs of maturity.

"Avery..."

Realizing I was staring, I blinked and looked away. "Sorry."

"It's okay. You can look at me."

My lashes lifted and there was something different in his eyes, a sort of exposed secret that wasn't there a minute ago. I didn't have guy friends and I pretty much kept to myself at school when other girls were around. Gavin wasn't necessarily my friend, but he was Drew's and the only person who might understand why today was so hard.

My hand lifted and stilled. I hesitated, glancing into his watchful eyes. He gave a slight nod that I read as permission. My fingers combed through his hair, and my lungs seemed to expand in my chest. It was so soft.

His eyes closed, and his head tilted into my touch. "That's nice." His voice was a breathy whisper that danced across my teary cheeks.

It was different than the hair on his face. My fingers traced over the stubble at his jaw and gently trailed to his lips. His eyes opened, and I stilled. "Should I stop?"

"Only if you want to."

I didn't want to stop. His warm skin thawed the chill inside of me, and I'd never looked at a man so closely. My fingers traced down his sleeves and over his chest.

"Guys are so hard."

He grunted and my gaze flicked to his, self-consciously checking to see if he was laughing at me. His lashes were low, hiding his eyes, but he still watched me. His arms shifted, and I scooted closer.

"I think you could get a girlfriend real easy."

"I think you're trouble."

My hand stilled, and I stared at his face. "Why?"

"Have you ever been kissed, Avery Dean?"

My head slowly shook. "Boys pay no attention to me."

"I bet they do. But you have this intimidating edge about you that probably keeps them at bay. I bet they watch you when they think you're not looking."

My brow pinched. I didn't want to be intimidating. I wanted to be love-

able. "Well, it doesn't do me any good if they're too chicken to say anything."

"You like being asked?"

I shrugged. "Asked what?"

"By a guy... You like when they ask you? Beg?"

I laughed. "I think begging is a little too extreme to set my hopes on. I'm not that popular. A wave or a smile would be nice."

His gaze dropped to my lips, and I shifted, not used to anyone looking at me so closely.

"What are you staring at?"

"Your mouth."

"Why?"

"I want to kiss you."

I frowned. "Why?"

His lashes lifted, his eyes turning almost pleading. "Can I kiss you, Avery Dean? I'll show you how a good kiss should feel."

"Are you screwing with me?"

He shook his head. "No. Just trying to salvage an otherwise shitty day. Say yes, Avery. Please." His breathing shifted, and something tightened in the air around us. "I'll beg."

Never expecting anything like this from Gavin, I nodded.

His eyes watched me as he moved forward. His arms loosely curled around my back. "Shut your eyes."

Everything went dark as my lashes lowered. His voice, a gravel scrape against my temple sent shivers down my spine.

"If you tell me to kiss you, I will." His arms remained around my back, cradling me to his front as his voice traveled to my other ear. "If you tell me to make you feel better, I can. Just tell me what to do. I can't bear to see you cry, Avery Dean. Tell me what to do."

My heart tripped out of beat and sped into double time. Licking my lower lip, I tried to remain still on his lap as excitement rushed through my veins. His words put me under some sort of spell, and though I was hardly moving, I was out of breath.

"Kiss me," I whispered.

The soft press of his lips warmed my mouth. His arms tightened, and I sucked in a breath. Pressure built in strange places, warm enough to make my outsides shiver.

His mouth firmed against mine, not hard, but undeviating, as if seeking to get inside. My lips parted, and his tongue teased like silk along the seam, pushing past my teeth and licking deeper.

A rush of blood raced to my heart, and I shifted on his lap. Our heads tilted, as our mouths played, pulling, tasting, feeling. I liked the way it felt. All of it. Especially his arms around me. In that moment I seemed the only person who existed to him. His focus became a drug I wanted to take again and again.

His hand lowered to the back of my jeans and nudged me closer. Something pressed against my crotch and I broke the kiss, looking down.

His mouth kicked up in a half grin. "Sorry. You're a good kisser."

I had brothers, so I knew about erections. I'd just never seen one before. "Should I touch it?"

He laughed. "Definitely not. Drew would kill me."

So? "Drew's not here."

His expression froze as he studied me for a silent second. "We can't have sex."

"Okay." I didn't want to have sex anyway. "Show it to me."

His mouth curved a second after I said those words. It was if they were magic words, words that filled him with the same feelings I had when we were kissing.

He slid me off his lap and lifted his hips, rolling down the zipper of his jeans. Flicking open the button, he reached inside, and my eyes widened. It was the first time I'd seen this part of a man, and it looked swollen enough to cause pain—to a girl and to him.

"Does it hurt?"

He laughed. "No." His fingers curled around it and slowly tugged.

"Wanna feel it?"

I nodded before I fully made up my mind.

He took my hand and wrapped it around his, and together we stroked. "It's warm."

His eyes grew heavy as my fingers explored, finding the crown to be the softest part. I gasped as a pearl of moisture transferred to my finger.

"Taste it."

My gaze jerked to his. "What?"

"Some girls like it."

"Really?"

He shrugged. "Men love having their dick sucked."

That wasn't exactly the same as women loving the job. I wanted to know if I liked it. "Can I try it on you?"

He watched me through the slits of his heavy eyes. "You're too curious for your own good. Will you let me try it on you if I let you do it to me?"

My underwear was wet, and I tried to remember which ones I put on that morning. "Okay."

He kissed me, and this time, it was different, deeper, more intentional. He eased me to my back on the couch, and my pants were suddenly open. I lifted my hips, but he only pulled them down to my thighs. As his tongue teased mine, his fingers swirled over my lower belly, drifting closer and closer to my underwear. I sucked in a breath as his fingers lifted the fabric and teased the patch of hair underneath.

"I'm guessing no one's ever touched you here."

"No, but that's okay."

He pushed my jeans down a little more and glided the tip of a finger through the seam of my folds. Damp skin parted, and a sound I'd never made escaped my throat. "Sorry."

His eyes lifted as his finger softly teased. "Noises are okay. They tell the guy if you like what he's doing." He pressed a little deeper, and I gasped.

My spine arched as I leaned back. "I think my jeans are in the way."

"I think it's best we keep them on." He lowered them to my knees, but no more. Looking up at me, he smiled. "Can I do it to you, first?"

Curious, I nodded.

"Lie back."

I looked at the ceiling and sucked in a breath as his tongue, velvet soft, traced over me. His hair tickled my hips and, when I glanced down, he was watching me, tongue on my privates, eyes heavy with something I didn't recognize.

He licked at a sensitive spot, and I squirmed. "Do you like it?"

"I'm not sure."

He slipped a hand between my thighs. "You'll like this."

I let out a startled sound as he pressed a finger inside of me again, this time deeper than before. His head lowered and his mouth closed over me, sucking as the finger started to move.

Sensation spiraled through me at a startling rate, and I twisted, unsure what was happening. "Gavin..."

He paused, and the feelings stilled, but my body throbbed. "Do you want me to stop? You're in charge."

"It feels like something's about to go very wrong."

"What do you mean?"

"Like... I don't know. You're doing something to me."

He laughed. "It's called an orgasm. Trust me. You'll like it. Nothing bad will happen."

I hesitated, unsure if I believed him. "Maybe we should stop."

"Please..." He licked. "Let me make you come." Another lick. "Please."

It wasn't necessarily what he was doing that tempted me, but the way he asked to do it like I was something to be worshiped, something he'd beg to touch. I relaxed, and his mouth and fingers stole my breath.

The silly sounds escaping from my throat were embarrassing. He was never rough, and there wasn't any pain, but I didn't like not knowing what was coming. I suddenly felt very out of control, like I was falling without a safety net.

"I can't." I scrambled out from under him.

"What?" He caught my jeans.

"I can't do it."

"Yes, you can."

I scooted to the pillows. "No, I can't. It's embarrassing. I don't want one. It'll hurt."

He ducked his head, dropping his brow to the bedding as his shoulders shook.

"Are you laughing at me?"

Lifting his face, his cheeks wore an amused flush. "Avery Dean, they feel amazing. Everyone wants one."

"Let me give one to you first." I'd have to see it before I made up my mind.

"Okay, but guys are different."

"Different how?"

"Messier."

"How much mess?"

"Like a sip. Some girls swallow it."

That was going to take a lot of begging. I grabbed a tissue from the table. "Sit the way you were."

"I think you like bossing me around."

I paused and smiled. I did like it. "Is that weird?"

"No, it's hot." He rolled off of me and sat up. "Is this how you want me?"

I wasn't really sure. "Is that the way people do this?"

"There are hundreds of ways to do it. It's whatever you like."

"I think I like you on the bottom."

He grinned. "Then you get the top."

I shoved my jeans off my legs because they were just in the way. Analyzing the area, I slid to the floor. "Should I touch you first?"

He leaned back, folding his hands behind his head. "I surrender to your desires. Do whatever you want. You're in charge."

THOSE WORDS. Those beautiful words. They didn't only apply to that day, but every day that followed.

Gavin didn't want to be responsible for anyone but himself. He wanted to get through the last mile and get the hell out. He liked pleasing me, and I liked letting him. We, like everyone else there, were desperate for company, starved for affection, and happy to find a hobby that didn't cost any money.

The loneliness ate at most people in Blackwater. It was a cancer as he said. But we found a way to fill a void. It hadn't taken long for him to change his mind about sex. And once Pandora's Box was opened, the lid never fit right again.

I stared at his bedroom, familiar yet vacant. My innocence was here. My fears, my secrets, my shaky confidence, and my euphoric screams, they all breathed to life in this room. So alive, they were stealing the breath from my lungs now.

"You're gone." My words intruded on this mausoleum of memories, ripping the scab of an unhealed wound on my heart. "You left, and now I'm all alone and still tied to this place."

A tear stumbled past my lashes, and I wiped it away, angling my blurred gaze toward heaven. "Nothing's made sense since you died. I don't know if I'm doing the right thing or fucking my life up worse than it was already fucked."

Rolling to my side, I covered my face as a harsh sob ripped from my throat. My heart jerked as memories punched into me. He was gone. He'd spent his whole life trying to get out and only made it a few months, never fully seeing all the things he wanted to see.

So much pain flooded me. I was drowning. I couldn't catch my breath or move. The sadness washed over me in waves. I gulped for air, but everything was drenched in tears of sorrow and fear.

I wanted the ache in my chest to go away, but it crushed me. I should have never climbed in his window. I should have never come back here. I could feel the hopelessness weighing me down, the fears and insecurities punching through my skull.

My stomach hurt. My teeth chattered. My life seemed so meaningless, a speck I feared would blow away without a trace, just as Gavin's had.

A while later, maybe an hour, maybe two, I laid in the silence. Shadows grew as the sunlight moved across the windows. Soon it would be dusk. Somehow, I needed to get myself up, dust myself off, and remember who I was supposed to be.

I couldn't stay here. I could never come back to this place. It was time to say goodbye. Avery Dean Mudd was gone, and I needed to get back to being Avery Johansson.

Again, I thought of the day Drew left. Looking back, I think I was more upset he hadn't offered to take me with him.

As I returned to my mother's, I took one last look around, feeling as if I should take some sort of keepsake from my childhood, but unable to find anything I wanted.

The scent of rubbing alcohol filled the air, and I knew she was drunk. Not the sort of drunk a normal person gets after a few glasses of wine or even a couple shots. But the kind of wasted a person gets when they're so intent on feeding an addiction they don't care about the poison they choose.

There was no choice here. Just waste. A wasted day. A wasted year. A wasted life.

"Where the hell'd you go?"

"For a walk." I found my coat and put it on. "I have to get back to the train station."

"I'm gonna need some money for groceries for the next few weeks."

I stared at the dishes she'd accumulated in my absence. In another few days, the house would be just as bad as I found it that morning. I wasn't a cruel person, and I'd never leave my mother destitute, but she was living off more of my income than I was.

"Why aren't you using your government card?"

"They don't take it at the Pinch and Save. I'd have to take a bus downtown to get to the big market."

"So take a bus. You're getting assistance that some people deserve and can't get approved."

"You saying I don't deserve my money?"

"I'm saying, be grateful you have what you have and stop being so lazy—"

A mug flew out of her hand, alcohol scented hot tea splashed everywhere as it shattered against the wall. I shielded my face as the ceramic exploded.

"*What the hell is wrong with you?*" I shouted.

"Me? What's wrong with *you?* I raised my kids. I made sure you were fed and clothed and vaccinated and put into school each year. You come here, in your fancy city clothes and call me lazy?"

"You'd rather beg for money than take a bus so you can access your own! If that's not lazy, I don't know what is."

"Selfish bitch! You'd have nothin' if not for me."

Fury raced through my veins as I stared at her in disbelief. "I have nothing *because* of you! The money I have left, I worked for. I got into college because I wanted it bad enough. You did nothing but berate me since the day I left, too selfish to want something better for me, your daughter. All you ever cared about was yourself! All I've ever heard is how your precious boys left you with an ungrateful daughter. Do you ever stop and think they left to get away from you? Look at this place! Why would anyone want to stay here?"

Her face darkened, and she shouted, "You will not disrespect me in my own home!"

"This isn't a home. It's a pigsty."

"And who pays your rent you self-righteous bitch? Whoring ain't dignified work, Avery Dean. So don't come here preaching like you're better than anyone else."

I snatched my purse off the chair. "I can't do this anymore. Only a fool would keep offering a helping hand to a mouth that only knows how to bite back. You have no concept of the things I've done for you. You'd rather rot in your own filth, living in squalor and waiting on a handout, than try to make something better for yourself. It's always everyone else's fault and never yours. Well, I can't keep saving you."

"I didn't ask to be saved! Get out of my house!"

Her words, though expected, hurt. My throat tightened around a lump as I bustled to the door, glancing back one last time to see if I'd forgotten anything. There was nothing.

"Goodbye, Momma."

"Good riddance. Don't come crying to me when you need somethin'." She stumbled into the kitchen, and I stared through the dingy glass on the door before pulling it closed.

She didn't register the finality of my goodbye. To her, this was just a usual fight with one of her kids, the sort we'd all endured since childhood. But for me, it was the end of everything I was before and the beginning of who I intended to be. It should have felt like a relief walking out of there, but all I felt was a hollow ache in my chest.

As I boarded the bus, I stared straight ahead, too distracted by my thoughts to open the textbook I'd brought. I didn't breathe a full breath until we were out of the town of Blackwater.

Staring out the window, I watched my reflection play over the passing homes and abandoned properties until we were barreling down an open highway. Catching a tear before it left my eye, I lifted my chin and swallowed against the lump in my throat. I wasn't going to cry.

Crying meant regret, and this was my decision. I chose to walk away once and for all, and I intended to stick by my decision. I was in control of my destiny. This was my life.

My finger rolled over my phone, opening my contacts. I stared at the number labeled MOM. Taking a deep breath, I blocked it.

I was done.

Still no calls or texts from Noah. I shut my eyes, waiting for the chill to escape my bones. Bit by bit, I cleared my mind, but the problem with removing emotional clutter was it made it a lot easier to notice the emptiness.

Walking back into my apartment building later that night was like coming out of a dream into a reality that had shifted off its axis and no longer felt the same. Everything hinted of change, as though someone came in my absence, moved things around, then put them back as they were.

It was late, and my back cried for my bed. As I approached my door, I stilled. On the floor sat a shoebox. I picked it up and slid back the lid. A pair of mittens—my mittens. A few bobby pins. And my T-shirt.

A piercing stab lanced my heart as I realized what this was. These were the few items I'd left over Noah's since we had started sleeping together.

Wiping my eyes, I gave up on my fight against the tears. I gave up on everything. I couldn't handle one more challenge.

Turning, I hurled the box at his door, no longer caring what anyone thought of me. I let myself inside my apartment and slammed the door. When I hit my bed, I truly fell apart.

36

AVERY

If not for my clients, the loneliness would have swallowed me whole. David took me to a great show. Christopher introduced me to escargot. Richard was his usual arrogant self. And Micah continued to hint at renegotiating our arrangement, but I continued to evade giving him an answer for reasons I didn't want to face.

I should accept his offer. It was the only option I had for companionship now that Noah had shunned me. And being with Micah wouldn't be a total loss. He treated me nice, understood I hadn't started in this social tier. But I didn't love him, and I wasn't sure I ever could.

Maybe I wasn't meant to fall in love or be loved. These were the sorts of thoughts giving me indigestion of late.

February became a month of preparation. Planning for something better to come seemed the only tolerable distraction I could find. I shopped for teaching clothes, prepared lesson plans, and exercised to the brink of collapse.

I hadn't seen or heard from Noah in weeks, but it made perfect sense for our paths to cross on Valentine's Day. My fate was just that cruel.

Waiting for Micah to park his car, I fed my key into the lock only to still at the sound of a door opening. Noah exited his apartment in a rush, just as my door opened. We glanced at each other and stilled, both frozen for a split second.

In his hand, he held a long-stemmed rose. Who was it for? My heart was suddenly in my throat, and as I tried to speak no words came out.

He recovered first, breaking all eye contact and looking away. He locked his door and went to the elevator, leaving me staring after him. I still hadn't moved as the elevator arrived and it seemed almost poetic that Micah stood on the other side of the doors when they opened.

My heart plummeted to the pit of my stomach. If Noah hadn't been through with me yet, this would certainly do the trick. He didn't meet my glance as he passed Micah and pressed the button to go down, nor did he utter a word in the other man's presence.

When the doors closed, leaving only me and my date, my hand trembled trying to pull the key from the lock. Micah and I were going to discuss his offer and come to a final decision. I wasn't ready, but with the dark place my head had been I wasn't sure I'd ever be ready, but I'd delayed the conversation long enough, and there was really no point in holding onto the past.

How involved did a guy have to be to give someone a rose on Valentine's Day? My stomach turned, and I quickly pushed all worries about Noah out of my mind.

Micah followed me inside, removing my wrap and I went to the stereo to put on some music. It was starting to snow.

Wandering to the window, I stared down at the street. Who was Noah meeting on Valentine's Day? Were they serious? He bought her a rose.

Micah brushed a gentle finger down my arm and handed me a glass of wine. "Come sit by the fire, love. It's cold by the window."

My feet wouldn't move. "It's snowing," I whispered, an unfamiliar sense of longing filling my chest.

"Tomorrow the streets are going to be a disaster. I can't wait for spring."

I used to think the same thing, but tonight, my thoughts were different. "I think it's pretty."

He led me to the couch, and I sat down, doing my best to focus on my company. "I know you've been sad since your trip home, Avery. Is there anything I can do to help?"

"No." And as much as cutting off the last of my family hurt, it wasn't the route of my pain.

"Have you put any more thought into my offer?"

I thought about it every day, but I never made any headway. "I have some concerns."

"Such as?"

"Would the arrangement include sex?"

If my question surprised him, he didn't let it show. "We would have a monogamous agreement. Intimacy would, of course, be open to discussion. Is that something you'd like to address now?"

How long could we possibly go without eventually sleeping together? Even a cactus needed water from time to time. "Isn't it something you'd require ... at some point."

"I think it's something we both would come to expect. But I can be patient."

There were so many ways to have sex. Everyone was different, and sometimes the most unassuming people were the most surprising. "What if we're not compatible in that way?"

"I think we'll manage."

It was the first time I felt wiser than him. We'll manage? He knew I had a bleak past, but I made it too easy for him to believe the fantasy. He didn't know me. He assumed the woman he spent time with was the basis of my character. It wasn't. I was nothing like my sugar baby persona. Eventually, he'd realize that and then where would we be?

"What would change for me?"

He raised a brow. "You'd have anything you needed. You know I never mind providing—"

"That's not what I mean. There are expectations. You want a certain kind of woman in your life. You're very specific. I do my best to be that woman—"

"You've yet to disappoint me, Avery."

"But that woman's not me."

He frowned. "Of course she is. People change. We grow. If we play a role long enough, it eventually becomes real."

Maybe that worked for Micah, but it wouldn't work for me. I didn't want to become this agreeable puppet that laughed at jokes that weren't funny and smiled through boring conversations. What good was a relationship if none of it was real? And where would the artifice end if sex complicated things? Would I be expected to fake orgasms, too?

I sipped my wine, wishing my glass held something stronger. I couldn't agree to this. I didn't want this to be my only option. And even if it was, I still didn't want it.

"Micah, I appreciate everything you've done for me, but—"

"You know I think you're a beautiful woman, Avery. I told you so the first day we met. My opinion's only improved over the years." His voice lowered. "Has nothing changed for you?"

I squirmed, somewhat uncomfortable with the question. "I care about you, Micah. You're very special to me, but I don't think we have the right sort of chemistry for what you're asking. It wouldn't be fair to either of us."

His glance drifted toward the door. "Is it him?"

The pressure in my chest intensified. "I… I'm not sure."

"Are you in love with him?"

I laughed without humor. "I don't know. I've never loved anyone." It didn't matter anyway. He didn't love me back. I was a scorpion. "If being in love feels similar to emotional agony, then I might be."

His hand rested over my knee, squeezing in gentle comfort. "When the person doesn't love you back, it can feel similar to agony."

Ouch. My insides clenched uncomfortably.

Maybe Noah didn't love me, but Micah didn't love me either. Not to say his feelings weren't real. But the object of his affection was a total phony. He loved a woman I made up.

His thumb dragged slowly over my skin. "I know you have reservations, Avery, but I'd never purposely hurt you. I could provide everything you need. I'd do whatever I could to make you happy."

"Micah..." The more he tried to convince me, the more certain I became. I couldn't accept his offer. This was supposed to be a means to an end. All of the luxuries were perks, but not necessary anymore.

I wanted a modest income making an honest living. I wanted to live outside of the shadows and make friends. I wanted to have dinner parties and join a book club and maybe even have kids one day. I didn't want to live by a negotiated arrangement anymore, and I certainly didn't want artificial love. I wanted the real thing.

My lashes lowered as I breathed through the ache expanding in my chest. I wanted to love Noah, but he wouldn't let me. I couldn't blame him. Nothing about my life was normal, and he didn't know anything about my past. He'd been so upfront about who he was and what he wanted. And I complicated things at every turn.

And now he'd moved on. Was it that tall brunette again, the one he kissed last month? My stomach turned and sloshed at the thought.

My vision blurred under the rush of unshed tears. I wanted a friend, and I made an enemy because no one wanted a relationship with the real me.

"I can't accept your offer, Micah."

He turned, his gaze measuring. "You don't need to decide tonight. We have time."

I shook my head. I didn't need time. "I'm sorry. I love you for helping me, but this was never meant to be long term. In three months, I'm graduating. The fact that I'll have no college debt is a miracle, but it's time for me to start living a normal life."

Maybe I'd move to the suburbs and find a summer job in retail while I looked for a teaching position. I could rent a modest apartment and save up for a car. My clothes would be mostly cotton, and my evenings would be my own.

"Are you saying you want to end things?"

Was I? My tuition was paid, but I had very little saved, and I still needed a place to live. "Not yet, but eventually. I need to stick to my original plan."

In three months, I needed to let all of this go. Including Noah.

"I can't say I'm not disappointed."

I met his stare. "Life would have been so easy if I could love you. But I'm not sure I know how to love."

His eyes softened. "You know how to love, Avery. But it's going to take a special man to earn it. Don't give anything to someone who has nothing to give back."

I smiled. He'd said those same words to me many times when teaching me the rules of being a sugar baby. Everything was a trade, according to Micah. Maybe that was why he'd found so much success. He didn't do anything without assuring he benefited someway in the end.

I wasn't sure that applied to love and matters of the heart. At the moment, I didn't need Noah to love me or even forgive me, but I needed him to know I was sorry I hurt him and that I cared about him more than anyone else.

Even if I'd lost him forever, I wanted to give him that.

37

NOAH

"Can I get you a refill?"

I slid my glass forward, and the bartender snatched it. Grinding my molars, I stared at the bar, silently calling myself seven kinds of fucked up.

I was doing fine and arrogantly thought things were better, but nothing had changed. She was still selling dates, and Micah was still a regular part of her life. As a matter of fact, the other man was getting awfully cozy at her place—or should I say *his* place.

A fresh cocktail landed in front of me, and I sipped it. I was a fucking idiot.

Getting blindsided tonight was my own damn fault. Realizing the guy wasn't just dropping her off and had actually parked his car ... yeah, that sucked.

Guess she was moving on—just like I was supposed to do. Just like I was doing, sitting here with the rest of single Philadelphia drinking my fucking loneliness away.

"Noah?"

Pivoting on my stool, I did a double take. "Lucy?"

My assistant gave a shy smile. "Are you meeting someone?"

She didn't look like her normal self. Gone were the cardigan and bad shoes. And where had all that cleavage come from? "No, I'm here by myself."

"Me too."

My brow tightened. She wasn't wearing her glasses, and her eyes looked huge. The way she had her makeup done... "You look pretty. You're not on a date?"

"Th—thank you." She climbed onto the stool beside mine, but still only came up to my shoulder. "No, no date. I don't know what's worse, sitting home alone on Valentine's Day night, or getting dressed up and going out alone."

I had to admire her choice. Most people would sit at home and mope. That had been my original plan.

"Well, you're not alone anymore. What are you drinking?"

"Um, how about a banana daiquiri."

I stilled. Was she fucking with me?

Uncertainty flashed in her big eyes. "Sorry, is that weird? I don't usually drink. I guess I'll just have a glass of beer or wine."

Grateful for her company, I decided she should have whatever she wanted. "Can we get a banana daiquiri, please—with an umbrella?"

She smiled, and I was glad to see her confidence return. "Thanks."

"My pleasure."

The blender ground up the fruit and Lucy grinned like a kid at a candy shop when the bartender slid her tall, tropical cocktail in front of her. She sipped and sighed, her long lashes lowered in pleasure.

"Is it good?"

"Delicious." She took another sip than slid it away. "How come you're alone tonight? You usually have me make reservations for you somewhere." Her gaze remained on the bar.

"I didn't feel like spending the night with someone meaningless."

Her lashes lifted, her gaze traveling to my eyes. "Oh." She sipped her daiquiri. "Do you want to hear something silly?"

"Sure."

"Every year on Valentine's Day, I get dressed up like this. I buy a new outfit and new shoes and spend extra time on my makeup and hair, but I never make plans with anyone."

"Why?"

She blushed, her lips twisting into a shy smirk. "Because I think it would be especially romantic to meet the love of my life on Valentine's Day. I fantasize about telling the story about how I met my Mr. Right and everyone who hears the story sighs because it's so romantic." Her smile faded. "I've been doing this since college, and you're the first guy who's ever actually bought me a drink."

"That can't be true."

"But it is. I know what men want. They want long legged bombshells. They like confidence and class. I'm awkward and mousey."

"You're smart and dependable, Lucy. I'd call you a tiger before I'd ever call you a mouse. The office would be lost without you. I know I would be."

"Thank you. But it would be nice to get a guy's attention for a change without the help of my resume."

"I think most men go after the wrong women anyway. Don't take it personally. And as far as confidence goes, you just have to put yourself out there, which you seem to be doing."

Her shoulders shifted with a deep breath, and she twisted to better face me. "Noah, can I tell you something else?"

"Sure."

"If you asked to take me home right now, I'd say yes."

Every sound silenced as the thoughts skipping around in my head skidded to a stop. Was this a joke? Was someone playing some sort of prank on me? I swallowed, trying to find my voice and laughed nervously. "Pardon?"

"I'm sorry if this is inappropriate, but..." She drew in a deep breath. "I like you—a lot. I have for a while. I know you're my boss, and I hope my job's not in any danger by me telling you this, but I thought you should know."

Ohhh, it was awkward... "Lucy, I'm flattered..."

"But?"

"But you work for me."

If she was disappointed, she hid it well. "Okay." She lifted her drink and took a long sip.

It wasn't okay. I felt terrible. "I think you're amazing. I wouldn't want to lose you because things got complicated."

She put down her empty glass with a shaky hand. "Please don't make excuses. I'm fine. As a matter of fact, I should be going." She scooted off her stool and took her purse. "Thanks for the drink."

"You don't have to leave."

"I do. I have an appointment I forgot about. Have... Have a good night, Noah. Happy Valentine's Day."

Fuck. I threw some money on the bar and went after her.

The place was packed, and she was so damn short. I lost sight of her. Exiting the bar, I rushed onto the pavement and searched the people walking by. When had it started snowing? A small figure turned at the corner.

"Lucy, wait." I raced after her, my leather soled shoes slipping on the dusting of snow. "Shit. Lucy, slow down." When she didn't stop, I sped up. "How the hell does she move so fast on such short legs?"

I turned the corner and came to an abrupt stop as she stood on the other side of the building. I winced at the sight of tears. Fuck me.

She pulled a red shawl tight over her shoulders. Her bare arms and legs must have been freezing.

"I'm sorry," I said, unsure how to make this better.

"I told you I'm fine, Noah."

"But you're not. I... I didn't know."

Her head tipped to the side as she looked at me. Stepping close, she closed a hand over my sleeve. "It's okay."

"It's not okay! Nothing is okay!" I forked my fingers through my hair, leaving it standing on end. Work was my escape, the one thing that took my mind off Avery. I couldn't have stress there as well. And I couldn't risk Lucy quitting. "Why does everything have to be so fucked up?"

"I..." She shook her head, genuine concern reflecting in her eyes. "I don't know."

"You like me. She likes him. I like her. Can't anyone get it right?"

Her eyes turned startled and wide. "I don't know who you're talking about."

"Why does everything have to be so damn complicated?"

Her teeth were chattering, and her breath formed a cloud of vapor between us. I'd been so out of it when I left my apartment, I didn't even have a coat to offer her.

Cupping my hands over her arms, I tried to warm her skin. "I think you're great, Lucy. The reason my company works so well has as much to do with you as it does with me. And I think you're pretty. Some guy is going to—"

My eyes widened as she lifted to her toes and pressed her lips to mine. I broke the kiss and stepped back.

My hand covered my mouth as I stared down at her with a startled gaze. "Uh…"

"It doesn't always have to be complicated, Noah."

Oh, yes, it did. "Okay, let's not do that again."

"Sorry."

I held up my hands. "It's cool." My voice took on a higher pitch. The wind cut through my clothes, and I shivered. "How about we walk for a little bit?"

She nodded, and we strolled through Rittenhouse. Her little heels ticked along the cobblestone as I tried to think of something to say. I couldn't say goodnight until I was certain things wouldn't be awkward in the office between us.

"How long have you felt this way?" I asked.

"Since the first time you called me at home on a Saturday and said you needed me. I think that was about two weeks after I started working for you."

Shit. That was over three years ago. "I do need you."

"I know. And I love feeling needed like that, so I might misread it from time to time. Maybe I tend to romanticize things, and I'm sorry. But … please don't fire me. When you called me at my nephew's party, I would have come to you. It didn't matter what you wanted. You're the only person who makes me feel … important. You're the only person who actually needs me to be there on a regular basis.

And so long as I remain necessary, I matter. I know it sounds stupid, but—"

"It's not stupid."

I wondered if she realized how many men in the office deferred to her. She was my second in command, my right hand. At four foot eleven, she managed to hold authority over the entire staff and keep them in line. And tonight, she took control of her situation by putting herself out there.

"I'd never fire you. But I think you were wrong at the bar."

"About which part?"

"You said men want women with confidence, but you said it like you see yourself as insecure. You're confident, Lucy. And the whole office *needs* you, not just me. You run the show when I'm not there. An unconfident woman wouldn't be able to do that. I think you know how much you matter, regardless of whether I tell you I need you or not."

She stopped walking, and I realized we'd made it to my apartment building. "But we all like the reassurance of seeing how necessary we are, Noah. Even the most confident person has doubts. Every time you need me for something, it validates my importance. I'm human enough to depend on that validation."

No one needed to tell her that she often ran the show more than me. It might be my ideas and my name on the door, but I'd be nothing without her there to keep me organized.

"You know your job's safe, right?"

She blushed. "I guess." She smirked. "You'd be a disaster without me."

I smiled because she was right. I needed her to make the tricky decisions, and that equaled security in her mind. It made her indispensable to my life. She was indispensable because she was the one in control—of my schedule, the payroll, the staff. I'd be lost without her.

She was the boss. I was just ... the owner. And it worked.

"That's it."

She frowned. "That's what?"

"You know how important you are to me, Lucy, but you still like when I come to you to solve a problem."

"Of course I do. That's my job."

Actually, it wasn't. But she'd made it her job, creating a position for herself in my world that no one else could fill. It was why I'd never fire her and why I'd never risk our relationship by getting romantically involved with her. She was priceless.

"Noah, what's going on with you?"

My hands fisted in my pockets as my muscles bunched against the cold. "Nothing. I just realized something."

"What?"

"That women need to feel needed."

She pursed her lips. "So do men."

"Yeah, but with us, it's more about our egos. With women, it's more about security."

"You lost me."

"Keep putting yourself out there, Lucy. There's a good man looking for you, and sooner or later you'll find him. Just promise me you'll still keep my life in order when he shows up because I'll always need you."

Her smile showed how deeply the compliment resonated. "Thank you—"

The door to the building opened, and we turned. Winston stepped out, and I froze at the sight of Micah, my stomach dropping to my knees.

He'd been here all this time?

My knuckles cracked as my fist clenched at my side. He glared at me then glanced down at Lucy, his expression softening. I fucking hated him.

Lucy's head tipped up, her lips parting slightly as she stared up at the other man. "Hello."

"Good evening."

I scowled, wanting nothing more than to tell him not to talk to her. I could invite her in, but that would send the wrong message.

Luckily, he stepped past us and crossed the street, his headlights flashing as his car unlocked.

I glared at him, wishing a bus would come barreling down Delancey right as he crossed. As he glanced back, my eyes narrowed. *What the fuck are you looking at?*

Then I realized he wasn't looking back at me. He was looking at Lucy. And she was watching him.

"Do you want me to have the doorman call you a cab?" I asked, stepping in her view.

"That's okay. I think I'll walk."

"You'll freeze."

"I'm not that cold anymore. Goodnight, Noah."

I frowned as she turned and lowered her shawl, exposing the sharp curve of her shoulder as she walked away.

"Mr. Wolfe?" Winston stood holding the door open, his chest flecked with freshly fallen flurries.

I quickly crossed the threshold, and when I looked back, the road was empty. All signs of Micah and Lucy gone.

I took the elevator to my floor and dug out my keys. As I unlocked my apartment, I hesitated and glanced back at Avery's door. Before I realized what I was doing, my fist pounded on her door.

The wood jerked open, and she glared at me. "What do you want?"

"Did you sleep with him?"

"Oh, my God. Go away, Noah."

She tried to slam the door, and I caught the wood. "Did you? I have a right to know."

"What right? News flash, you have no right to me. You're just my neighbor. We aren't even friends."

"Answer the fucking question, Avery!"

She flinched, and all arrogance left her face. "No."

"No, you won't answer it, or no, you didn't sleep with him?"

Her long lashes fluttered, and her eyes shimmered. Voice small, she said, "No, I didn't have sex with him. But I'm glad you think I'm such a whore you had to ask."

My head tipped back in relief and regret. “I don’t think you’re a whore.”

“No? You sure it’s not in my scorpion-like nature.”

Massaging the bridge of my nose, I growled. “Why do we always have to fight? Nothing is easy with you!”

“Look, I don’t know why you’re suddenly at my door when you haven’t spoken to me in weeks, but...”

Her lips pursed, and the bridge of her nose flushed, the whites of her eyes a glassy shade of pink.

Her voice broke. “I ... I can’t do this right now. I can’t keep disappointing you by being exactly who I am. I’m sorry we broke up. It was my fault—all of it. I never meant to hurt you, Noah. If there was another way for things to have worked out, I would have tried it, but there’s not. I’m always going to be this toxic person. You’re better off not trusting me and keeping to your side of the hall until I move out. Lucky for you that won’t be that long from now.”

A tear tripped past her lashes, and she either didn’t realize she was crying or refused to acknowledge her tears.

“Goodnight. I have to go.”

She pushed the door shut, and the soft click seemed to send a fissure carving into my heart. I stared at the door, unsure what to make of everything she just said. She was crying. Women like Avery weren’t supposed to cry. She was strong. Tough.

So why did she look so broken? Staring down at the knob, I reached forward and turned, my eyes shutting in relief when the door opened.

38

AVERY

Hand on my quaking chest, I staggered into the living room and gasped for breath. I'd told Micah I'd stay, but after seeing Noah wearing a smudge of some other woman's red lipstick on his lips, I knew I couldn't stay here.

"Oh, God." I gripped the arm of the couch, letting my tears fall. I couldn't bear the pain escaping me in horrific sobs.

I gasped as strong arms closed around me. *Noah.*

"Shh. Don't cry." He twisted me away from the sofa and pulled me into his arms.

"How did you get in here?"

"You forgot to lock the door."

"Get out." I didn't want him to see me like this. "You're breaking and entering again."

"I'll let you use my phone to call the cops." He brushed the hair away from my face and pressed his lips to my temple. "Try to breathe, Avery. You're going to hyperventilate if you don't calm down."

I sucked in a jagged breath. Defeated, I let him hold me. "I can't fight anymore, Noah. You win."

"I didn't win." He lowered to the couch, pulling me onto his lap. "We both lost."

The agony I'd kept bottled up for the past few weeks erupted out of me like boiling lava. "I wish I could be normal for you."

"You are normal. You just have a terrible job."

"My job pays for college."

"I know, but what does it cost you in the end? I'm falling in love with you, Avery. Hell, I think I fell in love with you the first time I saw you get on that elevator. I want to be with you, and I don't want to share. If you'd just open up to me a little, I could help you."

My face pressed to his shoulder, his familiar scent seeping into my lungs and calming me. "I don't want you to know any of that."

"Any of what?"

"Anything about the girl I used to be. I just want you to see the good stuff."

"Why can't I see both? I'm not an asshole, Avery. But you make this part of you a deception. You hide it until your secrecy is all I can see. If you just were upfront with me about the bad stuff, it wouldn't matter so much. And I'd never lose sight of all the good."

Fear twisted in my chest, wringing a sharp whimper from my throat. "My real name's Avery Dean Mudd. I grew up in a dirt poor trailer park with an abusive, alcoholic mother, and I don't know who my father is."

His hand brushed over my hair, holding me close. "None of that's your fault, and I'd never judge you for where you came from."

"But you don't understand what it was like. You came from this picture perfect home with a mom and a dad. Your family had money, and you've grown up with so many opportunities."

"I can't help that. I'm sorry it wasn't as easy for you."

My words tangled in my throat. "Everything I am is fake. And when I let my guard down and show people the real me, they see nothing but problems."

"No, sweetie. You're wrong."

"I tried to let you in, and you called me a scorpion."

"I was angry. I saw another man kissing you, and I lost it. I wanted to hurt you."

"You succeeded."

He pulled me so I straddled him and cupped my cheeks so I'd look him in the eyes. "You are not a scorpion. It was an asshole thing to say, and I didn't mean it."

Leaning forward, he tried to kiss me, and I turned away, my face scrunching tight. "You have someone else's lipstick on your lips."

He hissed out a curse. "That was a mistake."

"Did she like her flower?" Maybe if I made light of him dating other women, it wouldn't feel like a dull, rusty blade was gutting me.

"What?"

"The rose you had when you left tonight."

"Ah." He let out a deep breath. "I didn't have the guts to give it to her, so I left it by her mailbox."

Yeah, I couldn't discuss this with him. "Oh." I pushed off of his lap.

"Where are you going?"

"I need a glass of water."

He let me up, and I went to the kitchen. As I turned to ask if he wanted anything, he lifted Micah's half full glass of wine.

"What does he want from you, Avery? Why does he have such a hold on you?"

He didn't have to clarify who *he* was. Carrying my glass of water back to the den, I lowered myself to the empty seat. "He wants a relationship with me, but I can't give him what he wants."

His expression was unreadable. "Because of a control thing?"

"No, because of a love thing. I don't love Micah that way, and I doubt I ever could."

Noah's Nordic eyes lifted, and he stared across the table at me. "You have no fucking idea how glad I am to hear that."

"I'm indebted to him, Noah. This apartment, these clothes, my books… The others pay my bills, but Micah supports me. I'd never have made it this far without him."

"Bullshit. Did he ever offer to set you up with a financial advisor, Avery? Someone who could help you figure out an ordinary student loan and maybe educate you about student housing? He wanted you to believe he was not only your best option but your only option.

With your background, you might not have known better, but he did, and he took advantage of you anyway."

"He's been more than generous—"

"Stop." He held up a hand. "You're never going to sway me. When I say I don't like the way you make a living, what I mean is I *really* fucking hate your job. Really."

"I swear it's just business."

"To you maybe, but not to them. You're their fantasy. I see how they look at you. I watch them try to touch you. Micah point blank told you." He turned out his palms. "Maybe a stronger man could handle it, but I can't. I'm territorial for good reason. My ex left me for my best friend. I swore, the next time I fell in love with someone, I'd make sure she fully belonged to me. All this time I've been single because I didn't see anyone I wanted that much, but then I met you, and I wanted you every second since."

"You want me?"

"Yes, I fucking want you."

"Still?"

He hesitated. "I want to know you're mine and mine alone. I can't fucking share you, Avery."

I placed my glass on the table. "How would that work, if I was yours?"

"What do you mean? We'd be in a relationship. No other women and no other men. *None.* We would be a normal couple."

"Normal." I tasted the word, my mind calculating the time needed for student teaching and the money I'd need to rent a new place. "I… I'd have to move."

"That makes two of us."

"What?"

"If you think I'm going to pay that fucking asshole rent, you're crazy. I've been looking for a new place for weeks."

He was leaving? I immediately knew I wouldn't be able to afford to live wherever he moved. "How far will you be?"

"Depends."

"On?"

He swallowed, his Adam's apple gliding beneath the pale stubble on his throat. "You could come with me."

"I can't afford it."

"You could once you started teaching."

"That won't be until September, Noah."

He smiled. "We can work something out."

What was he asking, that we move in together? "You mean we would be roommates?"

He met my stare but didn't answer. "Maybe we're getting ahead of ourselves."

I shrank into the chair, my arms folding around the uneasy feeling in my stomach. "Then let's slow down."

"Why did you sit over there?"

Confused by his question, I shrugged. "I thought we needed space."

"I don't want space. Come back to where you were on my lap."

I stood then stilled. Who made him boss? "I think we should talk this out—"

"Avery, get your fucking ass over here."

I moved around the coffee table and stood in front of him. He caught my wrist and tugged me to his lap. This time both my legs draped over his to one side, and he pulled my back to his chest. His palm pressed to my breastbone, his fingers teasing the neckline of my dress.

"We need to get some things out in the open if this is ever going to work."

My stomach tightened. "What sort of things?"

"I want you to tell me about the first time you took control in sex. How old were you?"

I shifted to face him, but he held me still. "Why do you want to talk about that?"

"Because I do and we're trying that new honesty thing all the kids are talking about."

I sighed. "I lost my virginity just before my eighteenth birthday."

"That's not what I asked."

"Well, that's the answer. With sex, I've always been the one in control."

His fingers stilled, then continued drawing circles on my flesh just beside my bra strap. "Who was he?"

"My brother's friend. Eventually, he was my friend."

"Why did you break up?"

"We didn't. He died."

He let out an audible breath. "I'm sorry. How old were you when he died?"

"Eighteen. I was in Philly when it happened. I didn't go home for his funeral. Last month was the first time I'd been home in years. I think it's the first time I actually processed his death."

"Next time you have to go home, I could go with you."

I rested my head on his shoulder. "Thanks, but I don't intend to go back." And I didn't want to think about home, so I continued answering his question.

"After Gavin, I tried dating for a split second. It didn't end well. I assumed everyone had sex the same way. I probably put that guy in therapy. He never called."

Noah chuckled.

"Then, I decided to do some research. The Internet could be a scary playground. I visited the most otherworldly corners of the World Wide Web until I was able to sort of piece together what I was."

"What did you think you were?"

I shrugged. "A Domme or a Dominatrix. The label never much mattered, but it helped me meet the right people. I hooked up with this guy Tucker. We met online, and we seemed to be searching for the same thing. We lasted about a year, but we never slept together."

"I'm sorry, what?"

I smiled at his confusion. I'd warned him I wasn't normal. Neither were my needs.

"It wasn't sexual with Tucker. Not as much as it was personal. We shared a puzzle piece we both needed to feel whole. He needed pain, and I needed power. When I hurt him, I did so with careful affection.

When he cried, it was beautiful, like poetry in motion. Our co-dependent relationship went deeper than fucking and was sometimes far more intimate than making love."

"Are you saying you're a sadist?"

"No. But I'm addicted to that feeling. It doesn't matter if I'm being tender or cruel, so long as I'm the one calling the shots."

Gavin wasn't the pain slut Tucker had been, yet we still fit together because he liked being controlled and needed someone to control him. I was that person. Same with Tucker, but with a lot more leather and toys.

"Why did it end with that guy?"

A bittersweet flutter teased my heart. "He fell in love." The irony was, once Tucker found Raoul, he claimed he no longer craved the pain as much. I envied him for that, wondering if I'd ever stop needing control.

"Who was next?"

I smiled, detecting that he expected my list to take hours. Wouldn't he be surprised? "You."

"That's it?"

"Sorry to disappoint you, but you're only the third person I've slept with."

He leaned forward to look me in the eye. "You're serious?"

I shrugged. "How many women have you been with?"

"More than three."

Ugh, why did I ask that? I didn't want to picture him with other women. And now we were just sitting in this awkward silence, and it was all I could picture. "Say something."

"I'm getting hard thinking about the fact that I was only your third."

"I can tell."

He nudged his hips forward, and I laughed. "Feel like taking care of that for me?"

"While you have some other woman's lipstick on your lips?" I grimaced. "No, thanks."

"I told you that was an accident."

"Did you trip and fall on her mouth?"

"No, but I stopped her the second she tried to kiss me."

Was that a dig at me for not stopping Micah? My smile faded. "I don't always know how to respond, Noah. The girl I was never got any attention. If you saw what I looked like—"

"Avery, I saw the pictures in your album. You were a kid. There was nothing wrong with your looks. You're still the same person." He gave me a little shake. "This is the real you."

"It doesn't feel real."

"Why don't you stop trying to be what you think others expect and just be you?"

Just be me? Sometimes I was. Sometimes I was just Avery, building a snowman with my neighbor, cuddling up on the couch, dancing around my apartment in my pajamas. "Sometimes I think you see the real me."

"That's my favorite part."

I glanced at him through my lashes and smiled. "You're sweet."

He drew in a long breath and let it out slowly. "Can I tell you my theory?"

"On?"

"You."

I stiffened, never one to enjoy being the center of attention, and even less of a fan of being psychoanalyzed by a non-professional. Why couldn't he just accept me for who I was?

It was an easy request, but even I didn't accept the real me. I was forever trying to change her or hide parts of her away from others. Maybe he could explain why that was. "Go for it."

His hands closed around mine. Maybe he feared I'd bolt at the first sound of something I didn't want to hear.

"I don't think it's about control, Avery. I think it's about feeling needed, necessary. If you set up a deliberate role for yourself, you guarantee that happens. Your role with your clients is the opposite, but specific enough that you can relinquish control. Maybe because you still feel desired. They hired you to fill a need in their lives.

"That's what it seems to come down to, Avery, feeling needed. The control isn't always necessary, so long as things stay within certain parameters. You trust me not to take things too far, I think. That's why your authority slips when you're with me, because you see how much I want and need you. You only fight for authority when you start to doubt things."

I could hardly blink let alone form words to respond. What if he was right and all this time I'd been wrong? I felt like an idiot, totally out of touch with myself. I should have spent some of my money on therapy instead. Maybe then I wouldn't feel like such a head case.

"Sorry if that was too much."

I shook my head. "I'm just processing."

"Well, I should also be honest about myself. Since meeting you, I discovered how much *I* like *taking* control."

"I've noticed."

"I told you about my ex. She really messed me up. It took a lot of rebounds to get over what she did, and I'm still messed up from it. With you, it's different. You and I have this gloves-off sort of chemistry where we can just go at each other and be ourselves, whoever we happen to be in that moment. You challenge me to always give you my best. I love being with you. I love trying new things. And I really love when you let me take the lead. You're so fucking intimidating, but you can be incredibly indulgent at times. I love getting you there, watching you surrender. And if I'm holding the reins, I know exactly where you are, emotionally and physically. It's so intense. When we're in sync like that, I feel... I might be holding you in place, but you're there by choice. It's so clear in those moments that every part of you is present—with me."

Control was a drug, and I knew the high he spoke of well. My body responded to his words, my breath turning heavy, and my breasts straining against my bra. "That's a great feeling."

"I love it."

"Me, too."

If I shifted my legs, arousal would gush to my panties, so I remained perfectly still. I swallowed, unsure of what to do or say.

The first time Noah took control, I saw it as a deliberate betrayal. I specifically told him I needed control, and he usurped it.

But after we slept together and came to an understanding, it was easier to switch back and forth. He no longer stole my authority when it was my turn. But I also enjoyed when it was his turn. Sometimes I forgot who was in charge and just let it happen. No matter what, with Noah, it was always good.

He turned my chin to face him. "You're not saying anything."

I didn't know what to say. My head was spinning. It was getting late, and my brain was on overload.

"Whose lipstick is it?"

He rubbed a hand over his lips. "I ran into an employee of mine, and there was a misunderstanding. I straightened it out."

"Were you on a date with her?" I couldn't hide the jealousy or accusation in my voice.

"No. But it's good to know I'm not the only territorial one."

There was still the matter of the flower. "The rose wasn't for her?"

"Avery, the rose was for you. If you don't believe me, check your mail."

"What?"

He let out a breath. "It was an olive branch. It's Valentine's Day. I was just going to leave it by your door, but you happened to be standing there. When I saw what you were wearing, I knew you were spending Valentine's Day with someone else. Then I saw him."

I lowered my head. "I'm so ashamed of everything I put you through."

"We're working it out."

"You must have hated seeing him with me tonight."

"Yeah." He didn't hesitate or sugarcoat his feelings. "I pretty much hate his guts, and now that I know he's trying to start some sort of relationship with you, I want him totally out of your life."

"I don't know if that's possible."

"Anything's possible—if you want it bad enough."

I wanted Noah. "Tell me how to have a normal relationship. I've never had one. What would our relationship look like?"

He returned his hand to my chest, his fingers stroking over my skin gently. "We'd be totally committed, so we'd eventually live together. It would make sense because I like to cook and you never have any food at your place. Plus, my couch is better for snuggling."

"Not true."

"It's bigger. We can do more on it."

I rolled my eyes. He was right.

"You'd be a teacher, and I'd get hard every time you dressed for work, especially when you wear your hair in a bun and those little glasses I like."

"I don't wear glasses."

"It's a new prescription and my fantasy, so stop interrupting."

I smirked and let him go on.

"You teach at the little private school on 17th Street, and since I pass it on my way to work, I drop you off each morning. You like long showers, so I'm in charge of lunches. Each morning when I drop you off, I hand you a little brown bag with your lunch and a note on the napkin, telling you what I intend to do to you that night. But you never wait until lunch to read it.

"Every day you text me around ten, just to check how my day's going. You love your job, and your classroom's real cute. There's a bulletin board with all the kids' names on the wall and little Sally with the lisp is your favorite.

"School's out at three-fifteen, but your day doesn't end until five. Most days I have to come find you at your desk because you don't like to leave until your lesson plans are just right.

"We drive home, and I make dinner while you cut out materials for some science project. We always have music playing—in the fall it's mostly jazz, classics like Louis Armstrong and Etta James. In the winter it's nothing but Christmas carols, because we're those annoying people who go all out for the holidays. And in the warmer months, it's whatever feels right.

"My parents love you, and sometimes I get jealous of how close you and my sister have become. We argue over stupid stuff like who gets the remote or the last slice of pie, but we never really fight. We never take each other for granted, and we made a promise to always be honest with each other, no matter what. Every night we make love and then talk until we fall asleep. And the next day we do it all again."

His description left me breathless. "Wow." I wanted everything he described, exactly as he described it.

"Yeah." He pressed his lips to my hair. "And the sex is incredible, but you already knew that."

Yes, our sex was incredible, but he didn't say we would end each night fucking each other's brains out. He said every night we would make love. I didn't know the difference, so it was a little hard to picture, but it sounded amazing.

My cheeks heated, and I ducked my face. "I've never made love."

His fingers stilled, just along my collarbone. "Never?"

I shook my head. I'd never been in love before either, but Noah was changing that.

Time suspended, as he seemed to consider this new information. I wanted to make love with Noah, but I wasn't sure if we were there or if we would ever be there. He was the only person I could picture holding me closely and looking into my eyes, the only person I wanted to share that sort of intimacy with. But maybe he didn't want to.

I suspected that wasn't the sort of sex where one person could boss the other around. *Stroke my hair tenderly! Look in my eyes!* I would have to be genuine, natural, totally of my own volition.

"I want to make love to you, Avery, but..."

I braced for his excuse, unsure if I could take it. "It's okay. I get it. It can't be forced."

"It wouldn't be." He untangled our limbs and sat me across from him on the sofa. "Making love to you would be as easy as breathing, but the morning after might kill me."

I lowered my gaze. "Because of my circumstances."

"Yes."

We were back where we started. "It's only a few more months."

"I don't know if I can sit around and wait for you to wrap up dating other men. I can put up with a lot of stuff, but not that. Consider it a hard limit."

"You learned what hard limits are."

"I learned a hell of a lot more than that. Consider Pandora's Box opened."

I smiled, but my amusement was short lived. This wasn't a joking matter. "I need to talk to Micah."

"Then do it. Call him and figure this out."

Micah wouldn't want to discuss this over the phone. He preferred to discuss such matters in person. I had more leeway in person as well, but I didn't want to upset Noah. "Do you trust me?"

"Yes, but I don't trust him or any of your other ... clients."

"Then give me until the end of the week to sort this out and let me do it my way."

He reached across the couch cushion and grabbed my hand. "Don't... Don't let him sway you, Avery."

He wanted me to break it off completely. I wanted Noah. The choice was obvious now that we discussed a future. But change was never easy. "I won't."

39

AVERY

The moment I started the conversation with Micah, he predictably insisted we meet somewhere to discuss our situation face to face. I refused, and he grew frustrated, claiming he needed to take another call. Fifteen minutes later he knocked at my door.

"I wanted to do this over the phone," I said, letting him into my apartment.

"That's ridiculous. We're going to resolve this like adults. Tell me what's wrong, and I'll fix it."

"Nothing's wrong. I changed my mind."

"Something changed, Avery. We were fine last night. We agreed to wait until graduation to decide—"

"I don't want to wait."

His lips firmed. "Is it your neighbor? I can evict him, or we could find you another apartment."

My hands gripped my head. "No. Don't you see? This isn't normal, Micah. I want a relationship, not a business arrangement."

"And you think he's the answer?"

"He might be."

"Avery, what security would you have with him? Relationships have a shelf life."

"So do business arrangements."

He crossed his arms over his chest. "Is that the way you see our association? Over three years and you see me as nothing more than a work colleague."

"Micah, I don't want to hurt you."

"Hurt me?" He scoffed and released my hand. "You can't."

I drew back at the cold tone in his voice. "I'm sorry?"

"I pay you to be at my beck and call. Everything you have, I provided. I was willing to give you more if it kept you content, but you'd rather be with him. What's he offering you, Avery? How will you afford to stay here?"

My insides literally shuttered. The gentleman I'd passed three years beside was suddenly replaced with a shrewd stranger. My chin lifted as I hid my uncertainty. "I'll move somewhere cheaper."

"You have three months of student teaching. That will be a full-time job, one with no salary. Where will your income come from?"

"I don't know. I'll figure it out."

"That's what I'm trying to get through to you. You need someone to take care of you. You're smarter than this, Avery. Use your head."

"Why are you being so mean? You always knew this wasn't permanent."

"Am I being mean? I was in the middle of a business meeting when you called. I dropped everything to check on you. The moment I realized you were upset and this was serious, I came here. Do you know why? Because that's the arrangement. I take care of you, and you keep the drama to a minimum. This isn't me being mean, Avery. This is me checking on my investment and deciding if it's time to cut my losses. You know what I want. I've made my wishes crystal clear. But before you say another word, you better be damn sure you know what *you* want, because the minute this is over, that's the end. It isn't cheap to skip the emotional bullshit, but I damn well paid for the right."

He'd never spoken to me in such a harsh way before. All at once, I felt cheap and replaceable. I couldn't do it anymore.

"How long do I have until you rent the apartment? I can disappear with little notice if you want to show it to potential tenants. But I need to know how long I have to find a new home."

His jaw ticked and his nostrils flared. "You're making a mistake." Pivoting, he snatched his coat off the chair and stormed out, slamming the door behind him.

I flinched and shut my eyes, grateful Noah was at work and not around to witness Micah's exit.

40

NOAH

"See this shot here?" I zoomed in on the bottom of the mountain, showing the jumper at a new angle. "We want more like that."

"Got it." Steve marked down the file location and removed the thumb drive from the computer. "I'll check the other feed to see if we have more like that."

"Good." We both stilled as voices carried. "What the hell is that?"

Steve frowned and I went to the door. Lucy came bustling down the hall. It was the first time I saw her since last night.

"Lucy, what's all that—"

"I'm going to find out." She kept moving down the hall, back in her sensible shoes and glasses.

The shouting continued, so I followed, as did Steve. Lucy made it to the end of the hall first, and her voice was that of a grade school principal's.

"Just who do you think you are coming in here and abusing our staff? If you have an issue, you can take it up with me or Mr. Wolfe. Leave the receptionist alone."

I turned the corner and came up short as Lucy stood toe to toe with none other than Micah. He glanced down at Lucy and did a double take. "*You.*"

This guy was becoming a royal pain in my ass. "What the hell are you doing here?" I snapped.

He pulled his scowl from Lucy and glared at me. "I need to speak to you in private."

When he stabbed a finger in my direction, Lucy scoffed. "I'm almost certain this man doesn't have an appointment, Noah."

"I don't need an appointment."

"*Everyone* needs—"

"It's fine, Lucy." She was like a tiny little guard dog.

Micah lowered his gaze and sneered at her.

"Oh, God, don't do that," Steve muttered. "She'll kill you."

Lucy huffed out a breath, her fists screwed into her hips as she let him by. Micah's head twisted, never breaking eye contact with her as he passed. Only when he was standing in front of me did he ask, "Is there a private place we can talk?"

"Follow me." I wanted him out of my building as fast as possible, so I turned into the first empty conference room. "Talk."

He shut the door. "What are your intentions with Avery?"

"I intend to keep you as far removed from our relationship as possible, including my motives. Next question."

"Do you love her?"

"None of your damn business."

He flashed his teeth and growled, "Do you see this as a long term thing, or are you just trying to get into her pants?"

Already got into her pants, and it was definitely leading to long term. But fuck him for acting like he had a right to that information.

"Look, I don't know how you found out where I work or what made you assume you were entitled to personal details about my life, but my relationship with Avery has nothing to do with you."

"You sure about that, boss?"

"I'm not your fucking boss."

"Yeah, well I'm hers, and I'm not leaving until I know what you want with her."

I drew back, appalled, and needing a moment to react. "Do you hear yourself? You're her *boss*? Do you know how pathetic that sounds? You *pay* her to act interested in you. Do you think she'd spend any time with you if money wasn't involved? It's all a fucking act. You don't know a thing about her, but I do, and it drives you crazy because I didn't have to pay a penny for her time."

"She doesn't know what she wants right now."

"*You* don't know what she wants!" I snapped. "Let me guess. She tried telling you today, and you couldn't handle it. Maybe just a little more money or a bigger apartment and you could buy a few more contented smiles. She's not your fucking employee, and she's not your fucking property. She's a human being!"

"I know exactly who she is! You're the one who's falling for the act. You don't know what she came from—"

"Because I don't care! None of that matters to me. But we all know it matters to you. You love the fact that she moved here with hardly any life experience. How else would you have taken advantage of her and convinced her this was her best option?"

"She's never had to struggle because of me."

"Stop acting like you gave her something! You made her dependent on you for survival, and now that she wants to try to live on her own, you're losing your fucking mind!"

Too far. His complexion darkened as my words hit the bulls-eye.

I closed my hands into fists, just in case, not wanting another fight but also refusing to back down or take my accusation back. It was spot on, and he fucking knew it. "You gonna hit me now? That'll win her over."

"I should—"

"It's not going to change how I feel about her. You can beat me to a pulp, and I'd still stand up for her because that's what a real man does. He doesn't take advantage. He takes control. He lets his woman know that even when she can't take care of herself, her needs will be met. Well, I'm the self-appointed gatekeeper of all things Avery Johansson from here on out. I'm meeting her needs just fine, and she no longer needs you, so feel free to turn in your badge on the way out the door."

He sneered and pivoted away. My muscles slowly unclenched as his anger appeared to fade. Thank God. I wasn't a pussy, but the guy had some sort of jujitsu background I couldn't outmaneuver.

He paced to the other end of the hall and rubbed a hand over his dark, bald head. "I never wanted to manipulate her or take advantage of her. I *care* about her."

"Then let her go. Let her finish out the semester in her apartment and give her your blessing to finally start her life as planned. For God's sake, man, let her be happy."

His eyes narrowed. "And you think you can make her happy?"

"I know I can, but we need you out of the picture."

His nostrils flared as he continued to glare. "I'd never leave her homeless."

"Does she know that?" There was a reason she feared ending things with this man.

He sighed and rubbed two long fingers to the center of his forehead. "I just need to know that you aren't messing with her. I feel ... responsible for her."

"She's not your job. You were hers."

I didn't care if he was only looking out for her. Avery wasn't his concern anymore. She was mine, and I intended to see to all her needs.

He dropped his hands to his side and glared at me. "I don't like you."

"Feeling's mutual."

The tension dissipated, the climate of the room noticeably shifting. I waited him out. Eventually, he'd admit defeat and leave.

There was a knock at the door, and I opened it, finding Lucy fidgeting on the other side. "What's up?"

She peeked around my side and whispered. "Is everything all right? I can call the police if—"

"Everything's fine."

She looked up at me with big eyes. "You're sure."

"Positive."

"Miss?"

We both turned to face Micah. Neither of us spoke.

"I owe you an apology."

Lucy's chin lifted. "You owe our receptionist one as well."

The side of his mouth quirked and I frowned. Micah didn't strike me as a man who smiled often.

"I'll be sure to stop by her desk on the way out."

"And mine?"

"Pardon?"

"You said you owe me an apology, but I haven't heard one yet."

This time he fully smiled. "How about I take you to dinner and make it up to you?"

I rolled my eyes.

"I bet some women find you charming."

My head whipped around. "*What?* Lucy, don't fall for his bullshit."

"Easy, Noah." She pressed a hand on my sleeve but kept her eyes on the other man. "Bad manners aren't rewarded where I come from. But I'll take the apology when you're ready."

With that, she twisted on the heel of her sensible shoe and left the room. I hid a smirk and turned in time to see Micah staring after her in shock.

His expression snapped into a grimace when he recalled I was watching. "What are you staring at?"

"Just savoring your rejection." I crossed my arms over my chest. "I think we're done here."

His glare intensified and he took a threatening step forward. "You hurt her, and I'll know."

I held his stare but didn't say a word. Responding only put me in a position that needed his approval. I didn't need anything from him. Neither did Avery.

Realizing we were through, he shoved out of the room. I went to find Lucy and didn't have to go far. She was waiting in the next doorway.

"Hey—"

"Who was that?" she asked, cheeks flushed.

"No one you should concern yourself with. I'm taking the rest of the day off. I need to go home and take care of something."

"What should I do about your appointments?"

"Handle it."

"Is everything okay?" she followed me to my office.

"Everything's perfect." I pulled on my coat. "I also need you to see that the last shoot gets overnighted to Steve so he can start the edits in the morning."

"Okay."

I went to the door and paused. "And Lucy?"

"Yes?"

"Remember when I told you the right guy was out there?"

She nodded. "Yes."

I pointed over my shoulder toward reception, where Micah was likely apologizing. "That's not him. Understand?"

She nodded again but didn't form a verbal reply.

"I'll see you tomorrow."

41

AVERY

I perched on the bed, still in my towel and holding the phone. I wasn't sure what changed since Micah left, but something happened.

He called just as I was getting out of the shower. The first words out of his mouth were an apology for storming off. He then spent the next five minutes telling me not to worry about finding a new place, the apartment would be mine until the end of June—longer if needed.

When I asked what made him change his mind, he only insisted on sending me a severance package—he said to call it an early graduation present, something to help me get on my feet.

As soon as I ended the call, I checked my account. He'd deposited five thousand dollars electronically, more than enough to get me through summer.

I felt strangely lighter, as if the last of my debts had suddenly vanished. The loss of weight on my shoulders knocked me off balance. I guessed I could call my other Daddies and let them know I was through taking appointments.

It was over. I was just a normal girl again, free to do whatever I wanted whenever I wanted.

I laughed, unsure what I wanted to do first.

"Avery?"

My front door opened and closed, and I stood, gripping my towel around my chest. "Noah?"

"You have to start locking your door."

"Why aren't you at work?"

He stepped into my bedroom and dropped his gaze to my body, his determined strides faltering as he stopped to take my measure. "You're naked under there."

"Why are you here?"

He kept his stare on the towel and slowly approached. "Micah paid me a visit at work."

"What? When?"

"A little bit ago. He told me you quit."

Micah went to Noah's work? Did they get in another fight? He didn't look like he'd been in a fight. "Are you okay? What happened?"

"First..." He pulled me close and kissed me slowly.

Lifting to my toes, I sighed, luxuriating in his familiar taste and scent. It had been so long since he kissed me like that, and having his lips on me balanced my world again.

"Sorry." As he pulled away, his gaze held mine along with a promise for more. "I had to get that out of the way."

I no longer cared about Micah. I only wanted Noah to keep kissing me and holding me. I missed the feel of his arms, the touch of his body.

Leaning into him, I nuzzled my nose to his clean-shaven throat. "I missed you."

He caught my chin, kissing me once more. "I missed you too. Do you think you can put on a robe so we can talk? You're sort of distracting like this."

I laughed but obliged. Once I wore more than a towel, Noah told me about Micah storming into his office and how his little assistant stood up to him. I couldn't imagine anyone speaking to Micah like that, let alone a woman only four foot tall—though I suspected Noah exaggerated her short stature.

He told me how he refused to give Micah any personal details about our relationship, and I loved that he called it a relationship. I also loved that Noah wouldn't budge when it came to our privacy.

"No one's ever defended me like that before."

He stared into my eyes, his fingers pulling at the terrycloth belt around my waist. "I'll always defend you, Avery. You're my girl. We're gonna be the cute couple everyone hates that's weird about Christmas and annoyingly affectionate all the time. I'll be damned if I let anyone stand in the way of our happiness, so get used to it."

I wanted all of that. Everything he described last night and all the surprises in between. All the aches and insecurities inside of me shifted into something warm and pleasant. As I stared into his eyes, a sense of belonging stole through me, and I wondered if this was what others felt when they came home—to a happy home.

I sensed his desire, felt the evidence of his attraction, and saw deep satisfaction in his eyes. I did that. I filled him with all of those things, and he did the same for me.

My emotions spun like a flurry of feathers inside, tickling and teasing as so many obstacles disappeared. It was as if the stars had aligned just for us. I couldn't recall ever feeling this ... happy.

"Noah?"

He kissed my neck and tugged open my robe. "Hmm?"

"I love you."

He lifted his head and stared down at me, a smile tempting his beautiful lips. "You do?"

I nodded slowly. No one ever made me feel as significant or safe as he did. No one else had ever been able to overlook my past with an eye on the future. And no one had ever turned me on the way he did. "I do."

"I love you, too, Avery."

I knew that as well, because Noah wasn't complicated. He was straightforward and honest, and daring, and everything I never knew I wanted, but I needed him as much as my next breath.

"Will you make love to me now?"

His eyes dilated as he stripped off his clothes, never once breaking our stare. His fingers caressed as if touching me for the first time, worshipping me, loving me. Every kiss lasted a hundred years, an imprint on our souls that would connect us always.

Nothing was rushed. When I touched him, his fingers curled around mine, holding, guiding, and together we breathed, sharing the same air as much as we shared the pleasure.

When he filled me, our gazes held, locked in promises and implication. He trembled, as did I. And though we'd been together many times before, this was the first time I'd ever felt anything like this.

Every stroke of his body left a tattoo on my soul. When his chest pressed to mine, his arms cradling me tight, I could feel our hearts beating as one. The soft kisses and whispered words of love added to the intensity. I felt every shiver, every shift, and every hitched breath of pleasure. I felt his love.

It didn't matter who took the lead or assumed control. Neither of us had any authority over the feelings we shared. Love was the driving force that pulled us together and the reason why being apart ripped us to shreds.

I'd probably always get a thrill out of dominating a strong man, but from here on I'd only want one man. Because as much as I loved control, I loved Noah a million times more. I needed him, and he needed me. It was the safest feeling I'd ever known. Scary and exciting, but dependable. The moment we pushed the obstacles out of our way, the path was clear. He'd be there for me—always—if I let him in.

"I'll never keep you out again, Noah."

"Damn right, you won't." His lips nuzzled my throat. "I intend to know everything about you, Avery. No more boundaries, no more secrets."

"It's not all pretty."

"That's where you're wrong. Everything you are and everything you've ever been makes you the beautiful Avery you've become. You might be less sugar than spice, and you might not always be nice, but you're real, and I'm only interested in the real you. That's all you ever need to be for me. Understand?"

I just needed to be myself. "I understand."

"Good girl."

He seamlessly took the reins, but I didn't panic. He knew what I needed and would eventually hand them back. A relationship was about give and take. It was about taking turns. It was about being there for each other, in any way necessary.

He'd get me at my best and sometimes my worst, but I believed he'd love all of me, without conditions and without cost. And I intended to love him the same—passionately, completely. So long as he continued to need me, I intended to be there—loving him.

EPILOGUE
NOAH

Bobby Helms belted out *Jingle Bell Rock* as I held the front door for our neighbors. They stomped their feet on the mat and shook the flurries off their coats as they hung them on the overflowing coat tree in the foyer.

"That's great!" Keith laughed, pointing to my sweater that had Santa dancing in a thong. "Where's Avery?" He handed me a bottle of spiced rum.

"She's around here somewhere." I pressed a kiss to his wife's cheek. "Merry Christmas, Katie."

"Merry Christmas, Noah. Is Laurel here?"

"She's around somewhere." I shut the door and took the rum to the bar where Avery had made a huge bowl of eggnog. "There you are."

I placed the rum with the others and stole a quick squeeze of her ass. I loved when she wore those leggings that showed off every curve. These ones happened to have candy canes all over them to go with her hideous holiday sweater.

"Keith and Katie are here."

"Oh!" Avery turned, her hair in a spunky ponytail on top of her head making her look far too cute. "I have her earrings. She left them at the last game night."

I trapped her in my arms before she could go running off. "Pay the toll."

She smiled up at me and pressed her lips to mine. I breathed her in, taking another squeeze of her ass while I had the chance. "Mmm... You taste like Christmas cookies."

"Get a room, you two!" My sister grumbled as she caught us.

Avery slipped out of my arms. "Laurel, have you met my brother, Drew, yet? I should introduce you."

I hung back as she took my sister's hand, pulling her into the dining room. It was nice having Drew around, though I wasn't sure if I wanted him taking notice of my sister. Still, he was the only family member Avery reached out to and reestablished a relationship with, so I didn't object.

"Knock, knock."

Recognizing Lucy's voice, I returned to the foyer. She was buried in wool accessories and holding some sort of casserole.

"I'll take that." I relieved her of the dish, and she pulled off her hat.

"It's taco dip. Avery doesn't have to heat it or anything. I have chips." She reached into her bag, withdrawing a file, and said, "Quick, sign these before Avery sees. You know how she hates when we talk work, but you forgot to sign these before you left the office."

"Where would I be without you?" I scratched my signature across the form.

"Lost somewhere asking for directions."

"True story." I lifted the dip and chips. "I'll give this to Avery. Bar's in the living room. Help yourself."

Carols continued to play as the house warmed with laughter and familiar faces. Bright lights shined from the front lawn, as we spent weeks making sure our yard had the tackiest display of all suburbia. Inside, guests voted on ugly sweaters—the grand prize was a basket of cheer.

Once things were rolling and everyone had a nice buzz, I clanked a fork to my glass. "Can I have everyone's attention for a second?"

It took several tries to get everyone somewhat quiet. So I let out a loud whistle.

"Where's Avery?"

"I'm in here!"

I shook my head. "Will someone get her out here?"

Everyone shouted for her and she came into the den, holding a bottle of whipped cream and wearing a frazzled expression.

"*What?*"

"Come here."

She rolled her eyes and handed the whipped cream to Laurel. "I was making up the pudding shots."

"The pudding shots can wait. Get your ass over here. Where's your drink?"

"I lost it."

I snagged her hip once she made it through the sea of guests and pulled her to my side. Holding up my glass, I said, "I want to thank all of you for joining us tonight in our new home. And I want to thank my beautiful Avery for putting together yet another great gathering of friends." I kissed her cheek, and she blushed adorably.

Everyone lifted their glasses and toasted Avery. I swallowed the last sip of my cocktail and placed it on the end table.

"Keith, can you kill the music for a second?"

The room silenced and filled with curious, expectant looks. I turned back to Avery and took her hands.

"Avery, it was a little over a year ago that you walked into my life and threw my world off its axis. I haven't been the same since. I've been better, happier, and every day that I wake up next to you, I wake up with a smile. You're the woman of my dreams, and I want to wake up beside you for the rest of my life."

I reached into my pocket and removed the small velvet box. Dropping to a knee, I looked up at her and laughed. She was wearing an expression I'd never seen her make before, a cross between shock and disbelief and terror and joy.

"I love you, Avery. Will you marry me?"

There were several *awws* from the crowd, but Avery covered her mouth and didn't say a word. Her eyes glazed with tears and she shook her head—it was enough for me to fear this might not go the way I planned and suddenly I felt as if I were jumping out of a plane.

Seconds expanded, and my heart raced. I cracked open the box, showing her the ring and held my breath. Her shoulder shook as tears dampened her lashes, her face hidden behind her fingers. I started to tremble as well, and then I was falling to my back, tackled to the ground as she kissed me.

My fist closed over the ring box, and I wrapped my arms around her, holding her tight. The music kicked on—one of her favorites—Mariah Carey's *All I Want for Christmas is You,* and everyone cheered.

At the pop of a champagne cork, we pulled our lips apart and I smiled. "Is that a yes?"

"Yes, that's a yes."

"I love you."

She brushed her mouth to mine. "I love you more."

I bit at her lips. "Impossible."

She sighed. "I want you."

"Wanna sneak upstairs?"

She smirked and nodded. "I want to model my ring for you—while wearing nothing else."

That sounded incredible. "Mmm. And then what?"

"I'll let you know when I decide."

I no longer scrimmaged for control when she wanted it because as it turned out, there was room for both of us to take turns switching it up. No matter who was calling the shots, being with Avery was always incredible.

I stood and helped her to her feet. Several of the guys clapped a hand on my back, congratulating me. When I looked to the far corner of the room, I spotted Micah standing alone. He raised his glass, and I tipped my chin. That was as far as our interactions went. He was here for the simple fact that Avery asked and there was nothing I wouldn't give her. But I still hated the guy.

Taking Avery's hand, I pulled her toward the banister, and we slipped upstairs. We could only sneak away for a few minutes. I followed her into our bedroom and softly shut the door.

"Pants off, Mr. Wolfe. We have a house full of guests and only about ten minutes before they realize we're missing and I want to make every second count."

I loosened my belt. "Who said you're in charge?"

She arched a brow and pulled off her hideous Christmas sweater. "Me."

"Good enough." I dropped my pants and flicked off the lights. Within thirty seconds she had me begging, but tonight she'd be the one on her knees.

We were married the following spring, not wanting to waste time on a long engagement. Over our honeymoon, I took her skydiving and got the whole thing on tape. She screamed the entire time but also loved the rush. Although she claimed she'd never do it again, I knew she would. Avery was one of the bravest women I'd ever met. And she loved a challenge.

In the end, I had the woman of my fantasies. She was perfect in every way. Adventurous, gorgeous, silly, dangerously competitive, and my best friend. Pleasing Avery was as easy as breathing.

And she got me out of the deal, which she claimed made her the winner. I didn't understand her thinking, but I didn't need to. So long as she was happy with the outcome, I had everything I needed, because that meant I had her.

Avery got everything she set her mind to and sometimes it was fascinating to watch her succeed, even when approaching the seemingly impossible. But she was also incredibly easy to please because it didn't take much to make her happy. She had the job she wanted, a home that came with a fifteen-year mortgage in a decent school district, and an average, mid-sized sedan. Avery loved pretending she was average even if she'd never qualify.

I loved letting her believe the fantasy, too. But I knew the truth. And if one of us was the winner in this situation, it was me.

My wife was no average woman. She was extraordinary. Perfection personified, in every way. Easily the classiest woman in any room, but also the filthiest in the sexiest way possible—no matter the situation, there was always something dirty on her mind. And as far as fulfilling roles went, I especially like when she wore mismatched clothes and farm animal slippers.

She'd been a lot of things in her life, a bombshell, a student, a daughter, a sister, an average girl. But she'd always be so much more to me, because I got all those parts as one messy, sexy, unparalleled woman.

That was the real Avery.

And she was mine. Forever.

THE END

For more from Lydia Michaels visit
www.LydiaMichaelsBooks.com

ABOUT THE AUTHOR

Never miss another book release!

Click here to sign up for Lydia Michaels' Newsletter.

Follow Lydia Michaels on Instagram and Facebook!

What to Read Next?

Click here to claim your FREE Book from Lydia Michaels!

Billionaire Romance

Falling In | Sacrifice of the Pawn | Calamity Rayne

Small Town Romance

Wake My Heart | The Best Man | Love Me Nots | Pining For You | Almost Priest

Emotional Favorites

La Vie en Rose | Simple Man | Wake My Heart | Sacrifice of the Pawn | Forfeit

Romantic Comedy

Calamity Rayne

Erotic Romance

Breaking Perfect | Protégé | Falling In | Sugar

First Books in Binge Worthy Trilogies and Series

Almost Priest | Falling In | Wake My Heart | Forfeit | Original Sin

Paranormal Vampire Romance

Original Sin | Dark Exodus | Prodigal Son

LGBTQ+ & Menage Romance

Broken Man (MM) | Breaking Perfect (MMF) | Forfeit (MMF) | Hurt (Non-Consensual) | Protege

Sexy Nerds & Second Chances

Blind | Untied

Teacher Student, Workplace, and Age-Gap Love Affairs... Oh my!

British Professor | Pining For You | Breaking Perfect | Falling In | Sacrifice of the Pawn

Single Dads & Single Moms

Simple Man | Pining For You | First Comes Love | Controlled Chaos | Intentional Risk

-

Dark Psychological Thriller & Tortured Hero Romance

(TRIGGER WARNING)

Hurt

Non-Fiction Books for Writers

Write 10K in a Day: Avoid Burnout

About the Author

Lydia Michaels is the award winning and bestselling author of more than forty titles. She is the consecutive winner of the 2018 & 2019 *Author of the Year Award* from *Happenings Media,* as well as the recipient of the 2014 *Best Author Award* from the *Courier Times*. She has been featured in *USA Today, Romantic Times Magazine, Love & Lace*, and more. As the host and founder of the *East Coast Author Convention*, the *Behind the Keys Author Retreat*, and *Read Between the Wines*, she continues to celebrate her growing love for readers and romance novels around the world.

In 2021, Michaels released the groundbreaking, non-fiction series, ***Write 10K in a Day,*** to commemorate her career in the publishing industry. She looks forward to many more years of exploring both fiction and non-fiction writing, teaching about the craft, and learning from the others in the author community.

Lydia is happily married to her childhood sweetheart. Some of her favorite things include the scent of paperback books, listening to her husband play piano, escaping to her coastal home at the Jersey Shore, cheap wine, *Game of Thrones*, coffee, and kilts. She hopes to meet you soon at one of her many upcoming events.

You can follow Lydia at www.Facebook.com/LydiaMichaels or on Instagram @lydia_michaels_books

Other Titles by Lydia Michaels

Wake My Heart
The Best Man
Love Me Nots
Pining For You
My Funny Valentine
Falling In: Surrender Trilogy 1
Breaking Out: Surrender Trilogy 2
Coming Home: Surrender Trilogy 3
Sacrifice of the Pawn: Billionaire Romance
Queen of the Knight: Billionaire Romance
Original Sin
Dark Exodus
Calamity Rayne: Gets a Life
Calamity Rayne: Back Again
La Vie en Rose
Breaking Perfect
Blind
Untied
Almost Priest
Beautiful Distraction
Irish Rogue
British Professor
Broken Man
Controlled Chaos
Hard Fix
Intentional Risk
Hurt
Sugar
Simple Man
Protégé
Forfeit
Lost Together
Atonement

First Comes Love

If I Fall

Something Borrowed

Write 10K in a Day

FOLLOW LYDIA MICHAELS

Facebook
www.facebook.com/LydiaMichaels

Instagram
www.instagram.com/lydia_michaels_books

Twitter
www.twitter.com/Lydia_Michaels

Made in the USA
Las Vegas, NV
08 December 2022